Stone Virgin

Books by Barry Unsworth

AFTER HANNIBAL
THE HIDE
MOONCRANKER'S GIFT
MORALITY PLAY
PASCALI'S ISLAND
THE RAGE OF THE VULTURE
SACRED HUNGER
STONE VIRGIN

BARRY UNSWORTH

STONE VIRGIN

W. W. Norton & Company
New York · London

Printed in the United States of America

First published as a Norton paperback 1995

Manufacturing by the Haddon Craftsmen, Inc.

Library of Congress Cataloging-in-Publication Data
Unsworth, Barry, 1930–
Stone virgin.
I. Title.
PR6071.N8S7 1986 823'.914 85-24897

ISBN 0-393-31309-3

W. W. Norton & Company, Inc., 500 Fifth Avenue, New York, N.Y. 10110
W. W. Norton & Company Ltd., 10 Coptic Street, London WC1A 1PU

3 4 5 6 7 8 9 0

Madonna Commissioned 1432

He brings me writing materials without asking for money but he does not speak, I cannot be sure what his motives are, whether he has seen my worth and wishes sincerely to help me or whether he is merely acting on orders from his superiors or it is possible he has believed my promises to reward him when I get out of this hole, but whatever the truth of it I take this chance of reaching you, noble lord. I beg you to find out who are my enemies and speak for me; I mean those behind my accusers. From you a few words would be enough. I am innocent of the girl's death. I swear it by all the saints. Ask me to make any solemn oath and I will do it. I was in another part of the town when she was drowned. Those who say I was with her are lying; they have been paid to lie. You are my generous patron, you are one of the Three Hundred, you obtained for me the commission from the Supplicanti, having seen my work at Bologna. My lord, please help me now or I will sink under this weight of false witness. Why would I kill a girl for no reason? Besides, she was a whore. I will tell you everything I can about Bianca and the carving of the Madonna.

My landlady Maria Nevi has said in her deposition that I have a violent nature giving as evidence threats to her and threats to the boatmen on the day they brought the block, however she was not present on this occasion, she was buying fish in the market, so already she is perjured, because she has said on oath that she witnessed this scene. Why has she done this? I know the hag dislikes me — I always called her Fiammetta as a joke, though she is more than fifty and half her teeth gone and her thing pickled in its own vinegar. But there is more than dislike in this.

I remember that day well because of the beauty of the stone and my own fury. At the last moment, before swinging the block across from the barge on to the *fondamenta,* everything ready, myself standing there on the edge to help guide the block over, at this moment the boatmen began to demand more money, two of them at least, the third remained silent. Perhaps he was ashamed — or dumb. These two spoke in turn, encouraging each other.

I see them quite clearly in my mind's eye, the days in this cell have done nothing to cloud my memory, I always from childhood had the faculty of remembering well, not merely vividly but in detail. When I worked as an apprentice stone cutter for the Carthusians at Pavia — having run from the life of goatherd in my village — I was known for my ability to copy window moldings and all the details of *modanatura* from memory. (Umberto of Bavagna was my master then, I learned the elements of my trade from the monks and even some Latin along with the stone cutting.) One was young and smooth-faced but he had a diseased eye; the other older, spitting frequently over the side; both gray with the dust of the depot. In loud voices they explained to me and others who had congregated — Venice being at all times of day full of people with nothing to do but stare — what labor it had been to transport this block of Istrian stone from the *terraferma*.

My lord, they had been paid already. I would have given them something, *una bene andata,* but they were asking for a whole scudo. My eyes became confused with anger. Fortunately they were out of reach, God thereby saving me from violence, which he has done often before, otherwise they would have repented their insolence, sons of whores. I will confess that I am passionate by nature, my elements of heat are not properly blended. I was conceived in July, the worst possible month for the passions. My mother was barely eighteen, too young even for the limited balance women may achieve, Vegi tells us this, a woman cannot be *ragionevole e intendere,* even *secondo donna,* until she is twenty at least and moreover I suspect that my father was too eager and intemperate in his approaches to her, though naturally evidence for this is lacking.

So in this heat of the moment I may have said unwise things, but nothing against Venetians or the state of Venice, that I can swear to. But there was hostility toward me in the crowd because of my Piedmontese accent. A crowd had gathered now: my neighbors the saddle makers, Marsuppini father and son, who have since given evidence against me, two lads with trays of cakes, various idlers. But I never said anything against them. I have the highest regard for the citizens of this great Republic.

They saw my weakness, that spitting rogue and the other with the crusted eye, and they exploited it to the full— typical Venetians. A *barca* loaded with grain was seeking to pass but could not because the *rio* is narrow and the barge took up the space so the oarsman of the other boat grew quickly impatient and began shouting. I threw the silver down into the hold. This was money the friars of the Supplicanti had paid me on signing the contract for the Madonna, money to live on while I executed the work, not to throw down for these animals to scramble for, but they did not mind the indignity, being creatures of a low order, and were now all smiles and made haste to swing the block over, and I myself forgot everything else, seeing the stone settled on its rollers and maneuvered into place on the workshop floor, workshop that was also living room and sleeping place to me.

It was still with smiles that they left. The third wretch, who had said nothing, was smiling too. Reverence and awe is what they should have felt, seeing me left alone there, understanding what a guest I was left with. They were men after all, though thieves. But they departed grinning.

When they had gone I examined the stone again. There were the bruises from the quarrying but the grain was perfect and I knew that I had chosen well and I gave thanks to God who had whitened this stone in the darkness for my use and His greater glory, and I repented of my sin of rage and crossed myself, as I do now again. Anger that is past leaves a mood of vacancy sometimes, and so it was now and in this vacancy I stood at the window and I looked round the room as if seeing it for the first time — the block made everything else seem unfamiliar. It was warm, though still only March, and there was sunshine in the room and dust moving slowly in it and reflections from the canal also moving slowly — over the walls and my workbench and the pallet in the corner and the rat tracks in the dust of the floor. Light moved freely inside the room, having passed without damage through the membrane of the glass. So the Holy Ghost entered the chamber of Mary's womb as it is explained in the teachings of the blessed San Bernardo where he says that as the brilliance of the sun fills and penetrates a glass window and pierces it *con una sottigliezza impercettibile,* so the Word of God, the splendor of the Father, penetrated the virgin chamber without hurt, *senza ferirla.* But there was more, my lord, because into the chamber of my room I realized that God's seed had entered, the stone was God's seed waiting to be transformed into an image that would glorify His Incarnation, and it seemed that I could hear this dumb stone crying for its form and with a cry that was everywhere in the room like the light and inside the walls of my being and it was loud and silent. Then my body lost its weight and my mind became mingled with the light that was inside and outside and the pleading of the stone.

When I came to myself again the Angelus was ringing and there was the *fondamenta* and the bridge and the older Marsuppini outside his workshop, bald head lowered over his work. Cutting and stitching all day long. Who needs horses in Venice? But now that our new Doge is leading us to glorious acquisitions on the *terraferma,* people will have estates and so horses.

I hear his step, he comes for the papers now that the light is fading and he takes them at once, not giving me time to finish. I will ask for a lamp.

I could not stay longer there with the mute stone, in the dying light, but it was my misfortune to meet Fiammetta as I came out onto the street and at a moment when she was already heated by an altercation with the fishmonger.

We met at the corner of the Marsuppini *bottega* just a few yards short of the *sotoportego* that leads off into Campo Sant'Angelo; five paces more and I would have been under the archway and missed the hag altogether. As it was, we met face to face on the corner and she at once began raising her voice. Five lire, eight soldi, she screeched at me. It is her usual practice to utter the exact amount of my debt loudly and repeatedly like a parrot, not listening at all to anything I might say in reply and in this way she achieves several of the triumphs to which her hag's life is devoted, for example causing others to overhear and thus offending my dignity; and also by showing such an exact knowledge of the amount she puts herself in a commanding position — or so she thinks, but she is mistaken, *io me ne frego*, and God has justified this through the gifts He subsequently made me, which I am not at present free to reveal, not even to you, noble lord. And the poverty is not my fault but caused by the unfair practice of closed guilds here in Venice so it is impossible for anyone not native to the place to set up his own *bottega*.

So I merely felt sorry for her as she stood ranting there clutching the mullet to her breast and her face working, she is a hysteric also. I mention this to show that her evidence is not to be trusted. Five lire, eight soldi, she shouted again; he thinks a poor widow can live on promises but promises will not put sausages into my mouth. (Marsuppini has said in his deposition that I answered her lewdly and obscenely at this point but that is lies.)

Still she railed on. This great *maestro*, she said, when will he pay it? She put this question to the sky, it seemed, looking upward, her jaws working and her eyes blinking but she gets just as excited talking with the fishmonger, and I paid no special attention. Here is a great fuss, I said. But she was not listening; she was laughing falsely up at the sky exposing the interior of her mouth in which many teeth are lacking, clutching the fish as if I was threatening to despoil her of it. Here is a great fuss to make out of a few paltry lire, I said, speaking calmly, but again the demon rage was climbing up, my face had become suffused with blood. Have I not told you about this new commission? I said. The block has come. I shall have money when the Madonna is finished. (I did not mention the advance they had paid. I needed all of it.) What is five lire? I said, and I tried to get past her into the *sotoportego*. Five lire, *eight soldi*, she screeched straight into my face with her breath of sour milk. The *capomaestro* is a great man, he can forget about the soldi, but I am only Maria Nevi.

Go and fuck your fish, I said. Imagine my feelings, confronted by this detestable crone upbraiding me in the full hearing of others though of course I am indifferent to the opinion of others as I have said, but she was raising her voice more and more and I was trapped there, once again base talk of soldi dinning into my ears, the block of stone in the workshop, my great task all before me, my first independent commission in Venice after seven years — yes my lord seven years of servile work at others' bidding, trimming stone, laboring over obscure details of decoration, jobs no one else wanted to do. It was from this you rescued me; thanks to your good offices I had the commission from the friars of the Supplicanti, a Madonna Annunziata for their new church soon to be consecrated, destined for a prominent place on the façade, a work of high and holy importance and one in which I should express my veneration for the Santissima Vergine, the Mother of God, and through her the respect due to all women. And here was this hysteric hag with her mummified cunt and her withered tits in their black fustian of a fictitious widow, the husband never existed, she is a poxed-out *puttana.* Go and fuck your fish, I said to her, I have no more time to waste here; and I got round her into the *sotoportego.* Scum of Piedmont, I heard her shout after me, but I took no notice. Other things too she shouted; threats. She has said I told her to go and fuck her fish, and this is true, but I did not push her aside and I did not invoke the devil against her by making the sign of horns. However, it is true that I told her to go and fuck her fish, which profanity I regretted when my anger had cooled.

I did not notice which way I walked at first owing to the disturbance of my feelings, but there was a strong light everywhere. I remember that evening for the brightness of the light on everything, on the water and on the buildings, and yet the sunset bells had rung some time before — I had heard them while still in my room — and so there is something difficult to understand about these memories of light, but I cannot be mistaken. I think now that I was bestowing this light on things, that it was in me, this evening was the beginning of God's gift of light to me, which remained with me all the time I was carving the Madonna and accompanies me still, even here in this prison. (When I close my eyes I can feel the sweetness of this light within me and sometimes, in certain conditions, I see it on the surface of my skin.)

So I walked for some time at random. Campo Sant'Angelo, then over the *rio* but by the long bridge, Ponte dei Mercatori, I must have wandered south a little. They were working on the façade of San Zaccaria, hammers and bells and the booming of the cannon as the ships coming into the Bacinto saluted the image of the Virgin on the Basilica of San Marco. The city was crowded with visitors come for the Spring Fair — more than a hundred thousand it was said. It was Wednesday, the market was open, sausages and cockles and the smell of sawdust and wet fish. *Pan buffeto.* I remember everything about this evening on which I met Bianca, even the prices of things. Prices are nostalgic for men in captivity my lord. Ten snails, four soldi; a *secchio* of wine, thirty-five soldi. I had the friars' money in my pocket that day and I had hopes.

In one corner of the Campo Santa Maria Formosa there were actors performing on a platform hung with lamps and I stopped to watch. They were good, especially the Pantalone, he was a good tumbler, dressed all in red, with a fierce mud-colored mask and he had Turkish slippers too large for him which he kept tripping over and falling onto the platform with a great clash of bells; he had bells inside his clothes somewhere. He wanted to creep up and spy on two behind a screen who wore the masks of lovers. The one with the male mask was trying to put his hand up the skirts of the other and just as he succeeded every time a crash of bells, and they sprang apart. The people in the crowd were laughing and some were shouting advice of an obscene nature.

After this I began crossing the square toward the north side. For no particular reason I turned down that street about midway across which is called after the church and leads into the warren of the San Severo district. As I was thinking to retrace my steps I heard a woman singing somewhere above me, not very loudly but distinctly enough in a voice low in register but very sweet and the notes lingering, a haunting song, not Venetian by the sound of it.

Tu m'hai promiso quattro
O mocatura, o mocatura

I looked up, but the street was narrow and the balconies were high and I saw no one. I had to go to the end and then turn to look before I could see her. She was sitting at the edge of the balcony, looking over the street, and she was in a red dress with her shoulders bare, her hair dyed gold, and her face painted. She was smiling a little as if she had pleasing thoughts. But this was the habit of her face, as I learned later; she had few thoughts. This was my first sight of Bianca. I knew she was for sale. How else could it be, alone there, in that exposed position, and singing to draw the gaze? But that was not important in my mind. Also she was very beautiful, but it was not that. She seemed pleased and self-conscious like a child dressed up. My lord, I had never seen her before but I knew her — it was that which kept me there. I stayed gazing, but she did not look toward me. People were passing, they stared at me, a thing I hate, and still she did not look; she was lost in some dream. I had to move away but her face stayed in my mind. There was a tavern on the corner with a sign of crossed silver keys and so I entered, not to go too far away, not expecting trouble of any kind. It was chance that I went there. It is true that a man came in who was known to me but after seven years it would be strange indeed if I had no acquaintance in Venice. This was Rodrigo Nofri, who used to be a painter of masks, a bad one, and now is in the silk trade and making money. The dog has made money out of this business, he has testified that I uttered treasonable sayings against the state of Venice and in support of her enemies, particularly Francesco Bussone, Count of Carmagnola, and that I caused an affray. My lord this was in March it was before the arrest of Carmagnola. I said nothing against Venice and as for the fighting it was the Florentines who began it. There is a web of false evidence against me, I am enmeshed in it. I beg you to find Nofri and question him privately. I know he has been bribed. Not only that; he has been frightened. With him there was another man and his name I think was Bechine, from Murano. I did not discover his occupation but if from Murano almost certainly to do with glass, a big man, rather taciturn but not quarrelsome, none of us was quarrelsome, it was the Florentines who began it all. I will tell you what happened.

I had fish pie and radishes and a . . .

Conversations with him have always the same form. He does not speak of his own accord but he makes responses, always the same, so it is like a litany, he is my congregation of one. I remind him that we have our agreement and I watch his large head nod slowly and I wait for him to say yes it is so — he has a harsh voice and a thick accent of the Veneto. I ask him if it is certain that these papers of mine are being placed directly into your hands and he says it is certain. And without the knowledge of anyone else? Yes, without the knowledge of anyone else. And no reply yet? No, not yet. But he will bring it to me when it comes? You have my promise, he says. Once I give my word to a man it is sacred with me. Yes, I say, you are a man whose promises one can trust. Besides, you will be well paid. Sometimes it comes into my mind to try to overpower him and attempt an escape but I am enfeebled by these weeks in prison, and the brute is strong. He is an ox and cannot read; therefore I can abuse him in writing at least.

This time I surprised him by asking for a light, explaining that if I had a small lamp or perhaps candles I could continue my writing after dark. His first response was not favorable. It seems that it is no small thing that I have asked for. He says that he cannot give a man light without permission otherwise he will be out of the job on his ass. But he will see what can be done and meanwhile I should make good use of the daylight. So I do my lord though it comes late into this pit and leaves early.

When I was dragged out of the tavern and thrown onto the cobbles that coward Nofri was nowhere about, it was the Muranese who helped me and he told me afterward that the girl saw it and felt sorry for me and called to bring me up off the street before the *signori di notte* arrived on the scene, but he did not do it. It was the same girl.

He would have come the whole way home with me but as I walked I felt better, the bleeding stopped, and we parted at the Merceria. He is a good man and if he could be found I know he would give a true account of the evening. Andrea the first name and I think Bechine the second, from Murano.

Once back in my room again I lay down on the pallet and almost at once sank into sleep but woke with the first light because of my bruises and did not sleep again but lay there as the light strengthened. I could see the dark bulk of the stone in the middle of the room. Her face came to my mind, faintly smiling. It is difficult to explain, but I wanted to keep this memory of her face separate from everything else in her whore's life.

I never paid her a single soldo for sexual favors, whatever that prying crone Fiammetta claims to have seen through my window. She was the model for my Madonna.

I knew from that same morning that it would be so. I think I knew it from the time I got up to light the lamp, having grown impatient or alarmed, as I said, and being unable to sleep again. The block of stone was lit up, its crystals glittered along the planes where it had been cut; it shone brighter for its wounds as also Christ did. I thought again of the illumination of her face. Slowly it came to me, like music, God's intention, the quarrel with Fiammetta which upset me so that I walked without seeing, then the light everywhere about me and the impulse that made me choose that street to walk down, the song that made me linger, her face above me. It was clear to me in that moment that God had guided me to her. That was the evening when the light began also. Besides, what other explanation could there be?

It was early still when I made my way back. I knew the house was one of those opposite the tavern. There were three doors that could have been hers but I chose without hesitation and it was the right one and that is a further proof that my actions were being directed from above. I mounted the stairs and knocked, and a woman answered, middle-aged. She was wearing kerchief and apron and seeing my impatience smiled, mistaking the nature of it and she made a remark about the *uccello* that rises early. This was Bianca's doorkeeper. She closed the door on me and kept me waiting there several minutes, ten minutes or so, during which time my impatience grew so that my breathing was affected. I have said that my nature is excitable.

Then she came back to admit me. Bianca was standing at the balcony window with the sunlight around her. The floor coverings had been rolled aside and the planks were shining wet — the woman had been cleaning the floor when I knocked. On the wall a caged goldfinch, struck by the sun, was singing in brief phrases. There was a music stand with a sheet on it and red wall hangings. She was holding a book, which she must have just snatched up.

She did not move toward me. Good morning, she said. Did you bump into something on the way? I did not understand this at first but then I saw she meant my bruises. She was smiling, she too I think mistaking the purpose of my visit and my haste, haste that caused me to stumble a little as I went toward her, but the smile soon went when I spoke. You have been chosen by God, I said, wanting to impress her with the seriousness of the matter but it was too sudden and she was frightened, as also perhaps by my stumbling entrance and swollen face and I have no doubt the light was shining from me. So I stood still and tried to smile and I told her not to be alarmed. This is good news for you, I said.

You are the one outside in the street last night, she said. She crossed her arms over her bosom perhaps out of modesty, seeing I was not a customer. She was still holding the book. She had dressed hastily and carelessly. Her hair was up on her head but some golden strands had fallen loose and hung down. She was wearing a blue gown drawn together at the front with white string. I saw that she had been roused by her attendant and had dressed and prepared herself hurriedly, and this touched me even at such an important moment, this dutiful effort to get up and play the hostess; it was in keeping with the music stand and the snatched-up book which I do not think she could read.

Don't be frightened, I said. You must realize that this is a great compliment. Out of all the women in Venice you are the chosen one. And I explained to her about my commission for the Madonna Annunziata and about the block of stone waiting there.

Then she laughed but still with distrust. She kept her arms crossed over her body. Me for the Madonna? she said. Me for the Santissima Vergine? You will be beautiful, I said to her. You will live forever in the stone. The power of my talent will transform you completely, you will be immortal. Think of it, up there on the facade of the church for everyone to see. Also there will be dressing-up to do, you will dress up in the robe and headdress of the Madonna.

She liked this idea, as I had thought she would. Her hands slipped down to her sides. White, she said, and the robe should be high-waisted and it should have a full skirt. *Brava!* I said. And the face as nature meant it: no powder, no paint, no beauty patches.

She laughed again. Listen to him, she said. Everybody knows the Holy Virgin didn't use those things.

I will pay you, I said. I will give you one whole scudo for every hour. In advance.

This offer of money decided the matter, as it does most matters, coming on top of the favorable circumstance of dressing up. All the same she was not laughing when she finally agreed. She sounded sad, or resigned rather, as if she had lost some argument. Yes, as you like, she said. I will come.

She came that same afternoon bringing items of her costume in a beadwork bag. She was wearing a beauty patch at the corner of her mouth and . . .

She came decked out in her best, a puff-sleeved gown of blue and crimson with a brocaded corselage, a lace shawl over her shoulders, red silk stockings, and little gold shoes with those block heels which are so much the rage now in Venice, God knows why; the women can hardly walk in them. I complimented her on her appearance, reflecting that she must make some money from her trade to dress so and have an apartment and employ a *ruffiana* to keep the door and it surprised me because though beautiful she was not very clever and harlotry is competitive in Venice, this *terra delle donne*. In obedience to my instructions she was not wearing any paint but she had not been able to resist a beauty patch at the corner of her mouth and I asked her to remove this. Then she introduced a commercial note by asking for some money in advance

I have just the one room, not so very large, with the privy at one end of it, so there was nowhere else for Bianca to change into her *cose di Madonna,* as she already called them. I wanted nothing underneath, no bodices, no petticoats, nothing to spoil the line. She showed some modest reluctance about undressing in these unfamiliar surroundings and for this unusual purpose and seeing this I kept my back to her and busied myself moistening the clay. When I turned to her again it was a revelation: she was transformed. She was standing in the middle of the room beside the block of stone. The full white gown — it was a nightgown she had brought — covered her from neck to ankle. She had arranged the headcloth a little toward the back of her head, no doubt with an instinct of vanity, but I saw at once that it was exactly what was needed, it framed the face and showed her wide brow, her brow is not high but it has good width, and the front part of her hair was also revealed. The gown itself by fortunate accident was traditional in style, gathered high at the waist and fitting quite closely over the upper part of the body. The line of Bianca's shoulders and the full shape of her breasts were clearly visible, but the cloak, which I clasped at the throat, concealed the bosom partly, as was becoming.

She saw my approval but misunderstood the nature of it I think. She looked down at herself; she was pleased at being dressed up. She had that smile on her face, secretive somehow. Half the time she was in a world of her own. I want you to put your hair down, I said. Take out the combs. Perhaps she heard something of awe in my voice not for her but for the Holy Virgin who she now represented, because her own face became more serious, though that inclination to smile never leaves her face, it is in the shape of the mouth. Excuse me my lord that I speak of her sometimes still in the present. I do not always remember that she is dead. I never went anywhere near San Maurizio the night of her death. I was in my room. Those who say they saw me with her have been bribed to lie. My lord I beg you while there is still time to have the witnesses questioned privately.

She did as I asked her and her hair which as I have said was dyed gold and curled with tongs fell down over her shoulders concealing the sides of her face. No, No, I said, use the combs to gather the hair behind, at the back of the neck. Then the hair will be loose at the temples but off the face, I want to see the sides of your face. She did this and I arranged the headdress as I wanted it and I set her at the window, where the light could fall evenly across her face.

The pose was difficult. Here is a girl, a virgin, she has just been told that she is to be the mother of Christ, a shining archangel is standing before her she cannot be unmoved she cannot be simply a monumental detail for the decoration of a church facade as we often see these days. Well, I said to Bianca, the Angel Gabriel has just announced to you that you are to bear the Son of God. You are in your house reading the Bible and in these familiar surroundings, quite unexpectedly because you have had no warning at all, you are quite unprepared, the archangel appears bright and resplendent, possibly he reduces his splendor because shining beings are able to contain their light, I know that from my own experience, but a startling sight in any case. He gives you the news. How do you behave?

Bianca paused to give this her consideration. I saw the faintest of frowns mark her brow. Then her face cleared. I say the Magnificat, she said. No, no, no, I said. You say nothing. You have a desire to run away but you cannot, because after all he is a visitor, a holy one, you have your duties. And then, you are a virgin, you are confused at this talk of conceiving a child.

But it was useless to explain. She liked posing and pretending, but she had no imagination; she could see herself only as the Queen of Heaven. I wanted that drama of the pose I had seen as a child in country churches in Piedmont, they were crude but they had life and movement. I made her stand with the right leg advanced and the trunk turned away slightly from the announcing angel though her face regarded him still, her right hand laid over her breast, the left against the side of her thigh — this I changed later. I did not know at this stage exactly what I wanted except that drama of the turning body and to show the inadequacies of Bartolomeo Bon, who carries all before him here in Venice with his uninspired carvings, where you can simply see the original shape of the block and the arms either touching the sides of the body or joined to it by drapery and all outlines smooth and continuous, completely primitive. He goes on with this because it is all he can do and the people have no sense of what might be better and so he is rich and has a big workshop and many assistants.

So I spent time getting the girl into the right position. I took her shoulders and turned them to the angle I wanted. Now look toward me, I said, and when she did so I experienced a surprise almost like a shock at the gaze of those eyes of hers, dark brown flecked with lighter color in the sunlight from the window, she had beautiful eyes, vague-looking — she may have been shortsighted. As I moved her this way and that I remembered it was her trade to move her body in ways that men wanted and this thought disturbed me because she was also my model for the Madonna and was wearing the Madonna's robes.

And so I began to handle the clay and while I molded and kneaded it to make sure the moisture was properly distributed and adding sometimes water from the bowl I had there and played with the clay as I always do before I start the modeling to get the right feel of it and get my hands used to the texture and also to warm the clay because no one can make a living form out of cold clay, God warmed the dust before he made Adam. Afterward, when I began on the figure, we talked. She was always — I hear his steps outside, he comes early for the papers now.

She talked to me, once the first constraint had worn off. Her voice was low, not much inflected, and so rather monotonous to listen to, not grating but it was easy not to attend to it or I mean only attend intermittently and that is why much of what she said I cannot now remember or only imperfectly. Also I was absorbed in modeling the clay, which was of excellent quality, just stiff enough, and I had bound it with jute fiber to make it hold better. The figure being complicated I had made a wire armature and this was fixed to my workbench. I was molding to one-fifth life size, building up the form by addition — I never cut the clay though I have seen others do it.

It was gossip mainly. She stood at the window, posed as I had posed her, in the white clothes, the headdress, the high-waisted gown with the silk girdle, the cloak fastened at the neck, her face peaceful and self-absorbed. She spoke about her neighbor Corsetta who was there on the night of the quarrel in the tavern when my only offense was to defend Carmagnola against those pigs of Florentines. He was Piedmontese my lord as your lady wife is and as I am, and for this I was knocked senseless and thrown out. Corsetta is a whore too. That will be a *nom de guerre,* not her real name. She lives on the floor above, or did then — these girls come and go but if she could be found she might be able to throw some light on Bianca's movements the night she was killed. They were friends, so Bianca said. And there was another girl she mentioned whose name I have forgotten or perhaps I was not told it but called Sfregiata because of her scars; she had been slashed on the cheek for coming late to an assignation — only some minutes, according to Bianca — she had been visiting an aunt at the Convent of the Convertite though that seems unlikely, but in any case the man thought she had been with someone else during the time he had paid for. Bianca herself had been beaten once at least and badly though no bones broken. For laughing, she said, but I cannot remember the circumstances. She laughed often. Also, but she spoke of this later I think, she had once been subjected to a form of the *trentuno,* but only by six. The man had taken her for a pleasure trip to Chioggia, given her a good dinner and wine to drink, treated her like a princess she said then afterward she was pushed into a room with six of his friends waiting and they all fucked her some of them twice. I asked her if she had given the man offense, and she said no he had done it for a joke.

As you see my lord it was trivial matters she talked of. I try to remember anything that might help you in your efforts on my behalf but it was tittle-tattle of the streets. This was in March my lord you will remember that they had just executed the transvestite known as Rosso and the girls were talking of it as he had been an attendant of the courtesan Masina; they had paraded him through the streets in women's clothes slit up the front to show his genitals and after that he was garrotted in the Campo di Santa Maria Formosa and his body burned. He was weeping, she said. What, I said, while they strangled him? A man cannot fight for breath and weep at the same time. No, she said, before, when they led him through the streets. She had not stayed to see the execution. I wish now I had not joked though it was funny to think of tearful Rosso in his skirts with cock and balls hanging out but I am sorry I joked now that I know what happened to Bianca. They strangled her half to death before they drowned her.

Later, when I had started on the stone, she spoke of others, and this is more to the point, my lord. She made references to a protector, a rich man with an illustrious name, also to a pimp known as Strascino because he drags one leg as a result of syphilis. He took money from her perhaps for protection which she with her grand ideas called a fee, *un onorario,* and she called him her *mezzano* as if he were a conversationalist and connoisseur instead of a leg-dragging syphilitic *puttaniere* but it was typical of her to call things always by higher names and this was not exactly lying because she persuaded herself of the truth of it. All this was mixed up with her ambitions, more like daydreams, she wanted to be thought of as a *cortigiana,* not a common whore. Also, as I have said, she liked to make mysteries about herself. She spoke of Strascino always with some fear and once she forgot he was supposed to be the *mezzano* and she told me he and another had broken a girl's ankles and the bones never set properly. She did not give his real name but I think he is that Stefano Benintendi, described as trader, who has testified that he saw me with Bianca in the area of San Maurizio the night she was killed. A tissue of lies from beginning to end my lord. A common pimp, and they take his word against me. Alone and unsupported he would not have dared. There is someone behind this Strascino and I think it is the same one that Bianca spoke of, calling him usually her protector, sometimes her uncle. I know this man visited her at regular times because she once had to leave me hastily when his visit was due. She was frightened on that occasion of being late; she was more afraid of him than of this miserable Strascino. Bianca's fears were numerous but none of them deeply lodged or so it seemed, she could not hold things long in her mind; for example, fear would quickly turn into something else, some coquetry or private dream or gossip of the day and so I did not always pay attention.

The weather was very hot and the smells of the canal came in with the low tide. I was sweating as I worked on the clay. I worked in shirt and drawers only and still I ran with sweat. Molding clay is hot work my lord. She was standing at the window as usual in her *vesti di Madonna.* She had been telling me that her mother was connected to a noble family — by birth, she implied. The stone block was there where they had left it in the middle of the room. It cast a straight shadow between us. I did not believe what she said about her mother and in this I was right, because later when we got into the habit of fucking she told me her mother was a serving woman. She never spoke much of a father and I do not think she knew who he was but she once said he was a French officer, which also I did not believe. It is possible that her mother was a servant in a noble house and if so she may have procured Bianca for some member of the family and that would explain the apartment and so on but Bianca invented so much it was difficult to separate truth from lies and there was no reason then for making the effort. But I sometimes felt an impulse to shake her out of all this fantasy, give her a sight of more important things by telling her about God's favor that had been shown to me and about the light I carried within me and which sometimes shone from my skin though only certain people could see it.

However I refrained which was a good thing because I did not need to boast; Bianca knew it all the time, not perhaps as visible light — she was not able to see that — but she was affected by the power that came from me, and this was proved before long. She had been telling me about these fictitious connections of her mother's. I told her to be silent, as I did not want her mouth to move. But after a while she exclaimed and made a groping gesture and then she slipped down onto the floor and her face was as white as her gown and her eyes were closed. I gave her some water, raising her head so she could drink, and I loosened the ribbon that held her gown together at the neck. Her eyes opened but they were not looking at anything and she began trying to sit up but she could not and making groping fumbling movements with her hands. Then I suddenly saw that this feebleness was the result of my power that God had given me, so I became excited at once and I began to kiss her. Her lips were cold. Her eyes were able now to look at things; they were on my face. I was myself unable to see properly because of the heat that had risen to my head. I lifted up her gown of the Madonna and I was pulling her legs apart, they had no resistance, she gestured to me to wait, I think to inspect her to see that she was free from disease, the usual courtesy of whores but I could not wait. I threw her back and mounted her at once. Her body was cold; she cried out when I went into her — a cry of pain, my lord — and I knew this was a certain sign from God that she had become a virgin again for me. After that we did it often. If she was cold that first time she was hot always afterward, she was *solis filia* and *calida* if not *callida*. (You will remember the pun of Lipsius, my lord.) Bianca had a gift for love. She was not clever, *una cervellina,* but she knew how to give pleasure. Always she would keep on her Madonna things because I wished it so. I never saw her naked when we fucked only when we washed each other afterward from the bucket. And she took no money except for the time spent modeling.

All this was afterward. I had started on the stone then; I had made those first cuts that are so terrible. It was a good piece, freshly quarried, free from flaws, with no hard outer skin. A block should be set up and carved according to the lines of its bed; otherwise, it will split and break off. But this was a fine piece. All that summer I labored to release the form contained in the block. I worked nearly naked but still the sweat came off me. I used an iron point for removing the spawl you must keep a steady rhythm of striking with the point, because this is less tiring also by a regular stroke your life is moving at the same pace as the life of the stone your thoughts keep exact pace with your material as God's did when he made the world and that is why men can have some understanding of the nature of God, as is explained in the writings of Origen. So therefore carving is rhythm my lord no man can carve well who has no rhythm in his strokes either with point or claw.

The claw was no use for this hardest of stones. I used a granite axe, bouncing the blade on the surface of the stone, bruising the stone to give tooth for the chisel. Day after day striking at the stone. You must not cut too early with a fine tool, this closes the surface, takes life from the image. I would work with the sweat coming into my eyes and this tension of breaking the stone down to free the shape imprisoned within it because the stone resists it aspires to be itself always and this struggle I felt in my body through the shudder of the stone and the joy of it I discharged on her, on Bianca. She was there in her robes. I would feel my cock growing and this was a sin because I was shaping the Holy Virgin but I could not prevent it, the heat rose to my head, I could not see. My elements are not well mixed, owing to the circumstances of my birth. I made her lie down with me in the dust of the floor. So in this way the work went on and by the Feast of the Assumption of Our Lady I was within half a finger's breadth of the final form and ready to begin with the narrow chisel. Bianca came almost every day. There was no need for her to come so often but she did. She would put on the *vesti di Madonna*. Sometimes she brought things, Trebbiano wine, galantined meat, red muskmelons from the Litto Maggior, almonds coated with sugar. Once a big basket of cherries. She would sweep up the room, bring a wet cloth for my face. Often she sang as she moved about. All that time she must have been frightened. They took me to see her drowned body. I saw the marks of the cord. I would not have hurt her, I needed her for my model. She . . .

RESTORATION ONE

◇

The Lower Draperies 1972

I

Some feeling of superstition prevented him from looking up at the Madonna as he approached, as if it might be unlucky to have a premature view of her. Even mounting the narrow ladder he did not look up, not until there were only three or four rungs left and his eyes were level with her knees. Here for a moment or two he stopped, obliging Steadman to stop also, and below Steadman, Signor Biagi, the contractor whose men had put up the scaffolding. These two stood on the middle rungs of the ladder, flapping slightly in the March breeze, while Raikes gazed up at the statue.

Everything that was known about her he knew; nevertheless her appearance at these close quarters came as a strong surprise, almost a shock. She was imposing, of course, even awesome, seen thus from below, but it was not mainly this, nor the appalling damage to her, the bemonstering accretions of time and chemical pollution — these he had expected from his study of the photographs. What he had not been prepared for was her unprotectedness, the license of the air around her, something none of the photographs had conveyed. She stood clear of the façade, as subject to weather as any rock on the shore, but in a way that her human image made seem stoical, and that Raikes found unexpectedly moving. It was as if her disfigurements too, the blackened, blinded face, the crusted robes, were part of this patience and endurance.

Becoming aware of the men waiting below him, with their own brand of patience and endurance, he started climbing again, leaving the ladder at last to set his feet on the wooden platform, no more than five feet square, bolted firmly to its scaffolding poles against the wall, too close, Raikes noted, too zealously flush with the façade — the boards had skimmed the brick, scraping a band of fresher pink. No point in mentioning it now of course: Biagi was a key figure in the enterprise and had to be kept well disposed.

By now the others had climbed onto the platform beside him. "Well, here she is," he said to Steadman. "Isn't she terrific?"

Steadman nodded with his usual gloomy sagacity and after a moment said, "Poor bloody cow, she's had a pasting."

The deliberate impiety of this and the flat, noncommittal tone irritated Raikes, seeming to accuse him of emotionalism. He had known Steadman for some years now, but it continued to strike him as extraordinary that a man who at thirty-one — two years younger than himself — was an authority on Venetian Gothic should go on affecting this hard-boiled manner. You'll be talking out of the corner of your mouth next, he felt like saying, almost said.

He kept his eyes on the Madonna. Her face with its badger stripe of bleach was averted, glancing away across the rooftops to the pale rim of the Lagoon; but her body was inclined toward him, right arm laid across the breast, left held low and slightly extended inward, as if to ward off some threat. She had turned her body, though not her eyes, from the vehement archangel who had come to her with the news. Gabriel would have been on the other side, presumably; one of the several mysteries about her was that her Gabriel was not known to exist anywhere. "I hadn't realized," he said, "how far her trunk turns from the plane. Unusual for the period."

The judicious tone of this had been intended as a rebuke, but he saw now that Steadman's eyes were not on the statue at all; he was craning to look over the near corner of the *campo* below them. Down here among the café tables pigeons were going through routine mating procedures, the males strutting and fluffing themselves out and trying to hop onto the females, who placidly sidestepped and foiled them. Both fluffed and unfluffed paused frequently to peck around for crumbs. Love and bread together, Raikes thought vaguely. Could it be the pigeons that Steadman was interested in? Then he saw one of the Tintoretto people, Miss Greenaway, whom they had met earlier, pass rapidly round the corner of the church, a whisk of plum-colored pullover, jeans, short fair hair. She disappeared, presumably into the chapterhouse, which had been turned into a workshop, since it was the only neighboring building large enough to accommodate Tintoretto's vast canvases. Restoring these was the main British project at the church; his affair was a mere sideline.

So Steadman had been craning his neck for that. He looked with some curiosity at his colleague, who returned the gaze seriously — Steadman almost never smiled. Behind him he heard Signor Biagi shifting his feet. He turned and said rather awkwardly, *"Può scendere se vuole."* He had been discourteous, he felt suddenly, in not speaking to the contractor before, in allowing himself to be so absorbed by the statue. *"Va bene,"* he said, smiling. "Everything is fine."

Biagi smiled good-humoredly and began moving toward the ladder. "Oh, there is another thing," Raikes said, and he began in his careful Italian to explain that he would need material of some kind, tarpaulin or heavy plastic sheets — plastic would be better; it admitted more light — something that could be secured to the scaffolding to make an enclosure, thus affording privacy and also protection from the weather, especially in the early days. *"Farà freddo qui,"* he said. "The wind comes across from the Lagoon."

Biagi assented at once. *"È la parte esposta,"* he said, inclining his narrow, handsome head. "It is the exposed position."

These words of the contractor's lingered with a curious resonance in Raikes's mind. "You may as well go down too, if you like," he said after a moment to Steadman. "I'll stay up here a bit longer." His sense of awkwardness persisted. Steadman was there in an advisory capacity, not in the least as a subordinate. But his presence had become somehow oppressive. With relief he watched the two disappear, one after the other, over the edge of the platform.

He waited for a few moments, then moved up close to the Madonna, obeying some obscure impulse to engage the eyes which had seemed to avoid him; but they were without direction or regard, blind with soot, gummed by the long process of sulphation to mere slits in the face. Not eyes to greet joyful news, certainly; and joyful the news was always said to have been. On the other hand, perhaps not. She had not applied for the job, after all; presumably had not even known she was in the running . . . Signor Biagi's words returned to him. *La parte esposta,* the exposed position. Perhaps that was why the blocked eyes distressed him so. In *la parte esposta* one would tend to keep the eyes wide open . . .

He turned to look over the square. The fact that he knew precisely where he was did not lessen the strangeness of being there. He knew he was standing at the dead center of the façade, eight feet above the arch of the main portal, thirty-two feet above the ground. Across the square the rows of tall Renaissance houses closed off the view, but to the east he could see clear across the rooftops to the pale rose *campanile* of Madonna dell'Orto, the water of the Lagoon, and the white walls of the island cemetery of San Michele. Below him the pigeons continued their ploys, undeterred by the few people now sitting at the tables. No sign of either Steadman or Biagi. A stout man in suspenders, wearing a large white apron, stood in the doorway of the *gelateria* opposite. Three men emerged from the *sotoportego* that led off the square toward the canal of the Misericordia and the Ghetto Nuovo. They were talking together gravely, in the way of Venetians. One looked up toward him, peering slightly in the mild sun. Raikes was glad to think that he would soon be screened off.

He took a final look at the polluted stone of the Madonna. Some of this damage of course was irreparable: corrosion as severe as this would soften the detail forever; no one would ever see her now as she had been when she left the sculptor's hand. But he would restore her as well as it could be done. *I will give you back your face,* he thought, looking at her. *I will make you whole again.*

These last words, too portentous for his own habit of thought, seemed to have been uttered elsewhere and implanted by some agency in his mind. At the same time he felt the salt breeze from the Lagoon on his face and in his hair; and as in moments of high solemnity nothing seems accidental, so this sudden quickening of the breeze seemed not to be, and his ardent isolation. And the devastated stone itself seemed at that moment to take on some extra fixity of stillness, oddly like a tremor, as if here too his vow had been registered.

The sense of having made a promise stayed with him for the rest of the day, and it was still there in the evening when he came to make the first entry in his diary. He was tired but he had resolved to keep detailed notes of his progress from day to day, and he was faithful to his own resolves almost always. The diary would constitute a full and complete record; provide material for his report when he came to write it; perhaps even, suitably edited, prove a seminal study for those who came after.

Sitting at the table, against the window of his small apartment, Raikes felt elated at the prospect before him. This would be pioneering work. He was proposing to use on the Madonna a type of air-abrasion instrument, which had not as far as he knew been tried on any stone sculpture *in situ,* certainly not in Venice. At the end of the sixties they had used ultrasonic dental equipment on the face of St. Christopher, who like the Madonna was of Istrian stone and in an exposed position, being high on the façade of the Madonna dell'Orto, and this had been successful, removing the black tears from the saint's cheeks without damage to the stone below. But it was equipment designed for human teeth, not stone surfaces. The process had been too laborious; it had taken too long. It would have taken decades at that rate to deal with just the most spectacular damage. And Venice did not have decades: time was running out; much of her exterior stonework was past saving already.

Then in 1971, quite by accident, he had heard that air-abrasion techniques were being used at the Smithsonian Institution in Washington to clean American Indian buckskins. He had followed this up, found a firm in Oxford that made the machines under license. It was a jeweler's instrument, really, designed to cut quartz into pieces small enough to put into watches, but it could clean as well as cut if used properly. He had tried it out in England, at the museum where he worked, on various fragments of corroded stone, and he had been dazzled by the results. It was the thought of this miraculous quartz cutter that excited him as he sat there. He would get to work with it as soon as the initial water spraying had been completed. There was the hope too, which he had mentioned to nobody, of casting new light on the Madonna, concerning whose history and attribution there were certain unresolved and puzzling elements. He drew the diary — a stout, stiff-backed affair — toward him, and made the first marks on the first page.

She exhibits the blotchy black and white appearance typical of Istrian stone undergoing transformation through combined weathering and air pollution. The degree of transformation in her case is advanced because she is high up, carved in the round, and in a very exposed position. As one would expect, it is in the recessed areas that the calcium sulphate and carbon crust have formed. The exposed convexities show bleached white where magnesium carbonate has been lost; for example, on the middle of the forehead, front of nose, upper lip, chin. There is a roughly straight bleached stripe, about three inches wide, from brow to the bridge of the nose. Similar effects of sooty deposit in the recesses and bleach on the salient parts are apparent throughout the draperies on the whole figure. I intended to start the spraying process tomorrow and we shall see what effect that has.

In the afternoon went as arranged to the offices of the Soprintendenza alle Gallerie for my interview with their representative, Signor Manatti. He was affable enough, but I was surprised at one point to hear him express doubts about the wisdom of restoring stonework in Venice — or anywhere else, I suppose he meant. Frammetersi *was the verb he used: to tamper. Rather offensive. The beauty of time-worn objects and so on. This is an unenlightened view but unfortunately still common, though as I say I was surprised to find it here. He actually spoke as if the decay itself were in the nature of a protective covering, a* patina del tempo, *as he called it. Quite erroneous in the case of Istrian stone. It turns out he has not been to see the Madonna personally, though the scaffolding has been up for some weeks now and he could easily have done so. It isn't a patina at all of course; it is a disease.* Malattia del tempo, *it should be called. You might as well say leprosy is a patina. All this was before we looked at the photographs to-*

gether. He was impressed, as he was bound to be, by the details of the actual disfigurement, which are quite horrendous in close-up.

The photographs were on the table beside him and he glanced at the top one now, as if to find confirmation in the streaked, encrusted draperies, the masked face. It was outrageous, what had been done to her, this insensate pumping of SO_2 into the atmosphere.

He looked away, at the dark surface of the canal below his window. It was not very late, but the narrow *fondamenta* that ran alongside the canal was silent and deserted. The house was in Canareggio, a quiet district, with an air of sadness and abandonment about it that Raikes found congenial. An American named Wiseman, whom he had met three years previously when working at the Madonna dell'Orto, had found the apartment for him, and he had liked its high ceilings and sparse, somber furniture from the first.

Outside there was a thin vaporous mist in the air, and light from some source he could not identify lay over a section of the canal. He watched the gleaming water lap against its containing wall, sidling at the wet brick, gently but at the same time urgently, lapping into light, falling back into mist, with a persistent rhythm.

He felt obscurely disturbed by this rhythmic motion. Suddenly, unbidden and unwelcome, Steadman's face came into his mind, and that craned head, awaiting Miss Greenaway's return. Was it pigeons or sparrows that Aristotle said were addicted to venery? He must have seen her go or he would not have been expecting her to come back. She would probably have been to the public lavatory just off the *campo:* by great good fortune there was a well-kept one there. So all that time, he thought, while I was absorbed in the Madonna, Steadman was holding himself in readiness for a brief flash of Miss Greenaway returning from the loo; while I was contemplating damaged stone, his thoughts were centered on undamaged flesh, albeit engaged in lowly functions. Or virtually undamaged, I suppose. Was that why I found his presence there suddenly irksome, because he had debased my first communion with the Madonna, intruded thoughts of a carnal nature? No, not the intrusion itself, but my vivid perception of it. I was invaded by his thought processes, as if my own mind had no walls. Miss Greenaway means nothing to me. Yet for those few moments Steadman's yearning to get inside her knickers became my yearning. Was it repentance for this that led to my vow?

It was his habit, when troubled or alarmed, to take refuge in intricate thoughts; and he did this now, thinking of the tugs and runs of the currents out in the Lagoon, the unimaginably complex motions that had resulted in this small eddying here, this lapping love of the water against the brick. The sea was like a preoccupied god, whose main concerns always lay elsewhere. He was calmed by this sense of an indifferent ocean, and after a moment took up his pen once more.

As the statue is restored it should be possible to make further attempts at an accurate attribution. In the last fifty years she has been credited to a number of sculptors, among them artists as different as Arturo Rizzi and Pietro Lombardi. The best-argued case is probably Memmer's. He attributes the Madonna to Bartolomeo Bon on grounds of stylistic analogy with the statue of Justice in the superstructure of the Porta della Carta, which is indubitably Bon's. But his work is heavy and inert, to my mind at any rate; it has none of the tension of the Madonna. Of course he ran a big workshop and employed numerous assistants, some of them more gifted than their master. In Memmer's day it was at least possible to see the statue. How terrible to think that all this havoc has been caused in little more than twenty-five years of industrial belching.

In my view the main problem lies in determining the early history of the statue. I am convinced that if this were known it would lead us to the man who carved her. We know she was not intended for the place she occupies now. The church has clear early Renaissance features and is fifty years later at least. So why was she put there? And why was she not installed at once, in 1496, when the church was consecrated? Why did she have to wait so long — more than two hundred and fifty years? And where was she all that time? We know she was put there in 1743. Dalmedico is quite specific on the point in his Annals, *and there are also references in Sanudo and Verci. Dalmedico's account is the fullest, but he does not say where she came from. Presumably he didn't know. All three mention that she was thought to have miraculous powers.*

Raikes paused again. He was consumed with eagerness to solve these problems. Dalmedico described the benefactor as a merchant of pious life and good repute, but this was a mere formula. He did not supply the man's name, and there was no inscription anywhere inside the church. All the information available concerned the ceremony of installation, the Bishop of Venice officiating and several civic dignitaries present. It amounted to very little, really. Of course he had been writing a hundred years or so after the events described, but he would have had access to ecclesiastical records. There was plenty of detail elsewhere in his monumental work. Why so little here?

Raikes sat back. If the records had existed at all, there were only two possibilities: between 1743 and the time Dalmedico came to write this section of the *Annals*, the relevant documents had been either lost or suppressed . . .

At this moment there came a light tap on the door, and his landlady, Signora Sapori, entered and stood just inside the room, asking him if he would care to have some coffee and a piece of apple pie. *"Torta di mele,"* she repeated, thinking he had not understood. *"È casalinga;* it is homemade," she said, smiling in the doorway. She was a little wizened woman in her early seventies, quick in movement, with bright inquisitive eyes, like a squirrel's, dressed always in black, with a brief, immaculate white apron across her meager loins. "He will try it, the apple pie?" she said.

Raikes was touched by this kindness. Snacks in the evening were no part of the arrangement. Wiseman had said, in recommending the place, that Signora Sapori was a very kind and nice person. He was returning the smile and beginning to say that he would like some, yes, and how kind of her, when quite suddenly and unexpectedly, and in a way most uncharacteristic of his normal reticence, he was assailed by a strong impulse to put his hand up Signora Sapori's skirt; worse than that, to throw skirt and apron up and over, to strip away whatever lay beneath, make free with her wasted delta. The eagerness of this impulse and the terrible tumescence that attended it he felt must show in his face, but apparently not, for Signora Sapori's expression did not change. "In a few minutes, then," she said, nodding, pleased that he wanted some.

Good God, Raikes muttered to himself when she had gone. What on earth is the matter with me? He felt feverish. This grandmother with the little white apron. Was it some association with apple pie? He tried to retrace his mental steps. The apron had reminded him fleetingly of a girdle. Mary's, which she had loosened and thrown off, on her Assumption?

In the stress of these thoughts he moved again, sharply, and caught sight of his own head and shoulders lurking in the dark shine of the window beyond the table lamp. Light from this threw a pattern of broken loops and ovals over his reflection, like loose metallic ropes. Above these encumbrances he could make out his cheeks and nose and high, austere forehead, but his eyes were lost in shadow and the lower part of his face was gagged with light.

For some moments Raikes regarded with distinct unease this masked, fettered, curiously watchful acquaintance. Then he looked back toward his diary, but there seemed nothing for the moment to add. He had omitted the date and he entered it now at the top of the page: *March 20, 1972.*

2

It happened on the third and final day of the spraying, though Raikes did not think of it as an event exactly, anyway not at first: rather as a protracted quiver of the optic nerves, strained after so much peering. That there were elements in it that could not be explained in this way he hardly realized at the time.

He was standing inside his enclosure of plastic sheets — Biagi had been commendably prompt with these — aiming with a half-appalled sense of violation straight into the Madonna's face, driving minute particles of water at point-blank range and high velocity into her eyes and mouth. The water hissed as it issued from the nozzle, broke against her face with a flatter, softer sound and fugitive gleams of light, the two sounds fusing into a steady sibilance of assault. Water ran blurring over the temples and cheeks, brimmed the eye sockets, sowed pearls in the clogged mouth, clung in beads to the fungoid deposits below the chin. She was so wet it seemed the water must come from within her, vomited from the mouth, wept from the slits of eyes, dripping from folds in draperies saturated by long immersion, as if she were newly dredged up, still running with the waters that had drowned her.

Raikes straightened and stood back, closing off the nozzle of the spray. Some of the carbon had come away, there was no doubt about it; when she was dry again it would be easier to see how much. In any case he did not intend to go on with the spraying much longer, just an hour or two after lunch, probably; she had had three days of it, quite long enough. He glanced at his watch. It was gone twelve. Steadman would be waiting for him — they had arranged to meet in the square for a drink before lunch.

He moved close to the Madonna with the intention of leaning the metal tube against the wall alongside her. In fact he was beginning to bend forward to do this. His eyes were on the statue still, but he was on the point of looking away to where he intended to place the spray. His face was very near the folds of the Madonna's robe, where they gathered at the waist, too near to see any form or human likeness, only the ancient enduring grain of the stone. It was then, at the moment he had relaxed attention and was on the point of looking away, perhaps had already begun to do so, that a sudden sense of being quite in the open, without protection, descended on him, accompanied by a strong sensation of space and silence and a feeling of threatened balance that made him clutch for the rail. He had a fleeting impression of light, but he was not in it, or not quite in it — a long straight shadow across the light, two human bodies, naked and gleaming wet, part in light and part in shadow, standing together, but not very close, and some sort of echo or resonance, perhaps of voices, but no words. The impression was a strangely piercing one, perhaps because of the hush that seemed to surround it, but it was over at once, before his own body had achieved a stiffening of surprise. He found himself holding tightly to the scaffold rail. The wet Madonna was again before him. With conscious care he leaned foward to place the spray against the wall.

It was surprise he felt chiefly, mixed already with a sort of doubt, as he slipped out of his overalls, changed out of his Wellingtons for gym shoes — the cubicle formed by the plastic sheets had become changing room and frequently eating place as well as workshop to him — and began to climb down the ladder. His first steps on firm ground were attended by a sense of insecurity, even a remote sort of panic. Then he became aware of people around him, saw pigeons fly up. Steadman was sitting alone at one of the outside tables, and Raikes moved across the square toward him, remembering to smile only when he was almost there. "Sorry I'm late," he said. "Forgot the time."

"You're a dedicated fellow," Steadman said, in his flat laconic tone. "What are you having?"

"Beer, I think." Raikes looked across the square. The impulse he had felt to tell Steadman about his experience died quietly. He had sensed something derisive in the other man's brief words, not unkindly so but sufficient to put him on the defensive. He had no gift for irony himself and was highly vulnerable to it, his own nature tending always to enthusiasm. His usual defense was to assume a more distant air, and this sometimes made him seem cold or priggish. He knew Steadman regarded it as odd and excessive that he should have elected to do all the work himself from beginning to end, even these messy and laborious preliminaries, which he could easily have got an assistant to do. Steadman had no sympathy for more extreme natures, which was why sarcasm came so easily to him and why the two had never become very close.

The beer came, and Raikes busied himself pouring out a glass. Of course, he thought, she was wet, running with water. Some association of memory had perhaps been responsible. Common enough, wet bodies; perhaps archetypal. Tired eyes and some involuntary association. Perhaps he had straightened up too suddenly, just before. That would explain the feeling of vertigo . . . "Well," he said, "what have you been up to?"

"Just pottering about," Steadman said. "I've been trying to get some good pictures for my book. It's bloody amazing how few good photographs there are of Venetian sculptures. I'd like one of her when she's all cleaned up." He nodded in the direction of the church. "Odd creature, she is," he added after a moment. "Quite untypical."

"Typical, untypical," Raikes said. "That is all art historians seem to think about these days. No one makes value judgments anymore."

"Safer not to. Preferable, anyway."

"But why?" Raikes felt the slight fluttering in his stomach that always preceded direct conflicts of opinion with others. "Why?" he said again. "It is a human duty to make distinctions of value; it is one of the things that make us fully human."

"I should have thought," Steadman said," that we had all had enough of being fully human for the time being. It would be better simply to be sensible instead and not make so many judgments of any kind."

"Just because it's risky," Raikes said excitedly, "we should steer clear of it. Is that what you're saying?"

"Not exactly." Steadman seemed about to go on with the argument but checked himself, perhaps disliking Raikes's combative manner, and after a moment said in different tones, "Anyway it's not true of all of us. Take Sir Hugo Templar, for example. He'll rattle off value judgments for you nineteen to the dozen. Have you met him?"

"Not really. He's been to give lectures at the museum."

"Pleasure in store," Steadman said.

Sir Hugo Templar was the chairman of Rescue Venice, the organization funding the British restoration project. He was also an authority on European Baroque. He was coming from London to preside over a working conference due shortly, a combined progress report and pooling of information.

"I'll have to be there, I suppose." Steadman looked gloomily into his glass. "I'm not going back till two days later. Just my bleeding luck."

"What did you mean when you said she wasn't typical?"

"Your Madonna? Not typical of the Venetian sculpture of the time, I meant. That was still fairly primitive, you know."

"Well, of course, I know that. But he could have trained somewhere else, couldn't he?"

"I don't think there was a native Venetian capable of it at the time. My guess is that he came from the north, Lombardy perhaps.

There are Tuscan influences too. It's not a flamboyant style; it's a more naturalistic type of Gothic. If you look at the original shape of the block of stone, which you can see from the base, you'll notice that it had no real effect on the composition of the figure. The knees and feet are more or less aligned with the block, but the upper torso cuts across one corner. This is quite untypical of Venetian Gothic. I noticed it at once."

Launched on his subject, Steadman had forgotten that he was supposed to be a tough guy. His voice had taken on warmth; his tone had quickened; he was looking quite eagerly at Raikes. "Her arms, too," he said. "The right hand is conventional enough, pressed to her breast to show how unworthy she is. And of course the extended left hand is common in Romanesque and Gothic sculpture, but hers is held very low and *across* the body. It gives a curiously sexual significance to the pose. That might be accidental, of course. Or one might be quite mistaken, simply a perverted modern. The trouble is, we don't know enough, and we never will now. Artists were constantly on the move; a sculptor of the time might work in half a dozen cities in the course of his career. There was a lot of cross-fertilization going on; most of the work has no documentation. The difficulties of attribution are enormous."

"But you think a northern Italian who had worked in Tuscany?"

"Not necessarily worked there. It would have been enough for him to come into contact with Tuscan artists, like the Lamberti or Nanno di Bartolo, who are known to have been in Venice in the 1420s. There was a lot going on here at the time. Foscari was extending the Ducal Palace, an enormous building project. The Republic was rich, the pay was good, people came flocking from all over the place."

"I wonder where the Gabriel is," Raikes said.

"The messenger boy? Dismembered in some mason's scrapyard or lurking about in a cloister somewhere. Perhaps he was never made. One thing's certain, though."

"What's that?"

"Whoever the sculptor was, if he really intended that left arm to seem to be guarding the pudenda which is certainly what it looks like, then it's unique among depictions of the Annunciation, she has a unique left arm."

Steadman paused, looking across the square. "That in itself would be profoundly original," he said. "Oh God, here come the Stakhanovites."

The Tintoretto people were trooping diagonally across the square toward them, in loose arrowhead formation, with their leader, Barfield, at the head. All were wearing navy blue boiler suits.

"Those things must be special issue," Steadman said. "Birmingham City Galleries, boiler suits navy, art restorers for the use of. They've had their sandwich in the sacristy; now they're coming for their coffee."

There was a certain sourness in his tone. His efforts to detach Miss Greenaway from the tribal unit had not so far met with much success. None of the Tintoretto team was ever seen without the others: they conversed almost entirely among themselves, and their days seemed to follow a pattern of ritual observances.

Having reached the café enclosure, they seemed to be about to make for a separate table, but Steadman called out a greeting and after slight hesitation they approached and began to commandeer chairs from the tables around. "How's it going?" Steadman said when they were all seated.

Miss Greenaway laughed briefly and mirthlessly, as if thereby hung a tale. She seemed, however, flushed, Raikes thought, and he wondered if she was more aware of Steadman's interest, and more responsive, than her rather bluff and forthright style indicated.

For a while after this laugh there was silence among the group, as if that might be thought sufficient response. Then Barfield, whose title was scientific officer, a neat, sallow man with a visionary way of widening his eyes, said, "You are not going to believe this."

"Try us," Steadman said.

"It has taken us all this time just to get the paintings off the wall. I tell you no lie."

"It has been a rush," the other assistant said. Muriel Hagerty was older and grimmer than Miss Greenaway and had a perm and a wedding ring. "It has been a race against time," she said.

"My God." Steadman compressed his lips and nodded slowly. "Racing to get them down," he said. "Who said the epic is defunct?"

This sarcasm was so crude that Raikes immediately became hot with embarrassment, thinking how much it would wound the Tintoretto people, but to his surpise he saw that they all seemed to be taking the remarks at face value.

"They started taking up the floor today," Owen, the fattish art consultant, said, his glasses shining. "That didn't help, I can tell you. It did not help, did it, Gerald?"

The waiter, whose name was Angelo, came to take the order, and while this was going on Miss Greenaway, still looking flushed, began to undo the top buttons of her boiler suit. She was wearing a white T-shirt underneath.

"Taking the floor up, were they?" Steadman said. "My God. So your footing was threatened, was it?" But his heart wasn't in it now; he had been distracted by Miss Greenaway's unbuttoning. Angelo too seemed interested, remaining at their table some time after the order had been given.

"The workmen are in there now," Owen said. "The Soprintendenza alle Gallerie are doing it. Italian funds, apparently."

"They are going to put in a completely new floor," Miss Greenaway said. "Christ, it's hot, isn't it?" She slipped the upper part of her boiler suit off her shoulders and allowed it to fall over the back of her chair. Beneath the close-fitting T-shirt her breasts were outlined, beautifully large and round.

"I hope the water-main services won't be affected," Raikes said. In the midst of these words, without warning and therefore without possibility of control, an intense and turgid interest in Miss Greenaway's bosom invaded him. It seemed like an invasion, a quick-shooting spore of lechery, wafted on a resistless breeze from he knew not where, sprouting almost at once into speculation as to whether Miss Greenaway was wearing a bra and into the attendant impulse to slip a hand under the T-shirt to ascertain the matter. As before with his landlady, it was not the thought so much that bothered him — such thoughts come and go — but the feverish intensity of it. Blood fluxed in his loins. He felt himself distending. He said desperately. "We shall need good pressure for the spraying."

"Well, you won't get it," Mrs. Hagerty said,with a slight snap of the lips. She seemed cross about something.

"Yes," Barfield said, widening his visionary eyes. "Not one word of a lie do I tell. Just getting them off the wall has been the problem so far."

"Apart from anything else," Owen said, "the sacristan kept getting in the way, didn't he, Gerald?"

"And his language," Miss Greenaway said. "Considering we were in church. I know enough Italian for that. Oh, he was cursing us, all right."

They were firm enough, there was no sag, but that softly mounded effect argued against an integument of any kind, however gossamer thin, as did the way in which the nipples, perfect and palpable, pricked against the cotton of the T-shirt . . . With a dangerous plunge of appetite, Raikes found himself wondering how much of one of Miss Greenaway's naked breasts he would be able to cram into his mouth. He felt constricted inside his trousers. Whose cannibal heat was this? Three other men at this table, he thought . . .

It was Miss Greenaway herself who restored him, with her reference to papers. "Of course he was annoyed," she said, "because he had that clearing-out to do. They promised to clear the place completely, but there were still these two old cupboards in there full of odds and ends, files and so on."

"We need the space, you see," Owen said. "We can't have bloody great cupboards in the way."

"Files?" Raikes felt his agitated blood subside.

"The smallest of the canvases is seven meters long, you know. Isn't it, Gerald?"

"Seven point three," Barfield said.

"Not as much as that surely," the other assistant said.

"What did he do with them, with the stuff in the cupboards?" Raikes said quietly to Owen, who was sitting next to him.

"Carted it all off. What annoyed him, you see, was that he had to empty the cupboards before he could move them. He took everything through into the sacristy."

"They weigh half a ton each," Barfield said. "What am I saying? *The Murder of Abel* on its own weighs thirteen hundredweight."

"They'll be a good bit lighter when we get the old linings off."

"Getting them off the stretchers is going to be the real sweat."

The Tintoretto people had reverted to their group identity, talking among themselves, sipping eagerly at their coffee as they did so — except for Miss Greenaway, he noted, who was having a separate, low-voiced conversation with Steadman. He heard her utter again that brief, rather barking laugh.

There might just be something there. The chapterhouse had been unused for ages, certainly for most of the century. Or even longer. A convenient dumping ground. Very damp, though; some of the windows had no glass in them. Still, if the cupboards were reasonably airtight . . .

"No, it's a good six meters," he heard Owen say. "I'm talking about *The Sacrifice of Isaac.*"

"So am I," Barfield said. "It is five point six five."

"You're wrong there, Gerald."

"I have always thought it pointless," Raikes said, "to argue about things that can easily be verified."

It was the sort of self-righteous remark that made him disliked. A certain resentful hush fell over the table. Raikes got to his feet. He had not really intended the words as a rebuke. "I'll be on my way," he said. It would be a good time to investigate the sacristy. But regret at having offended the Tintoretto people made him linger. Fatally, he sought to make amends by expounding further. "All this measuring is a curse," he said. "It was Ruskin who began it, creeping about. Everyone says what a breakthrough, but I don't think so at all. His slide rule wasn't much use to Effie, was it?"

His own incoherence, and the total failure of his joke — none of the Tintoretto people seemed to know what he was talking about — distressed him further. "Measuring instead of pleasuring," he said. "All our excitement we reserve for matter. We are interested only in *things.* All of us here . . . If you measured a corpse, do you think you would learn more about death? We're all pygmies, that's the trouble. One of Tintoretto's working days would have flattened you," he said, looking at Barfield. "And he kept it up for *years.* Me too," he added hastily; "it would have flattened me."

Nobody said anything. "Well," Raikes said heavily. "I'll be getting along." He left silence behind him. Going back across the *campo*, he lingered some moments before the Palazzo Dorvin. This was one of the houses he could see from his cubicle, and the details of the façade were now familiar enough to act as a sort of visual incantation, soothing and reassuring: the Donatellesque relief of Virgin and Child above the doorway, the roundheaded windows, the clear carving of the foliation surmounting the pilasters, the porphyry discs so exquisitely placed. Late Quattrocento — same period as the church, more or less. Nothing special about it, in this city of exquisite houses . . .

A mystery all the same, Raikes thought. Calm descended on him. The proportions of this house, the passion that drove Tintoretto, the presence of death. That's what I was trying to say, that is what I meant.

3

He went straight into the church, eager to see the contents of the cupboards that the sacristan had been obliged to move. But it was evident at once that this would not be possible, at least not then: there were too many people about. The floor was being taken up, not in the perilous fashion the Tintoretto people, with their relish for crisis, had described; but a double row of marble slabs on the north side had been lifted out, there were planks across, and a number of workmen stood around in the main body of the church, with a young man in charge of them. Raikes stopped to pass the time of day and the young man introduced himself. He was an architect employed by the Commune and his name was Benedetti. There were a number of other people in different parts of the church who seemed to have no business there other than to observe the progress of the restoration. To crown everything, the sacristan himself was in attendance, hanging around the chancel with his inflamed nose and bad-tempered expression.

A direct request to this man to be allowed to go through the papers might well be refused, Raikes thought: the sacristan gave the impression of morose self-importance often found in persons of small office; he might put obstacles in the way, insist on some time-consuming official procedure. It was not worth the risk.

Raikes sauntered up the south aisle past the two enormous canvases of Tintoretto resting against the wall and fenced off by chairs. It was a strange experience to find oneself on the same footing as these, eye to eye with the naked couple on the wrong side of the gates, and Cain aghast at what he had done. He paused beside the marble group of the *Pietà* at the entrance to the sacristy and looked inside. The floor was cluttered with various objects that seemed to have been dumped in the course of the restoration work — some planks of wood, metal buckets, a stepladder, boxes. Down the center was a long trestle table with an array of tubes, bottles, brushes of various shapes and sizes, a pile of what looked like metal brackets. This stuff belonged to the Tintoretto people, presumably. The usual inhabitants of the sacristy surveyed the unsightly clutter from on high: *The Virgin and Three Saints* by Sebastiano del Piombo above the altar; the large canvas of *The Visitation* attributed to Palma il Giovane; the panels of women saints and martyrs. No sign at all of what he was looking for. Except the boxes . . .

Picking his way, he advanced across the floor. But the boxes contained only chipped terra-cotta tiles. There was a chapel beyond, dedicated to St. John the Almsgiver. Raikes stood at the entrance and peered in. The light was not good here, but almost at once he saw the two broad cupboards against the wall. Surmounting them and on the floor around was miscellaneous débris of cardboard boxes and files. Finding the sacristy too crowded, the sacristan had lugged the things in here. No wonder he had cursed. As Raikes had hoped, he had not bothered, after such exertions, to lock the papers up again. Presumably he would, before long. Clearly, speed was of the essence. But there was nothing to be done for the time being.

Turning to retrace his steps, he was disagreeably surprised to find the sacristan watching him, standing where he himself had stood before, beside the marble *Pietà*. Raikes nodded and said *buon giorno,* and with some confused idea of giving his activities a more natural look he stopped to talk again to Signor Benedetti on the way out. The architect was voluble, and Raikes had difficulty in following the rapid Italian. It seemed that the task of relaying the floor had been complicated by the discovery of an earlier floor in red and yellow terra cotta, destroyed some time in the nineteenth century to make way for the marble slabs. There were, of course, Benedetti explained, remains of still earlier floors, one of Venetian terrazza, crushed stone laid in concrete. Three floors at least, then, and the whole mass sinking as the tides went on scooping underneath. They would have to lay gravel down to a depth of some forty-five centimeters at least to try to distribute the water evenly. It was going to be a long job, Benedetti said, smiling cheerfully.

The sacristan was now nowhere to be seen. Probably he had returned to his post near the chancel. Raikes returned Benedetti's smile, wished him *buon lavoro,* and made his way out of the church.

It was not until that evening that the obvious solution came to him. He had got back to the apartment fairly early and almost at once started on the day's diary entry. Sitting at his table near the window, he wrote eagerly.

The Madonna has had three days of spraying now — something like twenty hours of it. I used a very fine jet and warm water — not too hot, about twenty-five degrees. Of course this must not be mixed with soap or detergents of any kind; the calcium carbonate would combine with it and deposit a water-resistant coating on the stone, which would simply attract more dirt. Like covering the whole surface of the statue with fly paper.

Some particles of carbon came away, but the general appearance remains unchanged. It is unlikely that the spraying will do much to remove the corrosion — I never expected it to. The purpose is to soften the encrusted area, making things easier when it comes to the actual abrasion of the surface. I intend to make a start on this as soon as she is dried out. In fact I am aiming to begin on March 25, the day after tomorrow. This is the date of the Feast of the Annunciation, so it seems appropriate; perhaps it will be a good augury. Just at present working hours are curtailed by loss of light in the early evening, a situation which has been made rather worse by the enclosure of plastic sheeting Signor Biagi installed for me — he is proving most cooperative. I am going to ask him if he can provide me with a good strong light to work by — maybe he can take a cable up there.

I was thinking again about what Steadman said about the artist. There is no reason to think he came from Lombardy except that there was an influx of Lombard artists in the early part of the fifteenth century. He could just as easily have been a native Venetian who had spent periods of his life elsewhere. He was influenced by International Gothic, that is certain, not so much in the draperies but in the setting of the Madonna's hair and the headdress. Perhaps he had worked in Milan at some time, on the cathedral.

Raikes paused. He felt physically tired as he sat there, after the hours of crouching and stretching. Voices came to him from outside, people calling to or shouting at one another, friendly or angry he could not determine. He leaned forward to look out, but there was no one on the *fondamenta* immediately below. A small group of people crossed the bridge over the canal at the farthest extent of his vision. A family group, father, mother, three children, dressed for some special occasion. He watched them mount the steps, the brickwork parapet for some moments concealing all but the heads of the parents. Then they were again in full view, crossing sedately.

He had forgotten what an intensely *processional* city Venice was, how people were constantly offering profiles, parading across the line of sight, passing briefly before one, necessary but irrelevant, too, somehow. It was a consequence of all the intersections of street and waterway — no other city made one realize quite so much how coincidental human beings are to one another, or encouraged nostalgia for more acquaintance, more knowledge, always frustrated.

He continued looking for some time after the family had disappeared. On the brickwork, immediately above the arch of the bridge, were three stone heads set in a row, humanized lions or leonized men — salt and damp and chemical agents had eroded the differences. Or perhaps, he thought, the travesty was intentional, evidence of that taste for visual jokes the Venetians had always displayed.

It was light still, but the sun was low, too low to reach the surface of the canal. This was dark green and almost motionless. Already on the water and on the damp-darkened brick of the lower walls opposite there was some thicker graining, approach of night; but the upper stories of the houses were still in sunlight. A covered gondola, moored almost directly below him, was rocking very slowly in the thin shadow of the wall. The prow rail of its nearer side reared up, caught some faint light along the brass, dipped again. Raikes watched the slight pelvic jockeying, as if the boat were gathering itself, then the next strange blind upward motion — strange in effect where there was no sound and little apparent movement of the water.

He thought of the face of the Madonna running with water too copious for tears or rain, her drenched garments; then the alien grain of her body as he brought his face nearer, the ancient indifferent stuff of which she was made . . . The memory to accompany this came back at once. It had been near the surface of his mind all day: sensation rather than memory, the hush, the sense of sound or echo, not voices but the aftermath of voices, a quivering resonance; the long straight shadow and the two wet bodies standing quite close together. Man and woman? Yes. They were washing each other or putting water on each other. Summer light but indoors . . . He had been afraid afterward, not at the time; not exactly afraid, but as if he'd escaped something, some danger perhaps.

Raikes stood up abruptly. Nothing wrong with my nerves. Then the idea came to him, an adventure for a man whose nerves were in good order. He had a key to the side door of the church; each of them had been given one. He had a flashlight. He could go out and eat something; then he could let himself into the church and get a good leisurely look at these papers. As soon as this idea came to him he knew he was going to do it. And tonight was the night — delay would only increase the risk of the papers' being locked up again or moved elsewhere.

It was not that he really believed he would find anything new about the Madonna. On any sober assessment this was unlikely. Of course there was always the chance that something had been overlooked; people did not always realize the significance of what they saw. However, it was faith of another kind that spurred him on, some sense that he had been given a sign, that a message had been distilled for him from the otherwise tedious talk of the Tintoretto people. In any case, was he not doing this for his Madonna, his stone lady? It was a chivalric exploit he was engaged in, an *avventura*. His key and flashlight and the rubber-soled shoes he chose to wear were the accouterments of knighthood. Knights were not supposed to worry about the odds against success.

All the same, emerging onto the *fondamenta* he obeyed to begin with a certain impulse of timidity, taking a direction away from the church, toward the Grand Canal. He had to wait for the dark, he reminded himself. And there was food to think about. As he reached the San Marcuola landing stage a *vaporetto* came in, its bow making fiery way through the bronze sheen of the water. On an impulse he got on and bought a ticket to the Rialto. There were not many passengers at this time of evening, between work and pleasure; a few people who had been working late and a group of German tourists who had probably come down from the station — they had their luggage standing beside them. All these people stayed on the covered section of the deck, and Raikes was on his own standing at the stern rail.

It was chilly out on the water, and he turned up the collar of his raincoat, watching across the glinting surface the marvelous succession of buildings over on his left, beginning with the Renaissance splendors of the Palazzo Vendramin; then church, *scuola, palazzo,* in superb procession, their fronts faintly flushed in the dying light. Again he thought how processional Venice was, how everything one did here seemed to fall into some recognizable ritual. Of course it was because Venice had not changed much, only decayed. This dirty noisy boat of theirs followed a time-hallowed triumphal progress, showing itself to the façades, which paraded themselves in turn. Like many ardent, lonely people, Raikes possessed a strong vein of melancholy, and now he thought how sad it was, how very sad, this endless celebration of its own beauty the city indulged in, so long after the glory and energy had departed. It was something that could not be translated into human terms without heartsickness — love diminishing in the midst of protestation.

The *vaporetto* passed under the Rialto Bridge and deposited him at the landing stage. He walked back, crossed the bridge, and found a small restaurant about halfway along the Fondamenta del Vin with a view over the water. Here he sat over a half liter of Grignolino and a pizza quattro stagioni, watching the flush gradually fade from the buildings opposite. The brick darkened, the stone paled, the water took on its leaden-rose hue — even tones of color had their own ritual here. Then the lights began to come on, destroying the delicate melting equipoise of slate and rose on the water; lanterns on the marking poles out in the canal, the triple-headed street lights along the *fondamenta,* the prow lamps of gondolas.

It was half dark when he left the restaurant. He crossed the bridge again and lingered for a while in the Campo San Bartolomeo in front of the statue of Goldoni. There was a pigeon on the playwright's jaunty tricorn hat and another on his shoulder. Through the gathering darkness he looked down, Venice's favorite son, streaked with pigeon droppings, blackened by corrosion, the genial cynicism of his expression still showing through. Humorous, indulgent, gregarious — Raikes found it difficult to imagine a man more different from himself.

It was after nine o'clock, and quite dark, when he let himself in through the side door into the baptistry. He used his key to lock the door again from the inside, wincing nervously as the key repeated its grating sound in the lock. His light played a wavering beam over the base of the Romanesque font, and in a sudden shaft he saw turbaned profiles of adoring kings, the patient back of a donkey, angels' wings. It was a strange experience to see these fragments of the Christian story so briefly and tremulously illuminated. A faint light from the street lamps outside came through on the north side of the church, but Raikes remembered that the floor was up on that side and kept clear.

He proceeded up the south aisle, his heart beating quickly, light and eyes directed downward at his uneasy feet. He caught the flesh tones of guilt and sorrow from the Tintorettos as he went by, the ghastly sprawl of dead Abel; Adam's rib cage; Eve's long flowing hair. In the sacristy he was obliged to negotiate once again the rollers, the trestles, the litter of objects everwhere. He caught sight of Saints Dominic and Benedict looking severely at him. In the hush of the chapel he stopped to caution his heart before moving to where the files and cardboard boxes lay stacked on top of the cupboards and against the wall, below a painting by Vivarini, he noticed now; no mistaking that style. *Nativity of the Virgin.* Be still, he told his heart. You are not a thief, you have a key.

He knelt down below the mummy-swaddled, stunned-looking

infant Mary and began to look through the files on the floor. These contained papers of various kinds jumbled together without apparent order and not seeming to offer anything of interest: receipts for the most part or handwritten notes of expenditure without any signature on them, records of payment for oil, candles, repairs of various sorts, none of them going back earlier than the 1930s.

Raikes looked through them quickly, with a gathering chill of disappointment. What he had been expecting to find he could not have said, but he had assumed it would be somehow immediately significant, that his hands would fall on it, just as his ears had caught the intelligence that files of papers were on view here.

The folders were fairly new, he noticed. So was the tape. Someone had simply bundled the papers into them, tied them up, and shoved them in the cupboards, probably in the course of preparing the church for the restoration. It looked as if they had been lying about loose before this — but somewhere dry; there was no mold on them, though many were frayed and discolored. Certainly they could not have been long in the chapterhouse, where it was very damp indeed. There were loose papers stacked against the wall, programs of regattas and concerts of sacred music, yellow with age.

He was looking, not very hopefully, in the cardboard boxes when he came across a batch of papers with dates in the mid-nineteenth century, the same type of thing as before: small financial records, faded and difficult to read. Below this were some old account books. There were more account books in the next box, and several smaller notebooks with stiff black covers. Raikes fished one of these out at random, opened it, and found himself looking at details of small sums of money paid, for reasons he could not make out, to one Andrea Carpello, in October 1759. With revived excitement, a sudden prescience of success, he began to turn back the pages. There was no entry for June 1743, but there was one for the 28th of April. Two ducats had been paid out on that day, it seemed, in payment for services, though these were not specified. There was an address written against the sum, of which Raikes could make out only that it was in the San Giovanni Crisostomo district.

He was kneeling on the hard floor, looking earnestly at this and trying to see some connection with the Madonna, when he heard

— and it was quite distinct in the silence of the church — the grating sound of the side door being unlocked. He heard the door creak open and he heard steps and some moments later voices, a man's and a woman's, cautious and low.

In two simultaneous movements Raikes seized the notebook and switched off his flashlight. He was dreadfully startled. He stood in the not quite complete darkness of the chapel, his heart loud in his ears, more breath to expel than his lungs seemed able to deal with. His first thought, and it was a very disagreeable one, was that the gleam of his flashlight had been seen and persons in authority had come to investigate. But these had not been the voices of investigators, no light had gone on, the steps were cautious. They were coming up through the church toward him. Now he saw glimmerings of light from beyond the sacristy entrance. The woman uttered a brief, annoyed-sounding exclamation. The man spoke in low tones. The words were indistinct, but they sounded like English.

Raikes stood motionless against the chapel wall. Were they thieves? Should he challenge them? He had left it rather late. They were inside the sacristy now and seemed to have come to a halt. The beam of their flashlight behaved erratically for some moments. He heard rustling sounds as of garments and a sort of intermittent murmuring, a swarming, summer sound, strangely inappropriate in that place. Then the man spoke, quietly but quite distinctly. "Hold the light, will you, Muriel," he said. "I'll clear a space on the table. Otherwise things are going to get broken."

The voice was familiar, the reasonable tone, the Midlands accent. Raikes could imagine the visionary widening of the eyes. It was the Tintoretto man, Barfield. "A square meter will be ample," he heard the voice say.

"We'll do ourselves an injury one of these days," the woman said, "clambering about on tables." Raikes recognized the cross-patch voice: it was Mrs. Hagerty.

There was no escape, no way out except through the sacristy. Raikes attempted to close his mind to what he was hearing and about to hear by tracing the lineaments of the Vivarini *Nativity of the Virgin* on the wall above him. All that was visible were the areas of white, and these only faintly; the headcloths of the women and the swaddling bands of the baby made a diagonal line from left to right, with the head of the infant almost but not quite in the center. He tried to remember the faces of the women attendants, distraught with excess of reverence, the dazed-looking bobbin of a baby . . .

"Muriel," came Barfield's voice again, "do you think you could spread yourself a bit? The angle needs to be increased by about five degrees. As things are at present I can't get in."

"I'm hanging off the bloody table already, "Muriel said. "Wait a minute . . . *Ooh!*"

"That's better," Barfield said. "That's much better. Hooray!"

"Ooh!" Muriel exclaimed again. "Oh, Jerry."

"Now you bitch," Barfield said with sudden savagery. "Now I'll teach you. Take that. You slut."

"Jerry, Jerry, Jerry," Muriel moaned. "I'm sorry, Jerry."

"Think I'm a bloody geriatric, do you?" Barfield said through clenched teeth, and this was quite the most appalling pun Raikes could ever remember hearing. "Think I can't fuck you on a table without doing myself an injury, do you? Take that and that." Some object fell with a slight crash to the floor. There was a woeful preliminary groan from Barfield, interrupting his furious abuse. Raikes stood amazed in the darkness. He could hardly believe it even now. There in the sacristy, in the presence of *The Virgin and Three Saints* above the altar, the marble *Pietà* behind them, Saints Dominic and Benedict on the wall, all the women saints and martyrs in the panels, objects of sacred devotion all round them, Barfield and his assistant were knowing each other carnally, acting out strange roles, different from those of every day, combining tones of rage and pleading.

It seemed to take a long time for this performance to run its course, sounds to abate, clothing to be readjusted. Barfield, restored to his usual pedantic mildness, made one or two anticlimactic remarks, and Muriel answered snappishly. The sound of their steps receded. For quite some time longer, Raikes remained where he was, motionless in the dark. It was an effort for him to switch on his flashlight again. Finally, still clutching the notebook, he crept out of the church and set himself toward home.

Speculations crowded his mind as he walked back. Why had they chosen the sacristy? Did the element of blasphemy add to the pleasure? Was Barfield activated only in the near vicinity of his restoration project? Perhaps there were people for whom cluttered tables and cramped positions were essential preconditions. A sort of variant of bondage sex, he thought vaguely. His own experience provided little help, but no practice, however outlandish, could lack for devotees somewhere surely, sexual habits being in that respect like religious cults . . .

These thoughts did not finally disappear until he found himself once more in his apartment, with the curtains drawn, looking at the notebook by the light of the table lamp. It was not a proper account book; the lines had been ruled by hand and the widths between them varied. It seemed more like a casual record of small incidental payments, perhaps made out of petty cash, which would be totaled and entered under a single heading in the official ledger. The writing was in ink, a spidery copperplate, much faded — and effaced altogether in places where there had been some friction in the pages. But the entry he was interested in was reasonably clear, except for a word in brackets in the cash column. The address was in San Giovanni Crisostomo: 5169 Calle Guanara. It seemed an improbably high number for the house . . .

Raikes was gripped again by the excitement he had experienced on finding the notebook and which had been overlaid in the interval by the behavior of the Tintoretto people. He tried to enjoin caution on himself. The entry in the notebook might not have anything to do with the Madonna. There was really only the date to go on, and that could be — quite probably was — purely coincidental. But it was in vain. He thought of the circumstances in which he had found the notebook, the haphazard way in which it had come about, as if vouchsafed to his blundering fingers, revealed to his vague eyes. What if I have been chosen? he thought. What if I am the one chosen to clear up the mystery?

Restless, he got up and went to the window. He parted the curtains a little and looked out. It was high tide. In the light from the *campo* along the bridge he saw the water washing over the steps of the house gate opposite, almost at the level of the *fondamenta* —

another six inches and it would be flooding right over. Water covered the top step, leveled for a few seconds in a translucent skein over the stone, slopped gently off again. There was to his sense in this brief steadiness of the water, its momentary unrufflement as it lay across the step with the pale stone shining through it, something devotional, something sacramental, though he was aware of that surprise, and even faint alarm felt before in Venice at the sight of water where water had no business to be, water creeping among the abodes of man in the silence of the night, disregarded. It was as if these steps and walls and the quayside itself, all this washed and accommodating stone, though seeming to be fashioned for man's purposes, now in his absence had reverted to its own, which was the celebration of the beauty and supremacy of the brimming water, whose levels were rising year by year and slowly drowning the city . . .

He returned to the table and stood looking down at the notebook. There was no other entry on this page, only three altogether for April and none at all for the previous month, confirming his belief that the sums were from some small fund for occasional expenses. But only this entry, as far as he could see, had a bracketed word in the cash column. This was difficult to make out, especially the first part of it, because the paper had worn smooth there. *Denari,* he had taken it to be, the Italian word for money. But it seemed to have more letters than that. The lamplight reflected from the worn patch, making things more difficult. Acting on sudden impulse, Raikes went down on his knees and held the page up against the light. Afterward he was to wonder whether it was the filtering light itself or heat from the lamp operating in some way, but the imprint was now quite clear and unmistakable. The word was *Fornarini.*

4

"That is a *very* old name," Wiseman said. "Goes back a long way. They were one of the original twenty-four, or so it is claimed. My gosh, yes." He blinked and chuckled at the thought of this. Venice was his hobby and his passion.

Raikes smiled in response, glad to find that Wiseman knew something about it, delighted by the other's enthusiasm, which he recognized again now after the years in which they had not met; it was the quality they shared and which had kept them friends. "Who were *they?*" he said. Here in this sheltered spot, the sun warm on his face, digesting his *spaghetti alle vongole* and veal cutlet, half the Merlot still left in the bottle, he felt a sense of well-being and expansiveness. "Sounds like a magic number," he said. "Were they the founders of the city?"

"They were the original families who ruled as tribunes over the Lagoon islands. This was before there was any Venice at all, at least as we know it now — there was no settlement on the Rialto yet. We're going back to the seventh century, a fairly misty period, which is why a lot of the claims can't be authenticated. The Fornarini, for example, claim a semimythic ancestry going back to the founders of Rome. That's nonsense, of course. Still, they are one of the oldest."

Raikes nodded. Wiseman's voice, the New York accent softened by travel and by the gentle temperament of its owner, was very soothing and lulling. The wine too had relaxed him. His eyes fell on two Italian women in early middle age, both slender and smartly dressed, sitting at a nearby table. One of them raised herself slightly in her chair in order, it seemed, to smoothe her skirt against the back of her legs. This slight lunge of the woman's pelvis gave Raikes an unexpected and poignant pang in the genitals. He felt his face and body go hot. He looked away hastily, nibbled some cheese, poured Wiseman and himself more wine. What would Wiseman say, he wondered, if I told him that since my arrival in this city, since starting work on my Madonna, I have had what seem to be hallucinations, my level of sexual awareness has been so topped up that I have intimations of orgasm in everything I see, I cannot look at a fork in a tree without feelings of restlessness? It would only embarrass him, of course. It occurred to Raikes that he did not really know what Wiseman's sexual propensities were — or indeed if he had any.

"They have the crest feathers of an eagle on their coat of arms," Wiseman said. "Only six Venetian families were allowed to display lilies or eagles on their arms. Seven if you count the eagle's foot of the Malipieri. They called themselves the Case Vecchie, the twenty-four I mean, or their descendants do. The old houses. They were a sort of caste within a caste. I'm planning a chapter on it, not on the history of the families, but some of the anecdotes about them."

Wiseman was in charge of the UNESCO office that had been established in Venice after the 1966 floods. In the time left over from official duties he was writing a book entitled *Venetian Byways*, a sort of compendium of historical gossip, exactly suited to his tastes and interests, which were antiquarian without being systematic. He was corpulent, and his rather full cheeks and small mouth gave him the general appearance of a cherub.

"The fact is," he said now, blinking mild eyes in the pleasure of having things to impart, "there are gaps in our knowledge, enormous gaps. There is the *Libro d'Oro*, of course, which is still in existence — it's in the state archives — but it goes back only to 1506 and in any case contains just certificates of marriages and legitimate births. No references to origins, no pedigrees, no blazons. A lot of the ancient registers with details of titles were probably destroyed in 1797 at the time of Napoleon's invasion of Venice. So really we have to rely mainly on the genealogical works compiled before 1797, based on state papers that were afterward destroyed. The best book on the subject is probably Marco Barbaro's *Origin and Descent of the Patrician Families*."

"Where could I get hold of a copy?"

"You could probably get one through the university here." Wiseman hesitated for a moment or two; then he said, "As a matter of fact I have a copy of the 1926 edition. You can borrow that, if you like."

"That is really very good of you," Raikes said warmly. He had not failed to notice Wiseman's struggle, and he was touched by this evidence of friendship. "I'll take care of it," he promised.

"Of course," Wiseman said, as if wishing to retract, "it wouldn't be much good for the eighteenth century, you know. The Fornarini family had sadly declined by that time. There might have been twenty or thirty people with that name, very few of them possessing any money. No, they were at their peak in the fifteenth century, when your statue was carved."

"Still," Raikes said, "I'd like to have a look."

"Of course. I'll drop by with it. Or I'll send someone. Not where you're working, though — it's too messy there."

"I'm not working this afternoon. I'm making a start tomorrow, the twenty-fifth."

Raikes instantly regretted saying this. He did not want Wiseman to know that he had been waiting for the Feast Day of the Annunciation before beginning; it seemed to reveal too much of his own private rituals. Wiseman was kind and sensitive and sympathetic, but he looked always for quirks and oddities; he made everything into anecdote. It was why Raikes had not given the real reason for wanting to know about the Fornarini — the last thing he wanted was to see the Madonna featured in Wiseman's *Byways*. And it was why he had never talked much about personal feelings to the other man, distrusting the quality of the understanding that Wiseman would give him.

However, he realized after a moment that Wiseman saw no significance in the date. No reason why he should, of course. I must stop attributing my own obsessions to other people, Raikes thought. "Shall we have some coffee?" he said.

"I suppose we'd better. I must be thinking about getting back. It's pleasant here, isn't it?"

"Very."

They were on the Riva degli Schiavoni, looking across to the marvelously fabricated shape of San Giorgio, with its line of little boats along the front, like beading. Earlier, when he had been on his way to meet Wiseman, there had been a powdering of mist in the air, thicker on the broader water where the Giudecca Canal opened into the basin of San Marco, obscuring the lines of the church, softening the outline of dome and *campanile*. Now, something like two hours later, the light was clear and sparkling on the water, every detail of Palladio's design was radiantly distinct, the whole thing, church and island together, seemed like a single artifact, resting improbably on its bed of mud and sand. There was shape behind shape here, hanging with distance, Giudecca beyond San Giorgio and beyond that the long sandbanks of the Lido.

There were a number of small boats out on the water. A motor launch went past at speed, its prow rising and dipping like the upper blade of scissors cutting horizontally. The surface seemed hardly disturbed by this, resuming its calm almost at once, canceling the passage. But just below them, under the planks of the landing platform, among the mooring posts of the gondola station, Raikes saw that the water was wild demonic green in the shadow of the timbers, swirling with a sort of secretive violence against the poles. He was struck by this clandestine, treacherous behavior of the water, and was about to draw Wiseman's attention to it, when the latter said, "As a matter of fact I know someone here in Venice called Fornarini."

"Do you really?"

Wiseman was again looking immensely pleased. It always gave him innocent pleasure to be in possession of facts and able to impart them. "Oh, yes," he said, and chuckled slightly. "Met her and her husband a year or so ago. She is Chiara Litsov now, but she was Chiara Fornarini before her marriage."

"That is most interesting," Raikes said. Wiseman must have been saving this up all through lunch, he thought, waiting for the most effective moment to come out with it. "Of course, you know everybody," he said.

"I think they would remember me. Would you like to meet them?"

"Well . . . yes. Yes, I would."

Raikes's hesitation had been caused by the fact that he had no real reason for thinking there was any connection at all between the Fornarini family and his Madonna. Mistaking its nature, Wiseman said, "They are an interesting couple. He is an artist, a sculptor, very talented, beginning to be successful. They don't live in Venice itself, but on one of the islands in the Lagoon, rather remote. You have to get a boat from Burano. But they have a telephone. Litsov himself is something of a recluse; he doesn't often leave the island. In fact he told me when I met him that he had been away only twice in the previous six months. She is more sociable. She is a remarkable woman, I think."

"I'd like to meet them very much," Raikes said, more firmly. Something might come of it after all, he thought. And there would be no harm done in any case.

"And so you shall, dear boy," Wiseman said. "Leave it all to Uncle Alex."

On this amiable note they parted, Wiseman to return to his office off the Calle Larga San Marco, Raikes to carry out a purpose that had been on his mind since the previous evening, since first his wavering flashlight had settled on that page.

He had been already that morning to the Central Post Office to check on the address, and it was fortunate he had done so, as neither street nor number was now the same. There had been a reorganization of the whole system in the 1930s, and Calle Guanara did not now include the house, which was known as Casa Fioret and given as being on the Calle dei Savi, number six.

It took him something like an hour to walk it, proceeding northward from behind the Piazza San Marco, steering roughly by the glinting water of the Grand Canal, constantly glimpsed on his left and lost again. The street ran between the church of San Giovanni Crisostomo and the Malibran Theater. It was narrow, with tall houses on either side, bounded by a green and malodorous canal. Casa Fioret was the last house on the right, its doors opening onto the street and the canal running at the side, immediately below its walls. There was no bridge; the street ended at the stone steps that led down into the water. From the third-floor balcony of Casa Fioret to the corresponding balcony of the house opposite, there was a double line of washing.

The street door was massive, six or eight feet across, with a high rounded arch and stone pillars at the sides with acanthus-leaf decorations. On the facing of the arch, in the center, there was a huge lion's head showing a snarl that had weathered into amiability; and set into the wall at one side, like guardian eyes, twenty-eight bell pushes in a rectangular panel — Raikes counted them as he stood there. Twenty-eight separate groups of people now lived in Casa Fioret.

The promiscuous sheets and pajamas and petticoats waving overhead, the evidence of multiple occupation staring Argus-eyed at him, gave Raikes a chilling sense of anticlimax and futility. What could all this have to do with the Madonna? He had assumed at least some sort of continuous occupation, somebody he could question. He felt like a gambler who had suddenly run out of luck.

The heavy door was not locked; it swung open to his push. He passed through and found himself in a large paved area like an interior courtyard, with a marble well-head in the center and a flight of stone steps, leading presumably to the upper floors. The stairs had a carved banister, made of heavy dark wood, with large smooth bosses at intervals. There was a smell of damp and urine. A baby was crying from a room on his right, and from somewhere above he could hear the sound of a radio. He stood for some moments examining the design of lions' heads around the rim of the well-head. The manes had been blended with the triangular patterns of foliation between the heads in an original and attractive manner which he could not remember seeing before. A woman with a shopping basket came down the stairs and went past him without speaking. He noticed now that the bosses on the banister were in fact human heads worn almost featureless.

At the far end of the courtyard there was a double door standing open, a sense of space beyond. Raikes passed through it into an area surrounded by brick walls, which he thought must once have been the garden of the house, though it had been leveled and paved over. It was rectangular in shape and extensive for Venice, with a wrought-iron gate at the far end. Three very small boys were squatting over something near the wall that ran by the canal, and a little girl with bare feet swung a disheveled doll. There were more lines of washing and two women standing talking together. It seemed to be a communal area used by the tenants. No one took any notice of Raikes at all. He stood for some moments, dismayed by the neglect and poverty visible everywhere: the rusty metal fire escapes clambering from floor to floor, the rotting eaves, the crumbling, discolored brick. It must have been a beautiful house once, with all the space, that courtyard, the long garden running beside the canal. The design was visible still, of course, and the proportions, the spacing of the windows with their high rounded arches, the elegant stonework of the balconies, the exquisitely decorated *campanella*. There were so many houses like this now in Venice, hundreds upon hundreds of them, tenements for the poor, rotting away along obscure side canals. Few if any would ever be restored.

Depressed by these thoughts, Raikes walked to the gate at the end, which gave onto an alley running down to the canal. Immediately opposite, beyond the wall on that side, there was a church, ruined and abandoned-looking; he could see the *campanile*, the dilapidated pantiled roof, the upper curve of the apse. Though sizable enough, the church seemed to have no grounds or precincts. It was hemmed close by other buildings all around.

He passed through the gate and turned down toward the canal, but there was no bridge across; the alley simply terminated at the water. He had to retrace his steps. Unwilling to go back the way he had come, he followed the alley, which he discovered came out after a few hundred yards on to the *salizzada*, close to the Fontego Canal. From here, disgruntled, disappointed, full of an obscure distress, he made his way to the Rialto boat station, and so home.

Wiseman had been as good as his word. Marco Barbaro's *Origin and Descent of the Patrician Families* was waiting for him. But he had no heart for it that evening.

5

Some sort of humility, and a fear of his own clumsiness, kept Raikes off the Madonna's face to begin with. All stone as she was, her face was more tender; it was here the human likeness was concentrated. It is no easy thing to bring a cutting instrument to the surface of a face, particularly such a one as he had in his hand now, with its steady pulse of power, its voracious hissing.

So he crouched down, like any devotee, and began on the hem of her robe. At first he held the instrument too far away to be very effective, being nervous still about the result. It was the first time to his knowledge that he had used the quartz cutter on stone of this antiquity, certainly the first time on an acknowledged work of art. He was inhibited to begin with, too, by his accouterments, the cable which he had looped over his shoulder, the plastic face mask which he was obliged to wear, covering eyes and mouth — for the infected stone was reduced to powder immediately, at the first assault of the cutter, and the dust flew upward into his face.

Gradually his confidence grew and he began controlling the distance better, aiming the cutter with more delicate precision, feeling its energy now allied with his own. All his doubts, and the discomfort of his crouching position, were forgotten in his delight at seeing the polluted crust thin out and disappear, centimeter by centimeter, as the microscopic grains of glass with which the cutter was loaded delicately blasted away the efflorescence of disease, leaving the uninfected stone intact. There was something in the nature of a continuous miracle about this transmutation: one moment there was the corroded stain; the next, as by the warm breath of a god, it was fanned away, leaving the pale and pristine stone beneath. Raikes was lulled by the process into a mood of calm delight. He worked steadily, constantly adjusting the distance of the cutter, holding its stem between fingers and thumb like a fountain pen.

As he worked, his thoughts reverted to his strangely demoralizing experience of the previous afternoon: the rotting tenement, the quarreling children, the wash lines, the sense of a dead trail. He began deliberately to recall the details of his visit, as if in retrospect he might discover some clue not apparent at the time. The listless child with her disheveled doll. The two women talking, indifferent to his presence, or so it seemed. The festooned washing, colors reflected in the dark green of the canal, also reflected the symptoms of decay, the peeling *intonaco,* the dark red of the rotting brick — there had been a tide mark six feet up the wall on the canal side. Damp course of Istrian stone far too low for present levels. The courtyard paved with terra cotta. Stone lintels carved with diamond patterns. Then the lions' heads in relief and that cunning pattern of foliation. Bumps that had once been heads. Another head somewhere he had seen . . . Most dispiriting of all that paved enclosure, once a garden. And the cramped, deconsecrated church across the alley. Deconsecrated presumably, yes, but why that word? There had been no cross anywhere visible. Something else tugged at his mind, something he had registered but not yet described to himself, something about the church . . .

He had switched off the cutter and straightened up. His mind was still on the church. Some combination of significance was seeking to engage his understanding. Suddenly, without preliminary warning, Raikes felt again that curiously piercing, swooning threat to his balance, not giddiness, a sort of dream fall that left him still standing in a hush, a resonant aftermath of voices, and he seemed to glimpse the Madonna, but white and clean, half hidden among foliage, at a distance and somehow as if roofed over, so that she was half in light, half in shadow, and lustrous, as if with rain or dew. He recognized the pose, the hands, the angle of the head. There seemed to be a distant landscape beyond her, with buildings of some kind on the crest of a hill. Then the plastic sheets were around him again, the corroded stone a foot from his eyes, dust still swirling in the enclosure. There was no disturbance to his breathing, but he was gripping the cutter tightly. As before, it was surprise, a slightly alarmed sense of escape, that possessed him. It was as if he had stepped off the curb without looking and something had swerved and just missed him, quite soundlessly.

Slowly Raikes removed his mask. He would have some coffee from his flask, he decided — Signora Sapori had kindly made up a flask for him. Before he did so, however, he bent down and touched the part he had cleaned, running his fingers along it. An event, this — the first reclaimed stone. It was smooth and cold to the touch. He could feel the slight sweat of the crystals under his fingertips. She had been under an arch of some kind, something constructed, not just vegetation; the shape had been too regular for that . . . The alarm persisted. It occurred to Raikes that he ought perhaps to go to see a doctor.

By the time he got home that evening, a good start made on the lower draperies, he had, if not dismissed this thought, at least confidently distanced it. It was not as if he felt ill at all; on the contrary, he could not remember feeling better. He was conscious of his body, of an energy and a sort of voluptuous tension throughout his limbs. It would be absurd to go to a doctor. He would feel a fool.

He was in a mood of confidence in any case when he returned to the apartment, having had a fair amount of Barbera with his dinner. He had dined with Steadman and an Italian couple who were friends of Steadman's — the man an authority on Byzantine influences on early Venetian sculpture — and he had enjoyed the evening and the talk, as people solitary by nature do enjoy such things.

It was late, but he conscientiously made his diary entry, recording his successful start. Afterward he had a look at the book Wiseman had lent him.

He had not intended to read long, merely to find his way about in the book, but he was soon absorbed. The *Origin and Descent* was much more than an official account of the patrician families of Venice. It contained a good deal of gossip and anecdote and personal reflections of the author — which was why Wiseman liked it so much probably, though he had been wrong about one thing, Raikes soon discovered: the Fornarini traced their origins not simply to the founders of Rome, but through eleven emperors of Constantinople right back to the founders of Athens, which was tantamount really to saying that there had always been Fornarinis, they were eternal. However, it seemed they could actually prove a progenitor in the eighth century, which was impressive enough.

Certainly they had had their ups and downs. In the year 1170, when Venice was at war with the Emperor Manuel I, the menfolk of the family followed their Doge to the Levant. While they were in winter quarters in Chios, a fierce plague broke out among the fleet, the Doge returned with only sixteen ships out of a hundred and twenty, and the family was almost wiped out. But God, according to Barbaro, gave the surviving males such potency and fertility that their women conceived at a glance almost, and the family was soon restocked; by the middle of the fifteenth century there were as many as fifty different branches of the Fornarini, and two hundred nobles of Venice bore that name.

The political power of the family had been founded by Marcantonio Fornarini, Venetian ambassador to the court of Naples in the early 1400s and afterward state inquisitor. In the period of their greatness the Fornarini produced two doges, three admirals, numerous high officials, and one saint — Francesco, first Patriarch of Venice, a man of irreproachable life, whose body had not been subject to putrefaction. In the sixteenth century they were prominent members of the celebrated Company of the Hose, so called from the tight-fitting breeches the companions wore. The uniform of a certain Nicolò Fornarini was described by chroniclers of the time as "having the left leg crimson and the right divided lengthwise in azure and violet, and embroidered with a cypress bough."

This seemed to have been the high point. Thereafter the decline was steady. By the time Barbaro was writing, only four branches of the family remained. The last appearance on the public stage was not edifying. Giorgio Fornarini collaborated with Napoleon and urged surrender on the Senate, a shame and a scandal in the opinion of Barbaro for one of such lineage, particularly as it was done not out of any patriotic motive or desire to protect the Republic from the consequences of invasion but out of revenge for loss of office: he had been dismissed for what the author with tantalizing vagueness referred to as "shameless misconduct."

This motive of revenge, a certain arrogant and implacable vindictiveness, ran like a dark thread through the history of the family. One Lorenzo Fornarini, arrested by the night constables in 1323 for brawling in the street, had refused to pay his fine, and when an official of the court came to his house for the money, he had threatened the man's life. Because of these menaces his fine had been increased by one hundred *lire di piccoli.* Six months later Lorenzo, aided by a runaway slave named Jacopo Saraceno, to whom he had promised money, waylaid the official and stabbed him to death. It says much for Venetian justice at the time that no distinction was made between patrician and slave: both were publicly garrotted. Then there was Andreolo, who in 1509 killed a lady's steward, an elderly man quite unknown to him, because the lady had repelled his advances, and he knew she valued the man. And there was Naufosio, who while campaigning in Lombardy against the Visconti put to the sword all the male citizens of Lodara because the town had held out against him — a usage most uncommon among Venetian commanders, and for which Naufosio had been recalled . . .

So Raikes read on, learning a good deal about the Fornarini family and something more about the past of Venice. But it was nearly two o'clock in the morning, and his eyes were heavy, when he stumbled on one small fact which seemed to him worth all the others put together and irradiated his being with joy.

Barbaro had reverted to the sainted Patriarch Francesco, extolling his virtues, praising his life of austerity and chastity, which shone like a beacon amidst the turbulence of those days. The greater was the pity then that the only other Fornarini to hold high ecclesiastical office should have so signally failed to follow his illustrious forebear's example, should indeed have so far failed as to have been notorious for his profligacy, and that in a licentious period.

There was a footnote to this, and Raikes, looking down to the bottom of the page, discovered that the prelate referred to was a certain Piero Fornarini, Bishop of Venice from 1737 until 1752, when he had choked on a chicken bone and died.

6

It was a day of bright sunshine, clear enough, though the sun was softened by the remnants of the night's mists. Once past San Michele and Murano, they were in the open, the great expanse of the Lagoon before and all around them, a vast glimmering sheet, patterned by its shallows, streaked here and there by rippling flashes where mudflats broke the surface; elsewhere unblemished, pale blue, with a soft shine to it as though wiped with oil.

The boat steamed northeast toward Mazzorbo, following the staked-out line of the deep-water channel. Raikes strained his eyes eastward across the shifting glimmers of the surface to where the brightness gathered and dazzled. He could make out the long shape of the Lido and the *campanile* of San Nicolò. Small islands, mere mudbanks tufted with vegetation, were discernible on both sides; others, more distant, were half lost in the haze, darker impurities in the clouded liquid of the horizon. To the east a mile or two away he thought he identified the island gardens of La Vignola and Sant'Erasmo, which supply Venice with vegetables. He considered asking Wiseman about this, then decided against it, not wanting to accommodate the information that Wiseman, once asked, would undoubtedly pour forth — he had a chapter on the Lagoon in his *Byways*.

The boat passed close to an island he remembered, the sad, abandoned San Giacomo in the Marsh, with its broken walls, grassed-over mounds of rubble, and listing birch trees. "Appropriate name," he said to Wiseman. "It looks like a marsh, doesn't it? A marsh that someone was once foolish enough to build on."

They were standing toward the stern, where it was roofed but open at the sides. Wiseman had turned up the collar of his light tweed overcoat. With his hair ruffled by the sea breeze and his cheeks rosy from the fresh air, he looked more than ever like an older-generation cherub, a worn Cupid caught in light, inconsequential currents or some sportive billows aimed by Venus. "It had a population of several thousand at one time," he said. "Hard to believe now, isn't it? The church was built by Carducci. They didn't keep up the sea walls. Shortage of cash, or so they say — it's the province of the Magistratura alla Acqua. There are drowning islands all over the Lagoon, and quite a few underneath the water, of course, like Costanziaca, for example, which was a flourishing place long before San Marco was thought of, with churches and monasteries — it was a place of pilgrimage famous throughout Italy. Then the tides just slowly made a marsh of it. The waters closed over it some time in the eighteenth century, I think."

They were approaching Mazzorbo now, with the *campanile* of Santa Caterina rising immediately before them. The *motoscafo* turned at right angles up the wide canal, stopped at the Burano landing stage, where it deposited Raikes and Wiseman. They stood for some moments on the jetty, watching the boat nose out again toward Torcello.

"What we need now," Wiseman said, "is a *sandolo* to take us to San Pietro. We're at the end of the line here, more or less. The water-bus services don't go beyond Torcello. Mrs. Litsov offered to pick us up here, but I said we'd make our own way. They'll bring us back, I imagine."

They went down to the busy little harbor, where the colored reflections of hulls and houses rocked on the water, and almost at once found a man who was willing to take them — he was making for the mouth of the harbor, about to set off on a fishing trip.

"You need someone who knows the waters," Wiseman said rather nervously as they stepped down into the boat, though perhaps the nervousness was for his balance, Raikes thought, rather than the uncertainties of the Lagoon. He was more than ever impressed by Wiseman's kindness in braving all this for the sake of introducing him to Chiara Litsov, *née* Fornarini. And he felt guilty in a way, or as if he were going on false pretenses. Still, she might be able to tell him something. His discovery of the evening before had definitely linked the name of Fornarini with the statue — and therefore, in his own mind at least, with the house in San Giovanni Crisostomo.

Something of the excitement of that discovery returned to him as they turned eastward beyond the harbor wall in what he thought was the direction of the open sea. The light was hazier now, and the long strips of the *lidi,* those essential ligaments of the Lagoon, were no longer visible. With Burano left behind, they were without immediate landmarks, moving on a calm waste of water, prey like everything else to its perpetual glimmering reflections. Astern, in the distance, a darker mass rose above the flats, and Raikes guessed this might be the cypresses of San Francesco del Deserto, which he had read about but never visited, where there was a monastery still, and where St. Francis of Assisi was said to have put in during a Lagoon storm. Though where coming from or going to, he could not remember. He had planted his stick and a pine had sprung up . . .

The boatman stood upright in the stern, propelling them fairly briskly with a rhythmic forward thrust on his single oar. He uttered a regular heavy breathing sound, like a quiet grunt, not a sound of exertion but seeming in the nature of self-encouragement, as another might sing. That, with the creaking of the rowlocks and the faint slap of the wash, was all the sound there was. Silent gulls probed for clams in the shallows not far away. The light flashed on their breasts as they turned. They were wading, not swimming, Raikes noticed — the water was no more than a few inches deep there. Beyond them, glistening mudbanks rose clear of the surface like a shoal of enormous amphibians basking half submerged. Here obviously both skill and knowledge of the channels were necessary; occasionally their oar gashed mud, releasing dark liquid to stain the surface.

"The water's rising, I think," Wiseman said. "All this is covered at high tide, of course."

They were coming again into what seemed deeper water, with little tufts of islands here and there, some with ruined walls on them or the remains of what might have been gardens, still precariously clear of the surface, though half drowned already, as was evidenced by the tidal detritus caught high in bushes and trees, a tangle of seaweed and bleached sticks.

"San Pietro," the boatman said suddenly, looking back toward them. His tone was one of doubt rather than affirmation. *È un'isola abbandonata,"* he said. He rested on the oar for a few moments, smiling and shrugging slightly. It was as if it had suddenly occurred to him to doubt the whole enterprise. *"Nessuno qui,"* he said. "There is nobody there."

"Somebody lives there," Wiseman said. *"Uno straniero. Uno scultore."*

"Ah, sì." The boatman appeared suddenly to remember. *"Americano, inglese?"*

"Inglese."

The boatman nodded. *"La moglice è italiana,"* he said. Apparently quite satisfied now, he returned to his rowing.

"He knew all along," Wiseman said to Raikes. "I've noticed the same thing before. It's as if they were testing one."

"It's not an English name," Raikes said.

"Litsov? No, his parents were Polish, or perhaps only his father, but he was born in England, I think. He's beginning to do very well now, as I told you. He seems to have taken off in the last three years or so. Before that they were very poor, I believe. Now a Litsov bronze can fetch four or five thousand pounds. I know that for a fact. He's a rising star, no doubt about it. Not that it seems to make much difference to him. He hardly ever goes off the island. She's the one who looks after things; well, you'll see when you meet her . . ."

As Wiseman continued, Raikes allowed his mind to drift from full attention. That sense of the fabulous descended on him which always lies in enclosed waters that have been intimate with man for long centuries yet still guard their remoteness. These shallows and salt marshes had provided a refuge for the people of the mainland fleeing from barbarian invaders something like fifteen centuries ago. They had been continuously inhabited ever since. It was possible because of this to imagine more willing collusions here than elsewhere between water and sky, more complex blends of light and reflection, more melting and fusion of forms. And yet the waters were no tamer than they had ever been, still responding to the elemental movements of the tide . . . .

"That's it now, on the left," Wiseman said.

Raikes turned to look in the direction indicated, saw the low shape of the island, with ragged thickets of trees, quite dense, on the left, the western side, and a ruined bell tower standing isolated against the bright haze of the sky. As they drew nearer, he made out ruined walls, an arch hung with ivy, two or three tumbledown *casone* — low wattle huts made by local fishermen. On the other side, the side they were approaching, it was barer, without trees. A cluster of black stakes marked the moorings.

"You can't see the house from here," Wiseman said.

The boat moved slowly forward toward the landing boards. In the shallow water dark weeds slowly waved their fronds.

"No sea wall here, either." Wiseman nodded to where the water moved among the rocks of the narrow shore.

They stepped out onto the tarred planks. Wiseman, extracting bank notes from his wallet, asked the boatman what time he was intending to return from his fishing. "Perhaps you could give us a shout?" he said. *"Può passare da qui?"*

The man nodded, pocketing the money.

"Litsov will bring us back, I expect, as far as Burano," Wiseman said to Raikes. "But it's as well to make sure. There are others today, by the look of things." There was a smart and very expensive-looking blue and white speedboat tied up alongside and beyond this what was presumably the Litsovs' boat, a long narrow *sandolo* with an outboard motor.

Raikes nodded vaguely. He was taken up with the loneliness and silence of the place. When the creak and slap of their boat had died away, there was no sound anywhere at all.

They began to mount the steps up from the jetty. From the top a rough path led off through low scrub. Raikes could see the chimney and roof of the house now, against a background of trees. The path turned sharply in this direction, bringing the house in full view and with it the Lagoon water beyond, and Raikes became aware simultaneously of a woman standing some way ahead of them, higher up, and of two men much farther off, near the house, outlined against the pale water. The woman, on whom his attention immediately became concentrated, was wearing a dark red head scarf. Raikes had the impression that she had just straightened up from a stooping position, thus rising above a low fence of crossed cane that made a triangular enclosure there.

The path was still rising, so that the woman was on a level some feet above them. It was a picture Raikes was to remember, composed of few but striking elements: the lonely figure against the sky, the vivid scarf, ragged pines beyond, the pale stone of the house.

"Mrs. Litsov, hello," Wiseman called, raising his arm in something between a wave and a salute.

She stood for some moments longer, motionless, watching them as they approached, and in this brief space there was communicated to Raikes some of the involuntary reserve or distrust that people have who live in lonely places. Then she came quickly down toward them, through a narrow gap in the fence. She was smiling, a pleased smile it seemed, but from the moment she was within three yards or so Raikes found his interpretive faculties disabled; he ceased altogether to be an observing and deducing creature. An overwhelming sense of her beauty flooded his being — it was like some fruit crushed against the palate of his brain, flooding every gallery. This impression was mysterious in its first effect, not depending on any conscious assessment; he was too stricken to register any but basic components — dark hair, high cheekbones, full mouth, eyes unexpectedly pale. It was more like a recognition of something. She was wearing a man's pullover, large and shapeless, and loose blue trousers, and she moved lightly. She was tall for an Italian woman. He braced himself for the introductions.

"Mr. Wiseman," she said. "Alex, isn't it?" The voice was low-pitched, rather deliberate-sounding — the only sign of foreignness.

"You remember me, then?"

"Of course I do. I can't shake hands; my hands are dirty."

As she reached them she did something that Raikes was always to remember. She raised her hands and ran the palms down the sides of her body from armpits to hips in a lingering gesture that was careless and exuberant and voluptuous at the same time.

"My hands are covered with soil," she said. "So, if you will permit . . ." She drew close to Wiseman and kissed him on the cheek.

"Permit?" Wiseman's smile was no longer merely social. "I must try always to catch you at your gardening," he said. "May I introduce my friend Simon Raikes?"

Later that day, in the lamplit silence of his room, his diary before him, it was to occur to Raikes that he had been scrutinized rather, though smilingly.

"It was good of you to ask me here," he said, looking for the first time directly into her eyes, which were very clear and steady.

"You are very welcome," she said.

He did not offer to shake hands and she made no move toward him.

"Are you doing some planting?" Wiseman said, breaking a silence that might have extended.

"Well, yes," she said. "Would you like to see?"

She led them up the slope and into the area formed by the cane fence.

"I have been putting in the seedlings for the zucchini," she said. "I grew them from seed, you know." She pointed to the spaced row of light green shoots against the fence, mounded up with black earth. Elsewhere in the enclosure Raikes saw tomato plants, eggplants, a straggling double row of artichokes. Along the side exposed to the sea there was a hedge of rosebushes in bright new leaf.

"You do the work yourself?" Raikes asked, and was once more lost in the woman's gaze.

"Oh, yes," she said. "Litsov is not interested in gardening. He is always too busy with his work. I like it, you know. And you see we are a long way from any shops, so it is useful to have a supply of vegetables. On the other side of the house, there is my herb garden. I'll show you afterward. I expect you would like a drink now?"

They passed once more through the gap in the fence and walked in file along the path toward the house, with Mrs. Litsov in the lead. She was talking still about her garden, turning frequently to look at the men behind her. It was only as they came up to the house, a long single-story building of rough stone screened by thickets of pines, that Raikes remembered the two men he had seen and wondered whether one of them had been this woman's husband.

7

The living room was spacious, with a large square window at the far end, overlooking the Lagoon. Light flooded in from the shadowless expanse of water outside, creating such plenitude that the white walls seemed permeated with it, and the several polished metal sculptures in the room gleamed with reciprocal reflections.

Raikes had been at once aware of these gleaming perspectives, though at first too busy with other impressions to register them fully — impressions mainly to do with the woman's movements about the room as she got the drinks ready and brought them, vermouth for Wiseman, white wine for him. The wine was perhaps not quite as cold as it should be, she explained. It had been in the cellar, of course, but they had no refrigerator, they had no electricity. Sometimes they had ice delivered . . .

"Now I must go and change and so on," she said. "You will think me rude. The fact is I stayed too long over my gardening. I did not forget that you were coming, but I forgot the time. And I thought my husband . . . But he is working still. I will not be long. There is someone else for lunch: Richard Lattimer. Perhaps you know him?"

"I have met him," Wiseman said.

"He is here too, but he may be in the studio with Paul. I will not leave you alone for long."

"Remarkable woman, the way she manages," Wiseman said when she had left the room. "It can't have been easy, especially in the winter. Of course they can afford to have help now."

Raikes nodded. "I would find these distinctly disturbing," he said.

"The sculptures? They are all her, I believe, in one aspect or another. It seems that he has had no other subject since they married. It is quite touching, in a way."

He was at it again, Raikes thought, composing a sentimental story. Wiseman seemed to take all the phenomena of the world on one plane only, including the evidence of obsessive vanity all around them.

For it *was* vain and it *was* obsessive, he insisted to himself, to use your living room as a showroom for your work. One or two pieces, yes. But he had counted nine disposed about the room at different levels, semi-abstract shapes, though all, as he looked more closely, derived from the nude female body. Only one of the pieces had a face, and the face was Mrs. Litsov's.

They caught the light, setting up in that long room a bewildering multiplicity of images, organic yet incomplete, the model only guessed at, fugitive, as if these forms had been caught at some moment of metamorphosis, line of shoulder or thigh, slopes of the breast, cleft of the buttocks, complex abdominal folds, subtle panels of the mons venus. Had Chiara Litsov been the model for all these, standing, kneeling, crouching, lying nude for him, supine or prone, hers the whole consummate shape these were the fragments of or clues to? Raikes sipped his wine, keeping these thoughts at bay. The work was erotic but there was nothing salacious in it: that was lost in the beauty of the molding, the fugitive nature of the human likeness. Wherever the eye paused, that part could be dwelled on as pure form, quelling lewdness in the way Daphne's change quelled Apollo.

"That must be Lattimer's boat," Wiseman said.

"Did you say you knew him? Of course, you know everybody."

Contrary to his usual habit, Wiseman showed no pleasure at this remark. He said, "I've met him before. He's an art dealer. He has a small gallery here, run by a man called Balbi, and another, bigger one in London. He specializes in sculpture — any period, any style, as long as it's good. He is supposed to have a fantastic eye. He's rich, of course. He owns a house here in Venice, somewhere in Canareggio — not far from you. He has contributed very generously to Rescue Venice. Quite large sums. That's how I know him — he made his first approach through UNESCO after the 1966 floods. I didn't know he was handling Litsov's work."

"Perhaps he isn't," Raikes said. "Perhaps he's just a friend."

"He's not that kind of man. You'll see what I mean, I think."

At this moment, as if on cue, the door opened and a fair man in a well-cut gray suit and a noticeably beautiful yellow tie came in. "Hullo," he said. "Has she left you on your own? I see you've got a drink at least. Oh, hullo, Wiseman."

Until these last words Raikes had thought it must be Litsov himself, judging by the ease of manner, the evident familiarity with the house, though the elegance and the handsome, cold composure of the face had not seemed in keeping.

"This is —" Wiseman began, but before he could say anything more, the newcomer announced his own identity. "I am Richard Lattimer," he said, as if it were too important a matter to be left to Wiseman. His face had broken into a narrow smile — the features seemed too perfectly regular somehow for a wider one.

"Simon Raikes," Raikes said. Lattimer's hand was cold and his grip surprisingly strong, so much so that Raikes was conscious of having to exert a countervailing pressure in order to avoid being engulfed altogether. For a moment or two he looked directly into the other man's pale blue eyes.

Then Lattimer moved to the table, took up the bottle of wine, and looked at the label. "Orvieto 'sixty-seven," he said. "*Not* a good year. Still . . ." He poured out a glass, and Raikes watched him, struck by the quick unerring way in which he handled both bottle and glass, a deftness in which there was something respectful too, almost caressive . . .

"Well," he said to Wiseman, "still helping to preserve our artistic heritage?"

Wiseman did not smile. "One does one's best," he said. It sounded pompous — which Wiseman was not.

"We were admiring the sculptures," Raikes said.

"Marvelous, aren't they?" Lattimer said at once. Glass in hand, he took a step forward and touched the nearest piece, which was the most naturalistic in execution, the armless torso with Mrs. Litsov's face. Lattimer ran a white, thick-fingered hand over the features and the breasts, showing the same confidence of touch he had displayed with the bottle. The face was briefly obscured, then stared ahead, wide-eyed and serious, while the hand caressed her breasts, arousing a strange sort of recognition in Raikes which he could not for the moment understand. Being without arms made her seem curiously defenseless and exposed, an effect that Litsov had exploited brilliantly by his sensuous treatment of the breasts and nipples, the care he had taken to render the tension between the downward pulling weight of the flesh and the upsurge of life.

"Litsov has genius," Lattimer said.

There was something definitely odd about Lattimer's face, Raikes decided. It was too reposeful somehow, unnaturally so. Before he could speculate further, Chiara Litsov re-entered the room, apologizing for the delay. She had changed into a pale blue dress of some material Raikes, always vague in such matters, thought might be silk. It caught the light, shimmering as she moved toward them, becoming itself a reflecting surface among the metal ones there — it was oddly, to Raikes, as if on entering the room she had become at once included among the various versions of herself all around them.

"Oh, there you are, Richard," she said. "You've introduced yourselves, I suppose? I hope he has been looking after you properly?"

"May I pour you a glass of wine?" Lattimer said. "I've been in the studio talking to Paul."

An immediate and unmistakable impression of familiarity was conveyed in this brief exchange. Lattimer seemed proprietorial almost. Probably his way always to seem so. But there had been something else in the tone, or the inflection, something that sounded cautionary, or perhaps like a reminder of some kind.

"He'll be out soon," Lattimer said, looking directly at Mrs. Litsov.

"I'm very glad to hear it," she said. "Before we all starve to death."

She returned Lattimer's look for some moments, smiling, and again Raikes had the feeling that something more particular was being conveyed. Then she moved the smile across to Wiseman. "And how is your book?" she said.

That she had remembered he was writing one visibly delighted him. In the warmth of her interest he lost his appearance of cherubic worldling and became eager, vulnerable even; and Raikes, seeing the transformation she had effected so effortlessly, was visited by a vague sense of premonition, gone as soon as felt.

He himself said little, able for the first time to look at Chiara Fornarini steadily, now that her attention was elsewhere. If he had been expecting some degree of high-bred frailty or aristocratic languor, he did not find it. Her face was wider at the temples and cheekbones than was consistent with strict proportion, and strongly molded; the lips were full, well shaped, amused-looking. It was the eyes that were most remarkable, wide-set, with a slight upward slant, gray-green in color, very striking against the dark hair and the light olive tint of the skin. It was a vivid face, consonant with the strength that was evident in the body, a strength seen as much in the grace of her movements as in the full limbs and straight shoulders.

Wiseman, in full flight now, was talking about the legend of St. Ursula, explaining that in the accounts of her pilgrimage to Rome she was always said to have been accompanied by eleven thousand virgins. This error, which he was dealing with in his *Byways,* sprang from a misreading of the original inscription, the letter M standing for *martire,* not *mille,* as was popularly thought. "It is eleven virgin martyrs, not eleven thousand virgins," Wiseman said. His face was glowing, his hair had somehow become disheveled. "Even Pignatti," he said, "writing in 1958, falls into this same error."

"Well, but I have seen the paintings," Mrs. Litsov said. "They are at the Accademia. If you go and look at the Carpaccios there, you will see that in his painting of this scene there are many more than eleven virgins kneeling with Saint Ursula at the Pope's feet. There are not eleven thousand, admittedly, but he could hardly have put them all in."

"I was going to mention that," Wiseman said, though he added nothing for the moment, seemed somewhat dashed in fact.

"Perhaps a few tagged along," Raikes said. He met Mrs. Litsov's eyes. Something in their innocent steadiness told him at once that she was aware of Wiseman's slight discomfiture, amused by it, and inviting him in as an accomplice. Suppressing all sense of disloyalty to Wiseman, he allowed himself to smile. The exchange of glances was over in seconds but it left Raikes feeling leagued with her.

Lattimer laughed suddenly, a rather barking laugh which did little to disturb the immobile set of his face. "Yes," he said, "she probably picked them up as she went along. On the swarming principle. She was the queen virgin, you know."

"I see the whole thing as what we would now call a demo," Mrs. Litsov said. "It was a mass protest of virgins."

"No, no," Wiseman said, without smiling. "Carpaccio himself didn't know. That is the whole point. That is the point I am making in my book."

"In that case, old chap, the mistake goes back a long way indeed," Lattimer said coldly. "The story of Ursula's mission and martyrdom is told in *Legenda Aurea,* compiled by Jacobus de Voragine round about the middle of the thirteenth century. That's two hundred years before Carpaccio's time. He got the account from there."

"Quite so," Wiseman said, "but he wouldn't have seen it in that version. Carpaccio couldn't read Latin. There was an Italian version published in Venice in 1475. My whole point is that Carpaccio —"

But here Lattimer, obviously sensing he might lose the argument, deliberately and indeed brutally interrupted, launching into a lengthy disquisition on the various treatments of the subject in late medieval art, the fourteenth-century frescoes of Tomaso da Modena at Treviso, Memling's beautiful reliquary shrine in the Hôpital Saint-Jean at Bruges, both of which he had seen. His knowledge was remarkable, his memory too, and his fluency admitted no pauses. Wiseman sat flushed and silent.

Raikes could not remember having seen before, in the course of an ordinary conversation, such self-assertion, such disregard for the rights of others, as Lattimer was demonstrating now. He was shocked by it, and it occurred to him to wonder why Mrs. Litsov did not in some way intervene. He stole a glance at her but her face bore no particular expression. This would be a good time, he suddenly thought, to raise the question that had brought him. All thoughts of poor Wiseman fled. "I don't know if Wiseman told you," he said, leaning toward her and speaking quietly, "but I had an ulterior motive in coming to see you today."

"Ulterior motive?"

For a second or two Raikes met the serious eyes fixed on him.

Again he was aware, not of scrutiny exactly, but a sort of speculation, as if something about him were being assessed. With a confused sense of turning the occasion into a compliment, he began, "If I had known, of course —" But this was wrong; it would seem patronizing. He stopped abruptly. Her eyes were on him still, but he could see only the same cool interest in them. "There were one or two things I wanted to ask you about," he said.

Before she could reply, a tall, fair-bearded man in a faded denim jacket came into the room. He did not approach anyone but stood quite close to the wall, looking at the visitors, it seemed uncertainly or perhaps diffidently.

"Here is the *maestro*," Lattimer said. "Now we can have some lunch."

"You remember Mr. Wiseman, don't you?" Mrs. Litsov said. "And this is Simon Raikes."

"How do you do?" Litsov said, making no move to approach anyone. "There was something to finish," he said, looking at his wife.

"When was there not?" she said. "Well, we can go and have our food now. Maria has been waiting with it for quite a while."

The dining room was reached through the door Litsov had entered by, then down a short length of passage. It was smaller, with the same roughcast walls. No sculptures in evidence here, Raikes noticed. Very little decoration of any kind. Various hors d'oeuvres had already been set out: olives, prawns, *aquadelle*, fried squid. There was more of the Orvieto.

Litsov began talking immediately but not about anything that concerned his guests. He had not looked directly at any of them yet. "Richard has told me that Adriano is still out of action," he said, still looking at his wife. "He still has this glandular fever."

"That seems to be so, yes," she said. "But I understood he was getting better. Isn't that so, Richard?"

"He is definitely on the mend," Lattimer said. "He expects to be working full out again in a matter of days."

"It is nearly three weeks now," Litsov said. "I am sick of it."

"He will not entrust the casting of your work to anyone else." Mrs. Litsov smiled. "It is a compliment, *caro*," she said.

"That's all very well," Litsov said. His voice was deep, with a note of irritation in it. "Meanwhile, no one casts my work," he said. "It is piling up there at Mestre and nothing happens, just excuses. I will not give him much longer. There are others on the mainland who can do the work as well as he can."

Neither Mrs. Litsov nor Lattimer replied to this, and their silence seemed to irritate Litsov further. "You think that I will do nothing," he said. There was definite anger now in his voice. "But you are wrong. I give him one more week."

"Everything will be all right," Lattimer said. "I will take care of it."

Litsov brooded for some moments, looking down at the table. Then, perhaps sensing he had caused embarrassment, he looked up. With an obviously deliberate effort to be more sociable, he said, "You have dressed up for us today, Chiara, I see," and he smiled at her.

The smile destroyed his face more or less completely. In repose it was handsome, with the broad fair brows, strong nose, blue, prominent eyes, full beard below; but jaws and chin were fashioned on a smaller scale, belonged on a child's face almost, and when the mouth smiled it collapsed into the beard, and only the white, voracious teeth survived. "It is nice to see you wearing a dress," he said. "Lately it has been trousers, trousers."

"I was surprised I could get it across my shoulders," she said. "I am developing muscles, Litsov, on this island."

This was said without coquetry, but the effect of her words was in some sort to focus the attention of the four men on the concealed mechanisms of her body as she sat there in the long-sleeved dress.

"Muscles!" Litsov moved his large head slowly as if this were a new thought for him.

Wiseman was merely arch. "I assure you," he said, "it doesn't show to any marked extent." He turned a cherubic smile on her.

"Where are they, then, these mighty muscles?" Lattimer demanded, and beneath the assumed jocularity there was atavistic condescension. He looked at her with his narrow smile, his handsome, small-featured, immobile-seeming face — not so much composed as artificial-looking, Raikes thought. As if it were not quite his own . . . That was it, of course: Lattimer had undergone plastic surgery at some time or other; the skin of his face had been stretched.

"You should show us," he said, in the same jocular tone. He glanced round at the others. Encountering Raikes's gaze, his left eyelid flickered in a brief, incongruous wink. "Give us a chance to judge," he said.

It seemed to Raikes, who was sitting beside her and looking at her closely, that some slight shadow passed over her face — impatience, distaste, perhaps only resignation. It was gone in a second; her expression was again clear. She seemed about to speak, but at this point Maria came with a great dish of *lasagne verdi*. Under cover of the polite business of serving and passing round, he asked her about life on the island.

It had been hard at first, she said, and especially in the winter. Everything was a problem to begin with. Fortunately there was good water. With children it probably wouldn't have been possible. They had been lucky to find Maria, who came over from Treporti twice a week, weather permitting, and looked after them in all sorts of ways. Litsov of course was not practical at all. He had been concerned only to fit out the studio. She smiled as she said this, without hint of blame.

Raikes looked down the table, saw traces of Litsov's unpleasing smile, saw the large face revert to customary staring gravity — there was an official dignity and gloom about Litsov's face, like that of a president on a foreign postage stamp.

"The place was never intended for day-to-day living, I suppose," he said, looking back toward Mrs. Litsov, nerving himself for the impact of her eyes. These had gold flecks on the iris, he had discovered, giving them a slightly tawny look.

"No, it was a kind of shooting lodge," she said. "People used to come here to shoot ducks. Or you say duck, don't you, in the singular? It belongs to my uncle, as a matter of fact — the island, that is. But it was my grandfather who came here. The family lived in the Veneto at that time. We had an estate near Castelfranco. My grandfather kept up the place while he lived, or so they tell me — I never came here then. They had parties here in my grandfather's time, when he was younger. Some of those alleged hunting trips were quite orgiastic, I believe. That was in the seventies and eighties of the last century. My grandfather died when I was four, and my uncle wasn't interested much in shooting ducks or having orgies, I suppose. Anyway, there was no money: everything had to be sold; my father went to Rome, where he got a job as a bank clerk. No one came here anymore except a few fishermen. Even the ducks don't come anymore; the motorboats have driven them away. Still, Litsov and I got a rent-free house. We couldn't have done anything without Richard. It was his idea in the first place. He had the whole place done up for us, practically rebuilt. He spent a fortune on it. He would have installed a generator, if Litsov hadn't taken a stand against electricity."

Raikes nodded. Litsov had to be humored, it seemed. However, Lattimer did not impress him as a philanthropist. If he had spent money, it must have been to get money back. Or had he more sentimental reasons? This was a curiously disagreeable thought, and Raikes shifted in his chair as if in physical discomfort at it.

"What did you mean?" she said suddenly, "before, when you spoke about an ulterior motive?"

Raikes glanced round the table. It was a propitious moment. The other three men were talking, or rather Wiseman and Lattimer were — Litsov listened, head broodingly lowered.

"Well," he said, "I thought you might be able to help me." He began in a low voice to tell Mrs. Litsov about his attempt to establish a connection between the Casa Fioret and the Madonna. He was aware that he was looking rather deeply into her eyes as he spoke, but in the interest of the subject he felt no shyness at this. He told her about the account book he had found — though not the precise circumstances of his finding it — and the entry with the date so nearly corresponding to that of the Madonna's installation in 1743, and the address, and the name Fornarini; how he had thought it possible that the statue had been kept there, in the house somewhere or in the garden, and transported from there to the church. He told her of his visit to the house, the present state of it, his disappointment. "I felt I was barking up the wrong tree," he said. Then he had discovered from his reading of Marco Barbaro that the Bishop of Venice, who had officiated at the installation, had been a

Fornarini, was perhaps the one referred to in the notebook, and so his hopes had begun to rise again; he was beginning to think there must be a connection. He spoke with a sort of fevered frankness, keeping his eyes on her face, deeply aware of her attentiveness.

"And so," he said, "when Wiseman told me you were a Fornarini, I thought . . ." Having reached this point, he did not know how to proceed. What did he want from her? What did he expect? He could not have said, in any definite way. He wanted her to keep his hopes alive. "I thought you might be able to throw some light," he said at last.

Mrs. Litsov shook her head in a way that seemed genuinely regretful. "I don't know of any connection," she said. "You must remember that I have spent most of my life away from Venice. In Rome first and afterward in London. And really I am not so interested in the past. Probably you think that is terrible."

"No, no," Raikes said, startled at the notion of fault in this radiant creature.

"Even my own family," she said, and quite suddenly made the second gesture he was to remember from that day, raising her left shoulder and reaching across with the right hand to stroke her upper arm in a lingering, self-consoling way. There was something childlike about this movement, which touched Raikes, though out of shyness he pretended not to notice it. "Perhaps I got too much of it," she said. Evidently the gesture had been involuntary: there was no change in her voice or manner, nor was it cold in the room — there was a good fire burning. "Of course, there were always stories," she added after a moment.

"What kind of stories?"

"Well, for example, they say the men of the family have a special grace to produce male children."

"Males? I thought it was just children generally. It didn't work a hundred percent in your father's case." He was aware of considerable gratitude that this was so.

"I am the only girl, you know. In fact there were generally more boys than girls. Then there is Francesco, who became a saint — there were a lot of stories about his goodness — and Jacopo, who was skinned by the Turks rather than become a Moslem, and Marcantonio, who was offered the crown of Naples but preferred to return to Venice and serve the state . . . The stories are always to their credit. It is just folklore really."

"That would be the Marcantonio who was Venetian ambassador to Naples early in the fifteenth century?"

"Yes. Probably a complete gangster. You have been studying the family history then?"

"I've been reading Marco Barbaro."

"I have an aunt in Rome, who is unmarried; she has all these books and papers, anything to do with the family." Mrs. Litsov smiled. "She thinks of herself as the guardian of our name," she said. "I could write to her, if you like. She might know something."

"I don't want to be a nuisance. I don't even know whether there *is* any connection between the statue and the house. It would be more logical to look for a church."

"Oh, she would be pleased, poor thing. She would be glad someone was showing an interest. The family papers are in America now, those that could be found. They were sold to Boston University long ago, to pay the rent I suppose. But I will write to my aunt."

Raikes hesitated for a moment; then he said rather awkwardly, "I'd be grateful if you didn't say anything about this to anyone. I'm trying to pursue these inquiries privately, you know. I haven't told anyone else about it, only you." Once again he became aware that he was looking at her too intently. She smiled and said, "You don't want to see it in your friend's *Byways,* for example? Of course I will not say anything."

"It really is very good of you to help me." He would have expressed his feeling of gratitude at rather more length had he not suddenly realized that silence had fallen on the table, that his face was too close to hers, his manner too confidential, that Litsov's solemn gaze was on him.

He sat back. The need to seem relaxed and affable led him into an ill-considered speech. "I'd like to say how impressed I am by your work," he said to Litsov. "The sculptures gain so much strength from being together." He realized at once that this implied some reservation about the works considered individually, which had not been his intention. "Most impressive," he continued hastily, "this balance you strike between organic form and pure abstraction."

Litsov's face showed no gratification at this whatsoever; if anything, the solemnity of his features deepened. And it was this, perhaps, this failure to make a civil response, that began to annoy Raikes — coupled with a sense of his own clumsiness. "Deeply impressive," he said, still valiantly smiling.

"All art tends to abstraction," Litsov said finally and magisterially. "The individual creature is only a means — a way through. We look at it and we dissolve it. It is submerged in the world of forms."

"Oh, no," Raikes said, combative warmth rising within him. "The individual is not submerged or dissolved. That is dangerous doctrine, I think. And it is a 'she' in this case, I gather, not an 'it.' "

"Paul is speaking figuratively," Lattimer said, in his cold, deliberate voice. "Surely you can see that? He is speaking as a creative artist."

"You say that as if it meant the same as *ex cathedra,*" Raikes said. He glanced at Mrs. Litsov. She was regarding her husband closely, with an oddly speculative expression. "Many people," he said, "and among them creative artists, would take a contrary view, and argue that truthful adherence to the particular is the way to universality."

"One body cannot be all bodies," Litsov said. "That is —"

"It is there I disagree," Raikes said quickly and warmly.

"Self-evident," Litsov said, as if there had been no interruption. "I have adapted Plato for my own use. Let me remind you what he said, Mr. Raikes. He said that when the artificer of any object reproduces its essence and virtue by keeping his gaze fixed on what is self-consistent and using that as a model, the object thus created is altogether beautiful. But if he looks toward the world of becoming and uses a created model, the result is not beautiful."

There was an impressiveness about this, uttered in Litsov's rather deep voice and accompanied by slight movements of that massive head. It was obviously by way of being a credo, for one thing; and the archetypal resonance of the phrases for once made the man's solemnity seem appropriate, rather than merely self-important. Then he looked toward his wife and smiled, and his lower face collapsed once more and his teeth showed, naked and white. "I have used a created model," he said, "but I have kept my gaze fixed on what is self-consistent in it."

He looked back at Raikes. The smile still lurked, but there was now, suddenly but quite unmistakably, an offendedness in his expression that he had possibly been trying to dissemble. "You think that I belittle my subject?" he said.

"No one could think that, Paul," Lattimer said. "No one in his senses could think that."

Raikes paused, unforgivably. He had not meant to go so far, but the challenge rendered him obstinate. And the lady was near.

"No," he was beginning, "no, I don't say that —"

Then Mrs. Litsov spoke, in clear tones, looking at her husband. "Mr. Raikes is not an artist," she said. "He cannot be expected to understand the creative process. Don't forget, *tesoro,* that he is merely a restorer of other men's work."

These words, which wounded Raikes more than he could have thought possible, immediately restored Litsov to good humor. "Is that so?" he said. "A restorer? I suppose mainly of works in stone . . . yes? That is why I like to work in bronze, the glory of changeless metal, as William Butler Yeats has it. Polished bronze, especially. I am not interested in texture, not at all."

Raikes could think of nothing to say. It was too soon to contemplate leaving. There was the coffee yet, another session in the living room, among the glory of changeless metal. Even before that, it seemed, there would be more to endure: Litsov had begun to speak again, and his tone now was condescending and assured.

"Well, Mr. Raikes, I used to think as you do; but everything in nature assumes autonomous and natural forms — trees, animals, insects. Why not art? Have you thought of it that way? Why should art imitate other orders of things, as to be like a bottle or a house? Art is a fruit of man and must take its own shape, just as other fruits do. Otherwise, what is it? I will tell you. Merely a substitute for nature, nothing else."

"Oh, I don't know about that," Wiseman said mildly. "It could be called a celebration of nature, couldn't it?"

Raikes, seeing the beard turn toward this latest contestant, was profoundly thankful for the interruption, which he felt fairly sure Wiseman had contrived expressly for his sake — he had been feeling like a caned schoolboy who must still stand and listen to the headmaster's homily.

However, the pain of the snub stayed with him for the rest of the visit. And though he behaved with what he hoped was proper poise, he addressed no more remarks directly to Chiara Litsov, nor looked at her oftener than he had to.

8

When, later on, in the silence of his room, he was bringing his diary up to date, he found he could remember very little of the conversation after Wiseman's remark about art and celebration. It was as if he had been downed and counted out. Visual details he could remember: sunlight of late afternoon falling through the big, square window of the living room, where they had returned for their coffee; sunlight on the woman's hands and the front of her dress and gleaming on the polished fragments that lay about the room like some marvelous wreckage. Only Lattimer had seemed somehow uninvolved in the sunshine, as if moving in a pallid luminescence of his own. Litsov had a nervous habit, noticed only then, of jiggling a foot or tapping with lightly clenched fist against the side of his thigh.

At odds with that noble brow. Raikes experienced a faint return of animosity. Of course as far as she is concerned I am a mere mechanic; she made that clear enough. But there was an atmosphere there, a curious sort of tension, difficult to define. There had been no chance to compare notes with Wiseman; Lattimer, in a white cap and a beautiful gray anorak, had brought them the whole way back in his speedboat, which he handled expertly, an exhilarating experience. Why did her words hurt me so much? he wondered. Because she put to public use what I had told her privately? But one's occupation is not such a great secret. And she could not have known that a sculptor was what I wanted more than anything else to be. No, it was because I had entered the lists for her and she knew it . . .

I must be mad, he thought. A complete stranger. She saw her husband being attacked and she defended him. What could be more natural? But that was not it either. Raikes sat back, obscurely puzzled, listening to the silence. Why did I take it upon me to defend her? His complacency of course antagonized me, but even then I was beginning to think that more apparent than real. It was the sight of her in the midst of all those metal versions of herself, trapped among them, only half acknowledged by him, raw material for his abstractions, nothing else. And then this care to placate him . . .

Lattimer too had shown the same concern, and Lattimer did not seem conciliatory by nature, far from it. Even before the great man appeared, there had been some sense almost of apprehension between them. And in fact he had been out of temper at first. Why was it so important to keep Litsov in a good mood? That rubbish about art being a fruit of man — enough to make one cringe. She was just a good wife, then, keeping his vanity fed, cooking for him, modeling for him, mediating for him with the outside world, since he so rarely left the island. A paragon.

With the word came feelings of skepticism. Raikes drew the diary toward him as if for reassurance. About the Madonna there were questions too, but with patience one might answer them. It was Mrs. Litsov's beauty that made for doubt. Was it doubt or hope he was experiencing? It was the virtuous nymphs, after all, who had to be saved by metamorphosis. Even her beauty had now become in a way questionable, something others might not acknowledge, so totally was her face and form to his own liking, not hitherto dreamed of, but instantly recognized . . . He looked down at the pages open before him. Here at least there was cause for satisfaction: he had kept to his intentions; the material was mounting up day by day. He paused for a moment or two to gather his thoughts, then embarked on the day's entry.

Tomorrow, back to work on the Madonna. The lower folds of her robe have been done now, up to a level just above the knees. All this is white and splendid. I am nervous still about the upper parts, especially the hands and head. But the quartz cutter is working wonderfully well. One must of course restrain the impulse to hurry. It is natural to want to get the whole form renewed. But any smallest area missed or skimped now will not absorb the conserver and that could jeopardize the whole value of the restoration. So patience is the order of the day. She *has been patient enough, after all.* È la parte esposta, *as Signor Biagi said. No sickliness there about fruit. Christ of course the spiritual fruit of the Madonna's womb. But she was not supposed to be an individual, merely a set of attributes for veneration.*

Her right leg, the one that is advanced, is given a definite prominence against the drapery, and the limb itself is quite robust and substantial and molded very plastically, almost as if it was done by abrasion rather than cutting. Great care has gone into the molding of this right leg, and the only significant movement of the drapery in the area is a long diagonal fold, not very deep — five or six inches — going from just below the kneecap to the beginning of the convex line of the calf, on the inside of the leg. This fold does nothing to conceal the details of the leg. In fact it rather sensuously emphasizes them. The left leg of course is masked by the drapery and not articulated.

The Gothic movement is implicit in this right leg and in the way the drapery is used not to enhance volume, as it was in the Venetian sculpture of the time, but to accentuate the line. Something of Nino Pisano there in the clinging lines of the robe? Certainly Pisano influenced the Dalle Masegne brothers and they worked in Bologna and Venice. Milan too, I think. So a line from Pisano through the Dalle Masegne to some northern Italian sculptor of the next generation?

Raikes paused and looked up, with a sudden feeling of discouragement. There were so many possible lines. Still, it was remarkable, and a kind of clue, that among the host of undistinguished monumental Madonnas of the day this one should exist, with its grace of feeling and movement. Made to a formula they had most often been: recipient of tidings, receptacle for the Holy Ghost, vehicle for Christ. Yet someone, whose name nobody knew, in early-fifteenth-century Venice, had fashioned a woman like no other.

She was there in the darkness now, looking across the roofs toward the dim expanse of the Lagoon, as she had done every night for the last two hundred and fifty years or so. And before that?

A mood of wondering speculation descended on Raikes, vague yet intense, absorbing, like the half-incredulous wonder we sometimes feel at the sheer fact of our existence in the world, when the details summoned as evidence, though true, seem somehow to make certainty less. He thought of Chiara Litsov and her gardening, the green shoots and black earth, the two figures glimpsed so fleetingly — the other man must have been Lattimer . . . He thought of the steps that had led to this visit, his discovery of the notebook, Barfield's peevish request for five more degrees in the devotional gloom, the spidery outline of the name in its suffusion of light, the house by the canal with its damp and echoing courtyard, the hemmed-in, disconsolate building of the church. Hemmed-in. The steady pulse of recollection missed a beat, stayed. *More logical to look for a church.* This church was deconsecrated, had therefore been abandoned or suppressed at some time. The original precincts must have been much larger. That was it, of course: the church land had been sold to the house opposite, or acquired in some other way.

With peculiar deliberation Raikes found himself dwelling on that view from the gate across the narrow alley. The words of his conversation with Steadman came back to him. *Lurking about in a cloister somewhere.* Why had he so easily assumed the alley to be the true dividing line? It could have been made much later. Easy to see why the owners of the house would want to acquire the land — that long, rectangular piece running alongside the canal would make a beautiful garden, and gardens were rare in Venice, gardens large enough actually to walk about in. Yes, easy to see . . . Steady now, he cautioned himself. Let us go step by step. Supposing the Madonna was made for this church and then for some reason never put in the intended place; supposing she was just left in the church precincts, and if then subsequently the church was deconsecrated . . . There would have been no means of retrieving her, or perhaps the priests did not want to, so when the land was sold . . .

In his excitement at these thoughts, he jumped up and began pacing back and forth across the room.

He was thirty-three years old, unmarried, physically strong, with an ardent, innocent nature and some tendency to hysteria. The Madonna was five hundred and forty.

FIRST INTERLUDE

Coronation

1793

In the spring of 1793, when Ziani began writing his boastful, scandalous *Mémoires,* the Madonna was three hundred and sixty-one. He was seventy-four and dying. The previous year a stroke had disabled him down one side and stretched a corner of his thin mouth. He could not walk far now and had a permanent expression of distaste. But his memory was clear as ever — clearer, as though distilled by the body's decay. The airs of the past came to him, warm with malice, spiced with lechery, scented with self-congratulation.

Day after day he sat huddled at the card table he used for a desk in one corner of the vast apartment on the third floor of his mortgaged house, writing by the light of the window, though reflections from the canal below troubled his eyes and sometimes disturbed the vengeful and erotic flow of his thoughts. Apart from his own meager person in its soiled blue satin robe, and his table and chair, and the couch he slept on, everything in the apartment was draped in dust sheets. Neither house nor furniture belonged properly to him; he lived on there by agreement with his creditors.

His eyes were failing; he could not see with any distinctness to the far end of the apartment; his gaze lost itself among the sheeted forms. All his energy went into the writing. When he came to the section of his *Mémoires* that dealt with the statue, the seduction of Donna Francesca, and the cuckolding of skinflint Boccadoro, he wrote with more care than ever, wanting to lacerate his personae and stimulate his readers in equal measure.

In that April of 1743, having recently returned to Venice from Rome, where I had fallen out of favor, and penniless as a result of those speculations described in a previous chapter, I was obliged to seek temporary employment, and found after a short while, through the influence of my family, a post as secretary in the house of the merchant Tommaso Boccadoro, who employed me because of my name and also because I had attended the University of Padua (though obliged, because of the unfortunate involvements related elsewhere in these *Mémoires,* to leave without obtaining a degree). Boccadoro also agreed to house and feed my faithful Battistella, who has been with me through so many vicissitudes and is with me still, in return for duties about the house, though he refused point-blank to pay him wages, thereby revealing early in our relationship his inability to rise to an occasion or make a generous gesture.

Though described as secretary, my main task was to restore to order the very considerable collection of books. Boccadoro had taken the house in part payment of debts, just as it stood, including the contents of the library, from a branch of the Longhi family. As the other part of the payment he had taken in marriage Francesca Longhi, a girl of eighteen. The Longhi had been spending more than they possessed for many years by that time, and they were desperate for money; otherwise, they would never have agreed to marry her to him. The family live now, what is left of them, in San Barnabá.

So as I have said, my main duties concerned the library. Boccadoro, while scarce knowing one end of a book from the other, had aspirations to learning, but the books had been kept without particular system; those who had accumulated them no doubt knew where to find what they wanted, but my unlettered employer blundered about among them, lost. I was to catalogue the books and make an index with brief summaries of their contents.

The work was not disagreeable, but the position of paid employee was galling to my pride, extremely so, and I found solace from the first, when dealing with Boccadoro, in a certain deliberate falseness of speech and manner. This took the form of praising virtue, but should not be thought of as hypocrisy, as I had nothing to gain at that point, other than, by saying what I did not believe and seeing him agree, to mark the difference between us and feed my contempt.

So I smiled on Boccadoro and spoke in praise of virtue. He listened to me in spite of my comparative youth. For one thing, he was innocent; and then my lineage exercised charm on a man whose father, it was said, had humped crates of fish on the Zattere. What also weighed with him was the rumor that had got about somehow or other, and which I did nothing to confirm or deny, that I had been pursuing theological studies in Rome with a view to taking Holy Orders.

He listened to me, as I say; he even sought me out. His trouble was that frequent one which afflicts hot old men with cool young wives, though I did not understand this at first, and certainly not the extent of Francesca's coolness.

Ziani stopped to wipe his eyes, peer across the apartment. He thought he had heard some sound there. These days he was haunted by small sounds and movements, most of them illusory. As always, his gaze grew perplexed among the whitish mounds. He caught a flicker as some loose fold of drapery stirred in a draft — the apartment was prey to a system of currents oceanic in complexity.

As his eyes strained, so did his mind, across the long interval of years, to the morning Boccadoro had confided in him. Sunlight caught and held in the enclosed space of the garden. May — the acacias were in flower. He had been there some weeks by that time. There was dew on the narrow leaves, and the pebble walks were glistening. Early in the day then. Some shouting or singing from the direction of San Silvestre. Singing or shouting? A quarrelsome note in it. They were setting up the fruit barges along the *fondamenta*. The statue there in her arbor, modest and provocative, with that arm guarding herself. And the old man shambling toward him, long-shanked, powerful still, violent, and ridiculous. No wig. He was not yet dressed for going out. He was in robe and skullcap. Ziani began to write again, every detail clear in his mind:

It was in the garden that he first spoke to me about his situation, the banality of which naturally he did not see, as our misfortunes seem always to be uniquely ordained. At the moment he approached, I was standing at the entrance to the arbor, looking at the statue; and it can therefore be truly said that this comedy begins and ends with her. I was wondering what she was intended to represent.

The garden was large for Venice, running a good way behind the house, ending in a high wall with a gate set in it; beyond this there were the precincts of an abandoned church. On one side of the garden, back toward the wall, were the ruins of a stone arcade, three arches still standing; and it was within the last of these, the one farthest from the house, that the stone lady dwelled. At some time the former owners had planted roses here, white on one side, red on the other, and they grew up the shafts of the columns to the height of the arch, where they met and mingled colors very prettily; and a grape vine that looked old enough to be a cutting from Eden, lacing with the ruins of the masonry, formed rafters with its thick stems and a roof with its leaves to make a bower for her. There was a wooden bench inside, where one could shelter from suns that were too burning. She was made of white stone, but in the light of the vine leaves she had a faint hue of green, and as always she was smiling, a slight smile, difficult to interpret. At that time we had no idea what she was.

Then Boccadoro came shambling toward me. He spent some time in preliminaries, glancing at me with his fierce little eyes. "My friend," he said, "you are young, but you have a good head on your shoulders. I have often noted it. I am speaking to you because you are more nearly of an age with my wife, though of course there is some difference of years, the more so because of this fact, which, as I say, I have noted. Do you not think so?"

"What fact is that?" I said; he had lost me. "Why," he said, "to be sure, this very fact of this excellent head that you have on your shoulders. And then, you have attended one of our very best universities . . . I have a deal of acquaintance, a great deal, but there are not many who are close to me, not many that I can call friend."

I did not see cause for astonishment in this after his lifetime of usury. Now I tried to combine in one regard modest acknowledgment of this praise and respectful interest in what was to follow, with what success

I do not know — but nothing did follow; nothing more came from him. He began to stare about the garden; caution — or pride — had intervened.

It was now that I took the first of many gambles in this affair. It was that species of gamble called a bluff by the practitioners of *spigolo,* the attempt to make your opponent think you are stronger than you are, the penalty for failing being full exposure of your weakness. "My dear sir," I said, "I understand what you are referring to. Believe me, you have my sympathy."

His face lost all expression for some moments through undiluted wonder at my words. I have often noted that when men are in distressful situations or situations of perplexity, however common these may be, however patent to view, yet will the smallest insights into them on the part of others seem wondrously perceptive to the one afflicted. So much is this the case that often, as now, the mere pretense of such an insight will suffice to unlock a man's tongue. "What," he said, "you have sensed it then?" "How could I not?" I said. "How could I not?" "She wants an increased allowance," he said. "She wants to rent an apartment of her own, a *casino.* She tells me she feels foolish among her friends through not having one."

"This fashion for *casini* is the curse of the age," I said. "It has been the ruin of many families, as I know for a fact." This was it, then: having bought the merchandise, he was now complaining at the price. But there was more. Encouraged by my nods, he came out with it. It seemed that ordering his house was not compatible with Donna Francesca's sense of dignity. She neglected to supervise the servants. She did not appear when he had guests.

I thought of the lady as I had seen her first, on the day of my arrival in the house. I had stood waiting in the interior courtyard, where there was a circular well-head, decorated with lions' heads round the rim. Their manes had been carved to resemble foliage, and I was admiring the inventiveness of the carver when I heard the rustle of her clothes and looked up and saw her above me, descending the staircase in a pale blue gown high at the collar and low cut in the front, in the fashion of those days, with the shining coils of her hair dressed high on her head, the gaze of a well-bred Venetian girl, equable, intrepid, without undue boldness, however; and a figure whose shape and suppleness the stiff brocade could not conceal. I had not expected her to be so well favored — perhaps because beauty of any kind in conjunction with Boccadoro was not a thought easily entertained. I had seen her before, in the street with her brothers once, when I still lived in Venice; but she had been no more than a schoolgirl then. She was more now, certainly.

These thoughts were in my mind as I looked at Boccadoro. It was all I could do to control my face. He was proposing to make this high-mettled creature, luxurious and willful, as all our Venetian ladies are, into an adjunct of the parlor, a devotee of the spinet, to soothe his unlovely brow when he returned from the countinghouse, and serve grenadines to his grotesque cronies as they sprawled grossly, wigless and unbuttoned, after dinner! Truly those whom the gods wish to destroy they first make mad . . . Then it occurred to me: Why did he not go to them, to these same farting cronies, for advice? The way to deal with an unruly wife, that would be within their scope and range. Why did he come to me?

"It is the chief affliction of the age," I said, "and one to which our women are unfortunately all too prone, to think of pleasure as something to be sought outside the home rather than in it. This constitutes a reversal of all traditional values."

"Yes, yes," he said. "Exactly so. You are a very Cato. Or perhaps Cicero is the one I mean."

I replied that I would not scorn comparison with either of these *signori*. A kind of excited suspicion was beginning to stir in me.

"Maria, her maid, grows insolent," he said, "and Donna Francesca refuses to check her."

"Refuses?" I allowed myself a tone of gentle wonder. *"Refuses?"*

That I stressed this word was no more than a fortunate accident. I had meant only to keep my ascendancy over him. He bridled and reddened and I thought I had gone too far; but then I saw how his eyes avoided mine. Here was not anger, here was shame. Stronger, more definite came the scent of his misfortune, rising to my jubilant nostrils like a savory steam. Where women are concerned there is only one refusal that matters. What if Francesca's went farther than the drawing room — higher, I should say — a flight of stairs higher?

As I hope will have been apparent to the reader before this, I am a sensitive man and an observant man and a man of acute perceptions, and now, as I talked to him, suspicion became conviction almost at once. This was why he had come to me. From colleagues he would fear derision — an old man with a young wife. But he was paying me for my services; and to Boccadoro's primitive sense, that restored the balance.

It would be difficult to exaggerate the pleasure this notion afforded me. I am willing to recognize that it was not, to speak strictly, Boccadoro's fault that I had been reduced to taking wages. We were products both of changing times. Half the great houses of Venice were owned by men like him, who had come from nothing. Nevertheless, by employing me he had demeaned me, imposed a slight on me, fixed me in an odious relationship. All this demanded redress. Hitherto, until this morning, I had found this in my deliberate insincerities. In all our conversations I was fencing with him, scoring off him all the time. Yet it was less than satisfactory. He did not know it, for one thing; and then, a duel cannot be carried on by feints alone. Now, if I was right, not only had he exposed his vitals but also given me the means of delivering the thrust.

"Why should you have this to contend with?" I said. "A man does his work. He expects to find peace at home. They do not understand this."

"Everything is difficult," he said. "Everything requires argument. It is tiring and moreover it interferes with business."

"It is this endless quest for pleasure I have referred to, which undermines all our institutions. It is the ruin of the state. What is happening to all our fine and great traditions?"

"What indeed?" he said. "They are going to perdition."

"And it is the women who lead the way," I said. "We take our tone from them. They are the keepers of our morals, that is a well-known fact."

"By God, yes," he said with feeling. (If my intuitions told me rightly, his were being kept pretty well.)

"That is the paradox of it," I said. "They are the keepers of our morals, but they must still be guided by us. Guided, not coerced, as we are not barbarians."

"By God, no," he said.

"True pleasure, for women," I said, "lies in the performance of their wifely duties, omitting no smallest thing that can add to their husbands' comfort and pleasure. That is the secret of it."

Boccadoro was so delighted by this that he rubbed his skullcap back and forth over his head, causing some of his scant gray hair to stick out from under it. He was a man of violent and impulsive gesture. "My dear fellow," he said, "I only wish she could hear you now." He paused and I saw an idea born on his face — his eyes were reddish-brown, deep-set, and normally quick-glancing, but they became fierce and staring when any calculation was involved. "But she could," he said. "She could hear you."

His considerations were clear to me, though I did not at first believe he would closet us together. I was near Francesca's age, as he had begun by saying; and he was wondering if I might sway her, bring her somehow to a sense of duty — including the duty of the bedchamber. I, Sigismondo Ziani, the moral voice of my generation, advocate of the conjugal couch! There was something so innocently hopeful in his staring shrewdness that almost my heart warmed to him — almost.

"There is one obstacle only," he said.

"And what is that?"

"My poor friend," he said, "she hates you."

Ziani laid down his pen and reached with mottled paw across the table for the brass handbell which, as essential to his survival, was one of his few possessions left unpawned. He held it at arm's length and rang it in sustained and querulous fashion, knowing however from experience so ancient even the rancor had gone from it, that Battistella would certainly not come at the first summons and quite possibly not at the second.

While he waited he grew pensive. Reflected light from the slopping canal moved in leisurely ripples over the walls of the apartment, the tented shapes, the faded baize of his table, his curled fingers, the stained satin of his robe — he spilled his food often these days, through tremulousness and the haste of his appetite. Reflections of light, sounds from the canal and *riva* below, these were the accompaniments to his days; with his view over the water, they were all that linked him to the world outside. He had not been out of the apartment for more than three years now. Poverty, misanthropy, growing infirmity, kept him immured. *There is one obstacle only,* his mind repeated, with self-delighting lucidity. *And what is that?* With sardonic interior laughter that moved no fraction of his face, he dwelled on the complacency of Boccadero's reply. *My poor friend, she hates you.*

He was commencing, with habitual imprecations, to ring for a third time when Battistella appeared and moved slowly toward him with his shuffling gait.

"Old fool," Ziani said, though his servant was a year younger than himself, "you are getting very deaf. When my *Mémoires* are published I shall buy a bigger bell. What ridiculous thing are you wearing?"

Battistella made no reply to this but stood surveying his master, mouth slightly open, breathing audibly. He was a spindly old man with inflamed eyes, very steady and direct. The short wig, which he hastily donned from old habit whenever he heard the bell, was rakishly askew on his brow. He was wearing a pink coat with silver embroidery in the fashion of thirty years before, very much too large for him, with sleeves rolled back and enormous ragged pockets so low as to be almost out of reach — he would have had to adopt a crouching posture to get into them. Below the flaps of the skirt his thin legs in their wrinkled hose seemed too frail, the patched shoes too narrow, to bear the pink and silver bulk above.

Ziani peered more closely. "I know that coat," he said. He felt a movement of rage. "You have been at my wardrobe again," he said. He at once regretted saying this, as it gave Battistella the chance, which he immediately took, to list his grievances, a thing he enjoyed doing: the dampness of the house, the lack of any proper heating, his bad chest, his wages two years in arrears . . . Battistella's face, throughout this wheezing catalogue, remained quite impassive. "Provide me with livery," he ended by saying — an old gibe, this — "and I will wear it, not only with pleasure, but with pride."

Ziani felt the eyes of his servant upon him. There was no denying that Battistella had scored a point. He assumed an air of languid superiority. "I am in the midst of composition," he said. "I have no time for trivial matters. I am relating the Boccadoro business. You remember that, I suppose?"

Battistella's breathing had quieted a little and he had become absolutely still. "I remember it very clear," he said.

"You always claim to remember everything. Do not imagine for one moment that you deceive me. This at least you should remember, as you were involved in it closely. I have reached one of the key points, that moment when with a sudden lightning flash of intuition I realized that Donna Francesca was not opening her arms to him." Ziani chuckled on a rising note, hee, hee *hee,* and reached for his snuffbox. "So to speak," he said. Triumph caused him to sniff up the rappee too vigorously. He sneezed violently and his eyes welled up with tears.

"As I remember," Battistella said, "begging your pardon, you mentioned that possibility to me soon after meeting the lady and subsequent to that you speculated several times as to whether Signor Boccadoro was getting his conjugals. 'Is he getting his oats, Battistella?' you said to me. 'That is what I would like to know.' So how can it have been a sudden bit of lightning?"

Ziani stared. His mouth fell open. This burst of garrulity, and the contradiction it contained, had been totally unexpected. His eyes were smarting still. He could think of nothing to say. The nightmare panic of being worsted descended on him. He took out his handkerchief and fell busily to wiping his eyes and blowing his nose. When the rather grubby cambric was removed, his face had recovered its lopsided composure. "My poor Battistella," he said. "You do not understand what it is to be an artist. Are we to include everything that occurs from hour to hour? Of course not. We must strive to render things dramatic. That is the art of it."

"Begging your pardon, sir," Battistella said, " but things either happened or they didn't."

Ziani raised his eyes to the ceiling. "What a blockhead!" he said. "Do you want me to say what waistcoat I was wearing? I compress all my suspicions into one moment. I am trying to present this business as a *campaign,* Battistella. Lightning assessments, bold courses, a master plan. My *Mémoires* will be faithful to the spirit of the age. And what is it, this spirit of the age?"

Battistella made no reply.

"You have no idea, have you? This is the age of the heroic strategist."

Still his servant said nothing. Using silence to indicate dissent or disapproval was one of Battistella's customary gambits; Ziani knew it of old. As always it vexed him and as always he was constrained to conceal his vexation. "Well, well," he said. "If anyone else had said that, you'd have thought it brilliant. Well, you needn't speak. You have no vision, Battistella. That is the difference between us. When these *Mémoires* of mine are published, you will change your tune. Did you take the sheets to the printer again yesterday?"

"Yes."

"And they still agree to make no charge for the printing?"

"They say they will take their costs out of sales."

"You see?" Ziani looked up in triumph. "The rogues can smell money," he said. "These are people used to assessing manuscripts. They see the genius in my pages. What is for dinner today?"

"For dinner today we have a good *torta*."

"Torta, torta," Ziani said fussily. *"Torta* can mean many things. You do not tell a man what is for dinner simply by saying there is pie." He looked expectantly at Battistella.

"This *torta* contains chicken pieces fried in good oil, and ham ravioli."

"And?"

"And almonds and dates. Also there is sweet wine from Málaga."

Ziani's eyes glistened. "I will admit," he said, "that you have managed excellently with food lately, my good Battistella. There was a time when it was *polenta* every day. Now the money seems to be going further. I congratulate you. As a literary critic you may lack refinement, but you are a good man in the kitchen. You will be rewarded, never fear. I am thinking of raising your wages. As you see, the printers have faith in me. Those people are not fools, they can see what will make a profit."

He paused for a moment, but his servant remained silent. "Well," he said, "you may leave me now. I am ready to resume."

"Yes," Battistella said, but for some time longer made no move, remaining silent and immobile, almost as if he had forgotten where he was, holding his master in the same fixity of regard.

This gaze, the way Battistella had looked at him, remained in Ziani's mind after he had gone. There had been a troubling quality in it. Of course he was losing his wits, *povero vecchio:* sometimes he did not seem to know quite where he was. This thought gave Ziani a brief sense of superiority. All the same . . . Battistella was his only link with the world, and dependence made him sensitive to any hint of change. Sometimes, these days, he had a sense that his servant was up to something. Age had slowed him down. He had become contradictory and moralistic. But he had been a considerable trickster in his day. Of course Battistella was just as dependent on him, in a different way . . . Fifty years now. Scrapes they had been in together . . . This brought him back to thoughts of Boccadoro, and he took up his pen once more, remembering that comical indecision.

I saw contrary impulses pass over Boccadoro's face, march, countermarch, skirmish briefly, withdraw to regroup. As I have said, though shrewd in business matters, he was ingenuous in all else — I never knew a man easier to read. If Donna Francesca in very truth hated me, as he asserted, my effectiveness as counselor would be greatly the less; she would not be brought to compliance by hated Ziani. On the other hand, and for obvious reasons, it increased his sense of security.

For my own part, I felt sure he was exaggerating the matter. After all, I was unoffending and the acquaintance was slight, even though I had been a month in the house. My days were spent in the library, for the most part. Finding the atmosphere oppressive, I dined out in the town whenever I could afford to do so, which was whenever I had money from my mother. Because of the unfortunate circumstances narrated earlier in these *Mémoires,* I was not welcome in my stepfather's house, but my mother gave me money sometimes. Even when I took the evening meal, however, conversation was not lively; there was no increase in intimacy, as there was always present, in addition to Boccadoro himself, his ancient deaf aunt, who lived in the house, and often enough Francesca's singing master, Signor Malpigli, or her dancing master, whose name I have forgotten — Buffo, I think. Sometimes even her dressmaker stayed to dinner. Boccadoro had the ungenteel habit of asking anyone in the house to his table.

It was probable enough that she disliked me, I thought; his praises would not have disposed her well toward me. But hatred is another matter. In the course of a career not unmarked by experience of the fair sex — as should be evident from the most casual perusal of these *Mémoires* — I have noticed that ladies render themselves vulnerable through declarations much more than do we, for whom matters of the heart occupy a less central place. Therefore their safeguard is in discretion and they know this well.

"However it may be," I said, "give me the chance to be of service to you. If what you say is true, she cannot dislike me more. Let me try what I can do."

For a moment I wondered if eagerness had throbbed too palpably in my voice; but no, his face broke into a smile. "If it produces results," he said, "by God you will not find me ungrateful." He meant money, of course. The promise shone from the yellowish teeth of his smile, offensive alike to dignity and all sense of elegance. Nevertheless, I smiled back upon him. "You have engaged more than a scribe," I said. "As I hope to show you."

The meaning in these words he did not see. He smiled still and nodded. At this moment the lady herself, accompanied by Maria, came out from the house onto the terrace which overlooked the garden. She had perhaps been intending to descend the steps but on sight of us she checked and turned aside. The two of them then began to walk the length of the terrace, a distance of thirty paces or so. During the rest of my conversation with Boccadoro they walked back and forth on the terrace — Francesca in a long-sleeved gown of some white material and her hair set with threads of pearls, which shone as they caught the light; Maria too in white, and carrying a white shawl, in case her mistress should feel cold, for it was early still, though with promise of heat later.

Ziani looked up from the page. Evening was advancing; the light was losing strength. His eyes were giving him trouble. Before long Battistella would bring his dinner, this famous *torta* that he was promised; also the great candelabrum, which could hold thirty candles but now held only three — all they could afford, or so Battistella said. Battistella controlled all expenditure now. He kept the candelabrum in his own quarters and would not bring it forth, no matter how much play Ziani made with the bell, until he judged the time appropriate.

Sockets for thirty candles, Ziani thought, and he allows me three. In the evenings, when the shadows deepened, the shapes of things looked threatening, and he longed for a good clear light that would leave no dark corners. He keeps the candelabrum in his room, he thought. When I demand it, he makes excuses and creates delays . . . He felt twinges of rage, too much resembling pain to be encouraged. He closed his eyes and breathed deeply. She, the maid, Maria, was carrying a shawl, a white shawl, yes, in case her mistress . . . promise of heat in the day, but it was early still. Scent from the cones of acacia flower, a scent normally rank, but the cool air chastened it. The stone lady was in her arbor, flecked by the sunlight that broke through the young vine leaves, patterning her face and headdress and robe and the arm that lay across her breast, defending and caressing — that ambiguity which intrigued me from the first . . . There were darker markings on her. Dew of the night? Yes, there was something of the night about her still — what was it? Why am I obliged to think so deeply about her, only a thing of stone?

Ziani opened his eyes. She had looked alert; that was it. As if her ravisher — or deliverer — might be near, the promise of the dark not yet over. She could have been a garden deity, a spirit of the seasons. Boccadoro and I stood near to her talking, the two girls pacing above. Girls they were still — for the servant was scarcely older than the mistress — and of a similar height. And dressed in white, and walking side by side . . . Was it then that the first rudiments of the notion came to me? About the germination of ideas it is impossible to be precise. Of course when they turned toward us it could be seen that Maria was darker-skinned and slightly fuller-bodied; she lacked the ethereal quality of Donna Francesca. But the general resemblance was strong.

Men in colloquy below; women parading above. It was as if some secret of life were contained there. He and I could have been attendant lords, or attendant saints, of that order who assist at divine occasions, miraculous events, hover at the margins of visitations.

We had perhaps arranged this occasion too, for so might the Queen of Heaven have walked, with a companion, in the cool of the morning, visible to mortals but indifferent. A wrong choice was made, he thought suddenly, on that morning or a morning like it, by me or someone else. It was not inevitable that I should end like this, captive, disabled, with no one to rely on or compete with but Battistella. Did I compound the wrong or merely inherit it, as I stood there with Boccadoro, watching them pass and repass?

This softening, almost like contrition, was unusual with Ziani, and he shifted sharply in his chair as if in an effort to be released from it. It was almost dusk now. He hoisted himself and leaned sideways, with the usual pain of such labor, to look down over the broad glinting surface of the water. From here, helped by the curving line of the canal, he could make out the blurred masses of light on the Rialto, the blanched reflections on the water. Strange to think that the house where these distant episodes had occurred was quite close by, that after all vicissitudes he had come back to die within a mile of it. Boccadoro was dust, gone with his horns to the grave, but the house was still there, with the narrow canal below the garden wall, the arbor empty now, unless some new tutelary spirit had been installed. *She* was still alive, married into the Bembo family. Living in some style, so Battistella said.

He could hear the loud bells of San Stefano, ringing the Angelus, signal to pleasure, not devotion. Venice was stirred with the rhythms of pleasure still: in that respect she had not changed. This was the time of promise, of encounters. He could remember, as if the feelings had belonged to another, the excitement of dressing to go out, in this same house, when there had still been money, and in other houses in Venice: the sense of a whole city, a whole population, preparing for pleasure, the bells, the flush on the water turning leaden. One set out as the rose turned to lead; augury of disillusion not recognized then.

The great houses on the opposite bank were lit up now. No shortage of candles there. Gondolas bobbed in the broken bronze reflections at the landing stages below the steps. While he watched, a party in white bird masks and scarlet *tabarri* came down from the Casa Loredan opposite and were helped into two boats. It was

Carnival time still — Carnival was almost continuous in Venice. In these beaked masks, tall hats, full cloaks, only voices and laughter distinguished men from women.

Some could afford to entertain, Ziani thought with bitterness. Some could afford considerably more. Battistella, his lifeline in this too, brought him the gossip of the coffee house as it was retold in the market. Had not Ludovico Marin employed the architect Selva, notorious for his high fees, to redesign the interior of his mansion and extend it as far as Campo San Salvatore? The Contarini had ten gondolas at their doors and fifty servants in livery. For the sake of a single reception, it was said, the Mocenigo family had gutted three adjoining palaces, giving them a suite of forty salons. All this while others, of descent no less illustrious, lived on bread and gruel in their new ghetto of San Barnabà — so many broken patricians in that district now that they called them Barnabotti — or crouched, as he did, in some corner of their pillaged ancestral homes. Ziani felt a rush of energizing malevolence. Revenge was as necessary now as it had been that distant morning in the garden, though the enemy was different. Scions of these noble families featured or would feature in his *Mémoires,* all in a scandalously discreditable light. Then we shall see who laughs, he thought, reaching for his handbell. Then we shall see.

It was Ziani's custom, every morning before resuming, to reread attentively what he had written the day before in order to make stylistic improvements. This morning, while reading the previous day's stint, he fell prey to very considerable disquietude concerning Francesca's "hatred" of him. All these years he had thought of this as a complacent exaggeration on Boccadoro's part, understandable and natural at a time when the old man himself was being deprived of sexual favors. But suppose the lady had really said it? He had never asked her, as far as he could remember. If she had indeed said this, disturbing reinterpretations of the whole affair became necessary, since it could only have been meant as a signal. As an expression of true feeling, it was too excessive on such slight grounds. Then she had wanted him to understand something by it. And how could it be understood but as an expression of interest, a kind of encouragement, something that invited a response? But that would mean . . . Ziani fell to stroking his jaws rapidly and repeatedly, in consternation. That would mean she had made the first move, fired the first shot. He, Ziani, master strategist, expert at plotting that route which led, deviously at first, afterward straight and clear between the lady's legs, had been all the time her dupe, instrumental to her purposes: she had led him by the prick . . . It was an appalling thought, a true monster of the mind, needing to be smothered at once, before its infant lungs became too raucous. He thought of summoning Battistella, but his servant's responses were unreliable these days: not only did he argue on matters of literary theory, but he could not always be trusted to corroborate the past. No, he would have to wrestle with this demon alone. Adopting his usual discipline, Ziani closed his eyes and took a series of deep breaths. The thought did not quite go away but he began to feel calmer. After some minutes of this he was able to take up his pen and begin again.

The first test, and the most crucial, was whether Francesca would agree to grant me audience. If she was as unbiddable as he said, she was capable of disobeying his express wishes; but I did not think this was likely. In fact I expected a summons through Maria; and wherever in our goings about the house our paths crossed, Maria's and mine, I waited for some sign. However, there was none. She looked boldly at me, made a sketch of a curtsy, and that was all. This Maria was a beauty in her way, and I will confess that had I not been set on the mistress, I would have been strongly tempted to assay the maid. Moreover she was ripe for it; I detected invitation in her regard. All men of the world will know what I mean when I say she had breasts that seemed impatient of her bodice. Some few trinkets would have clinched it, something for her trousseau.

When the moment came it was the lady herself who spoke, and in a way that seemed unstudied — though naturally she would not have wished it to be thought rehearsed. I was crossing the courtyard on my way to the library, which was on the first floor of the house, when Francesca came in from the garden. We met in the middle, at the wellhead carved with lions' heads, where I had stood that first morning and watched her descend the stairs. She greeted me and seemed to hesitate; my instinct told me to stop. She stopped too; talk between us thus became inevitable.

"I see that you are busy," she said: I had papers in my hand.

"Not at all," I said — how promptly may be imagined. "Not if you wish to speak to me, noble lady. What could count beside that?"

She paused a moment, still regarding me, though without much kindness. Then she spoke again, but now as though addressing the mild lions on the well-head. "It is not so much that I wish to speak to him," she told the lions, who seemed quite to understand. "I would not aspire so far," she said. "Only to look at him, to observe at close quarters this faithful steward, this *persona esemplare*."

"Persona esemplare?" I frowned, as if puzzled. This was a critical moment.

"Such a . . . paragon," she said, still to the lions, but there was a slight breathlessness now which betrayed her. As is universally acknowledged, women are frail and tender vessels, their containing walls are more porous, feeling finds its way to the surface less resistibly than with us, whose casing is tougher. So it was now with Francesca, in that catch of the breath, a slight, the slightest, quiver of the lip. (This tendency of theirs to self-betrayal is of great advantage to us, second only to their innate credulity.) However, I was not sure yet of the precise nature of her emotion.

"That sounds like a character in a play," I said. "A new type for the *commedia dell'arte* perhaps? A character who does nothing but moralize, and of course always at the wrong time. No, my name is Sigismondo."

It was effective. It made her look at me and abandon this absurd pretense of conversing with lions. It was important to dispel any sense on her part that she was mistress speaking to servant. We had both been bought by Boccadoro; I would not have her thinking she was higher placed. Victory is not victory if achieved by self-demeaning. Besides, my whole strategy was based on her being brought to see the natural alliance between us against jumped-up Boccadoro. After all, we were both *scaduti,* fallen ones. I planned to prevail on her virtue by exacerbating her desire for revenge. This had further advantages: when the citadel fell, I would have no mere compliant lump on my hands, gates flung open and nothing more to do, but a creature energetic, eager, inventive, shameless, seeing in my felicity her more exquisite vindication. Such at least was the plan. The reader will judge for himself how far I succeeded.

"You must be confusing me with someone else," I said.

I saw the slightest of frowns trouble her brow — a deliberate frown; she was like a child, wanting to show the adults she was puzzled. Then her face was smooth again and she wore the mask of youth, which is of all masks the strangest. "My husband continually sings your praises," she said.

"Then perhaps," I said, "it is he, your esteemed husband, who is confusing matters."

Now indeed I was on the brink. In what other game are the greatest risks taken at the beginning? I was about to reveal myself as a *persona* far from *esemplare*. If I had miscalculated in some way, misjudged her relations with Boccadoro, she would be prompt to make me suffer for it. With what haste she would repair to him, point out his faulty judgment, as all good wives so love to do! We were still standing in the same place, looking sometimes at each other, sometimes at the lions, sometimes at the walls. It was she who moved first, turning toward the door of the small salon that led off the courtyard, but turning leisurely so that I was sure to be included. She passed into the room immediately and advanced toward the casement at the far end. Obviously I was intended to follow, and I did so. We stood together in the embrasure, looking out toward the garden. We were in the full light and our faces were clear to each other as we talked. It was the first time we had been alone in a room together, and I wondered if she felt constraint. Nothing showed on that mask of her eighteen-year-old face.

"It is not only as a cataloguer of books that he praises you," she said, "but in all other respects too. He talks about you constantly. It is very tedious to listen to. Sometimes he compares you to Cato, sometimes to Cicero. Sometimes, in his enthusiasm, he compares you to a person called Catero."

"A noted sage," I said, and she smiled. Her smile was very beautiful. Once having seen it, a man would cast about for things to say to bring it back. Next moment, however, a look of annoyance came to her face and she gestured toward the garden. I glanced through the window and there, not many yards away, was the hulking form of Bobbino, Boccadoro's manservant, lounging insolently in full view, kicking at the gravel path. "My husband instructs him to wait within call," she said. "For my convenience, of course. I say that I have Maria, but that makes no difference. That is why I came to stand here at the window, so at least we would be spared the sight of his pig's face peering in."

My heart exulted: she was confiding in me. "Shall I send the oaf away?" I said. "Let me kick him round the garden."

"No, no," she said, "thank you." And she smiled again, though not by my intention this time — perhaps because Bobbino was so big. "Never mind him," she said. "My husband seems to think you could be a kind of tutor to me."

A kind of tutor I could be indeed, I thought. My eyes perhaps betrayed me, because her own expression changed and her chin lifted slightly, in a sort of defiance.

It was this, the sense that she had seen my desire, that brought me out from cover completely, made me throw myself on her good will. "I don't know where he can have got that idea," I said. "Perhaps it was at the theater."

This was said at random. The truth is that I was flustered. She had seen unregenerate Adam peeping out through my eyes, and I had been excited by the defiant quality of her response. Otherwise I would not have been so disrespectful to him. But at the back of my mind there still lingered thoughts of the *commedia,* and how Boccadoro resembled Pantaleone — it must be remembered that the old comedy with its stock characters and improvised dialogue still ruled supreme in the Venice of those days. This was fifty years ago, before the rise of Goldoni — he was just beginning.

However, that one word, uttered as I say too hastily, did more for my cause, I think, than a hundred prepared phrases might have done. (Perhaps, as I think now, it was inspiration, the kind of "accident" that happens only to talented persons.)

"Theater?" she said. For some moments her face remained set in its impervious cast of youth. Then she broke into a different kind of smile, one of contempt, for Boccadoro, for me. "Theater? He never goes to the theater. What would he do in a theater? And he does not want me to go, because it is a bad influence, so he says. For that matter he never goes to the Ridotto, either, not he, he would not risk a florin at the tables. So naturally I do not go. He does not rent an apartment, or even share the rent of one, which is often done nowadays, for meetings and conversations among friends."

Here was a catalogue of troubles indeed. "I am extremely sorry to hear this," I said. "It is medieval. It has a flavor of barbarity about it."

"Yes," she said, "four months married and I go out less now than when I lived at home with my brothers. I thought I would have more freedom, but it has happened the other way. No wonder —"

She stopped short on this and I did not press her. "Well then," I said, "you should choose a *cicisbeo* to escort you, if he will not go. That is common enough. There are many who would undertake it gladly, asking for nothing in return but the pleasure of your company."

"My husband does not believe this," she said, and she lowered her eyes. "Then there is this creature Bobbino," she added after a moment, following some train of thought of her own.

"Well," I said, "a kind of tutor I could be to you, if you consent."

"Oh indeed?" she said, very coldly. "And what kind is that?"

"The kind who talks about the theater," I said, and without giving her any time to reply, I began in fact to talk about the theater, which I had known well in the years before I left for Rome, the quarrels and the cliques, the great Arlecchino, Sacchi, who was later to become so successful as a manager, the love affairs of Carlo Gozzi and the comedienne Teodora Ricci, Goldoni's *Momolo Cortesan,* which had run for three weeks at the San Samuele Theater, and which had a written part for the protagonist. Goldoni himself was naïve, strangely so for one who created so many rogues on stage. I made Francesca laugh when I told her the story of how a trickster, dressed up as a monk, had succeeded in selling him a lace from the Blessed Virgin's corset.

I spoke mainly of things as they had been five years before, but that made no difference to Francesca. She attended eagerly to my every word. Looking at her absorbed face, seeing the laughter rising to it, I knew that my campaign was well and truly launched.

Ziani stopped to reach for his snuffbox. He was pleased with his delineation of this last scene. It had pace and profundity and penetration. How she had hung upon his words! And how adroit he had been, how quick to see the matter that would interest her! As often happened in moments of self-congratulation, he sniffed too vigorously and the coarse rappee made his eyes water and smart.

His window was open slightly, as the morning was warm, and he could hear the men working on the restoration of San Samuele — they were driving in new piles to replace those of the original foundation. Battistella, who crept around Venice like a feeble ant in his borrowed robes, gleaning gossip along with the groceries, Battistella had seen the old piles, the ones they had taken out; they were of larch and they were seven hundred years old. Fast in the clay for seven hundred years! Black as carbon but still strong. The men were singing the *"Bandiera Bianca,"* a song almost as old. The words came to him, barely distinguishable, punctuated by the rhythms of the work:

contro il gran turco — bandiera bianca
che l'enemico — segno di pace

It was not the Turk who was the enemy now, he reflected. The enemy was nearer home — vultures more local, getting the whiff of the Republic's decay. Revolutionary France, the Austria of the Hapsburgs, an unholy league of liberty and tyranny that would destroy Venice, who had kept these twin monsters in balance for so long — longer than those stakes had been bedded in the silt of the Lagoon . . .

He reached for the handbell and gave a prolonged summons. While he waited his thoughts returned with fretful obsessiveness to that room in Boccadoro's house, the two of them there by the window. Already his triumph had been eaten away by a return of nightmare doubts. *She* it was who had made the first move; *she* who had contrived the meeting; *she* who had directed and controlled the course of the conversation. All his theater talk had only been floundering, improvising — he was the one who belonged in the *commedia*.

With mechanical curses he rang the bell again. Why was it only then that he had begun to be conscious of desire for her? A month in the house, and he had not thought of her particularly in that way. Desire had followed his will: that was why his memories of her had this painful tension. Until he had possessed her there could be no room for tenderness; he had been too afraid of failing.

"You will not hear the trumpets," he said when Battistella finally appeared. "You will come crawling late on the Day of Judgment."

Battistella stood surveying him, breathing noisily. He was still in his pink coat, despite the warmth of the day, and his wig was as usual askew.

"What is for luncheon?" Ziani asked.

"There is a good rice pudding."

"Rice pudding, rice pudding," Ziani said, with customary pleasurable sharpness. "And how is it made, this rice pudding?"

"It is made with honey." Knowing how it pleased his master to protract these conversations, Battistella never revealed all the details at once.

"And?"

"It is cooked in milk of almonds."

"I am thinking seriously of raising your wages," Ziani said. "You may as well know that. And you may keep that coat, you may have it. This morning I have been describing my first *tête-à-tête* with Donna Francesca. I have managed it well, that colloquy, extremely well. Consummately. I have brought it home to the reader. The way I engaged her sympathies was brilliant. I have been wondering whence the initial agitation came, and it occurs to me now that she was aware of my loaded cannon right from the very commencement, she felt the danger. I was mesmeric to women in those days."

Ziani reached for his snuffbox. "It was a burden in some ways," he said. "One had to —"

"No, sir," Battistella said suddenly. "It did not lie there."

Ziani's hand jumped and he spilled his snuff. "What do you mean?" he said, staring.

"Begging your pardon, sir, she had no one to turn to but her maid. They sold her to him, her brothers did. Theirs were the debts, and she had to pay. It is not only pagans and Saracens and blackamoors. They would have shut her away or killed her, that family is well known."

Evidently under the impression that he had made himself clear, Battistella began his snail-like withdrawal.

"Where is all this tending?" Ziani said. "Who told you that, anyway?"

"Maria and I sometimes talked."

"Did you so?" Ziani said uneasily. "You are a sly dog, Battistella. I'd wager you did more than talk. But what is behind all this rambling, what point are you seeking to make?"

"She was looking to find a friend," Battistella said loudly and wheezingly from the door. "Nothing to do with mesmeric, nothing to do with cannon."

On this, he immediately disappeared. Ziani sat for a considerable time, staring before him. He was deeply offended by this brusque rejection of his theory. I must stop discussing these *Mémoires* with him, he thought. He has no sensitivity whatever, and always gets hold of the wrong idea. But who else was there? He had only Battistella. She had no one to turn to but her maid . . . Could it be true that she had come to him in need, and her first hostility was to cover that? That she might have been unhappy in that way had somehow never occurred to him. But the mask of youth could cover that as well as other things. So while I was laying my groundworks, my mind set on victory, master strategist Ziani, she was merely suffering and trying to keep that fact concealed? Of course she complained, but only conventional complaints . . .

He tried to shake off these disagreeable thoughts and recover his feeling of triumph, but it would not return. He had a sense of something incomplete in his memory. They had stood together in the window, glancing from time to time across the garden. The lout Bobbino kicking at the gravel. Sunlight on the boxwood hedges, the narrow leaves of the acacia, the apricot trees espaliered against the wall. She turned her back on spying Bobbino, and he moved round a little so as still to look her in the face . . . That was it: this change of position gave a view of the statue, half-hidden as she was by foliage, with the first roses of the year climbing round her. The outbuildings of the abandoned church rose behind her, looking from that angle like a distant background in a painting. Even though she was half masked by shadow and leaves her pose was striking, the face raised with that provocative alertness, the guarding hand held out. That faint smile of hers not visible from there.

Seen thus among the leaves she was like our first mother. He had known nothing at all then about the man who made her.

The conversation with Battistella unsettled Ziani for the rest of the day, as if he were the dupe of time and memory. Besides, he was beginning to feel dissatisfied with the pace of his narrative. It seemed to be dragging somewhat. Perhaps he was spending too much time on the description of preliminaries. He was impatient to get Francesca's clothes off, reveal her beauties, describe the tunes they had played together. His cold heart was stirred by the memory of these exploits; he crept to reach them, stalking them as it were through the thickets of his prose.

However, something held him back. In part he was handicapped by egotism. To sell the *Mémoires* and retrieve his fortunes, he was depending in equal measure on the scandalous and erotic. At the same time he wanted to be noted as stylist, as man of the world. He imagined the reader exclaiming aloud at the justice of his observations. Elements such as these are not easily combined. So far he felt he had managed things well: in Venice and elsewhere public figures and the scions of noble houses had been exposed and discredited, one revealed as a cardsharp, another as pimp to his numerous female relatives, a third as voyeur of his own wife and two footmen with her knowledge but not theirs — to mention only a few. This chapter, these episodes of Francesca and old Boccadoro and the Madonna, he had envisaged as one of the highlights. But some quality of reluctance had crept in, he knew not how. Dues of recognition had to be paid, slowing him down.

When he resumed it was with the determination to get to his conquest with the least possible delay.

In the days that followed we met quite frequently in different places about the house, and wherever we met we stopped to talk. These meetings had always an air of accident about them, but it has been my experience that at certain junctures of human affairs accident is aided by design. Certainly it is true that we met more often in those few days than during my whole stay before.

We talked of indifferent things and took care not to laugh together much. We were never really alone. For one thing, Maria was always in attendance. She kept at a distance and busied herself usually with some task of stitching; all the same, those eyes and ears of hers missed nothing. But it was Bobbino that was the real constraint upon us. Wherever we looked we seemed to see him, lounging idly, doing nothing in particular. If we walked in the garden, he would be there, not far away. If we sent him about his business, he would be back before long, on some pretext or other. When we were behind closed doors, he knew it and for how long. Thus we were obliged to speak gravely, for that was what Boccadoro would expect; and Francesca had to keep Maria by her for that same reason.

But there is a language that lies within and around what is spoken, and this developed rapidly between us precisely because of these constraints I have mentioned. In pauses, and in inflections of the voice, we talked to each other, with eyes on eyes, with hands that did not touch. Thus the supervision aided me, fretting Francesca, making us accomplices. I owed much to the lout Bobbino.

Boccadoro himself, for ten days following, spoke no more to me about the matter, either by hint or direct question. I think now, and must have supposed then, that Francesca was deliberately keeping him waiting for her "verdict." This allowed meetings in the meantime while she was supposedly making up her mind, confirmed him too in his laughable belief that there would be dislike to overcome on her part before the Ziani message of duty and morality could be brought home to her. These were the tactics of her cunning, not prompted by me. Nevertheless, I was the instigating force . . .

So it was that during this period the Casa Boccadoro resembled the physical universe, in which, as the Englishman Newton has shown, all bodies are bound together by a principle of mutual attraction or repulsion, either inclining to cohere in regular figures, or inclining to recede. All of us were held in balance: myself, Francesca, Boccadoro, Maria, Bobbino — even my Battistella, to whom I had complained of that animal's intrusiveness and who sought to distract and deflect him. (Battistella was an astute fellow in those days; now addled, poor soul.)

This celestial state was shattered when Boccadoro announced his intention of leaving for Verona, where he had business to attend to. He would be away for one night, he said. Bobbino was left behind, of course, to spy. All the same, I don't think Boccadoro had any suspicions; he was not a man to review judgments once formed. And this explains his fury later, when he discovered us.

He left early in the morning, but it was not until midafternoon that Francesca and I met. She kept to her own quarters till then, perhaps to mark the vulgarity of haste. For one so young she had a great sense of occasion.

Ziani paused, sighing. He had not known then what monstrously memorable forms her sense of occasion could take. That same night he was to know . . .

He had made up his mind to take her to the theater, this being the first thing in which they had found a mutual interest. However, he had spent his wages and had no money besides, or very little. He had borrowed two lire from Battistella, who could always, by means Ziani did not inquire into, feeling they verged on the miraculous, produce a little money, but it was still not enough. He had hung around Florian's for an hour or so before lunch in the hope of making a touch — there was only Florian's then; Quadri had not yet opened on the other side of the *piazza*. But it was awkward, after he had been away so long — awkward, on being recognized, to start asking for a loan. Bad policy, too. He had given it up almost and was walking on the Broglio, feeling dispirited, when by great good fortune he had met Pietro Gradenigo, who had been a fellow student and who at once agreed to lend the eight lire he needed. Enough, with what he had already, for a box at the San Samuele, also wine and biscuits. Yet after all this, with the well-known perversity of women, she had asked to be taken to a gaming house . . . Should I mention my poverty, he wondered, my stratagems to obtain money? No, it is incompatible with conquest. He took some snuff, wiped his eyes, resumed writing.

She wanted to go to the Ridotto, where she had never been in her life before. She wanted to do something she had never done before, she said, and she could not keep the pleasure from shining in her eyes. This was an occasion to do something *for the very first time*.

But what about Bobbino? We looked at each other for a moment. Then I asked if she could trust Maria. Yes, she said, she had complete faith in Maria's discretion. And I in Battistella's, I said, he is the most faithful creature alive. So let us take them into our confidence, let us appeal to them for help, let us throw ourselves upon their mercy.

And this is what we did, and at once, summoning them to us, holding a council of war. Neither was well disposed toward Bobbino: Maria because — and this I understand only from nods and compressions of the lips and salvoes of glances — he did not keep his dirty hands to himself; and Battistella — but this I knew already — because Bobbino was a bully and jealous of his position in the household. Jointly they begged us to have no further inquietude: they would take care of booby Bobbino.

We were set on the adventure anyway — less assurance would have been sufficient — but I felt relieved to have Battistella's support. In many difficult situations, before that time and since, I have benefited from his resourcefulness and sagacity. (He is less reliable now, through age, poor soul. His mind inclines to stray.)

We left by the street door, quite soon after dinner, while Bobbino was in the pantry still. We were masked, of course. Therefore once on the street anonymous, completely free from recognition and detection. Venice, alone perhaps of cities, confers this freedom on her children, because of the universal custom of masking, which in the middle years of the century was more widespread even than now, masks being commonly worn in public places, whether it was Carnival or not, and by people of all degrees. With this custom comes that other one of sexual debauchery, the casual trafficking for which our city has long been famous, even more than Rome, that *città delle donne*. The anonymity conferred by masks has been a potent force in our history, adding to the excitement of intrigue as it grants immunity from the consequences, emboldening the prick while it renders the cunt more yielding. I was sensible of boldness myself in that region, not to say effrontery. For her state I couldn't answer, but I hoped. She was elated and inclined to laughter.

The masks we wore were full-face, of that close-fitting kind, oddly like death masks, as it always seemed to me, white in color; and with them we wore the *bauta,* which had become very fashionable, more ample in those days than now, covering the head and shoulders. In these, and our loose-fitting clothes, we were well disguised.

Francesca's mood of excitement increased as we walked down the short street onto the *salizzada*. She made loud remarks about other passers-by and raised her concealed face often to laugh. She was determined, on this great occasion, to enjoy everything, right from the beginning — and of course she had to show it. I began to understand how high-strung she was. How violent she could be I had yet to learn.

From the Rio di Fontego we took a gondola toward San Marco, one of the best routes in the city in my opinion, the water broad enough and the way winding, with very varied views. The evening was warm, with a light *scirocco* blowing. The bridges and *rive* were all lit up, crowded with idlers and strollers and pleasure seekers of every sort, and those who live by them, whores, mountebanks, peddlers, pimps, all doing a brisk trade, Venice being full of strangers just then, come to see the celebrations for the visit of the King of Portugal. That day there had been a big regatta on the Grand Canal, and fireworks were promised for later. Hoping for more money, our gondolier began singing for us, *"Venezia, gemm' adriatica, sposa del mar."* He had a tenor voice, not very strong, but sweet. We kept the curtains of the cabin open so that we could sit looking out at the people and the lights. Francesca laughed and exclaimed less, and by this I knew she was beginning to enjoy herself. The moon, not quite full, was straight before us, low in the sky, over the Bacinto. We descended at the Ponte de la Canonica. I paid the man extra to avoid a wrangle and we made our way from behind the basilica into the *piazza*.

We began at once to cross the square in the direction of San Moise, where the Ridotto was. But I was worried still about money. I had about eleven lire in all, barely a ducat. It was possible Francesca had nothing with her — I did not want to use her money, in any case. Now at the Ridotto, even in those days, in order to play *faro* or *spigolo* one needed more than this; they did not play small games. And to play the numbers without enough to cover initial losses was to invite an abrupt end to our entertainment. I was hoping for a good deal from this evening, and I wanted no failures.

As we passed under the Nuove Procuratie I happened to notice the sign of the Guardian Angel, and I suddenly remembered the Moro coffee house alongside, which I had used to frequent once, with the two small inside rooms, where they had card tables and a *biribisso* wheel — the place has been closed down since. On the spur of the moment I suggested to Francesca that we should try our luck in there. The stakes would be lower. Besides, I thought, she should see something of the underworld of Venice there, which she would not have seen before. Had she not said that she wanted to do things for the very first time?

It was crowded and hot inside, the usual rabble of rogues and harlots, mingled with some of the best blood in Venice. There were faces I recognized: masks were obligatory here, but they were often too flimsy to conceal the features, mere tokens — the doorkeeper kept a stock for people arriving without one; an eye mask or a false nose was considered enough. The din was great; sexual commerce was incessant at the fringes of the tables, conducted by prostitutes and by women who had lost at cards and wanted to play again — for a few lire they would copulate standing up in the passageways off the gaming rooms, enveloped in the folds of their cloaks. The place throbbed with noise, smelled of sweat and wine fumes and sexual discharge. And Francesca loved it. She laughed as we jostled through to the tables, and her eyes were gleaming in that white mask.

Fortune favored us, as I shall relate. A man in a black mask that left nothing but mouth and chin exposed was making good use of that mouth at the *biribisso* table, boasting he had understood the system. His manner was truculent. His purse, which he made no attempt to conceal, bulged with sequins.

It was this casual display of gold that made me suspicious. I have a nose for dupes, and this was not one. It seemed to me that he was acting a part. He had begun by asserting loudly that the wheel went in certain runs and sequences, four on red, two on black, the third red always in the zone of the twenties — or some such thing — it is a long time ago now. The croupier — the only one without a mask — told him to play or move off. In a rage, real or simulated, he put down a handful of gold sequins on the middle band of the red. And he won. And he won again.

Since then I have seen the trick played often enough. Always there is someone who claims to be an infallible winner. Others are skeptical, but when they see him win they begin to believe it and they put their money with his. When there is enough on the table, everybody loses. The money of the boaster returns to the bank.

Simple enough, but effective. Then I had only instinct to go on. I gave my money to Francesca for luck and told her to put it with his. With eyes if possible more brilliant than ever she did so. We doubled our money twice. Then I took it up. At the next turn the bank took everything.

From that point onward everything went well for us. We played *faro* and won. We played *bassetto* and won. Francesca brought me luck. She sat beside me and sometimes played a hand, sometimes whispered advice. I asked her if she wanted to go on to the Ridotto, but she preferred to stay where she was, here where we were winning, amidst the uproar and the reek. She loved every minute of it — I never knew anyone to enjoy things as she did. . . .

When we finally rose from the table it was after midnight, and between us we had won some thirty sequins, over six hundred lire in the exchange of the time. It was more ready cash than I had had for years. We went out to the front room of the Moro and sat in a corner and took the masks off our heated faces and drank a bottle of champagne together, glass for glass.

What time it was when we left, I do not know. The Moro used to stay open till three or four in the morning. We walked arm in arm to the San Marco boat stage. There were still a good many people about on the Molo — Venice being then as now a city of inveterate noctambulists — and the gondolas were plying. It was quiet on the water, full tide — the level at the Molo was not more than a few inches below the bank. There was a thin mist, making the moonlight seem luminous. Where the oar broke the surface, the ripples gleamed. We were both slightly drunk: with champagne, with the elation of winning, with the sudden quiet and beauty of the night. Our boatman this time was silent, but in the distance, toward the Lagoon, we could hear singing, voices answering voices. Francesca herself sang, a snatch from an old song, *gentil mia donna*. She trailed a hand in the water. She allowed me to kiss her, on the cheek several times, once on the mouth.

We returned by the side canal that ran below the house. Thus it was that we came through the garden. We lingered there, and there the lady did something else *for the very first time*.

Ziani sniggered mechanically to himself and reached for his snuffbox. He was becoming increasingly uneasy. He sought to recall that nighttime garden of long ago. Not dark there but twilight — dawn was not far away. Scents of the garden, the roses, the acacia blossoms — musk smell of early summer. Deep steady smell of the roses. There was the brackish smell of the canal. The statue glimmering in her alcove — her form and the roses, the white ones, the only defined things in the garden, as if they were first to anticipate the day. And the oval of the girl's face. They had sat together in the dimness of the arbor, on the wooden bench against the wall, behind the statue — she was at the entrance, their guardian angel. No, he thought, I knew already that this had been a cloister, that we were on church ground. I knew she was the Madonna Annunziata; I had found Longhi's book by that time, in my delvings in the library, among those neglected volumes, though I spoke of it to no one. I knew who she was when I crowned her with the roses . . .

His uneasiness grew. If I had not done that, he thought, perhaps Francesca would not have done what she did. Before going into the arbor they had made a chain of roses for her head. Alternate red and white roses. She split the stems with her nails. Then he had laid this circlet of roses round the stone brows. He had addressed a mock plea for lovers to her, and genuflected, to make Francesca laugh, calling her Lady Venus, Our Lady of Lovers. There was an emanation of light about her, a light different from that elsewhere, or so it seemed — an illusion, trick of the mingling of day and night in the garden. The roses had smelled of their wounds as well as their perfume. The Madonna had seemed to listen . . .

I must get back to myself, he thought. Man of the world, stylist. What is needed now is some general observation on the nature of the fair sex, followed by a deft description of the romantic ambience, then graphic details of how I had her.

I have often remarked that when the ladies grant us their ultimate favors and surrender the keep, it is not because we have roused their appetites or dominated their wills, still less because we have convinced their minds, but because, generous creatures, they wish to make us gifts. It is in the arranging of suitable circumstances that the man of the world shows his mettle.

Our hearts were full to overflowing with the beauty of the night, our minds with the sensations we had experienced, the excitement of the tables, the return over the moonlit water, the tranquil garden with its sweetly mingled odors, where the last of the night contended with the first of the day. There was everything here that was needed to appeal to the fancy, touch the sentiments, incline the mind to thoughts of love.

We were sitting together in the arbor. I had kissed her earlier, but briefly and playfully, and she had evaded some kisses, allowed others. Now, however, when I returned to the assault, I found a warmer welcome. Far from evading, her lips sought mine. We began to kiss long and eagerly, myself in a seventh heaven of delight, still not quite daring to believe that the highest felicity would be vouchsafed, though now her mouth was opening to the kisses, and her lips had assumed that softness of consistency that a man of the world will recognize as denoting readiness in women. Ziani, my boy, I said to myself, the moment has come to sound the charge. I got my hand under the skirt of her gown, lost my way among her petticoats, found it again at the junction of hot flesh and stocking top. She pressed her legs together at first, made some attempt to ward me off, push my hand lower, but the gesture was halfhearted and feeble; and when I moved the hand up between her legs and touched her cunt, her own hand fell away, her thighs loosened, all resistance was at an end, she sighed, she was mine. By now I was vastly swollen in the nether part and impatient to make the breach, but held off a little longer, rubbing gently at the threshold, and especially that little nipple they so love to have fondled, while we kissed and she panted and the milk of her pleasure wet my fingers. Then, when further delay threatened my own equilibrium, I knelt before her, a position more suitable for prayer, but it was the only way the thing could be done on that narrow bench against the wall. I was unbuttoned and my weapon was out, rearing up, huge. (I had a huge one in those days and always rearing up at moments opportune and otherwise but now most opportune.) Because of my position and the indistinct light I don't think she was aware of this great spike that awaited her; she leaned murmuring to kiss me and I drew her downward, holding her in my embrace, pulling her gently forward until she slipped from the edge of the bench and so transfixed herself on my braced and eager *uccello*. As she slid down, I slid up, impaling her with one great resistless thrust.

All this I had intended for our mutual pleasure, but I heard her exclaim in a startled way as she came down onto me, and when our faces were level I saw hers twist with pain. My own spasms were not long delayed, but I realized in that moment that Donna Francesca, four months married, had just ceased to be a virgin, and that my versatile dagger, piercing her, had in the self-same stroke wounded old Boccadoro more grievously even than I had intended.

Ziani stopped, laid down his pen. He had grown excited, writing this; the ancient gristle between his legs had stirred. But that small heat soon died away, lost in the terrible doubts he had had since starting this section of his *Mémoires*. Had he simply been her instrument all along, a convenient length of piping? Such thoughts, the suspicion that he had been somehow a dupe — which of all things he most dreaded being — all this was difficult to endure. But there was more, much more: there was the thing she had done afterward, the thing that had put him in thrall, subjugated his memory ever since, destroyed his whole vision of that evening, the moonlight, the roses, his masterful importunity, her sighing sacrifice of maidenhood. She had dispersed these sentimental wraiths forever. She had shocked and frightened him.

While he still knelt there, spent now, his pride limp and flaccid, she had sat back from him and in his full view lifted skirt and petticoats, with deliberate gesture and smiling face — a pagan smile — touched her own torn parts, raised her hand so he could see on it, in the dawn light, the glisten of blood and seed, and holding this hand extended before her, had walked to the front of the statue — the Madonna! — and anointed her on the forehead, just below the crown of flowers.

RESTORATION TWO

◇

All Below the Waist

1

"When did the first attack occur?" The doctor leaned forward with polite interest, placing the palms of his immaculate hands together and resting them on the desk.

"About three weeks ago," Raikes said. "I wouldn't call them attacks exactly," he added defensively. He had made the appointment on Wiseman's recommendation. Vittorini was an eminent neurologist, with an international reputation, Wiseman had said, amiably glowing at being in a position, once again, to impart some special knowledge to his friend; tactfully forbearing to ask why that friend should be asking for a specialist in disorders of the nervous system. Moreover, he spoke excellent English, another advantage — Raikes had not wanted to leave matters to the hazard of his Italian. "I suppose that's what they are," he conceded now. He was wishing that he had not come. He felt ill at ease, sitting there without bodily ailment — or at least without feeling in any way ill. Vittorini's calm, chestnut-colored gaze made him feel afflicted and fraudulent at the same time.

"How soon was it followed by the second?"

"Quite soon — less than a week."

Vittorini made notes on the pad before him. After a moment he said, "So there have been four occurrences within the last month?"

"Yes."

"And all that has been since you began your work of restoring the statue?"

"That's right, yes."

"And you have had no recent accident or acute illness?"

"No."

"The hallucinatory content — you say that has been different, quite distinctly different, each time?"

"Well," Raikes said, "the sensation is the same, more or less, and the auditory part of it, a kind of echoing silence, if you understand what I mean, as if someone had just been laughing and the resonance of that was still in the air, but as silence rather than sound . . ." He stopped in some confusion. "It's difficult to describe," he said.

Vittorini sat back, rolling the pencil between his fingers. "Tell me again what you think you saw," he said. "Take your time. Try to include everything."

There had been some hint of skepticism in this, or perhaps merely professional reserve. Raikes did as he was asked, struggling with his own reluctance, taking things in order: the long straight shadow, the wet bodies, the distant glimmering view of the Madonna, the arch of foliage . . . It was difficult not to embroider, as when telling one's dreams; more difficult still to convey the sensation, that hush over things, the sense of exposure, the strange belated fear.

He did his best with all this, glancing sometimes at the walls, sometimes at the floor, sometimes at Vittorini's impassive face. When he came to the most recent of his "visions" — for it was thus ironically he persisted in thinking of them — he experienced, quite unexpectedly, some return of the fear, enough to dry his throat. Only the day before, while at work on the Madonna, he had seen — and it was an experience more disturbing, more protracted, than any before — a girl's drowned face, first looking up at him through clear water, then at a level with his own face, suspended in darker liquid, less distinct and smaller. He had had the impression of a necklace or band of some kind round the throat.

"It seemed to be in some kind of container," he said. "The second one, I mean. Like a jar or a small tank. But I know it was the same face." He looked at Vittorini with embarrassment. This was the experience that had brought him here, led him to endure what he was enduring under the doctor's attentive regard.

When he had finished there was silence for some moments while Vittorini wrote. If he had noticed Raikes's trouble, he gave no sign of it. "These things do not happen at any special time of day?" he asked, without looking up.

"No."

"But always so far in the vicinity of the statue, the immediate vicinity?"

Raikes hesitated for a moment or two. Then he said, "Yes, always."

Vittorini regarded him a moment. "Do you yourself know of any factor that would precipitate these attacks?" he asked.

"None at all."

"And the only warning is the threat to balance and the sense of enveloping hush you speak of?"

"Yes," Raikes said, "and that is quite brief, or at least it seems so."

"The attacks, are they followed by headaches or drowsiness or anything of that kind? No? Mr. Raikes, is there anything you can think of in your family history that might help to account for them?" Vittorini laid the pencil delicately on top of the pad. "Not to put too fine a point on it," he said, "is there any family history of fainting fits or mental disorders?"

"Not that I know of," Raikes said. He felt affronted, absurdly enough, though whether at the imputation of fainting or madness he could not have said. Below this there was an obscure but definite alarm. "No, certainly not," he said after a moment.

Vittorini was silent for a short while. Then he said, "It is interesting, it is unusual, this highly formed nature of the hallucinations, and the variety, as also that they occur always in the same place. Are you aware of any twitching of the limbs at the time?"

"No."

"Urinary incontinence?"

"Good Lord, no."

"Is there a feeling of familiarity, as if you were reliving past experience?"

"Not exactly," Raikes said. "The impressions are very vivid, but I don't feel as if I have been involved personally. It's not familiarity so much as a kind of certainty. Not complete, of course, but for example I know there is an object that is casting those straight shadow lines, even though I haven't seen it; I know those two faces are the same face, even though one of them is indistinct. That's not quite the same as familiarity, is it?"

"Perhaps not," Vittorini said. "Well, Mr. Raikes, it will be necessary to carry out some tests."

"Tests?" He was taken by surprise. What had he been expecting? Pulse, blood pressure, some words of reassurance, awkward talk about the fee.

"Nothing to worry about. Just a checkup, really. An hour or so of your time will be enough. It would be necessary to come to my clinic."

"Very well," Raikes said, concealing a certain dismay.

Vittorini stood up and extended his hand with a sudden and very charming smile. "You will make an appointment, please, with the girl in the outer office. Do not worry meanwhile. Try not to remain standing in the same position for long periods, and avoid sudden changes of posture."

Advice difficult to follow, Raikes thought to himself, emerging onto the street, peculiarly so, for a man engaged in restoring a life-size stone Madonna. Was it simply this then, a faintness caused by awkward position or sudden movement? But how could that account for the sensory disturbances? He had not been fully frank with the doctor, and this bothered him now, like some sin of omission.

Vittorini's office was in Calle Mazzini, not very far from where he lived, less than a mile in fact, as the crow flies, but a good half hour's walk in the labyrinth of Venetian streets. Still, there was no hurry. He had finished his work for the day. He was due at Lattimer's house for a drink that evening, but not until later on, after dinner.

His route brought him close to San Giovanni Crisostomo, but he resisted the temptation to visit once again the tenement behind it, the green murk of the side canal, the hemmed-in, abandoned church. He had been back twice since that exciting moment in the silence of his room when he had first realized the connection between the church and the house. There was no more for the moment to be found there.

It was late afternoon but the sun was hot still. Raikes took off his jacket as he walked. The streets between the Rialto and the Church of the Apostoli were crowded, making it impossible to go at any pace other than the prevailing saunter. Many of these people were obviously tourists, slung with cameras, dressed in light-colored holiday clothes — vanguard of the summer invasion. Stalls along the way were festooned with tokens of welcome — postcards, guidebooks, souvenirs.

Raikes was glad to move into the comparative peace of the Santa Fosca district. Venice has her lines of demarcation, like all cities, and the San Felice Canal is one of these; north of this there is what seems a resumption of quieter, more traditional life, hardly touched by tourist traffic. Gradually Raikes fell into that rhythm which is the great charm of walking in Venice, an alternation of enclosure and liberation constantly repeated, as one emerges from narrow streets into the sudden space of the *campo* or the levels of *fondamenta* and canal.

Back at his apartment, he at once got out his diary. The daily stint of words had become a necessity to him, though he had departed considerably from the strict account at first envisaged. The diary now included speculations concerning Lattimer and the Litsovs, about whom — and especially about Chiara — he had thought frequently since his visit; and he had also taken to recording his "visions" in as much detail as he could remember.

He dated the entry as usual in the top right-hand corner: *April 15*. Then at once, as though the incontrovertible fact of the date had released him, he began to write eagerly.

Went to see Dr. Vittorini this afternoon. Wiseman was quite right — his English is impeccable. It was a relief to be able to speak easily and naturally. All the same I'm not sure if I managed to convey the extraordinary sense of certainty, not déjà vu *at all, but a sense of conviction without deductive process, or only the very crudest. Anyway, the good doctor did not seem unduly surprised by anything I said. Professional manner, I suppose. I daresay he has heard it all before. I lied to him once and I think he knew it. That was when he asked me if all my attacks, as he called them, had happened in the neighborhood of the Madonna. I said yes, but of course there was the incident at the Casa Fioret, which I have mentioned already in this diary. Next Tuesday I have to go for those famous tests he spoke about.*

There is absolutely no doubt in my own mind that the long converted yard behind the Casa Fioret, running alongside the canal, was once part of the property of the church on the other side of the alley, that the Madonna originally stood in the church cloister, and that she became incorporated in the garden when the land — and the cloister with it — passed into private hands. There is no proof, but there are now four links at least in this chain, and they strengthen one another. When coincidences multiply beyond a certain point, they become implausible; we are obliged to look for a design. There is the notebook that I found in the baptistry of the Carità, the matter of the date, the name of Fornarini, the Casa Fioret. Now this abandoned church of the Supplicanti, which, thanks to Pardi's Annals, *I have discovered was consecrated in 1432, a time almost certainly when my sculptor — whoever he was — would have been active in Venice.*

I haven't been able to get into the church, which is in any case just a shell of a building, ruined and boarded up. But I have traced the line of the cloister, and it continues dead straight on the other side of the alley, forming what is now the outer wall of the yard. That is strong evidence in itself. Then there is the other matter.

Raikes paused. This was the matter he had not told Vittorini about. Why, he did not quite know. Secrecy, the desire to preserve something, some scrap at least, from the doctor's knowledge? Perhaps he had feared Vittorini's skepticism. He himself experienced something like disbelief when he thought about it.

He had retraced the steps of his former visit more or less exactly: the street door, the damp and echoing interior courtyard, the mild snarls of the lions. Everything had been the same, even to the gossiping women and the lines of washing hanging out. He had crossed the alley, tried the narrow iron gate in the opposite wall. There was a chain with a padlock, but this lifted off — the chain simply served to prevent the gate from staying open. No more than twenty yards to the rounded wall of the apse. On either side of the doorway eroded reliefs, one of the Annunciation, one of Daniel in the Lions' Den with a Greek inscription round the frame. Windows and doors all boarded up — there was no apparent means of entry. Through gaps in the boards a sense of darkness, a smell of damp masonry and the discharge of cats.

On his return he had followed the line of the cloister. The pavement was cracked but level enough. Parts of the roofing intact still, draped with ivy. Building materials had been left under here: bricks, gravel, some sacks of cement. The line of the cloister ended abruptly at the alley wall.

This time, by the merest chance, he had elected to return via the house. Just before passing from the yard into the dimness of the entrance hall he had stopped, on some impulse, and looked behind him. He had felt the warning hush that was now growing familiar. The section of the church visible from here — the roof of the apse and the upper part of the *campanile* — formed an ensemble he recognized: it was the background to the glimmering Madonna of his vision.

Even when, that slight, swooning threat to balance over, he had continued to stand there, looking; he had remained convinced: it was the same in every detail. Someone had stood where he was standing, while the Madonna was still there, in the garden, with leaves around her and the church buildings rising behind. He was still convinced of it. And he knew now why he had said nothing about it to Vittorini: it was his only defense against the fear that had been with him from the first and that his interview with the doctor had done nothing to relieve, the fear that somewhere inside his skull, beyond his control, a terrible process of derangement was taking place. It was with a sense of keeping this fear at bay that he began writing again.

The church is, or was, named the Santissima Annunziata. It was the foundation in Venice of an order known as the Supplicanti. There is an account of these people in Pardi's Annali Ecclesiastici, *and Romanin has something to say about them in his* Storia Documenta *(volume 3). I have been able to refer to these books in the library of the British consulate.*

The ground for the site was granted by Doge Jacopo Tiepolo in 1334, but it seems that the building was not finished until 1430, with the completion of the apse and cross vault. The Supplicanti were a flagellant order founded by one Matteo da Polenta in 1296, dedicated to poverty, with a rule of extreme harshness. By the early fourteenth century there were twelve communities in Italy. It seems to have been a numerous and successful order. Pardi says that in 1341, at its first general assembly, it numbered sixteen hundred brothers, with four hundred claimants for admission. The church of the Santissima Annuziata was consecrated in 1432. In 1494, before the end of that same century, within the lifetime almost certainly of some of the novice monks, the church had been suppressed, and the Supplicanti, on the advice of the Maggior Consiglio, expelled bag and baggage from Venice by Pope Alexander VI. The grounds are not specified in either of my sources beyond the customary phrase used in both: rilassatezza di costumi, *laxness of habits. Almost certainly sexual. But what can have caused such a rapid and presumably collective deterioration?*

Raikes looked up vaguely, possessed once more by the astonishment that this discovery had produced in him when he had first come upon it in the musty little room on the first floor of the consulate. In not much more than half a century this *rilassatezza* had become serious enough for the monks to be sent packing. The affair seemed to have been kept within church jurisdiction; he could find no reference to any criminal proceedings. The hearings had been held *in camera*. Transcripts must have been made, but it had been a papal process, and the relevant papers, if they existed at all, were presumably on some obscure shelf in the Vatican archives. As inaccessible, as far as he was concerned, as if they had been on the moon. There was a chance they had been published elsewhere, of course. The trouble really was that he had neither time nor scope for the sort of research that would be necessary. However, he had written to a former colleague in Cambridge — his first museum appointment had been at the Fitzwilliam there — asking him to find out what he could through the libraries of the museum and the university about the transactions of the Supplicanti in Venice. Something might come from that . . .

With a start, Raikes realized that beyond the lamplit zone of his table, beyond the membrane of his window, darkness had descended. He glanced at his watch: it was after nine. For three hours he had been sitting here, writing and musing. Now there was no time for the shower he had intended to take, no time for more than a sandwich on his way to Lattimer's house. Fortunately this was not far away. He was annoyed with himself; such lapses were becoming common with him these days, symptoms of his preoccupation. Or obsession, he thought uneasily. Now he would arrive disheveled and in disarray before a no doubt impeccably turned-out Lattimer. He had no idea, either, why Lattimer had suddenly phoned to invite him.

2

He followed the directions that Lattimer had given him. The house was on the north side of the Canareggio Canal, in the Ghetto Vecchio — no more than ten minutes' walk. The street lamps were lit along the *fondamenta*, and light from them flexed across the surface of the water. A grain barge passed Raikes, going northward, in the direction of the Lagoon, leaving behind it a sustained aftermath of sound, gentle slaps of water against the canal walls, squeaking complaints of strained rope as the moored boats sidled in the wash.

The house was in a street at right angles to the canal, a tall, narrow, three-story building with steps to the front door and a heavy brass knocker. The door was opened by a square-jawed, thickset man in early middle age, an Italian, gravely polite. He was leading Raikes across the short hall when Lattimer himself emerged from a door beyond. "Ah, you found me then," he said, smiling his narrow smile. Once again Raikes experienced that cold and vigorous grip, once again had to exert a countervailing pressure — there was a quality of steel in Lattimer's fingers. He was casually dressed, in cardigan and slacks, but there was about him none of the carelessness — either of the elegant variety or the merely sloppy — that the Englishman normally displays in such garb: the cardigan was close-fitting, the slacks sharply creased, the shades of blue carefully matched. Even in a society where nothing but the loincloth was *de rigueur,* Raikes thought, Lattimer's would have been conspicuous for the symmetry of its folds.

"Come in here," he said, moving to open a door. "Luigi will get us a drink. What will you have? I've got just about everything, I think, except hemlock; we've run out of that." He laughed in the barking fashion that Raikes now suddenly remembered.

"Whiskey, please," he said.

"What a good idea." Lattimer looked at Luigi. "Just bring a bottle of Scotch, will you?" he said. *"E soda e ghiaccio. Basta che li porti,* we'll help ourselves."

Luigi withdrew, with a barely audible *va bene.* He had a formidable breadth of shoulder, Raikes noticed.

The room into which Lattimer now led the way was long and high-ceilinged, with an arched alcove at the far end, and it immediately struck Raikes as beautiful. This was as much a sense of careful spacing and dimension as of the objects themselves, which were not very numerous in any case: Afghan carpet, all brown and gold and dull pink; Gothic Madonna in wood, with traces of gilt and red still on her, standing in a corner; a low table inlaid with blue tiles; a cabinet full of glass objects. His glance stayed on a gleaming skeletal bird in the alcove.

"That's an uncommonly accurate bit of work," he said. "It's a heron, isn't it?"

"Odd if it weren't accurate," Lattimer said, in the sardonic, point-scoring tone customary with him. "It is the very bird itself."

"How do you mean?"

"There is a man in France who does them. I ran a show for him last summer. It was a sellout. He gets the carcass, big dramatic birds are best, eagles, cranes, that sort of thing. Then he has a way of stripping them, some sort of acid bath, but he doesn't give the formula away, of course."

Luigi came in with the drinks tray, put it down on the tiled table, looked briefly at Lattimer, then silently withdrew. The tiles were matched in color but there was no overall design, Raikes noticed, each tile being decorated with its own pattern of leaves and flowers. They had obviously been collected separately.

"Iznik tiles," Lattimer said. Even engaged in pouring out the drinks, he had been taking note of where Raikes was looking. There was something curiously eager in this attention to a visitor's reaction. It was at odds with the manner, assured to the point of arrogance, and with the composure of the face.

"Fine work," Raikes said, with a sense of fulfilling expectations.

"I should think so." Lattimer passed Raikes his whiskey. "They have lost the secret of that blue," he said. "Tiles like that haven't been produced in Turkey since the seventeenth century. They were mosque tiles originally, I suppose you know."

Raikes nodded, swallowing some of his drink. He did not much like Lattimer, he decided. The fellow was overbearing even when he was merely offering information. He wondered once again why he had been asked. He had wanted to come, of course, mainly in the hope of learning more about Chiara Litsov. "You didn't finish telling me about the bird," he said.

"Well, he assembles the skeleton again and fixes it together, don't ask me how, fabricates various bits and pieces, seals the whole thing, gives it washes of metal solution. You end up with a chrome or steel or silver bird. Expensive, of course, for obvious reasons. They'll be copied before long, but I expect to clear up quite a bit first." Lattimer paused for a moment. He was smiling that narrow smile of his. "The glory of changeless metal," he said.

Raikes realized that this was a reference, rather a sly one, to the conversation at the Litsovs' the day he had gone there for lunch and antagonized the artist. But before he could make any rejoinder, Lattimer was asking him to pass his glass for a refill and the next moment he had begun to discuss the wooden Madonna in the corner.

"My pride and joy," he said, pouring out for both of them generous measures of Scotch. "I wouldn't part with her for any consideration."

Raikes looked across at the hieratic hands, the serene, slightly simpering face. "Well," he said, "it's a valuable piece."

"Yes, but it's not so much that, it's the way I got her. She was in a private collection in Rome. The family had always thought her an eighteenth-century fake — there were a lot of French fakes of Gothic wooden sculptures about, still are as a matter of fact, especially the Chartres style. But I knew as soon as I saw her that she was genuine. I knew who she was and where she had come from. I didn't say anything, of course."

Lattimer poured himself more whiskey. He had downed the last glass very quickly indeed; Raikes had barely touched his. "No, I'm not a fool," he went on. "They were selling up, you know. The beauty of it was that I knew everything about her. I knew she had been at one time on the north transept of the Abbey of St. Germain des Prés, together with various other pieces, most of which have never been recovered. It is supposed that they were moved to protect them from the excesses of the Revolution. I knew she had been in Lenoir's museum until the 1840's. Then she disappeared. And here, after a hundred years, she was. And they thought she was a fake. There was a kind of beauty in the situation. I got her for a hundred pounds."

Lattimer's face was quite composed still, but his eyes were shining at this triumphant deception. It was the first time Raikes had seen him look anything like moved or excited. "That's why I keep her," he said. "Not because she's worth a lot."

He was silent for some moments. Then, with a marked change of tone, he said, "Let me tell you this, Raikes. I respect the work you do; I regard it as highly important work. Invaluable."

Despite himself, Raikes felt a glow at this. He knew that the man before him, however exquisite his taste, was a bully. He had seen the way he had treated Wiseman, merely over a difference of opinion, and he could sense the same kind of almost brutal assertiveness in everything Lattimer said. Yet the praise pleased him, in the potent, corruptive way the praise of bullies pleases.

"That is not what Mrs. Litsov seemed to think," he said.

Disappointingly, Lattimer did not take this up. "More important than what a surgeon does, for example," he said.

"Oh, come now," Raikes said. "A surgeon preserves life."

"Life would still go on if there were no surgeons. There would be more suffering, of course, but life would not be threatened with extinction. Life can spawn more life. You can't spawn Gothic Madonnas. They talk about the uniqueness of the human individual. I daresay it's true. But why should it be interesting? What value has uniqueness got when you're talking about millions? I suppose the individual dandelion is unique too. I've always found the whole notion intensely boring. For a true concept of uniqueness you have to go to the artifacts of the past, to your Madonna, for example. Human lives are expendable, Simon. Works of art are not."

Raikes was not sure for a moment or two whether this was meant seriously. He was distracted, too, by the use of his first name. But Lattimer's eyes were on him, pale, staring intently. "I'm afraid I can't agree," he said.

"It's the truth of the matter, whether you agree or not. And people have always known it, whatever the pious platitudes. What do you think you are all doing in Venice? Do you really think all this money would be spent and all this concerted effort made if it were just a question of saving lives? Of course not. It is objects that we really care about. The floods of 1966, which were what really started all these international restoration projects and all these millions of dollars flowing in from abroad, they weren't such terribly serious floods as these things go. I mean, in the scale of cataclysms they would rank near the bottom. If it hadn't been Venice, if there had only been people to worry about, what would anyone have done? If it had been ten times as bad, and somewhere else, what would anyone have done? I'll tell you. They would have sent a few food parcels and forgotten all about it."

Lattimer paused to drain his glass. "I took that message in with my mother's milk," he said. "That's why I'm in this business. You can't go wrong. That's why I love Venice so much. That's why I keep a house here. Venice is the greatest storehouse of artifacts in the world. It is an artifact itself, more than any other city. Brick and stone, built on water. Here, let me give you some more whiskey."

He refilled his own glass. Raikes wondered if he usually drank so much, decided probably not. There was some sense of strain or tension in him, as apparent in the unbridled speech as in the drinking. Perhaps something had happened to bother Lattimer, make him want to let off steam. Perhaps, Raikes thought, I have been invited simply as someone insignificant, someone to talk to. He felt oppressed. There was something distinctly disconcerting, even alarming, about Lattimer, the fine-drawn immobility of his face, the pale eyes that stared so intently, the neatness of his person, the beauty of his house, the unrelenting dogmatism with which he expressed himself. Underlying all this, Raikes sensed an intention of friendliness, even perhaps some quality of appeal — though whether for sympathy or merely admiration, he could not tell.

"Well," he said, "it was a man who made my Madonna after all, and for me that is the most truly remarkable thing about her."

Lattimer remained silent for some moments, looking down into his glass. Then he said, "You work for a museum, don't you, one of the London ones?"

"The Victoria and Albert, yes. The conservation department."

"What do you call yourself? What's the job description?"

"I'm called a conservation officer."

"I don't suppose they pay you much of a salary, do they?"

"They pay me enough," Raikes said, rather stiffly.

"Far below your deserts, I'm sure. You know, Simon, I took to you the moment I saw you. The fellow you came with, what's his name, Wiseman, he's a lightweight character, but I saw something in you from the first. This man is *serious*, I said to myself. I like that. More whiskey? You're not drinking much."

"Wiseman is one of the kindest men I know," Raikes said.

"That may be." Lattimer's tone was contemptuous. He paused a moment, as if to allow ripples to die away. Then he said, "As you know, I deal in sculpture. Sometimes there are questions of authentication. It would be very helpful for me if I could have the backing of a great institution like the Victoria and Albert — I mean in the person of one of its conservation officers. In the person of Simon Raikes. It would help to convince the client, you understand. Of course I could not ask you to do that without a very substantial fee."

Raikes felt his face go hot. He had never been offered a bribe before. So this was why Lattimer had asked him. "I really don't think — " he began.

"No need to make up your mind now. Think it over. I said a *substantial* fee, remember."

Raikes was silent. He did not really know how he should react. His main feeling was one of embarrassment. He was casting about for some way of changing the subject when Lattimer did it for him. "What do you think of my house?" he asked suddenly.

"It's very nice."

"The reason I live in Canareggio," Lattimer said, "is that it's off the beaten track. Not so many unique human beings in the form of tourists penetrate here."

"Quite a lot of people about at present," Raikes said.

Lattimer nodded. "They're like flies," he said. "The temperature goes up a bit and they start to swarm."

"Some of those same flies might visit your gallery and settle on a Litsov bronze. Presumably you wouldn't object to that?"

"They would be clients," Lattimer said. "People with taste. Quite different. They'd better hurry up, though."

"How do you mean?"

"Litsov bronzes are a hot property."

"Has he always used her as his model?" Raikes was aware that this was rather a shift, but he was afraid the conversation would veer away again. Lattimer was looking at him steadily, with an expression that seemed in some way ironical.

"Always? They've only been married for about three years."

"Really?"

"I've been handling Litsov's work for six years now. Litsov is my creation. I have taken this talent of his, not so very considerable, and I have built it up. From nothing."

"You said he was a genius."

"I said he *had* genius. He has something that makes him different. That is quite a rare thing. I have built on that." Lattimer poured more whiskey for himself and topped up Raikes's glass. The bottle was more than half empty now. "Litsov is my creation," he said again. "For years I made nothing from him. For three years I even paid him a salary. Then last year I set them up here, in Venice. He isn't really interested in money."

"But he must owe a great deal to her, to his wife," Raikes said, still valiantly persisting. He was determined to speak of her. "He obviously owes a lot to her," he said. "Somehow I thought they had been married longer."

"She gives that impression perhaps." Lattimer was smiling that narrow smile of his. "I have known Chiara quite a long time too," he said.

Raikes found himself disliking this smile. So Litsov had been a rising star when she had married him. *The winters are difficult.* Had she said that? Something of the sort — something to suggest more than one. There had been a certain kind of knowledge implied in Lattimer's words that he did not want to analyze. He was suddenly unwilling to discuss Chiara Litsov with the man before him one single syllable further. In haste to get away from the subject, which he had been so eager to reach, he said, "Anyway, I hope his work is not still piling up on the mainland."

"His work?" Lattimer said sharply. "What are you talking about?"

The remark seemed to have taken him completely by surprise. The smile had gone from his face, leaving a drawn blankness of expression.

"I thought there was some trouble with the man who does the casting. Litsov was speaking of it that day at lunch."

"Oh, that," Lattimer said after a moment. "Yes, everything is back to normal now."

Raikes had a sense that these words were improvised somehow, as if Lattimer had temporarily forgotten his lines. The whiskey he had drunk was beginning to make him feel sleepy. It would be time to leave soon. "You know," he said, "speaking of surgeons, sometimes our work does resemble theirs, in a way."

He began to tell Lattimer about experiments he had been involved in some years earlier to consolidate very friable Carrara marble by forming new calcium carbonate in the pores. This was an attempt to reproduce the natural process, observable at San Filippo in Emilia, where the spring water, emerging saturated with calcium bicarbonate and carbon dioxide, deposits calcium carbonate — stone, in other words — on contact with the air. They had drilled holes in the marble, inserted glass tubes, fed in a solution of calcium hydroxide.

"We were injecting the marble with a sort of plasma," Raikes said, "designed to harden in the veins and reinforce the substance. It didn't work too well, I remember — too many unknown factors. The mechanism by which calcium carbonate is dissolved under some conditions and precipitated under others is not yet fully understood."

"I've been to San Filippo," Lattimer said. "Fascinating place. The spray seems to turn to stone as it comes out. You leave something in the water for a while and it gets a crust of stone on it. As a matter of fact, I brought back a souvenir from there."

He hesitated. An extraordinary smile came to his face, shy, secretive, painful-looking. He said, "Would you like to see it?"

"Oh, yes," Raikes said, surprised. "Very much." He had not somehow associated Lattimer with souvenirs.

"We'll just replenish our glasses." Lattimer was still smiling. "Come on," he said. "I'll show you."

Glass in hand, Raikes followed his host into the recessed part of the room. There was a door leading into a passage, a flight of stairs, another door. They emerged into the night. A lamp above the door behind them cast a misty swath over low bushes, the pale flowers of a wistaria, a gravel path, glinting faintly with mica. They were in what seemed a fairly sizable garden — sizable enough for Raikes, in this darkness, not to be aware of limiting walls. "You're lucky to have this," he said. The fragrance of the wistaria came to him mingled with some muskier scent, which he thought might be acacia flowers. What are we doing here? he wondered.

"Another advantage of living in an unfashionable district," Lattimer said. "Luigi looks after all this. Hang on a minute." His voice held a quality of eagerness or anticipation.

He disappeared along the path, leaving Raikes standing there at the dim verge of the lamplight, clutching his glass, aware of the silence of the house behind him, the darkness into which Lattimer had vanished, the enclosing strangeness of the garden. He made out, in the direction Lattimer had taken, the long low shape of a building, a shed of some kind. Light from this suddenly spilled out, and he saw Lattimer again, standing in the light at the open door.

"Over here," Lattimer said.

Raikes advanced, paused at the door, looked inside. There were no windows in the place. A long strip overhead gave brilliant light. He stood blinking in the doorway, confused by the light and by the extraordinary clutter of objects here, displayed on stands, on the walls, in cases along the sides.

"Come in," Lattimer said. "This is my museum."

Raikes stepped inside, speechless still, not with surprise really, but a kind of wonder. His first hasty glance revealed a polished human skull on a stand, a large and beautiful piece of stone, veined with green, lying on a table near the door, a framed bank note on the wall. He could see no order or principle among these things.

Lattimer went some way into the room, picked something up from a table, returned. "This is what I brought back from San Filippo," he said.

It looked at first merely like an irregular lump of pinkish-gray granite, about the size of a hen's egg. But a human likeness could be discerned in it; there was a face beneath, with features half obliterated by the growth of stone.

"That's a terra cotta head underneath," Lattimer said. "Head of a woman. I left it in the water for an hour while I had a drink, and that's how it came out. I have not shown this place to anyone else, you know."

This was obviously an attempt at a compliment. Lattimer's mouth stretched in the same painful smile. "Everywhere I've been," he said, "I bring something back. These are only the Italian things."

Raikes had an impression of long secrecy suddenly broken. Again he wondered if something had happened to disturb Lattimer. The man seemed drunk now: his eyes showed nothing, but his speech had thickened. He had started moving about among his possessions, the light shining on the smooth hair, the handsome, taut-skinned face, as he held up now one object, now another, for Raikes's inspection. He explained everything. There was the viper he had killed in the foothills of the Alps, near Torre Pellice; there were framed photographs of himself in various guises; there was a fencing sword with which he had won some tournament — it suddenly seemed appropriate to Raikes that fencing should be Lattimer's sport. On a table at the far end was a litter of military items: a forage cap, webbing gaiters, a pistol in a holster, a bayonet.

"Come and look at these," Lattimer said. "I was in the army here, you know. Sicily, Monte Cassino, Rome. Right through it. This is getting on for thirty years ago now. Monte Cassino, there's a perfect example of what I was saying before. A mutual massacre going on, and they spent weeks agonizing over whether to bomb an empty monastery."

There was a gold wedding ring among the litter. "That belonged to a German once," Lattimer said. He held up the bayonet. "This could tell a tale," he said, "but I mustn't boast."

The attempt at modesty — in the midst of these evidences of vanity and self-obsession — was crass enough to be ludicrous, but Raikes felt no inclination to smile. "I must be going, I'm afraid," he said. Turning toward the door, he caught sight of a shallow tray with a glass lid, containing tufts of fibrous-looking hair tied up with ribbon. He peered at these and Lattimer, seeing this, raised the lid.

"Trophies of war, old boy," he said. "A different kind."

Raikes looked down at the little bundles. He counted nine of them. There was not much range of color — from black to dark brown, with one lighter colored, reddish. The hair was very coarse, wiry-looking. It curled in all directions, not lying straight as a tress would have done. "It's human hair, isn't it?" he said, doubtfully.

Lattimer chuckled. "Human it certainly is," he said. "That is pubic hair, my boy. Every time I win through, I ask the lady for a token. All these are Italian specimens. The names are on the ribbons, but I know them without that. I could tell you the exact place and circumstances for every one of them. This one was in Rome." He held up the little fibrous bundle with its faded red ribbon. "She was hot stuff," he said.

"So that's what is meant by tuft-hunter," Raikes said. "I've always wondered." He felt slightly sick. "Good Lord," he said, glancing at his watch, "it's twenty past one, and I have a day's work to do tomorrow." Without waiting for Lattimer's response, he moved out into the garden and along the path toward the door.

Inside, he refused offers of more whiskey. Soon he was walking back through the deserted streets. The feeling of nausea lessened as he walked, but the cause remained, the thought that had pounced too swiftly to be anticipated or suppressed, the hideous possibility that one of those little bundles might be a sample taken from Chiara Litsov.

3

He worked at the statue in the failing light, straining to make sure that no square millimeter of her person was missed. He was kneeling before her on his little mat, involved in the intricate folds of her robe, as these clung to or fell away from her thighs. In fact he was working between her thighs now, in the region of mythic speculation. Here at this point, beneath the draperies, lay the gateway to the miraculous. The Logos entered here, he thought, wielding the quartz cutter with unremitting care and skill. As the brilliance of the sun fills and penetrates a glass window, in St. Bernard's simile. No damage to the membrane either on entrance or exit. It was a good image, apt both for conception and birth. Deriving of course from the beauty of medieval stained glass windows. Thus art replaces nature, he thought; the earlier symbols had been of rain or dew, penetrating and vivifying the earth. Before leaving England he had read everything he could find about the Annunciation.

He knelt back, switching off the instrument and removing his mask. The light was not good enough now. For reasons he could not fathom, his request for an electric cable to be laid up here had not so far been attended to. Biagi had been politely vague on the matter. The architect in charge of work on the church floor said he thought it was a matter for the Soprintendenza ai Monumenti. They had referred him to the Soprintendenza alle Gallerie, who said they would take the matter in hand. So far, however, nothing had happened. It seemed a simple enough thing, a good light to work by.

This particular evening it didn't matter; he would have had to stop soon in any case; it was the evening of the conference, when they were all due to congregate and report on progress under the auspices of Sir Hugo Templar. He would have to get back, change, collect his notes — he had agreed to say something about his work on the Madonna.

He knelt there for a while longer, looking at her. All was pure and splendid now from midthigh downward, her restored parts beginning to take on a faint, glimmering incandescence in this failing light. Above this was the coarse mottling of her corrosion, the blackened concave parts merging already with the slowly darkening air. He glanced up at the averted face, the badger stripe of bleach that ran from forehead to nose. He had a sense, not for the first time, that she was about to break into some movement or gesture. This hour of the changing light was the time the angel came to her, or so it was generally believed — no doubt why the church had enjoined the faithful to say an Ave Maria at the time of the eventide Angelus bells. By a coincidence in itself miraculous she had been reading Isaiah, chapter seven, verse fourteen, at the time: *Therefore the Lord himself shall give you a sign; Behold, a virgin shall conceive, and bear a son . . .*

Remembering Vittorini's advice, Raikes got to his feet slowly and carefully.

He had allowed himself an hour to wash, change, have some dinner. But when he returned to his apartment, the reply from Cambridge was waiting there and he could not resist taking the time to read it. His friend had been busy on his behalf. He had drawn a blank at the Fitzwilliam Library, and at first at the university library too — mainly because of the difficulty of categorizing the material. But then he had consulted an acquaintance at Pembroke who taught Italian history.

"You are lucky, really," he wrote. "Because the Supplicanti were in Venice for only something like seventy years, the episode has been a sort of focus of research. It's not often, apparently, that you get such a tidy period, cut off at both ends. It was a chance for some academic sleuthing. Not much seems to have come of it. All the extant records of their dealings in Venice have been collated several times, most recently in 1949 by a man called Masters. It's a perfectly ordinary record of day-to-day transactions such as were going on in religious foundations all over Italy at the time. There is nothing in them to show what went wrong. No one has ever been able to discover why the Supplicanti came to grief in Venice. The documents have never been traced and are now presumed lost. One thing, though, I think will interest you. There is a record of the commissioning of a Madonna in 1432 — which lies in the period you asked about. I am enclosing a photostat copy of the English translation."

The rest of the letter, the friendly sentiments, the professions of readiness to be of further help, Raikes barely glanced at. He immediately began reading the document that had accompanied it, a single sheet, cast in the conventional form of a contract.

> In the name of God, 16 March, 1432,
> Be it known to all who shall examine the present official instruments that the Prior and friars of the church and foundation of the Supplicanti in Venice were called together and assembled in chapter in the sacristy by order of the Prior and at the sound of the bell struck three times, according to custom. There were present the pious Friar Francesco di Niccolò of Rimini (Prior), Friar Giuliano of Foligno (reader and preacher), Friar Pietro Giovanni, and Friar Giovanni di Alemania, constituting the chapter. Also present were the worthy Nunno Cischi and Ser Uguccio Toschi, *operarii* of the church. These on their own behalf and on behalf of their successors in the said church give to the stone cutter known as Girolamo Piemontese, stipulating and receiving on his own behalf, and of his heirs, *et cetera,* the making of an image of the Holy Virgin Annunciate in white stone of Istria, to be done by his own hand and no one else. He is held to the same and to work at and perfect the image with his own hands and with the utmost diligence, vigilance, and perfection. And this is to be for the price of sixty gold ducats, in part payment of which the said master Girolamo, stone cutter, acknowledges receipt of the said witnesses, and me, the below-named notary. And he promises to do the work and finish it within the next six months, beginning today. And the said chapter promise to give the said master Girolamo bread, wine, oil, and wood for his maintenance, and he on the one hand and they on the other promise to observe all these conditions.

The meeting had already started when he entered. It was being held in a building near the Accademia Bridge, not far from the offices of the Ministeria delle Acque, an ancient place, once the guildhall of the Venetian mask makers.

He was surprised, on entering, to find a diminutive Japanese occupying the platform, speaking fairly fluent but oddly accented English. "Due to humidity, hah, yes," Raikes heard him say. He saw Steadman sitting near the back and made his way toward him. Steadman looked up as he approached and grimaced in friendly fashion.

"Hah, yes," the Japanese said. He had paused on Raikes's entrance. In the curiously opaque light of this cavernous room he appeared due to humidity himself, with his gleaming spectacles, the unnatural shine of his pale, lightweight suit. The lamps were high up in the ceiling, milky globes whose light seemed to lose all force in the spaces of air below; and Raikes had the impression that there was a further attenuation of this already exhausted light by some mist or vapor in the room, some impalpable thickening of the atmosphere, as if the whole place, though warm enough, was not properly sealed off from the moist breath of the night outside.

The eyeglasses of the Japanese shone steadily through this, and the high-pitched, crowing vowel sounds continued. He was reading from a script but interjecting his own remarks from time to time. He must have been asked to speak as a sort of courtesy, Raikes thought — the Japanese were not engaged in any collective effort of restoration in Venice, as far as he knew. Of course, Sir Hugo was a great believer in internationalism. There he was now, high-domed, nonchalant in black corduroy, seated to the right of the speaker. Perhaps he had simply lassoed the Japanese from a doorway? But no, listening further, Raikes understood that the man was an official of the Tokyo Museum of Fine Arts, where they had recently been dismayed by the deterioration of certain medieval saddlecloths in transit between Tokyo and Los Angeles. Discoloration had occurred round some of the stitch holes, and a loosening of the weave itself, especially at the edges. A serious matter.

"All you know the effect of humidity," the Japanese said, looking up briefly from his notes and making a small bow in deference to this knowledge on the part of his audience. "To stabilize atmosphere conditions in the galleries and museums, that is standard practice. But in world of today we must also consider art object in transit. There are two expressions for humidity, there is absolute humidity expressed by water vapor contained in given quantity of air, and relative humidity expressed as percentage rates of weight of water vapor in air to weight in same volume saturated air at same temperature. The effect of humidity on art object is related to relative humidity . . ."

Raikes sat back in his chair. This was really rather boring stuff and barely intelligible in any case, though he could appreciate the displeasure of the museum. A fourteenth-century decorated saddlecloth was in a sense more valuable than something like a Tintoretto painting, as there might not be more than two or three in existence, whereas there was no shortage of Tintorettos . . . That was heresy, of course. All the same, he thought with gratitude of his stone lady, delicate, hieratic, Gothic mysticism still implicit in her lines, drama in the *contrapposto* but no vulgar posturing, no sprawl, no Baroque "dynamism," thank God. *Girolamo Piemontese, stone cutter.* That stillness, not inertia, the stillness of arrested motion, unmistakably the achievement of art. One saw the same quality in the work of other sculptors then or a little later, people like Donatello, Nanni di Bartolo, della Robbia, however different they were in other ways. A mistake of course to read meanings into the work of artists so remote, but difficult not to see in that emblematic stillness some sort of metamorphosis from the breathing woman to the immobility of God's lodging. Perhaps that was why stone seemed so much the medium for Madonnas. In effect the Annunciation took Mary's humanity away as we would look at it now. Here was a young Hebrew woman, working-class, probably illiterate, told abruptly that she was henceforth mere sanctified womb, that her body, her whole being, was no more than a nutrient chamber. Enough to cause that terrible stillness . . .

He glanced round. Miss Greenaway was in front of him, with Owen beside her. He made out the unmistakable back of Wiseman's head up near the front. At the end of the same row he caught sight of Lattimer's fine-drawn, regular profile, felt some surprise at this, then remembered Wiseman telling him that Lattimer had been a substantial benefactor to Rescue Venice. An appropriate way for him to spend his money. What had he said? *It is objects we really care about.* And his own pleasure at Lattimer's praise for his work. Proof of original sin. He thought again, with a sort of wondering excitement, of the document, the contract, back in his apartment . . . *to be done by his own hand and no one else.*

There were something like a hundred people present and Raikes wondered vaguely who they could all be. Some of the number was made up of representatives of other restoration enterprises in the city. He saw faces he knew from Venezia Nostra and the Comité Français. There were some people from the new German project at the Church of the Gesuati — they had begun restoring the frescoes there. He recognized the huge, bald, sad-looking Slingsby, from the American Committee to Rescue Italian Art. All coerced or cajoled here by Sir Hugo. He wondered what sort of messages they were getting through their earphones; the Japanese must be presenting some problems to the interpreters.

"It is the air," the Japanese said, suddenly and it seemed disconnectedly. He had departed from his script again. He paused and uttered that curious crowing monosyllable in the back of this throat: *Hah.* "Even in box," he said, "air attacks art object." He made the shape of a box with his hands, then gave it a rapid and extremely professional-looking karate chop. "Air demolish art object," he said, suddenly smiling. "Even when in box."

He paused for some moments to allow the drama of this to make its impact. Then he went on with his reading. "From this it can clearly be understood that air of certain absolute humidity enclosed in closed vessel varies relative humidity when vessel made to travel through regions of varying temperatures . . ."

Again Raikes's attention wandered. He felt slightly nervous at the prospect of having to speak later on, but at the same time he was rather sleepy and there was a heaviness in his limbs, not unpleasant. It was a state he had become familiar with during the past week or two after working on the Madonna, not like the weariness he had felt at first, but with something almost voluptuous in it. Perhaps because of this, perhaps because of the vaporous atmosphere, he found it difficult to keep the two figures on the platform in distinct focus, and he began to have a curious sense of synchronization between the Japanese and Sir Hugo, as if he were watching a ventriloquist's act or some ingenious piece of puppetry.

This illusion was broken by scattered clapping. The Japanese was bowing, shuffling papers, descending. Sir Hugo rose, advanced smiling to the microphone, one hand in the side pocket of his jacket, the other elegantly raised. This was his public address posture, as hieratic in its way as that of the Madonna. Sir Hugo thanked the Japanese for his contribution and said that he personally found it deeply moving to see how truly international the efforts to save Venice had become. Venice belonged to the world. He enlarged on this, appearing to forget that the Japanese had not actually referred to Venice at all, but had spoken exclusively of Japanese saddlecloths. Two men with cameras made their way up the side of the room with that half-crouching gait of photographers. From below the platform Sir Hugo was briefly peppered with flashes. Of course, Raikes thought, he would not have omitted to invite the press. The presence of these cameras immediately began to change his ideas about the kind to talk he was going to give.

"We are grateful," Sir Hugo said, with his well-bred modulations, "that he should have come along and added his expertise to our think tank."

"Good God!" Steadman mutterd uncontrollably. His legs, in their gray flannels, writhed. "Have you ever heard such crap?" he whispered in Raikes's ear.

Raikes wrinkled his nose in sympathetic distaste. Still, he thought, it was people like Sir Hugo who got things moving. Below the modish phrases and the nonchalance lay a formidable tenacity of purpose and a very definite idealism. His sense of occasion was unerring; it would not be ill-lit halls and irrelevant saddlecloths that featured in the reports going back home, but international cooperation, progress, a case for more funds. All the same, *think tank* . . .

"And now," Sir Hugo said, "without more ado, I am handing over the stage to the distinguished team from Birmingham, who are making what promises to be an important breakthrough on the —"

It was Raikes's impression that the Tintoretto people — or one half of the squad at least, Owen and Miss Greenaway — were in motion before Sir Hugo had actually finished, that the platform was cleared and these two in position at the light switches while the ghastly close of that sentence — it could only be "Tintoretto front" — still hung unuttered in the air.

There was a slight pause. Then Raikes heard curious shuffling sounds behind him. In common with other members of the audience, he turned his head to look. It was Barfield, coming up the center aisle toward the stage. His right leg was encased in plaster and he was leaning heavily on a stick. In spite of this, he was making fairly brisk progress, perhaps eager not to lose the momentum set up by his assistants. He was carrying a rolled-up screen under his arm. He had trouble getting up onto the platform and attaching the screen to the wall, but this merely added to the impressiveness of that gallantly limping approach. Leaning on his stick, he began speaking at once, in his flat, didactic tones. He had no notes.

"The main problem in these early stages," he said, "apart from the enormous size of the paintings, which has made handling them very difficult, is the fact that Tintoretto, to get the dimensions he wanted, used a large number of canvases stitched together. We have found it a very tricky operation to remove this stitching. Very tricky indeed."

Perhaps forgetting his disability for the moment, Barfield took a step and stumbled a little. "It requires a light touch," he said, recovering. "It isn't only the stitching, of course. The old lining and the layers of decomposed glue have to be removed before we can reline the paintings. I can now report that this has been successfully accomplished with the first of the paintings, *The Woman Taken in Adultery,* by first applying a fine gauze along the seams as a reinforcement. Once we can consolidate the surface with a new lining, the actual cleaning process can get under way. This promises to be a very tricky operation. Very tricky indeed. To give you an idea of the complexities involved, I'd like to show you the photomicrograph of a cross-section through the paint surface of the woman's dress."

Barfield looked sharply to his left, then to his right. At once nearly all the lights in the room went out, the whirring of a projector made itself heard. "When you're ready Muriel," came Barfield's voice in the dimness.

But the beam of light, when it came, did not hit the screen. It fell above and to the right, lighting up a square of blank wall. Edged purplish by this light, still leaning on his stick, Barfield gave directions. As if in an uneasy dream, Raikes listened to this slightly peevish, reasonable voice.

"You need to change the angle, Muriel," Barfield said. "Up a bit and about three inches over to the left; no, *your* left, Muriel . . . That's better."

An abstract image of extraordinary beauty now appeared on the screen, bands of dilated blue and glowing orange, burning off at the edges to diffusions of crimson and ocher, with complex and exquisite interactions between the spreading color and the containing bands.

"There are seven layers of paint through this surface," Barfield said. "We are looking at them horizontally, highly magnified, of course — the actual paint thickness is point twenty-four millimeters in this section. No, wait a minute, I tell a lie, there are *eight* layers, if you count the nineteenth-century repainting here." The walking stick entered the zone of light, pointed briefly at dark lilac mist along the edge of the uppermost band.

Of course, Raikes thought, he might have received his injury by some other means, crushed under the weight of a Tintoretto, for example. That would have been in keeping with the hectic and heroic note he had sounded — in fact, all the Tintoretto people had sounded it — in the café that morning when Miss Greenaway had slipped memorably out of her boiler suit top, and revealed, along with the beauty of her breasts, the existence of documents in the sacristy. Or he might simply have fallen downstairs . . .

"We can't decide whether to clean off this repainted area," Barfield said, "until we are sure about the nature and quality of the original. This is a tricky business. Tintoretto used an extraordinarily wide range of pigment. Microscopical and chemical analyses of paint samples from this one painting have revealed just about all the pigments available at the time. In addition to lead white, carbon blacks, red, yellow and brown ochers, we have identified natural ultramarine or lapis lazuli, azurite, smalt, indigo, malachite, verdigris, copper resinate glazes, orpiment, realgar . . ."

The hypnotic effect of this litany of colors, delivered in Barfield's flat voice, combined with the glowing composition on the screen, lulled Raikes into a state of slightly somnolent reverie. He felt immune for the moment: while voice and picture continued, no calls could be made on him. He found himself wondering again why Lattimer should have chosen to show up here. So that his presence should be noted? So that Rescue Venice should be reminded of his previous generosity? He did nothing without a purpose, as Wiseman had implied, and as Raikes had discovered for himself; but the urges of the man's egotism seemed at least as strong as conscious purpose. It was impossible, for example, to know whether Lattimer had wanted mainly to offer him dubious employment, that evening of his visit, or to be admired and envied in the midst of his possessions, the souvenirs of war and business, the grisly trophies of his sexual exploits.

This brought him, by a process he did not pause to examine, to thoughts of Chiara Litsov, a resurgence of that slightly painful sense of her existence which had occupied some part of his mind ever since his meeting her, a feeling half curious, half sorrowful. He was not conscious of any desire in this. In fact the heat that had plagued him earlier in his stay, when Venice had tormented him with its endless suggestions of sexual possibility, when he had gone around in a more or less permanent state of tumescence, all that had ended now — since meeting Mrs. Litsov, he suddenly realized — stilled as effectively as a blow might still restless limbs, to be replaced by this painful mental scrutiny, this strange speculation which had no goal of discovery because no knowledge to proceed on, but fed on itself and was its own justification. She and the Madonna had been the twin bearings of his thoughts . . .

The glowing spectrum on the screen was extinguished. The lights went on. Barfield, clearly finished, limped to the wall and took the screen down, to the accompaniment of applause. Sir Hugo was on his feet again. Raikes waited until his name was uttered, then made his way up to the platform.

He had come armed with several photographs, blown up to poster size, together with weights to make them hang properly and a suction-plug device for attaching them to the wall. The first one he showed was of the Madonna as she had been when he arrived, exhibiting her travestied form and face, the encrusted sores of her disease. This public display of her, combining with his feelings of nervousness, affected his emotions. It was only with reluctance that he had agreed to speak; basically he thought of the whole affair as a stunt of Sir Hugo's and had a certain distaste for it, while conceding it was probably necessary; but the presence of the newspaper people and the number of what seemed ordinary members of the public had made him see that this might be something of an opportunity. When he turned from the photograph to face his audience, holding his single page of notes, he felt suddenly like the Madonna's champion, speaking out on her behalf, belied and disfigured as she was. This gave from the start an accent of feeling to his voice.

"This is the lady as I first saw her," he said. "No one seeing this, I imagine, would claim that weathering improves the look of stone sculpture. She is made of Istrian stone, which is a dense limestone of very common use in Venice. She is therefore an example of what is happening to the external stonework of this beautiful city.

"Weathering of course is a very long and gradual process. It may be broadly defined as the process of adjustment of minerals and rocks from the original place of formation to their present environment on the earth's surface. The same thing applies to human beings. Adjustment to life outside the womb involves a shock to the system."

This was a prepared joke, and there was some laughter at it, or rather that collective murmur which denotes audience awareness of humorous intention. Raikes paused, noticing here and there faces he knew. A camera flashed, recording this moment of pause.

"So," he said, "there was damage done to the Madonna even before she was made. There was the shock of the quarrying. The deterioration really begins there. Afterward, over the centuries, there was a long process of recrystallization, impaired density, increased solution rate. Helped, of course, by the carbon dioxide always present in the atmosphere. But it wasn't this that caused the appalling disfigurements you see in the photograph. She is suffering from a specifically twentieth-century disease.

"Many of you will be familiar with the process. Sulphur dioxide is given off when fossil fuels are burned. The chimneys of Mestre and Marghera have been pumping SO_2 into the atmosphere for a long time now. And Venice is a humid place, notoriously so. In winter, cold and humid; in summer, hot and humid. So we have a perfect formula for disaster. The SO_2 combines with the moisture always present in the atmosphere to produce sulphuric acid. This acts on all exposed stone surfaces to form calcium sulphate, which spreads over the stone like a tumor, rotting it to gypsum. Those are the encrustations you can see. Underneath them the decay is still going on."

Raikes replaced the photograph with one of a highly magnified stone sample and explained the process of the electron-microscopic examination done by sectioning. He pointed out the symptoms of soluble salts accumulated on the stone in the presence of water, the powdery deposits, humid stains, loss of cohesion; the deadly efflorescence — white needlelike crystals caused by dissolved salts sweated from the pores and crusting on the surface. Then he showed a picture of the Madonna as she was now, cleaned almost to the waist. He spoke about the progress of his work, the excellent results obtained with the air-abrasion instrument, his hopes for a complete restoration. At this point he paused. He had gained confidence in speaking, but now some of his tension returned. He was about to say something he knew to be not politic.

"This is just one statue," he said. "Venice is full of rotting statues. The Madonna shown here is about five and a half centuries old. If the rate of decay could be shown on a graph, there would be a very slightly rising line for the first five hundred years and an almost vertical one for the last fifty. The problem is one of time and human resources. It has taken one man rather more than one month to clean rather less than one half of one Madonna. To put the matter bluntly, Venice cannot go on relying to the extent she does at present on foreign enterprises. Unless more active steps are taken on the part of the authorities to recruit and train restorers at sufficiently attractive rates of pay, and to shoulder the financial burden of large-scale restoration projects, it will be too late. Quite soon it will be too late. The lady behind me was caught just in time. A few more years, and she would have had no fingers and no nose. A few more after that, and she would just have been a piece of limestone."

He was conscious of clapping as he took down the photograph and left the platform. When he walked back to his place he saw Muriel standing near the film projector. She had her left arm in a sling.

4

One of the people from Venezia Nostra spoke next, in Italian, about the work currently being done at the Palazzo Dolfin-Manin. In the course of his remarks he pointed out with noticeable emphasis that this was an Italian project, that all the people involved in it were Italians, that it was financed entirely by Italian funds. The same thing applied to the restoration of the Carpaccios at San Giorgio degli Schiavoni, recently completed. This too had been an all-Italian enterprise, he said.

Then Sir Hugo was to the fore again, one hand in pocket, one hand extended, making his final remarks, winding things up. There was some final clapping, and people began to leave. The room thinned out quite quickly. Raikes found himself standing with Steadman in the center. The representatives of Venezia Nostra were gathered around Sir Hugo, talking eagerly. None of them glanced in Raikes's direction. "I rather wish I hadn't made those remarks," he said. After the heightened emotion of his address, he was feeling depressed and slightly apprehensive now.

The saturnine cast of Steadman's face did not change, but his gray eyes below their dark brows looked amused. "It won't make you any friends at court," he said. "There's something about you that is distinctly self-destructive, Simon." He looked at Raikes for a moment; then quite suddenly he broke into one of his rare smiles. "Paradoxically enough, it saves you," he said.

Raikes returned the smile, rather ruefully. He was aware for the first time of genuine feelings of friendship between Steadman and himself and he was glad of it.

They were joined by Miss Greenaway, who said, "Enjoyed your talk, jolly good, made those Italians sit up." Her face shone with cheerful prejudice. She was wearing a green dress of thin woolen material, fitting closely, revealing the splendors of her breasts. They looked even more magnificent than usual. "Are we going to have a drink, Albert?" she said to Steadman. First-name terms — Steadman's gloomy persistence had paid off, it seemed. Miss Greenaway looked happy and her voice was quieter.

"Are you coming?" Steadman said. "We need a drink after listening to Sir Hugo."

Before any move could be made, the rest of the Tintoretto people came up, Barfield hobbling on his stick, Muriel with her arm held in its sling, Owen walking between them like an attendant taking two patients out for an airing.

"Accident?" Raikes said.

"One of the Tintorettos fell on them." Steadman spoke in hushed and reverential tones. .

It was obvious that Barfield did not find this at all funny. "We are soldiering on," he said. "It couldn't have happened at a worse time."

"Fall, was it?" Raikes did not know why he persisted with this questioning. Not malice, but a sort of fascinated politeness led him on.

"We were working late," Muriel said, in her usual snappish way. "Gerald got his feet caught in some rope. I don't know who left a coil of rope where anyone could get tangled up in it."

"It wasn't me, Gerald," Owen said.

"He brought me down with him," Muriel said, looking sternly at Owen.

Wiseman, in company with his fellow American, Slingsby, now approached to say appreciative things about Raikes's talk and to take his leave — he had some work on a report still to do. Slingsby stood beside him, taller by a head, nodding as if in full assent. It always surprised Raikes that these two were fellow countrymen, Wiseman being so cherubically elegant and urbane, and so gregarious that he seemed to move at more ease and with more grace and certainty in crowded places, as if he took on extra bodily accomplishment at such times; and Slingsby so huge and awkward in movement, in billowing crumpled flannel suit, with the pink countenance of a shrewd baby and vast pale hands, which he held unusually high up, at chest level, and which fluttered when he spoke in quick and surprisingly neat gestures in the air below his chin.

"I want to say how much I enjoyed your talk," he said to Raikes. "It was interesting, it was instructive."

"I don't know if you've met Steadman, have you?" Wiseman said. "This is Harold Slingsby. He is here in Venice with the American Committee to Rescue Italian Art."

"ACRIA for short," Slingsby said. *"Per acria ad astra."*

This was clearly a joke he had made before. He laughed in a whinnying, hesitant way. His small blue eyes were alarmed-looking. "Had an accident?" he said to Barfield.

"I got involved in some rope that had been left lying around," Barfield said, looking at Owen.

"We were working late on the picture surface," Muriel said. "He brought me down with him."

"I can quite categorically state," Owen said, "that I did not leave that rope there."

It was obvious from their silence that Barfield and Muriel did not believe this. There was a rather awkward pause; then Slingsby said, "Well, as I say, I enjoyed your address, Mr. Raikes. But as far as I am concerned, it was something that Japanese guy said that had my ears really flapping."

"Oh, yes?" Raikes watched Wiseman quietly and gracefully extricate himself and withdraw. "What was that?" he asked.

" 'It is the air.' Those were his words, Mr. Raikes. A short but very pregnant, extremely pregnant, sentence. It sums up the whole situation, here in Venice, in four words: 'It is the air.' " Slingsby made plucking motions with his large hands; his gestures never seemed quite consonant with what he was saying. "Not the water," he said. "Not bacteria. Not pigeon shit. *It is the air.* What is it your poet says? 'Into my heart an air that kills . . .' " He leaned forward and said quietly, "I do not like the Japanese."

Raikes was seeking for a response to this when Sir Hugo bore down on them, accompanied by a sensual-looking man of extremely small stature, virtually a dwarf, dressed in a brown velvet jacket and a pink bow tie. "Here are some of our restoration people," Sir Hugo said in his high, imperturbable voice. He looked distinguished and benevolently predatory, with his high-shouldered stance and long sweeps of hair. "This is Jonathan Beamish-Smith," he said. "Whom you will all have heard of. He is editor of *Fine Arts* and a regular contributor to reviews on the — er — London scene."

So he was hoping to get coverage in England, too, Raikes thought. Beamish-Smith had greeted the introductions with complete silence and immobility. He had heavy-lidded eyes and a moist, pouting mouth, very red, like a slightly unfurled rose. He came to the top button of Sir Hugo's waistcoat.

"He has been greatly impressed," Sir Hugo said, looking down at him benevolently, "by what I like to call this briefing session of ours."

Still Beamish-Smith said nothing. The lids were low over his eyes. Raikes, who was standing near him, caught a sweetish whiff from his person, something like incense.

"Greatly impressed," Sir Hugo said, after waiting in vain for a response from Beamish-Smith. "Have you two had an accident?" he said. "What have you been doing to your leg, Barfield?"

"It is broken," Barfield said. "No, as you were, I tell a lie, it's fractured. My colleague here, Mrs. Hagerty, has pulled something."

"Troubles never come singly," Steadman said, in a voice charged with folk wisdom.

Raikes found himself in danger of grinning at this, and he looked away in case things got worse. He met Sir Hugo's eye. "Excellent talk, excellent," Sir Hugo said. "Rather forthright."

Something in his glance and tone acted as a warning to Raikes; he knew at that moment he had blotted his copybook as far as Sir Hugo was concerned: he had exceeded his brief. A word from the president of Rescue Venice could affect his promotion prospects at the museum, perhaps seriously.

"I'm glad you liked it," he said slowly. "A drop in the ocean, really — like the work we've been able to do here. It's frustrating. I sometimes think that more publicity could get things moving. Unwelcome publicity, I mean. For example, press investigations into the way the Italian authorities are applying their funds. Of course, my position at the museum precludes that line of approach for the moment."

It was not much of a threat really; but it served at least to show that he had registered the rebuke and was not repentant. Sir Hugo nodded. "Oh, excuse me," he said, quite casually, after a moment. "There's someone over there I must catch before he goes." He made off fairly briskly in the direction of the platform.

Raikes was about to take up the question of the drink again — he felt distinctly in need of one now — when Miss Greenaway, who had been chatting in another part of the room, rejoined them, by chance taking up a position alongside the silent dwarf.

Afterward, recollecting in tranquillity, the nearest comparison Raikes could think of was with a caged bird when, touched suddenly by the sun's rays, it raises its beak and begins to chirrup and sing. As soon as the breasts of Miss Greenaway appeared before his eyes, Beamish-Smith's lids opened wide and he broke into lisping, musical speech.

"Great service to art," he said, apparently to Barfield, "restoring the Tintorettos, and I am thinking especially of his flesh tints. Tintoretto's flesh tints must be looked at in the framework of Venetian and indeed Italian painting as a whole. Correggio, for example, spiritualizes the flesh and makes it radiant, whereas Giorgione gives a happy fullness to it; he presents his ladies serenely, bathed in late afternoon light, when flesh abandons itself like a mystic savory fruit . . ."

Beamish-Smith paused and moistened his lips, still looking intently at Miss Greenaway's breasts. His eyes were like jewels. "Titian loved them with his sensual passion," he said. "He made them appear to be waiting on his own desire."

"What, the flesh tints?" Steadman simulated surprised inquiry. "I don't quite follow you there." He frowned and looked at Raikes. "Unusual notion, that," he said. "Flesh tints waiting."

This was nowhere near enough, however, to halt the editor of *Fine Arts*.

"He laid them," Beamish-Smith said, "with the help of Cupids, *et alia*, in a shady landscape or a mysterious alcove."

Slingsby had been looking round the room with vague and anxious eyes, not really listening. However, at this point, he took more interest. "Did he, now?" he said. "What, his models?"

"Glowing with animal warmth among their draperies," Beamish-Smith said.

The Tintoretto people, injured and uninjured alike, forgetting their differences, had closed ranks, united in disgust at such nauseating terminology — Miss Greenaway's mingled with self-consciousness at being under this unwavering scrutiny. "We shall have to dash off, I'm afraid," Barfield said.

"Queens in a realm of voluptuousness," Beamish-Smith said. "Sure of their offered bodies, and yet instinctively anxious, listening for the steps of some visitor, an angel, or some god perhaps." He smiled dreamily at Miss Greenaway. "Who knows?" he said. "Even his Virgins are profane with a terrestrial beauty."

"I've got a terrible feeling I left the kettle on," Muriel said. "You know, on the gas ring in the workshop. Having only one arm, you forget things."

Whether or not the others saw the logic of this, they were clearly grateful to Muriel.

"Better check," Steadman said. "I should go at once."

"I've got a suede jacket in there," Owen said.

"Suede jacket?" Barfield looked severely at his colleague. "There are Tintorettos in that building," he said.

"Tintoretto sought for a higher voluptuousness," Beamish-Smith said.

There was a general movement toward the door. But the exalted dwarf remained where he was. Raikes heard the voice chirruping on behind him: "The opulence of heavy, mature bodies, such as Rubens afterward remembered . . ."

In the narrow lobby, in haste to escape, he almost bumped into Lattimer, who had just come back in. "I left my umbrella here somewhere," Lattimer said. "Ah, here it is." He seemed anxious and was frowning slightly — the first time Raikes could remember seeing that brow at all marred. "I don't usually forget things," he said. "Happens once in a blue moon."

Raikes had the impression that the strained, frowning look derived from something more than this mere oversight. "Coming for a drink?" he said.

"No, I can't, I'm afraid. I've got one or two things that need seeing to. You must come round again one evening. I'll give you a ring."

Standing at the door, Raikes watched him walk away in the direction of San Samuele. As always, Lattimer was dressed with utmost appropriateness, in a light tweed suit this cool evening; the temperature had dropped and there was a feeling of rain in the air. He held himself very erect as he walked. Light from the street lamps, diffused in the misty air, shed a diminishing luster on his smooth hair and well-tailored shoulders. At the last moment, near the bridge over the Rio del Duca, when his form was half lost in mist and light, Raikes saw, or thought ne saw, another, slighter figure join him, someone who seemed to have been waiting there, a woman probably, dressed in a raincoat and dark beret. The two figures merged almost at once into the thicker mist that hung over the water. It seemed to Raikes that they did not cross the bridge but went off right somewhere, toward the Campo Morosini.

The impression was over quickly enough for him almost to doubt it; recent experiences had in any case inclined him to doubt his eyes, especially when, as now, the thing seen was at the farthest stretch of vision. Behind him, and approaching, he heard the carillons of Beamish-Smith. Rapidly he set off down the street to where Steadman and Miss Greenaway were waiting for him, looking at bags and belts in a shop window.

"Better get a move on," Raikes said as he came up to them, "or we'll be hearing some more about flesh tints."

"There's a little place a bit farther down here." Steadman nodded in the direction intended. "My God," he said as they walked along. "What a circus."

"I don't mind a bit of attention," Miss Greenaway said. "But he was overdoing it. I didn't know where to look."

"He did," Raikes said.

"He struck me as oversexed," Miss Greenaway said.

Steadman uttered a short laugh. "I've never known what that word means," he said. "Unless it's an expression of our own sense of limitation, like 'too clever' or 'too beautiful.' No, you can't blame him for staring at your tits, Pauline. They are absolutely staggering and he had them just at eye level. It was the stuff about mystic fruit and higher voluptuousness that choked me off."

It was not warm enough for them to sit outside, but the bar was not crowded, and they found a corner table easily enough. All three asked for cognac. There was some degree of poignancy in the situation, which Raikes felt. Steadman was leaving for England the next day and the relationship with Miss Greenaway had obviously progressed far enough to make this seem to both of them something of a separation. He would be back in three weeks, he said. He had some lecture commitments at the Courtauld and some research to do in connection with his book.

"The Madonna should be almost done by then," Raikes said. "All but the head, I should think."

"I look forward to seeing her. Things are going all right then?"

"I think so, on the whole. I'm having trouble keeping the glass particles in the cutter free from damp, especially in this weather we're having now. I don't want the thing to seize up on me at this stage."

"Well, this is a humid city, as you pointed out. Any more leads on the statue itself?"

"Not really," Raikes said cautiously. He had begun to like Steadman much more than before and he needed his help; but the habit of secrecy remained, and the jealousy. All knowledge of the Madonna was a gain in her favor, an intimacy granted; he had no intention of admitting rivals. Besides, Steadman knew nothing of his visions. He would have to give something away, however.

After a moment or two, he said, "There's something you could do for me while you're in England, if you like. You'll have good research facilities there. You could find out about any Piedmontese sculptors working in Venice, say between 1425 and 1435."

"Piedmontese?" Steadman looked at him curiously. "Piedmont was not exactly a thriving scene in the early fifteenth century," he said. He waited for some moments as if in hope that Raikes would enlighten him further. Then he said, "There is some Northern Gothic influence in the stone carvings and relief work in local parish churches, traces of the Dijon school. But there are no prominent artists; I can tell you that now. I'll find out what I can, of course."

"I'd be grateful for anything you could dig up," Raikes said. "Are we going to have another drink?"

"I don't think so." Steadman glanced at Miss Greenaway. "I've got packing to do and so on," he said.

Understanding this glance, Raikes nodded. "I wouldn't mind an early night myself," he said. He lingered, though, a little longer, aware of a fascinated desire to discuss the Tintoretto people. "Extraordinary bad luck," he said, "Barfield and Mrs. Hagerty injuring themselves like that, both at the same time. You'll have more to do now, I expect."

These last words were to Miss Greenaway, who compressed her lips and nodded emphatically. "It wouldn't be so bad," she said, "if Muriel didn't insist on her rights so much. She's the senior assistant, you know. I mean, she insisted on managing the film projector with only one arm. That's just an example. She's afraid I'll usurp her place in Gerald Barfield's favor. As if I'd want to! He's far too mild and straitlaced for me. I like someone with more dash."

"Well, his leg is straitlaced enough, certainly," Raikes said.

"She's really got a slave mentality, Muriel has, under that snappy manner. It's Jerry this and Jerry that, yes Jerry, no Jerry."

"There's more to the business than meets the eye," Steadman said. "Owen swears he didn't leave any rope lying around. There *was* a coil of rope, he says, but that was against the wall. Besides, Barfield let slip once that the accident happened in the sacristy. Yet by the time Muriel had got help, he was in the chapterhouse. Did he crawl there? And if so, why? The rope was in the chapterhouse, Owen says. This was around midnight, remember. They are all in the same hotel, you know; she's only a few yards away down the corridor."

"Strange business." Raikes got to his feet. He had begun to feel mean, sitting there, saying nothing; but it would have meant explaining too much. "Have a good trip," he said to Steadman, with a sudden feeling of affection. In the course of the evening he felt they had become friends; certain misconceptions had been removed; Steadman's habit of raillery, which he had feared, was on a par with his own assumptions of aloofness; different ways of reacting to awfulness, and Steadman's more attractive . . . "Mind how you go," he said.

Steadman broke into one of his rare smiles. "You're the one in need of that advice," he said. "It's funny; I used to think you a calculating fellow."

They parted at the doorway, Steadman and Miss Greenaway making toward the Accademia boat stage. Raikes decided to walk a little before getting the *vaporetto.* It was just after ten, a time of evening he had always liked in Venice. Away from main thoroughfares the streets were quiet; the lamplight took on a selective, deceiving quality, hiding much that was decayed, touching with sudden caress a stretch of canal, the perfect ellipse of bridge and reflection, the broken glitters where a boat had passed. Aided by this light one could ignore the damp and desolation emanating from ground-floor windows and ruined boat gates, abandoned as life retreated higher; see only the beauties of the Renaissance brickwork, the exquisite proportions of the house fronts. Time the despoiler had not much hurt the city's beauty, but this was best seen now in ambiguous lights.

He walked in the general direction of San Marco, keeping north of the square. After some time, he found himself at the bridge behind the basilica. A cruise boat, her decks hung with lights, passed slowly across his line of vision, emerging from the Giudecca Canal toward the open sea beyond. For a moment or two he saw her brilliant upper deck, towering behind the Bridge of Sighs; then she had slid noiselessly out of sight, cut off by the arcades of the Ducal Palace. Floodlighting lay in zones on the canal, flickering at the edges where the water lapped, like a message too rapid to be decoded.

He made his way down to the Riva degli Schiavoni with the intention of getting a boat back up the Grand Canal. However, in the window of the bar adjoining the Danieli Hotel he saw a thick arm in crumpled fawn suiting raised to beckon him, saw a large, pale, mouthing face — it was Slingsby. Too late now to pretend — he had already stopped and peered. Reluctantly, he walked over and went in.

Slingsby was sitting alone at a table near the window, on a chair not designed for such spreading bulk. "I saw you passing," he said. "What's your poison?"

This seemed to Raikes a curiously old-fashioned expression, as if

Slingsby had been reading boys' adventure stories. He was reminded suddenly of Lattimer's remark about hemlock. "I'll have a cognac," he said.

"I'm having gin," Slingsby said. "Hey, *scusi,* waiter." His face looked pinker, moister; the small blue eyes, though still containing alarm, had lost that affrighted glancing. "I like gin," he said. "It's *clean.*"

A graceful, olive-skinned youth came unhurriedly toward them; he was dressed in a red silk shirt and close-fitting black velvet trousers which held his genitals in a tight, neat pack.

"Ah." Slingsby brightened visibly at the sight. "There you are. For *mio amico* one cognac. He is a noted restorer of stone virgins." The youth smiled broadly, uncomprehending. "For me, *doppio* gin." Slingsby raised his large hands and made delicate, curiously irrelevant-seeming gestures in the air before him. "A double," he said.

Smiling, the boy made a gap between thumb and forefinger. *"Così, signore?"*

"Dead right," Slingsby said. He watched the waiter's tight-sheathed retreat. "My, that boy has white teeth," he said. "Real white. You married, Mr. Raikes?"

"No," Raikes said. With an instinct of caution, he added, "Still playing the field."

Slingsby brooded a moment. Then he said, "This evening was interesting, it was instructive. All those people come to save Venice from the elements. Totally forlorn quest. Germans, Italians, Americans, British, French. Has it struck you, Mr. Raikes, that the same peoples were at one another's throats just a generation ago on this same terrain? Were you in the war, Mr. Raikes?"

"I was nine months old when the war started."

There was no change in Slingsby's expression of shrewd, haunted baby. "I guess not," he said. "You must have been too young. I was younger then myself. Young firm bodies we had in those days. You married, Mr. Raikes?"

"Playing the field."

"None of them believes in God either. They have all come to restore works of art made to the greater glory of God, and none of them believes in Him."

The boy returned with the drinks, and Slingsby went through a pantomime of the gesture with finger and thumb. "*Così,* eh?" he said. "*Grazie, amico.* Say, what's your name? Antonio, Benito, Ricardo?"

"Giuseppe." The boy pointed a finger at his chest. He smiled from one to the other of them.

Slingsby followed his sinuous retreat. "Great sense of humor, that boy," he said.

"I don't think it's a forlorn quest," Raikes said, reverting to Slingsby's earlier remark. "Every single thing saved is a victory — I mean of course in the limited terms in which we can see it. Even just one thing . . . It's an expression of belief in the future. It is the most *pacific* thing anyone could do."

There was a drift of rain against the window. From where he was sitting he could see the row of triple-headed street lamps, their dark pink panes making a long looping pattern down the *riva.* Over to his left he made out the neon Campari sign on the Lido, glowing hideous in the distance. Another waiter, older than Giuseppe, was stacking the red and white canvas chairs round the tables outside the Danieli. He had just uttered, he realized, a statement of faith. "If I didn't believe in it, I wouldn't be doing it," he said.

If Slingsby felt this as a reproach, he gave no sign of it. "That Japanese guy had the answer," he said. "*It is the air.* Did you see him make that karate chop? In that chop the man's true nature stood revealed. I did not like to feel I shared my human nature with that chopper, Mr. Raikes. But that is not what depressed me."

Raikes said nothing. In the case of a man so prone to depression and dismay as Slingsby, he thought, particular causes could not add much in the way of illumination. Outside on the pavement, in the thin rain, two grave elderly men with umbrellas had stopped in conversation. He glanced at his watch. It was nearly midnight, high time he was making for home. There was no one but themselves there now. They would want to close the bar. Suddenly, disagreeably, he remembered again that tomorrow he had his appointment at Vittorini's clinic.

"That chop was the perfect illustration," Slingsby said obsessively. "The air is killing Venice. The air is a reservoir for aggressive impurities. The air is killing us. What is it your poet says?"

"I think you're exaggerating quite a bit," Raikes said.

"Exaggerating? Mr. Raikes, I am forty-eight years old. I have spent my working life looking at deteriorated stone in all sorts of places. I have just been in Austria looking at the aggressive effect of sulphate-rich water on their water tunnels over there — they used alkalic Portland cement in the concrete; fatal, of course. Before that I was in Edinburgh, looking at the headstones in some of your graveyards over there. Before that I was engaged in studying the weathering rates of basalt on Bohemian medieval castles. I have probably seen more decaying stone than any other man alive. It has affected me, Mr. Raikes. I won't deny it. It has played havoc with my life. Because, you see . . ."

Slingsby paused, making solemn plucking motions in the air before him. "I have realized that the same thing is happening to us," he said. "With every breath we draw. Inside we are the same, foul and pitted and polluted. And now I find myself in Venice, which is the most horrifying place of all. It is a nightmare. The place is stuck all over with images in the human form, doges and dignitaries, angels, saints, Madonnas — all riddled with bacteria. There couldn't," he said gloomily, "be a worse place for a man like me. I have asked repeatedly for a transfer."

Giuseppe had emerged from behind the bar and was wiping tables and arranging chairs. Slingsby's harassed eye lingered on his lithe bendings and stretchings.

"Of course," he said, "there are areas still relatively untouched. Recently quarried, so to speak. After about the age of seventeen the rot sets in. There are just a few precious years."

Raikes got up. "I must be on my way," he said. "Are you coming?"

"No, I'll stay on a while."

Raikes left him there in the deserted bar. Outside on the pavement, setting off for home, he gave a last look behind him. He saw Slingsby's hand raised in that pantomime gesture, signaling for another *doppio*.

5

Vittorini's clinic was on the Via Garibaldi. Light rain began to fall as Raikes was walking toward it from the Arsenale stop.

He was apprehensive, talking to the girl in the small reception room and later to Vittorini. The latter, no doubt seeing this, took obvious care to reassure him, though without explaining much, compared with what an English doctor would have felt obliged to explain. It seemed that medical mysteries were more jealously guarded here.

It was not fear of discomfort or pain that troubled Raikes but the feeling that he was somehow a *suspect,* a person under particular scrutiny. He had never had this feeling before, but he recognized it at once, in the affability with which he was treated, in the movements of the doctor's manicured hands; he was an oddity, one whose behavior might give rise to concern, who might need controlling. This unease persisted as he went through blood-circulation tests and skull x-rays, not allayed by the spacious, well-appointed room or the deft and friendly sister; but it mounted to definite alarm only with the electroencephalograph, which they gave him finally. Seated in the tall-backed chair while the little steel cups were attached one by one to points of his skull, he felt truly in the grip of interrogators.

Some jellylike substance was dabbed on his head before the electrodes were fixed in place. The sister perhaps sensed his tension, for she smiled and said, *"Non si preoccupi, è solo una pomata."*

Una pomata? he thought. Only a salve? That couldn't be true. It must be something to conduct the electricity better. They were treating him like a baby. Indignation contended with his alarm. Eight slender wires now led from the eight plugs on his head to a console against the wall. He sat there, skull jellied and studded, wired to the gently humming machine, while quite painlessly, without sensation on his part, the impulses of his brain were measured and recorded.

The apparatus was removed, the jelly sponged away — this last not by the sister but by an ordinary nurse, summoned for the more menial task. She spoke to him cheerfully in the accents of the Veneto. He made an appointment for the coming week, when the results would be made known to him. Within an hour of his arrival there, hair combed, umbrella remembered and retrieved, he was on his way back to the Arsenale.

It was not till much later in the day, with rain pricking the canal below his window, his diary on the table before him, that he thought in any conscious way about the business, and then it was with some return of that alarmed indignation. He remembered the lie about the *pomata*, the dab of the jelly, the wires trailing from his skull. He had been reduced to a mechanism, plugged in. What could such a contraption possibly have to do with the swift and marvelous motions of his brain? Yet something irrevocable had happened there. Evidence had been extracted from him. Uneasily he took up his pen and drew the diary toward him; as usual he cast about for something of a factual nature to begin with. After some moments he found it.

Problems due to humidity still continue. There is a constant interaction of cold air from the Alps and warm air from the Adriatic, and the two currents meet and contend over Venice. As I mentioned to Steadman, constant care is needed to prevent the glass particles from absorbing moisture and thereby clogging the machine. Time has been lost through the need to keep the beads dry. I have been wondering whether something less absorbent could be substituted for the glass. Aluminum oxide, for example, would not coagulate so easily. Must try this out when I return to England. The other main problem has been dealing with the dust. It is extremely dense and acrid, and even with the full face mask I am using, which goes down well below the chin, some dust is inhaled. Apart from being disagreeable, this is obviously dangerous to the health. Perhaps a larger mask could be used, though this would cause problems of air supply. It should not be difficult to devise some sort of vacuum pipe that could suck up the dust while the work is going on. Presumably the nozzle of this could be attached to the abrasion instrument somehow. Some improvements will have to be made to the process. While the work remains so laborious and physically uncomfortable, recruiting local assistants will be difficult.

He paused. Perhaps a jet, fixed somehow to the nozzle, a cone of nebulized water playing round the point of impact . . . He thought of the Madonna, cleaned now to the waist. Another month, five weeks, maybe. There was regret in the thought of her completion, as well as eagerness. An intimate connection would be severed, and not with the Madonna only. He tried as he sat there to review his "attacks," as Vittorini had called them, in the order in which they had come, but this was strangely difficult; he was impeded by memories of the accompanying sensations, the piercing light, the threat to balance, the intimate *knowledge* that attended the experiences. These, as objectively as possible, he had recorded in the diary already. But he had not so far attempted to interpret them. It was with the sense of taking a big step that he began writing again.

Could it be that I have really been seeing in this fragmentary and fleeting form true things about the past of the Madonna? That long straight shadow I saw lying across the room on the first occasion, when I was just beginning . . . There were two people there, in a room of sunlight and shadow; it was hot, they were washing each other, naked, a man and a woman, lovers therefore. And the straight lines — were these cast by the stone before she was made? *The mystery is not in what I saw but what it means. And the face in the water: every feature was clear; she was smiling slightly, as if at some pleasing thought. A beautiful face, mouth full but well shaped, level brows, delicate nostrils. There was a band of some kind round her neck.*

Discounting all this, what do I really know? She was commissioned in the March of 1432 by the friars of the Supplicanti from a Piedmontese named Girolamo. If I am right, she was delivered to them but not installed, remaining where she had been set down against the wall of the cloister until the church lands were sold. There she stayed, in what is now known as the Casa Fioret, through all its various owners, until 1743, when, in the belief that she had miraculous powers, she was installed on the façade of a completely different church, by a benefactor unknown, under the auspices of one Piero Fornarini, Bishop of Venice, who subsequently choked on a chicken bone.

So the friars must have rejected her. On what grounds? Why would they reject a work of such outstanding quality? There is the position of the left hand, of course, which is unorthodox. This Girolamo was a Gothic man, at least in sensibility. He would see things in more extreme terms than they did in the later Renaissance. I have been wondering whether he was influenced by certain of the early Fathers, who suggest that Mary's first reaction to the Annunciation was fear of Gabriel's magnificence. He came to her clothed in fire, after all. Could Girolamo have seen this as a sexual fear? The form below the draperies is very sensuously realized. I have mentioned already the molding of the right leg, which looks almost unclothed, so closely does the drapery follow the contours of the limb — almost as if the stone had been abraded rather than cut. But it is not only the lower leg. The line of definition, and the same effect of abrading, is continued up the line of the right thigh, leading the eye straight to the pubic area. This too, the pubic triangle, is very carefully sculpted, the same effect of clinging drapery, due of course to the way the skirt of her robe is gathered up toward the high-waisted girdle; but the result is that we can trace the actual slope of the flesh between her legs, and this, in conjunction with the outstretched arm and the contrapposto, *is erotic in effect. I don't believe I am simply being "a perverted modern," in Steadman's words, to think this.*

If she was rejected on those grounds, it is ironical that the Supplicanti themselves fell into disgrace within fifty or sixty years and for what must certainly have been sexual dereliction — probably institutionalized sodomy, for them all to have been sent packing like that. Almost as if the good friars in their turn were corrupted by this image of the flesh dwelling in their midst.

Raikes abruptly stopped writing and after a moment or two got up and began walking about, prey to a sudden, inexplicable unrest. Not suspicion exactly, but the monstrous shadow of it, had fallen across his mind, and he felt the kind of alarm that is experienced when associations form almost with violence, beyond control, in a sort of mental spasm. Why that phrase? he thought. *In their turn.* He felt flushed and feverish, as he had on the occasion when his landlady, Signora Sapori, in her immaculate apron, had offered him some apple pie. In a further series of spasms he began to think of Chiara Litsov, the lonely figure in the red scarf standing above him, the beauty of her eyes and brows, her smiling mouth, the fingers pressing at the black earth round the roots of the seedlings, that strange, self-loving, self-protecting gesture which had seemed so at odds with the openness of her manner . . . Had one of those trophy tufts been hers? Was she the figure in the mist, waiting for Lattimer?

6

Crouched against the Madonna's pelvis, through the dust-mottled visor of his mask and the dust-filled space beyond it, Raikes watched the diseased encrustation of the stone clear, blur, clear again, the skin emerging white, millimeter by millimeter. The instrument seemed to attack the contaminated surface with an appetite of its own, stroking off the dross eagerly.

He worked with concentration. No single diseased grain would be allowed to survive. However uncontrollably murky his thoughts, this work of his hands would emerge pure; his hands alone would achieve it; restored, she would be his creation, and his only. The faint hiss of impact, the hum of the compressed nitrogen feeding the cutter, signals of his own control and power. There was no sound in the enclosure, in the universe, but this, no sight but the slowly spreading whiteness — an absorption surely similar, he drifted into thinking, to that of the obscure artist who had made her, this shadowy Piedmontese. Yes, surely similar — it was a consolation to think so, to think that he had not given up all share in the creative process when he had lost faith in his talents as a sculptor, settled for the safe hierarchy of the museum with its salary structure and pension scheme. Loss of nerve, acceptance of reality: he would never know now. He had not wanted to be second best.

There were differences, of course, apart from the obvious one. It was difficult for modern man to feel at the heart of things, unless insane; but the man who had made this statue had seen himself not as a random particle of matter, but as second only to the angels, in a world that was the center of the universe, in a city that was the richest and strongest maritime power that world had ever seen. Marvelous to have that sense of centrality. The price, of course, was to be constantly in God's eye. Signor Biagi's words came back to him: *la parte esposta,* the exposed position. Strangely long ago that seemed now . . .

He was roused from these thoughts by shouts from below. He rose, moved rather stiffly to the edge of his small enclosure and peered down. He was wearing his mask still, and the plastic visor was dusty, moreover tended to distort vision slightly at distances greater than a yard or two. He made out a small group of figures standing below him, a little way out into the square, several workmen in overalls, a dark-suited man, a woman in a light-colored coat.

Even before removing the mask he had a certain breathless sense of who the woman might be. When he snatched it off it was as if his eyes were inundated with light. This flooding of the retinas, and the immediate recognition that the woman was indeed Chiara Litsov, combined somehow to impede his vision once again. He closed his eyes in a long blink, opened them, saw that the man in the suit was Biagi, that Chiara was smiling.

"Can I come up and see what you're doing?" She had put her hands to the sides of her face, the better to wing these words to him.

Biagi, no doubt thinking that such a matter had to be discussed between men, acted as mediator. *"Chiede se può salire,"* he shouted. "She asks if she may come up."

Raikes was aware of hush below, a suspension of activity among the workmen. All sounds seemed to have stopped. Suddenly he felt a wave of pride; she was asking for *him.*

"Vuole guardare il lavoro," Biagi shouted, continuing in his role of male herald of female desires.

"Come up if you like," Raikes called. "It's rather dirty up here. Be careful on the ladder. *Va bene, può salire,"* he added to Biagi, feeling obliged to carry on the official, male side of the dialogue.

He watched the contractor escort her toward the foot of the ladder. Then they were both lost to sight, cut off by the edge of the platform on which he was standing. Signor Biagi did not reappear: he would be intent on the *signora*'s progress up the ladder; so would all the workmen who happened to be outside the church at the moment. Raikes tried to remember, or perhaps he had not noticed, what she was wearing under the coat. He found himself hoping, in the moments of waiting that now followed, that it was not a skirt. Then her hand appeared above the edge of the planks and he went forward to help her.

She needed little help, however, but was up onto the platform quickly and lightly, with a grasp of his outstretched hand that lasted a moment only. "So this is where you do your restoring," she said. "I was curious, after hearing you talk about it. I was in town and so I thought I would come and have a look."

This came all in a breath and somehow prematurely, or so it seemed to Raikes, as if she were eager to account for this uninvited visit, or at least as if she were conscious, in the silence of his regard, of needing to make some defense. This gave him pleasure; he could not have said exactly why. If she was warning him not to presume, he was glad she thought him worth warning.

"I see you're wearing trousers," he said, for want of other notions of what to say, and because, in the terrific hush of her approach up the ladder, it had been on his mind.

"Yes," she said, rather vaguely. Then, perhaps catching some note of satisfaction in his voice, she smiled and said, "They are best when it comes to climbing ladders."

There was a pause while Raikes struggled to absorb this smile. Then he gestured toward the Madonna. "Well," he said, "this is my lady. She's in a bit of a mess at present, I'm afraid. You may not be able to get a proper idea of her."

It was true that the Madonna was unsightly, with the speckled dust lying over her, powdering her encrusted face, caught like dirty pollen in her robes.

"This is the bit I've done so far," Raikes said, pointing. "It is slow work."

She went nearer to inspect it. "There's a huge difference," she said. "This is the pure stone again, isn't it?"

"As pure as it will ever be." Was she merely humoring him, showing polite interest? The suspicion conflicted with his proprietary enthusiasm. He said, "Something is always lost, you know."

This had a pompous sound, even to him, but she did not look up. She had crouched and was running a slim hand down the line of the Madonna's right flank. "He knew what a leg looks like, didn't he? How white the stone is." Her hand had a warm pallor, almost vivid against the cleaned stone.

"It looks whiter by comparison, or so I am hoping. It should be a very pale cream color. In its pristine state, I mean. That is one of the things that is bothering me, whether this blasting process will take the warmth from the stone. It's Istrian stone, you know."

Somewhere in the midst of these words his feelings had quickened, changed course. Whether it was the sight of the woman's living hand on the stone, or the angle of her head as she crouched there, the dark hair falling forward to reveal the pale skin of her nape above the coat collar, something childlike and wondering about her caressing of the ancient texture of the limestone — something of reverence too, as if she were paying her respects. Somewhere among all this there was a factor not accidental, striking him with the sense of something foretold, fulfilled. She chose this moment to turn, throwing back her hair, and look at him; still not rising.

"Istrian stone," he plunged, "as perhaps you know, is a very dense form of limestone. When I say dense . . . the capillaries are very close together, much closer than in marble, for example. Marble is more permeable . . ."

He fell helplessly silent. In the pause that followed their eyes met. She seemed at first to be waiting for him to say more. Then her expression changed. She stood up and after a moment said, "I'd be really interested to see the work actually in progress. Would you mind very much?"

This request changed the quality of his hesitation — as perhaps she had intended. To refuse her anything was scarcely conceivable. On the other hand, there was the shining hair, her lashes and eyes, the clear skin of her face, her narrow hands even; and then the coat, obviously of good quality. All this must be protected, down to the last pore, follicle and fiber.

"It's rather a messy operation," he said. "The dust, you know."

"I could wear something over my face."

"Perhaps we could find you something to put on. I keep a spare mask here. If you really want to, that is."

"I do, yes."

The tone of this made further discussion superfluous. He left her there and began clambering down the ladder, his heart beating in his ears. In certain states of disturbance one becomes self-conscious, pausing where one would not pause, noting the trivial as if it were significant; Raikes found himself registering the paint-flaked rungs of the ladder and his own momentous feet, in their shabby tennis shoes, descending.

At ground level, however, consulting Signor Biagi, several of the workmen within earshot, dignity demanded a leisurely style, an attitude of good-humored indulgence toward female caprice. He hoped this was what showed on his face.

"They get these ideas," he said, smiling, trying to control his breathing. "*Si mettono in testa queste idee . . .*"

The sentiment was deeply familiar to Biagi, who shrugged and nodded humorously. "*Che ci possiamo fare?*" he said. "What can we do?"

"Strange creatures." A terrible impatience to be back up the ladder assailed Raikes. He shook his head, smiling indulgently. "*Non si sa mai,*" he said. "You never know what they will get into their heads."

One or two of the nearby workmen laughed and exclaimed approvingly at this. "*Non si sa mai,*" one of them echoed. Raikes became aware that his stock had gone up since Chiara's visit — here at ground level at least.

"*Che ci possiamo fare?*" he repeated, smiling and shrugging at the workmen, united with them in resignation and indomitable logic.

Biagi was so pleased with this that he went so far as to clap the Englishman on the shoulder. "*Non si sa mai, eh?*" he said, chuckling. "*Non si sa mai cosa gli salta in mente.*"

Raikes obtained some overalls and a reasonably clean-looking cap. Clutching these, calmed by social success, he began to climb back up the ladder.

She was looking at the Madonna's face when he returned, her own face held close. She was of a height with the statue, and when she turned toward him the two faces were level, close together, flesh and stone, the one vivid with life, the other blurred and streaked with ancient lamentation. Once again a fugitive sense of recognition stirred in him. Then she moved away and the moment was lost.

He helped her off with the coat, not touching her, aware of not touching her. The overalls were too large, slipping off at the shoulders, needing to be rolled up at the ankles. She pushed up her hair, bunching it under the cap with both hands, lowering her face at the same time, gestures hasty and careless, though piercing to Raikes. He gave her the spare mask and showed her how to put it on.

In the shapeless overalls, with the cap covering her hair and the mask over her face, she was unrecognizable, a creature metamorphosed. He stared at her for a moment, then put on his own mask and cap. First shaking out the cable to keep it clear of the cutter, he crouched before the Madonna, Chiara crouching beside him — they were shoulder to shoulder, almost touching, like devotees at an altar. The faint drone of the machine filled the enclosure, followed a moment later by the hissing assault on the stone.

Raikes resumed at a point slightly higher than where he had left off so that she would be able to see the contrast. Here, where the robe was gathered up to the high girdle, the folds were intricate. He advanced the cutter close to the surface, withdrew it as the encrustation thinned. Delicately, savagely, the glass crystals thrashed at the stone. Dust rose around them, glinting briefly in the light.

When he stopped a narrow strip of perhaps three inches had been reclaimed. He turned his head to look at her. Through dust-thickened air and misted planes of plastic, her face seemed suspended, indistinct, as if seen through some slightly opaque medium. Raikes felt that seashell resonance in his ears; he experienced a sort of swooning tremor and instinctively clutched for balance at the Madonna's knee. This passed at once. For a few seconds longer they crouched there, silent and motionless at the base of the statue. Then Chiara stood up, removed the cap and mask, shook out her hair. "That was really very interesting," she said. "Thank you for letting me watch."

Raikes got up slowly. "It's a long job, as you see," he said. Retrieving her coat from its polythene wrapper, helping her on with it, he felt, though more faintly, the usual belated fear, as of danger only recognized after escape. "Still, we're getting on," he said.

She turned to face him. "You must be very patient," she said. She had smiled as she spoke, but now the smile faded and she looked rather attentively at him, though she said nothing more.

"Yes . . . Well, I don't know if it is patience. A kind of crablike tenacity." In a few moments, he thought, if I don't do something to prevent it, she will be climbing back down the ladder. I will go down too, of course. At the foot of the ladder she will thank me again; then she will walk away, back to home and husband. Better do nothing, let her go . . . "Do you fancy a cup of coffee or a drink or something?" he said.

"What a good idea. A drink would be nice. As a matter of fact, I've got one or two things to tell you. Nothing very much, I'm afraid. I've had a reply from my aunt — the one in Rome that I told you about. The guardian of the family secrets."

It was exactly what Lattimer had replied, and in exactly the same tone, when he had asked for whiskey. *What a good idea.* "It was very good of you to bother," he said.

"Well, we can talk about it over the drink."

7

Sunlight below seemed stronger, dazzling almost. Pigeons fluttered round their feet as, watched by the workmen, they set off across the square. By unspoken consent they went past the café at the far corner, through the dimness of the covered passageway, out into the light of the *campiello* beyond. They crossed the Misericordia Canal and turned left along the *fondamenta.* It was warm here, in the shelter of the wall, and they walked slowly. Only occasional remarks were exchanged between them, but Raikes was not conscious of constraint, though he still felt a kind of astonishment at her presence; he had not succeeded yet in detaching her from the surroundings of their one previous meeting, so much had she seemed to be part of these, captive almost, though a splendid one, confined there like the shining bronze fragments of herself.

They were in the Rio Terra della Maddalena now, among what seemed a sudden density of people, tourists for the most part, thronging the way, clustered in thicker groups round stalls laid out with trinkets and souvenirs, Murano glassware, silk scarves, gondolier hats. He was again reminded, suddenly and disagreeably, of

Lattimer. *They are like flies.* It was true, in a way: there seemed, in the contrast between the moving throng down the center of the street and the fingering, exploratory stillness of the clusters at the stalls, some enactment of the pattern of insects. As if they had found some sweetness or decay, and settled . . .

"Crowded, isn't it?" he said. He was beginning to regret coming this way instead of making for the quiet backwaters of San Alvise, north of the church.

"The season is beginning," she said. "But the area around the Maddalena is usually quiet. It is off the beaten way. People go straight through to Santa Fosca."

"You know the city well."

"Quite well, I think. But I have not spent so much time here, really. What you have to do in Venice is to get rid of all notions of order and logic and rely on a primitive sense of direction. That seems to suit me."

"Why, because you are primitive?" Raikes said, smiling. "It's probably genetic. The Fornarini family must have Venice printed on their chromosomes by this time."

In fact the *campo* was almost deserted. There was a small café with two wrought-iron tables, one on either side of the door, looking toward the elegant Renaissance well-head in the middle of the square and the circular construction of the church beyond. One of the tables was occupied by an elderly couple, speaking German; the other one they took.

Here in the sunshine, facing each other across the narrow table, they drank Carpano and talked for perhaps two hours, though the experience had no dimension of time in Raikes's mind. Visual perspectives too were simplified or obliterated. Beyond their table, beyond Chiara's face and the words and looks they exchanged, the near world and the far — buildings, people passing, the waiter, the couple at the next table — lost all distinction. There was only the talk and the small, momentous events that accompanied it: clink of ice, slide of sunlight on the glasses, her gestures, the changing expressions of her face.

"My aunt," she said, "first of all, before I forget. I'm afraid there's not much to tell. The Fornarini family never owned a house in San

Giovanni Crisostomo, at least as far as she knows. The records are not complete, it seems, far from it in fact, there aren't any voting lists to go on or anything of that kind. So it's just possible. Anyway, it didn't belong at any time to Piero Fornarini, who was Bishop of Venice when the Madonna was installed. He seems to have been a licentious character. Even my aunt admits that, and she is very protective about the family name. The only mention, again according to my aunt, is in a letter he wrote to his cousin. There's a manuscript copy of this among the papers. It seems that the donor of the statue, presumably the original owner, had agreed to pay a fixed yearly sum to the church on condition his name was not mentioned. Piero suggests that since they can't call the man by his proper name, they could refer to him as Cornadoro, Golden Horns. He doesn't say why."

"If he doesn't say, the cousin must have known."

"I suppose so."

"And nothing about these miraculous powers of hers?"

"No, I'm afraid not. It's difficult to think of Piero in connection with miracles. There's a story in the family that he didn't choke on a bone at all but died laughing at what my aunt calls *una barzelletta sconcia*, a scurrilous anecdote."

"I wonder if he was listening to it or telling it."

"I don't know . . . I'm afraid this has not been much help."

"Oh, I wouldn't say that," Raikes replied. "If I can garner enough details, perhaps it will all come together, sooner or later. I know more than I did. I know to my own satisfaction at least that the Madonna was commissioned in 1432 by a monastic order recently settled in Venice and carved in that same year by an obscure artist from northern Italy. The monks didn't use her, I don't know why." He looked away across the square. "The thing is like a great sponge," he said with sudden intensity. "Saturated with the facts. I just don't know how to get hold of it, where to press." Yet he knew as he spoke that this was not it; it was not frustration he had felt but grief, a sense of loss, as if he had been cheated somehow of a dear possession.

She was looking at him curiously. "Does it matter so much to you? To find out, I mean?"

She herself, he realized, had not shown much interest in these details. She had told him once that she did not greatly care about the past."

"Well, yes," he said. "I have undertaken it, you see. It would be like leaving the Madonna half restored."

"And do you always do what you undertake?"

He could see no hint of derision in her face, only sympathy and interest. "Well, no," he said. "I abandoned my biggest undertaking something like eight years ago."

"What was that?"

Raikes hesitated again. Years of reticence made it difficult, but he had begun already, in a way; and the urge to bring her closer was very strong.

"I wanted to be a sculptor at one time. I was at art school, you know, not university — I didn't train as an art historian. St. Martin's, in London. I did sculpture there."

"What made you change your mind?"

"I didn't change my mind exactly. I mean, I didn't stop wanting to do it."

He looked away from her again, at the tall old houses lining the near side of the square, noting automatically the ogival door of the nearest one, with its reliefs of saints and angels above the arch. Late Gothic. "I realized that I wasn't good enough," he said, and found that his lips had stiffened a bit with some residue of the old pain. "It took me several years. I was always slow to realize things. Very tenacious, you know."

When he looked back at her face, he saw that it wore the slightly strained look of close attention that he had come to recognize as one of her expressions.

"I'm sorry," she said.

"No need. I got over it years ago."

"I don't believe you were no good."

He smiled, touched by this obvious intention to please him. "It was a mental thing," he said, "like everything with me. I think I saw it too idealistically. I saw it in terms of making a contribution and so on. The wrong attitude. A real artist doesn't think in those terms. The trouble is, or was, that I am bad at compromising, in that sort of situation anyway. When I went into museum work it seemed to me that I had made an absolute choice. I've never tried to sculpt since then. It was the kind of choice, you see . . . Not like other things. It was like choosing between two different ideas of oneself, two completely different modes of existence. What bothers me is that I *defined* myself. People shouldn't have to do that."

He paused, looking directly at her. "I remember the day I put in for the post," he said. "I felt I had turned to stone."

She was looking down at the table, the long dark lashes lowered over her eyes. "I don't know much about it," she said slowly, "but I have a feeling that the choice is not so final as you have thought. You are young enough to do anything you want. Besides, the work you are doing now is important."

Exalted by this, Raikes became unusually voluble. He told her about his work at the Madonna dell'Orto four years earlier — his first visit to Venice — how they had worked on the blackened cheeks of St. Christopher with an ultrasonic dental drill, the labor of it, the ridiculous slowness. "We had nothing else," he said. "It was like trying to paint Westminster Bridge with a toothbrush." He had known that something else must be found, had stumbled on this air-abrasion technique, which was much better but still not fast enough — not if you considered how much there was to be done. In London, before he came away, he had been experimenting with a chemical mudpack based on magnesium silicate, which you could apply and seal in and leave for a month or more, setting up a violent bacterial reaction that would devour the sulphated crust. "You could get rid of ninety percent of it like that," he told her eagerly. There was beauty in it, a kind of natural justice, harnessing the voracious bacteria, previously the very allies of decay.

All the enthusiasm of his nature came out. He talked to her as he had talked to no one for years. He told her about the Bologna Conference of 1969, the first of its kind ever to be held and one of the formative experiences of his life. It was there that he had heard the first full analysis of the chemical causes of stone decay, made by Giorgio Terraca, at that time director of the Center of Conservation and Restoration in Rome. Terraca had illustrated his talk with a set of pictures of stone samples magnified five hundred times. These had shown the fibers that made up the stone, tightly knit at first, bursting apart under the pressure of calcium sulphate.

"You saw the whole process," Raikes said. "I can't tell you the effect it had on me. It was like watching Armageddon in slow motion, literally like seeing the big bang that will end the world — not a whimper but a bang. Decay is the wrong word for what happens. The stone is blown apart. I understood then that I wanted the world to go on even after I had ceased to be a part of it. Not for the sake of our children and all that stuff." He floundered a little. "Just to continue, that's all," he said.

She was listening to him intently, that slight expression of strain back on her face. It was not to understand what he was saying, he suddenly saw, but to understand *him.* Me, he thought, incredulously. Me, Simon Raikes. Vaguely at first, only half perceived, like some shift in music, he felt the humility of this thought change and quicken. He looked at her face, the clear lines of the temples and cheekbones, the curve of the mouth, the long, strange-colored eyes. "I want it all to go on," he said.

After a moment or two she said, "I am not so interested in things if I am not there to see them. That is too abstract for me, that whole idea. I want to exist whether the world exists or not. Do you know the poetry of Biagio Marin? He lives in Grado, in the Lagoon. He sums it up for me. *'Che vaga pur a fondo le stelle e' l'firmamento . . . Me vogio êsse eterno.'* I have known that poem since I was a little girl."

"It's dialect, isn't it?"

"The Veneto dialect, yes. Did you understand it? *Vaga* is *vadano,* you see. "Let the stars and the firmament sink . . . I want to be eternal."

She looked at him, smiling slightly. *"Me vogio êsse eterna,"* she said again.

Their eyes met. Time and the world stood still for Raikes. "But you are," he said. "Don't you know that?"

Her smile deepened with some quality of self-depreciation. Then as she continued to meet his gaze she grew serious again. "We are getting metaphysical," she said. "Never my strong point. Litsov is the one for that."

Perhaps by some instinct of retreat she began to speak of her husband's taste for Platonic speculation, realms in which she soon ceased trying to follow him; and from this to some of the places they had lived in before they settled on the island. There had been spells in Greece and Paris and a suburb of London. "Southeast twenty-seven," she said with a comical shudder. They had not had much money. She had taught Italian, private lessons, badly paid. Things had got better since Lattimer took a hand. He had been the first to see Litsov's talent, she said. Saying this, speaking of Lattimer, she repeated the gesture he had seen before, passing a hand slowly down from her shoulder along the outer arm, a gesture at once consolatory and self-loving. It disturbed him now, as it had done before.

"Have you known him long, Lattimer I mean?"

"No, not so long . . ."

He had organized exhibitions for Litsov in London, Rome, New York. He had made sure the right people saw them, the right things got into the papers. He had built Litsov up. Seeing how Litsov was with money, he had organized all that side of things, too, so that a regular monthly sum came in. "Like a salary," she said. "Of course he handles all Litsov's work too. My husband is glad to be free of these bothersome things. He does not like business. He hardly ever goes off the island, you know. He dislikes telephones even."

Raikes nodded. This portrait was becoming familiar. She had the habit, rather unusual, of referring to her husband by his surname only, and in a tone that one might use for an institution. The tone she used for Lattimer was different; it made him uneasy yet at the same time had a sort of unreality about it; he was ready to discount it as not really relevant. The stirrings of love are both slavish and obstinate; for Raikes the reality was the woman he saw before him, her movements and glances, the way she touched objects on the table with fostering gentleness, the look of sudden, almost painful attention that would come to her face.

He walked with her as far as the Misericordia — she had decided to walk to the Fondamenta Nuova and take the Burano-Torcello *motoscafo* from there. At the junction of the canals they stood for a few minutes longer before parting. They had talked away the afternoon. The first flush of sunset was in the sky now, faint and diffused but unmistakable; it was the time of day when the sun loses silver tone and begins to take fire, more ardent as the air darkens, like some blossoming of survival. The water had in it already that sobering of lead-rose which infuses melancholy into the sensuality of the city.

"I wanted to say I was sorry," she said.

"I can't imagine what for."

"For what I said that day you came to lunch. You remember, don't you?"

Pride struggled briefly and subsided. "Yes," he said.

"I felt sorry as soon as I'd said it, for quite complicated reasons. When you told me you had wanted to be a sculptor, it made it seem worse."

"No need," he said. "You could not have known."

"Litsov is highly strung," she said. "He's an invalid, in a way."

Taking this to refer to Litsov's nerves, Raikes nodded. "That's not why you came, is it?" he said. He smiled and said rather teasingly, "You haven't gone to all this trouble, choked yourself with dust, bored yourself with my conversation, just for an opportunity to say you were sorry?"

It was a tone he could not have used before this afternoon. And the look she gave him in reply, steady, conscious of power, this too could only have come after what they had said to each other.

"Is that what you think?" she said.

"No," he said. "No."

He watched her walk away, watched till her figure was lost among the moving forms of others in the dazzle of light at the entrance to the canal.

Later, back at work on the Madonna for what remained of the daylight, he was thinking how strange it was, how extremely strange, that he should be up here at all, engaged in this obsessively meticulous work. What could there be in the circumstances of his life hitherto, the Cambridge suburb where he had grown up, loving parents still there, still the same, school, college, the world of the museum, friends, sweethearts, ambitions, dreams — what could have led to it? Nothing in it seemed likely to provide clues as to why he was where he was now, high above the ground, enclosed by sheets of plastic, involved in dust, harassed by visions and speculations, occupied by thoughts of two ladies, one of stone and one of flesh.

He was over the halfway mark, though head and torso still remained. It had been those voluminous folds of cloak and gown that had taken up the time. Another month at most. Sealing the surface against further infection, another few days. And then . . .

In sudden distress he straightened up, switched off the cutter, hooked it over the scaffolding, pulled off his mask. He turned from the Madonna with some instinct of flight or revulsion. A couple of steps brought him to the edge of his enclosure. He was able to look down over the square at the usual mild activity of early evening. He saw the proprietor of the *gelateria,* in new and resplendent suspenders, standing in his doorway. Pigeons puffed out their breast feathers in the hazy light. Directly below him two of the workmen were talking together, discussing soccer — their voices came clearly to him. Work for the day had finished. A party of small chattering girls in black and white, a young woman at their head, crossed the square in a straggling group.

Raikes felt a vague surprise at how quickly pain, or the prospect of pain, had followed upon that charmed talk in the sunshine. He looked over the weather-faded tiles of the roofs, the thickets of bulbous chimneys, the tall *campanile* of the Madonna dell'Orto, to the milky lilac of the Lagoon. With the sight of this encircling water it came to him again that he was after all on an island; Venice was an island, and within her there were others; he was in his plastic cell, in the enclosure of the *campo;* and the buildings that enclosed the *campo* were islanded in their turn. She too . . . She would be back at home again now. Three miles or so to the northwest, in a room, in a house, on an island, in the waste of the Lagoon — itself trapped there by the greater sea outside. She would be touching things, moving about. Pain at the thought of leaving merged with the wonder of her existence. Three miles of shallow water. Standing there, like a navigator seeking haven, he took a conscious and deliberate bearing on that luminous point.

SECOND INTERLUDE

Sanctification

Ziani peered at the blurred pink form of his manservant standing just inside the room. "Have the sheets come back from the printers?" he said. "Come closer, I cannot see you. Why are you lurking there? Where are the sheets from the printers?"

Battistella advanced slowly. "They are not ready yet," he said. The thin wheeze of his breathing was audible in the quiet room. His ancient dusty wig was set straight by some chance this morning, giving him a look of unexpected severity.

"Not ready yet?" Although this was the answer he had been expecting, Ziani felt an emotion of rage too pure and justified for caution. "Not ready?" His voice rose and cracked. "They have had more than two hundred pages."

Frustration at having no one but Battistella to upbraid increased his fury. "Blockhead," he said loudly. "Have you no more to say than that?" He slipped a hand under his robe and laid it over his heart; the violence he found there frightened him. "I will go elsewhere," he said, in a more subdued tone. "There are other printers in Venice. You think I cannot go myself, but I will surprise you Battistella, I will get out my stick. The Ziani family has produced men of action for a thousand years, we have furnished the state with admirals and ambassadors. Do you think that I, last of the line, am incapable of telling this rogue of a printer to go and fuck himself?"

"The master printer is ill, that is the reason," Battistella said slowly. "He has a fever."

"Ah." Ziani considered this. "Has he not assistants?" he said after a moment or two. "The best printer in Venice, so you say, and he has no assistants?"

Battistella paused for so long that Ziani began to think he had not heard. Finally he said, "He wants to do the work himself, he doesn't want nothing going wrong with it, he won't give it over to other hands. Don't you want to know what is for lunch?"

"Never mind lunch." Whether it was the long pause or this garrulous outburst — always a sign of disturbed feelings in Battistella — or the sudden change of subject, Ziani could not have said, but something here struck him as odd. This zeal of the printer came too close to what he wanted to believe; his appetite for flattery could not take such a gulp.

However, as he struggled with this, his agitated heart still not subsiding, Battistella began once more to speak about lunch and in particular a white sauce he had made.

"White sauce, white sauce?" Ziani said sharply, distracted by greed from his anxieties. "And what is it made of, this white sauce?"

"It is made of sugar and sour sherry." Battistella paused a long moment. "And cinnamon," he added slowly. "And cloves. And oil of almonds."

This soothed Ziani; his heart settled. Puzzlement remained, however, long after Battistella had been dismissed, there in the background of his mind as he resumed the story of Francesca and old Boccadoro and the Madonna. His narrative was going more smoothly now that the awful night of the Madonna's coronation had been dealt with; unwillingness to arrive at this had held him back, as he now believed, imposed those loops and meanders on his style.

He paused to gather his thoughts and concentrate his forces. White sauce and printer's fever alike receded. With calm and measured movements, he took up his pen, dipped it in the ink, and began to write.

My man Battistella and Francesca's Maria between them distracted booby Bobbino, the watchdog Boccadoro had left behind, one plying him with wine while the other smiled on him — he was asleep and snoring long before Francesca and I returned. After our success at the tables we were able to bribe him to keep silent. He had no real loyalty to his master, merely a jealous sense of his own position in the household. Reassured on this score, encouraged in his lecherous hopes by Maria's brilliant glances, bribed lavishly by us from our winnings, Bobbino ceased altogether to be a problem; in fact he was an asset to us, because Boccadoro, quite the poorest judge of human nature I have ever known, trusted him completely.

I must deal at this point with the comedy of his return from Verona. That same day, in the evening, he spoke to me. We were like characters in a play, acting a scene that was small but crucial to the plot, he red-faced after dinner, unbuttoned, his blunt head freed from the hot confinement of his wig, Pantalone complete; I the studious secretary at the desk, taking letters to his uncouth dictation. Suddenly he breaks off, looks over his spectacles at me, and says:

"Your medicine is working."

"Sir?"

"Donna Francesca declares herself impressed."

"I am glad to hear that, believe me."

"She had thought you a hypocrite and a time-server."

"Had she so? That serves to show the danger of hasty conclusions."

"Indeed yes. Now she has come to admire your mind, though I must tell you that she does not find you physically prepossessing. I say this not to wound you but so that you should understand her feelings. Still, that only increases your moral authority. My dear fellow, you have worked wonders already. She has come to me today and she has said that she no longer considers it important to have her own apartment in town. That is a step in the right direction, to say nothing of the savings. I congratulate you."

"It is nothing. She is disposed to virtue and needs only to be counseled well."

Pantalone scratches his bald pate with his thumb and pauses in momentary hesitation. "Use your influence," he says. "Follow this up."

He pauses again. His little reddish eyes glance here and there like those of a haunted ferret. I see now that the moment has come for some further avowal. He is an innocent in matters of feeling, as I have said before, having spent his life amassing money; his nature is trusting, outside the world of finance. But he is a passionate man, with violence in his nature, and strong, though old — I am surprised he has not tried to force her, but such is the case.

After a moment he says, "I have every confidence in you."

"I shall study to deserve it." The raised head, the steadfast gaze.

"Try to bring her closer to a sense of wifely duty. That is where you must aim."

I know where to aim; I have hit the target already, dead center; and it is not her duty, unless that is the name for what lies between her legs. But of course it is, for this Pantalone at least; it precisely does lie there. He is appealing to me. The moment has come.

"I have hesitated to speak of this," I say, "out of my delicacy, and respect for you. Believe me, I understand your situation, which is in no way your fault but springs from the perversity of this age, which brings discord and division even to the marriage bed. You need speak no further of it. Be assured that I have understood."

He is listening to me with all his soul, his eyes at last stayed from their roaming, fixed in wonder at my powers of divination.

"However," I continue, "there is one thing I will venture to say, one piece of advice I will presume to offer. Donna Francesca is beginning to see her error, as is proved by her retraction in the matter of the apartment. As you say, I have obtained a certain influence. The process is beginning. But it will be slow. An injudicious move on your part could ruin all. If she seems softer, less reluctant, in the days to come, you must still hold her off."

"Hold her off!" he cries. "Good God!"

"Absolutely essential. Call upon your reserves of fortitude. Maintain a distance. Leave her to her own devices. Above all, do not under any circumstances go to her room. Let her doubt her place in your heart. Believe me, this will be salutary. In the end she will come to you with gratitude and complete submission, she will do anything you ask."

His eyes are shining at this prospect. "A man must have dignity," he says. *"Ci vuole dignità."*

"Exactly. Women wish to submit in their deeper natures, but because of the corruption they derive from our first mother they must always seek first to turn us to their purposes. If they achieve it, they then despise us. That is the paradox of it."

"Strange creatures," he says. He has fallen again to scratching at his pate. "How can we know what ideas they will get in their heads?"

"How indeed? One thing there is to bear in mind and you have said it. *Ci vuole dignità.*"

"Dignity," he says. "By God, yes. Why should we be their playthings?"

"There is one thing more that works for us. More important than any."

"And what is that?" he says.

I pause for effect. I have been saving this ever since I came upon the book, waiting for the moment. I am about to enlist the Virgin's aid.

"You do not know what we have in the garden," I say at last. "That statue in the rose arbor, you thought perhaps it represented one of the Virtues of some spirit of the seasons?"

"Something of the sort," he says, staring.

"Well, she is the Madonna."

He gapes at me, grotesque in his surprise. The flush of digestion has faded now and the rouge shows against his sallow skin — he has taken to paint since his marriage.

And so I told him of my discovery. As I have said, the library where I spent most of my days has been greatly neglected. Books had accumulated during the period when the Longhi family owned the house, but for a long time now there had been no attempt to classify them or even to record what was there; they lay everywhere, on the shelves, on tables, in piles along the walls. Mildew had affected many, mice droppings lay among them; in some cases mice had nibbled at the edges of the paper. Now in my work of examining these books and making an index I had come across a manuscript volume, dated 1612, written by one Guilliamo Longhi, a history of his family from their earliest beginnings.

It was not a very distinguished story. The Longhi are an old family but they have not often risen to positions of power in the state. They made the mistake of involving themselves in the Tiepolo conspiracy of 1310 and had their palaces impounded as a punishment. They were readmitted into the nobility a century or so later, for services in the wars against Genoa, but never fully recovered their former position. However, they produced artists and men of letters and antiquarians — like this Guilliamo.

These facts were in the book, suitably dressed up, embedded in a mass of legend and hearsay and boasting. But what was of most interest to me was the Madonna anecdote, and it was this that I related to old Boccadoro: how she had been made for the church of the Santissima Annunziata by a sculptor Guilliamo does not name — perhaps not deigning, perhaps not knowing; how she had been sold to the Longhi, together with the cloister she stood in, when the family bought the land for their garden.

Guilliamo was writing within a century of this and he had relied on stories and old scandals. He says the friars did not want to put the Madonna on the façade of their church because in the same summer she was made the sculptor was involved in the murder of a town whore. Guilliamo asserts that he created amazement by proclaiming that light shone from him, from his face and limbs; and this others claimed to see too, and some even knelt as if witnessing a miracle, so great is the power of suggestion on simple minds.

All these are old tales that Guilliamo picked up here and there; but one thing there was that struck me: the Fornarini were involved in this affair too — the same family as this Piero, Francesca's uncle, who now has charge of our souls, God help us. At that time, and for a century after, they were one of the first families of Venice and wielded great power. According to Guilliamo, a certain Federico Fornarini, a member of the Consiglio dei Dieci, prosecuted the case himself, brought witnesses and so on. Why one so highly placed should have exerted himself Guilliamo does not know but piously commends such civic virtue. Ours is a more cynical age and for my own part I think it more likely that this Federico wished to conceal his own evil life by appearing as a guardian of morality, since a man's zeal in the exercise of public virtue is usually proportionate to the eagerness with which he pursues private vice. What the outcome was, Guilliamo does not say. Then in less than a century these Supplicanti were expelled — for notorious debauchery, as Guilliamo puts it, and unnatural practices.

It was little of this, however, that I told to Boccadoro, stressing instead the beneficent image of the Virgin, here in our midst, conferring grace.

"With the Blessed Madonna here," I said, "how can things go otherwise than favorably for us? If we add to my efforts on your behalf the invisible but potent effects of the Holy Virgin, protector of female purity, emblem of chastity, guardian of the sanctity of Christian marriage, we simply cannot fail. Follow my advice; curb your impatience, keep your distance a while longer. Above all, keep away from her bedroom.

Ziani paused, savoring the moment. How cleverly and eloquently he had spoken! What a triumphant occasion! He had seen his success written on Boccadoro's face — the old simpleton had swallowed everything whole.

For years afterward he had kept Longhi's book about him as a souvenir, through all travels and vicissitudes, only to have it stolen finally, along with the other contents of a traveling-box, in an inn in France, while he was busy with the chambermaid.

He took some snuff, then gave a prolonged ring with his handbell. These days, in spite of Battistella's unreliable responses, Ziani needed him increasingly as sharer in the climactic moments. When the *Mémoires* reached the world, he would have admirers in plenty, but just now — and with these delays at the printers . . .

This last thought darkened his mood. Moreover, his right leg was painful this morning, with frequent shooting pains, and his heart was agitated. He tried to retain the sense of triumph, but he could recollect nothing but Boccadoro's face and his own coldly attentive self, watching for signs of weakness, marks of pain. There was no comfort in this for him now. He rang again for Battistella, with mechanical imprecations at his servant's delay. He sat waiting, muttering to himself, among the faintly stirring draperies in that museum of sheeted exhibits. The tide was low — smells of slime and excrement wafted through the half-open window like a reek of the evil latent in matter. The horror of vacancy came to Ziani. He sought in the ashes of the past for something living still. After some moments of total immobility, he remembered a time shortly after this talk with Boccadoro when he and Francesca had contrived to visit the theater together. They had returned via San Marco. There had been some special occasion, he could not remember what — the *piazza* was brilliantly illuminated. All round the walls there were lamps, on the old and new Procuratie, set very close together so that they merged: the fronts of the buildings were clothed in sheets of light. The arcades were hung with tiny lamps; every curve and volute was defined by them, myriads of lamps, their flames wavering in the breath of the *scirocco.* White doves shot in alarm through these zones of light. For the sake of contrast, the *piazzetta* had been left dark; when the lights of the square became too dazzling, you could saunter there at the water's edge. That is what he and Francesca had done; they had stood together on the *piazzetta* with that great blaze of light on one side and on the other the dark water of the sleeping Lagoon.

There, where we stood together, Ziani thought, it was neither light nor dark. He thought of this with wonder. It seemed to him that if he could choose now he would stand forever in the full blaze of the square, bathe and bathe in the light and never leave it . . .

He could not bring himself to resume work that day. His disabilities, that *horror vacui* which had come to him, clouded his mind. He sat sick and disconsolate. After supper he played moody games of checkers with Battistella — games that grew moodier as he lost.

Next morning, however, it was better. Memories came fresh and strong to him. He wrote about his lovemaking with Francesca and how they had seen old Boccadoro kneeling in prayer before the Madonna. He was coming now to the climax of the story, and the sense of this made him write eagerly.

Francesca herself was totally shameless, reckless too. Her bedroom was just down the corridor from his, and so it was necessary to be careful, but she took no care at all. We contrived meetings all over the house, but the library was the main place. She would lie down on the floor fully dressed. Sometimes in order to excite me she would feign reluctance, resisting my attempt to undress her or open her legs. I would raise her skirt, underskirt, petticoats, uncover her patch of pelt — her pubic hair was fairer than the hair on her head, an unusual thing.

The throes she was capable of were amazing. She would be crying out as soon as I was inside her. She would pant and moan and cry out so that I thought the house would be on us. She didn't care. Even in her bedroom, not a dozen yards away from his . . .

Ziani stopped to consider. It was as though Francesca had wanted to be caught. There had been a dangerous, desperate quality in her abandonment. His mind strained across the interval of years to that charmed succession of days — ten days were all they had had. Yes, such recklessness was unnatural. She had kissed and caressed him on occasions when Boccadoro was present, when by turning his head the old man might have seen. Once she had done something worse. And yet, he thought, she did not seem really to know me or recognize me. There had been something impersonal in it. That heedless bright look on her face. Creature of light. Dangerous, destructive. He would have been content to let the intrigue run a course more placidly sensual, more discreet. It was a good joke, after all; the sense of having duped Boccadoro added to his pleasure. Francesca's cries and spasms flattered him. There was sport here for some time to come. But she had shown no sense of self-preservation, none at all. She had not behaved as if there would be other days, other lovers. Yet he had not felt she loved him . . .

In perplexity he rang for Battistella, ostensibly to ask for some coffee, in reality to sound out his servant's opinion about this abandonment of Francesca's. Misgivings accumulated while he sat waiting. The nightmarish suspicion returned to him: Would anyone have served Francesca's purposes, anyone with a prick that could stand to attention? Certainly she had loved to play with his, to fondle and caress it, observing it closely, like a new pet or a toy. Yes, that was it. That length of gristle which had been his pride, with its autonomous erections, its chastened dwindlings, sudden rearing recoveries, this marvelous mechanism had been no more than a toy to her. Useless now to anybody.

When Battistella appeared, he assumed as usual his expression of weary superiority. "I have been writing," he said, "about that period after old Boccadoro came back from his visit to Verona." He reached for his snuffbox. "By God," he said, "she was dying for it, she couldn't get enough."

He paused, remembering her dangerously exalted face, raised to laugh. She would do anything. Battistella had not replied and Ziani had an impression of extra stillness in him, as if he were waiting for something more. "She was possessed," he said. "Do you remember that time I told you about, when we came upon the old man praying to the Madonna? She made me do it there and then, while he was still at his prayers. I didn't want to, you know. We could hear him while we were doing it, begging the Madonna to make his wife love him. Francesca enjoyed that. She was cruel, you know. I'm coming on to that bit next, as a matter of fact."

"She didn't enjoy it," Battistella said suddenly. "Not what you'd call enjoy."

"What do you know about it?" Ziani said, staring. "Was it you that was having her or was it I?"

"Begging your pardon, she was sold to him. She blamed him for buying as much as she blamed them for selling — more, him being old and distasteful on top of it."

"I don't follow that reasoning," Ziani said, perturbed by this sudden loquacity.

"She blamed him more."

"Because he had married her?"

"Not only that. She blamed him for what she was doing with you. The more bad things she done, the more it was his fault. There are natures that carry things to extremes."

"There certainly are," Ziani said. "And yours is one of them. I've never heard such rubbish."

"The cruelty," Battistella said, quite undeterred, "the cruelty was because she was outraging herself, begging your pardon. Also, she wanted to show she was a human being, not a piece of merchandise. How can you show you are a human being and not a piece of merchandise?"

"I've no idea," Ziani said. "No doubt you will tell me."

"By embarking upon actions." Battistella paused, nodding slowly. "That was what she done with you," he said.

Ziani maintained an uneasy silence for some moments. Then, with sudden spirit, he said, "You are wrong, Battistella. Francesca liked being fucked, she enjoyed it, nothing to do with merchandise. She enjoyed the risk of being caught too, it excited her. And she was cruel too, nothing to do with outraging herself. Why do you try to explain everything in terms of something else? It is a very dangerous practice, especially in regard to women. If we go on like that, the time will come when women will not be held accountable for their vices at all. Then where will we be? Would you want to live in such a world?"

Ziani reached again for his snuffbox. Good humor had returned to him. He had come out on top in this argument, he felt. "It would be the end of civilization as we know it," he said. "I really did not think that at your advanced years you would fall into that intellectual trap, Battistella."

Battistella made no reply, had begun in fact his usual snail-like withdrawal.

"Do you remember that man in Paris who shot off his own *uccello* by accident?" Ziani said. "That was ten years later. That will come in the Paris section of my *Mémoires.* A practiced duelist too — he had killed six. I don't recall what the quarrel was about; an affair of honor no doubt."

"You were cheating at *faro.* He caught you dealing with a mirror in your lap."

"Walking toward me, coming up to the barrier, he fired his pistol somehow by mistake and shot off his own cock. You would say that meant something else — for example that he hated himself for having already taken six human lives, but I would say simply that he shot off his cock."

Battistella, arrested in his creeping retreat, remained obstinately silent.

"A young man," Ziani said. "Not more than thirty. He may be alive still. Forty years ago it happened. That would be forty years *senza uccello.* A strange fate for a man. Well, don't speak, damn you. You can't bear to be worsted in argument, can you?"

"Will there be anything else, sir?"

"No." Ziani strove to preserve a dispassionate appearance. "No, you can clear off. I have to get on with my *Mémoires.* We have discussed what there is for dinner, have we not?" he added rather wistfully — he would have liked to run through it again. But Battistella had gone or at least was no longer distinguishable among the billowing forms.

Left alone, Ziani thought for some minutes, focusing his memories. Then he began to write.

For some days after Boccadoro's return we led a charmed life, Francesca and I. We took risks but it seemed that the gods aided us. The old man must have listened to me, for he kept away from her room, though I never dared spend the whole night with her, usually leaving well before morning.

We had some narrow escapes. I remember that Signor Malpigli, her singing master, once nearly surprised us together in the garden — we still, out of gratitude, sometimes made love in the arbor of the Madonna. But the nearest thing was when the priest, Don Antonio, came on one of his visits. He used to come regularly to discuss the affairs of an orphanage Francesca took some interest in and — more to the point — contributed charity to, though of course it was all Boccadoro's money. This priest was a stout florid fellow greatly in love with his own opinions, with a pompous habit of rocking back on his heels.

On this occasion we had forgotten he was coming. It was midafternoon, with Boccadoro gone off to his warehouse on the Zattere al Ponte Lungo. Francesca and I were downstairs in her apartment with the door locked, half naked both, grappling together on the Turkey carpet, and she was just beginning to prick me with her claws — she had a delicate way with her nails when excited — when I heard a tapping at the door and it was Battistella come to tell us that Don Antonio was waiting in the anteroom.

Now there was no way out of the salon save by this anteroom and I was afraid that if we kept him kicking his heels there and then he saw me emerge, he might, out of pique, or duty, or a confusion of the two, find the matter of sufficient interest to mention to old Boccadoro. So I dressed with what speed I could and I snatched up some sheets of music and rolled them together in such a way that they might seem like documents and so I made haste out of the room.

There was a short passage, another door, then the small room where he waited. He rose to his feet when he saw me and with a bare greeting began to move toward the door. "One moment, padre," I said. I had to give Francesca time to dress and compose herself, to overlay with attar of roses that odor of sanctity which lovemaking bestows on the person, to allow the flush of our encounter to subside from her face.

It was now that I showed my superlative presence of mind. I knew that this Don Antonio was opinionated and fond of talking *dall'alto in basso,* and so I decided on the instant how to snare him. "One moment, padre," I said. "Donna Francesca and I have encountered a philosophical difficulty in the course of our conversation, and I would like to take this opportunity of referring the matter to your learned wisdom."

"Yes," he said, "what is it? I would not keep the *nobil donna* waiting."

"She will not mind," I said. "She would explain the difficulty herself, but asked me to do it. Ladies, as we know, are not at their best when dealing with abstract notions."

"That is true," he said. "What is it then?"

At this moment, glancing down, I saw to my consternation that I had omitted to fasten properly the points of my breeches. While not gaping open exactly, I was in significant disarray, and he would only have to look that way to see it and come to his conclusions.

To button myself before his eyes was impossible. I lowered my hands and covered the place with the rolled-up music sheets and held them there while we spoke. "Well," I said, "I take it you hold that the universe has a plan?"

"Certainly," he said. "Nature is God's own codex. This mighty maze of things cannot lack a plan, indeed it must have the best of all possible plans."

"Just so," I said, keeping the music in place — never did the vapid airs of Baldovino serve to better purpose. "Now I daresay you would call yours an optimistic view?"

"Certainly I would."

"Now here is the point, Don Antonio," I said. "One can have optimism as a result of mystical insight, at that level at which Spinoza could declare that *omnis existia est perfectio.* If we could see existence as perfect, we could achieve a miracle; we could cancel the gulf between the absolute and the fallen world. Do you see this as a possibility for human beings?"

"No," he said, rocking back on his heels in his self-important way. "By definition it is not possible for the creature to cancel distinctions between God and His creation."

"So then," I said, "either your optimism is simply contentment with the existing order of things, or you have an explanation why God, the

Perfect Being, generated this imperfect world of corruptibles, at the same time making it impossible for us to adopt the beautiful view of Spinoza."

He was looking less complacent now, perceiving the pit I had dug. I smiled upon him. "I think I have you there, padre," I said. "Yes, I think I have you there."

"Not at all," he said. "By no means. Aquinas has explained this matter. God's love did not permit Him to remain self-absorbed, without production of the creatures. Since the seeds of all things were latent in His mind, how could He deny them germination?"

"So," I said, "if I understand you aright, Don Antonio, God expresses His love for us by generating existences that not only in His sight but even in the sight of man must seem imperfect or evil. Is not this strange?"

"Not to me," he said. "I do not see your difficulty. The world had to be peopled. God shows His goodness through the number and variety of the phenomena. There is one great scale or ladder of creation and it is continuous from worm to seraph."

"Not see the difficulty?" I said. I decided to make an end of this charade. It had become tedious to stand there, obliged all the time ot keep myself covered. Francesca would by now have reconstituted herself. Besides, his complacency disgusted me; at least I can feel sorrow for the world. "Not see the difficulty? Don Antonio, you surprise me. This optimism of yours is not a hopeful matter at all. You deny our ability to see perfection in created things. You maintain nonetheless that God's goodness consists in cramming the universe with them. And where is man in all this? A creature clinging to a ladder between animals and angels, only there at all because of the requirements of plenitude. Then God loves abundance and variety better than He loves happiness or progress? This is not optimism, it is an apologia for the existing state of things, a recipe for inertia. No wonder we are ripe for revolution. It will come, Don Antonio, never fear, and it will sweep you away with it, cassock and all."

And so I left him spluttering there and made good my escape. Being discomfited already by my clear superiority in debate, he did not broach the subject with Donna Francesca, and so she did not know till later how I had contrived to delay him.

Ziani laid down his pen and wiped his eyes with triumphant self-congratulation. It had been a superlative performance on his part. I routed that porcine padre completely, he thought. What poise, what address, what presence of mind! Handicapped as I was, obliged to shield my open fly, denied all freedom of gesture with which to emphasize my remarks.

When, a little later, Battistella came in with his dinner, Ziani tried to recall the episode for him, but his servant seemed to remember nothing of it.

"Your powers are failing," Ziani said, tucking in his napkin at the neck. "You are not the man you were, Battistella." His tone was peevish; he had been hoping for some endorsement of his triumph. "In those days we were all optimists," he said, pursing thin lips to suck the hot soup from his spoon. "We believed that nature and reason went hand in hand. Now I know that is untrue. Now it is reason alone I believe in. I have embraced the Jacobin philosophy, Battistella. I repudiate the notion of human nature. I repudiate it utterly."

In the vehemence of this statement, his hand shook and soup ran over his chin. More quietly, he said, "The rules of reason and justice are applicable at all times and in all places. Man comes into the world with nothing but his own percipience; he is a blank sheet."

He had the impression that Battistella was now farther away, less distinguishable among the shrouded forms of the apartment. "Anything can be inscribed on that *tabula rasa,*" he said. "I have finished my soup. Where is the game pie?"

"Nature is nature," Battistella said as he came forward. "History is history, begging your pardon. They can talk about Jacobins. Is it reason and justice that is occurring in France, or is it barbarities? Your head would be off, sir, you would be a *tabula rasa,* begging your pardon. I will leave you to finish."

He had commenced his usual snail-like retreat. "We may come into the world with nothing," Ziani heard him say from somewhere near the door. "In France you go out of it short of a head. All the inscription goes into the basket."

"That is illogical, Battistella," Ziani said, peering across the apartment. He realized after a moment that his servant had gone, but he was not put out by this, replete as he was, still buoyed by his consummate handling of Don Antonio. That night, which was his last, he slept well.

Next morning he was at work early. He was eager to finish the affair of the Madonna and move on to the Naples section of his *Mémoires*. In fact, there was little left to tell. Barely waiting to finish his chocolate, he dipped pen in ink and began.

We managed on several occasions, with the help of the servants, to go into town for the evening. We went to the San Benedetto Theater and took a box at the top row and heard half of Gluck's *Ipermestra,* which was all the rage those days; the other half we missed, having grown excited by the music — we locked the door and drew the curtains and made love on the floor. We also went to hear La Zabaletta at the Incurabili and afterward to the Ridotto, where we gambled and lost.

Most enjoyable was the night we went to the Giudecca festival. The gardens of the island could not contain everyone, so they moored rafts out in the canal with banks of flowers on them, where people could eat and drink and listen to the music. The streets were strewn with flowers and all the houses decked out with flags and garlands. We danced the *furlana* for hours on end. Francesca had on a sleeveless red bodice and a white silk skirt. She danced with several men but came back to me. We had fritters and watched the clowns and the wrestlers. There was light in the sky when we got back.

That was not the night we came upon Boccadoro praying in the garden; then it was earlier, not much after midnight. We were returning from the Ridotto and had entered the garden by the canal gate. We saw his light and heard him muttering, alone there, kneeling at the feet of the Madonna.

I would have kept away, skirted the garden, repaired immediately to the house. It was she who wanted to go nearer, to hear what he was saying, so I was obliged to go too. Hand in hand we crept forward. I was afraid of making some false step in the darkness, disturbing him. But he was quite intent. He was saying Ave Marias to her.

He had set a lantern down beside him, at the base of the statue. Its rays lit up the side of his face nearer to us, some of his black velvet robe, the outstretched arm of the Madonna, the folds of her skirt. A paler light was cast upward, onto her bosom and her dreaming face. The old man's eyes were lowered and his lips moved reverently: "Hail Mary, full of grace . . . blessed art thou among women . . ."

He came to the end of this one and I thought he would begin another; but there was a silence and then he began to pray on his own account and in more halting tones.

"Blessed Mary," we heard him say, "Virgin and Mother, please help me. Holy Virgin, turn my wife toward me . . ."

As soon as she heard this, Francesca began kissing me hastily and rubbing her hand down the front of my breeches. She was in a great hurry; she wanted to do it while he was praying. She went down on her back there and then among the bushes and pulled me down with her. I wasn't ready, and besides I felt some compunction and this constrained me, but she was determined; she wrapped her legs round me and squeezed me in somehow. Then I began to stiffen inside her and I felt excited. I put my mouth on Francesca's to prevent her from making a noise.

Boccadoro was praying still: "Holy Virgin, help me to win my wife's affections. I will honor you forever. Not only that, Blessed Madonna, I will vote a yearly sum of one hundred zecchini. I promise it. Make her love me and I will vote a sum of one hundred and twenty zecchini for the rest of my life . . ."

Francesca was terribly excited. I clasped her round the buttocks and raised her a little so as to penetrate deeply. My own pleasure was mounting. All the same, even then, I could not help thinking how typical it was of old Boccadoro to bargain with the Madonna.

"Make her love me," we heard him say again, and then we came together and I kept my mouth on hers to stifle the sounds. We lay there while he said some more Hail Marys. Then he took himself slowly off with his lantern.

He could have taken it into his head that same night to go to her room; he would have found her bed empty and known something was wrong. It was only a question of time before some such thing happened. We were set on a course that could end only in disaster. Though apprehensive, I must admit that I viewed this prospect with relief: my eyes were beginning to sink into my head rather; Francesca was insatiable.

In fact our luck ran out three nights later. As usual I had given him time to retire, seen his light extinguished, waited until I thought he would be sleeping, then made my way to Francesca's room, which as I have said was not far from his.

The time was around midnight. She was waiting for me eagerly. We embraced and kissed. It was hot and in our ardor we cast aside the sheets. We were naked. I turned Francesca over. Coquettishly she pressed her body against the mattress while I stroked her beautiful arse and persuaded the portals to part. She soon grew impatient for my prick and raised herself, enabling me to enter. We were in this position, possibly of all positions the most blatant, in the middle of the bed, without covering or concealment, when the door suddenly opened, Boccadoro's voice said, "Are you awake, my love?" and the next moment his face, surmounted by a nightcap, illuminated by the lantern he was holding up, came peering round the door.

What had driven him — loneliness, suspicion, desperation — I do not know. Perhaps he was hoping his prayers had taken effect. He stood there for perhaps ten seconds, gaping at us slack-jawed, the light ghastly on his features. Then he let out a roar of terrifying volume and rushed toward the bed. Francesca sprang out on one side, I on the other. But it was I who was his object. He came rapidly round the bed, shouting like a man possessed. He seized me by the throat but the lantern impeded him and I struggled free. He was coming at me again. I saw Battistella in his nightshirt halfway into the room and Maria at the door. Francesca had put on her nightgown but I was naked still, having had no time. Boccadoro swung the lantern as if he would strike me with it. He had the face of one demented — congested and staring in the swinging light. Then an idea seemed to strike him. He shouted that he would kill me — his first coherent words — and rushed out of the room.

I could not see my nightshirt so I wrapped a sheet around me and made for the door. My first idea was to get back to my room but I met Battistella in the passage and he told me that Boccadoro was coming back with a sword he had taken from its place on the wall on the first landing. I could hear him shouting still. Francesca came out into the passage at this moment and together we ran down the back stairs and out into the garden.

There was a strange light out here, a sort of luminescence, though there was no moon. Even in my concern to escape Boccadoro's sword I noticed it. It was one of those summer nights that never get really dark. The Madonna was clearly visible in her arbor, glimmering there with this strange light upon her, a radiance that seemed to come from nowhere.

Boccadoro was in the garden now, sword in one hand, lantern in the other, calling on me to show myself. This I declined to do. The whole household was out here. Our white nightclothes were conspicuous, but it was hard to tell who was wearing them, a fortunate circumstance for me, I think, as Boccadoro pursued now one, now another, tiring himself, while I kept down behind a hedge. He was threatening death still, but there was a tearful quality in his rage.

Various neighbors, roused by Boccadoro's shouts, had joined us, also in states of undress; and a boatload of people, out late on the canal, had come in to see what was happening. The garden was suddenly full of forms and shadows and shifting lamplight, with this strange pallid radiance hanging over all.

"Come out, you coward!" Boccadoro shouted. His voice was hoarse.

"Have you thieves here?" somebody asked, and it was this that gave me my idea, and the strange luminous quality of the summer night that made her seem to shine with her own radiance and perhaps too my memories of other light on her, moonlight, lantern light, and the way she seemed always to attend, to be intensely present, though no doubt this was the genius of her maker. Besides, he was after my blood and this sharpens invention, as is well known. Then I thought of that wretched carver and how some had believed they saw light shining from him.

I stepped out into the lantern light, only the bedsheet to cover my nakedness. Boccadoro raised his sword and began to make a rush. "Stop!" I shouted. "I am not a thief. I am your secretary, Ziani!" I pointed at the Madonna. "We are witnessing a miracle," I said.

It was sufficient to stop him. They crowded round full of questions. "Can you not see it?" I said. "That heavenly light she is clothed in? It is a little dimmer now. Before, when I saw her from my window, she was radiant, there was a bright halo of light round her head."

"I saw her too," Francesca said. "She was gleaming with unearthly radiance. I could not sleep, that is how I came to see her. I was intended to see her — else why could I not sleep? I usually sleep well enough." She looked at her husband. "Don't I, *caro?*" she said.

"Yes," Boccadoro said. "Yes." He was panting from his exertions.

"My mistress rang for me," Maria said. "I went to her room and then I saw it too. A light on her such as you never saw in your life before."

"I heard the shouts," Battistella said. "I came out and saw her. She was shining like a thousand candles."

Booby Bobbino helped me more than anyone: in common with most brutish persons, he was highly suggestible. "I see it," he burst out suddenly, and he fell to crossing himself and mumbling prayers.

Boccadoro hesitated a long moment, the sword held down by his side. He had had time to think. There was a crowd of witnesses. Should they witness a miracle, or should they witness his horns?

"I thought it was thieves," he said at last. "Then I saw the Madonna shining."

"Put out your lamps," I said. "You will see her better."

They did so. It is true she was shining; there was a glow on the stone like very pale fire, like the edge of flame where it whitens into air. Trick of the light, effect of the pale stone of which she was made — fortunate for me, in any case.

We looked at her, the raised head, faint dreaming smile, the half-unwilling turn of the body. There was a scent of roses. Bobbino's mutterings continued somewhere behind me. On an inspired impulse, I sank to my knees. One by one they followed suit — every single person there in the garden, Boccadoro included. It was a triumph: in forestalling the vengeance of that *cornuto,* I had saved my skin and created a miracle at the same time.

It was a miracle that became official. Francesca's uncle on her mother's side was Piero Fornarini, Bishop of Venice at that time, a man of extravagant habits. Partly no doubt for the sake of protecting the family name, but more for the sake of Boccadoro's money, he agreed that the event should be accepted as miraculous. That is how the Madonna came to be sanctified; that is how she came to be installed on the façade of the Carità.

With feelings of triumphant self-satisfaction, Ziani picked up his handbell and gave it a prolonged ring. He was coming to the end of this episode now; not long afterward he and Battistella had left for Naples. A couple of paragraphs remained to be done; in these he would enlarge a little on his own ingenuity and resource.

"I have nearly finished," he said when Battistella appeared. "Tomorrow I hope to make a start on that Naples business. All the same, it has a beautiful symmetry, this affair. Perhaps you don't know the meaning of that word?"

Battistella made no reply, merely stood staring, breathing heavily.

"Think of it," Ziani said. "The Fornarini family, for reasons of their own, prosecute the sculptor and cause the Madonna to be suppressed; three hundred years later a Fornarini sanctifies and elevates her. The friars who reject her because of the sculptor's unsavory life are themselves expelled in an odor even worse. The archdupe Boccadoro, to conceal his horns, erects a monument to cuckoldry that will last for centuries. The Madonna, symbol of all that is chaste and virtuous in women, is rescued from obscurity for her services to adultery."

Ziani chuckled with delight and reached for his snuffbox. As was usual in moments of triumph or glee, he took too much and his eyes smarted and watered. "Only I," he said, fumbling for his handkerchief, "Sigismondo Ziani, stand outside this pattern. And do you know why, Battistella?"

Battistella, who was standing near him, seemed about to reply. At that moment they heard the heavy brass knocker of the street door sound loudly four times. It was a sound extremely rare these days. Battistella moved to the window, opened it, and craned down at the street. This brought his ancient smell close and also his wizened, dark-eyed face. Ziani had not seen his servant's face at such close range for a very long time. He now saw it change in a way that was quite inexplicable.

"It is the lady and a blackamoor with her, they are coming in," Battistella said. All at once he was wheezing again. He began to move as fast as he was able across the room toward the door, but before he could reach it they heard sounds below, a woman's voice on the stair. A moment later the door was thrown open, and an old lady, in a black satin dress and an elaborately curled wig, came stepping briskly into the room, followed by a tall Negro footman in silver and blue, the livery of the Bembo family.

She stood before them, holding in one gloved hand a silver cane, in the other a sheaf of written papers. "Retrieve these wretched scribblings, Jacopo," she said, pointing with the cane.

Ziani sat gasping, open-mouthed, while the Negro stepped to his table, swept up the papers there, and handed them respectfully to his mistress, who put them with the rest.

"Do you not know me?" she said. Her face was heavily powdered and rouged; age had thinned her mouth to a crooked line; but there was beauty still in the eyes and brows.

Ziani's heart stirred violently. He slipped a hand inside his robe to restrain it. Breath came from him in short gasps. "Those are my papers," he said with difficulty.

She raised them. "Here," she said, "we have that section of your ill-written *Mémoires* purporting to deal with my early life and my first husband. I could have destroyed these sheets piecemeal as your man brought them to me, but I choose to have it done before your eyes. Watch carefully, Sigismondo."

While Battistella cowered back against the window, and Ziani sat helpless and aghast in his chair, she handed the sheets one by one, gingerly, between finger and thumb, to the tall attentive Negro, who with pleased smile and downcast eyes methodically tore them into minute pieces and scattered them about the floor.

When all were destroyed, she nodded briskly once. "So," she said, "I have dealt with you as you deserve. You were always a self-regarding fool, Sigismondo. I knew it from the first, from the first time we stood together, there at the well-head with the carved lions."

Ziani was dumbstruck. He saw her raise her head, saw or thought he saw, in this face that was so changed, the same look of exaltation, that dangerous and destructive light it had worn half a century before when they were deceiving Boccadoro together.

"Yes," she said, "with your talk of the *commedia*, your vain air of having understood me, I knew what shape you were making me into, I could see it on your face. As I was their victim, so you were encouraged to think you could make me yours. I knew it but I needed someone. Besides, you did not succeed. I was always more than you thought me. All that is past. Now, after fifty years, you want this false shape revived, this product of your shallow brain and debased imagination, you want me installed in public view, a monument to your exploits, also largely imaginary — you were never much good, Sigismondo, were you? Did you really think I would leave my nature and my likeness in such care as yours? Would I consent to have my portrait made by an ape? You must be mad indeed to think it. Did you forget my mother's name?"

She fell silent and in the pause that followed a snatch of song in a man's voice came up to them from the waterside below: *"Venetia, Venetia, chi non ti vede non ti pretia."* Then she nodded again, this time to Jacopo, who moved instantly to open the door for her.

At the threshold she turned. "You won't rewrite those pages," she said. "You are too old. Don't blame your servant. His devotion is the only good thing in your miserable life."

In silence they heard the steps retreat down the stairs. Ziani fell back against his chair.

"You betrayed me," he said.

All trace of color had gone from Battistella's face. "May I sit?" he said. "How could I know she would come here?"

Ziani pressed his hands together in an attempt to stop their trembling. "You never took the sheets to the printers," he said slowly. "That was all lies. You gave them to her."

"I sold them, begging your pardon. We had no money."

"Sold them?" Ziani gave him a palsied stare. "All of them?"

"Not only to her. Various parties concerned was ready enough to buy them."

"Do you mean to say that you have been going around Venice selling parts of my *Mémoires* to different people?"

"They wanted to avoid the scandals."

"And the rest? The sheets you couldn't sell?"

"I have them below stairs."

"But the gaps," Ziani said. "How could I remember? I would have to rewrite everything." He knew he could not do it. "You have betrayed me," he said again. His whole head now was trembling. Battistella, he saw, was weeping — his cheeks were wet. "You have destroyed my hopes," he said.

"Where did you think the money was coming from?" Battistella said. "You never thought about it, begging your pardon. There was no more money. *Siamo su'n ponte.* The good puddings, the ravioli, the game pie, the sauces, where do you think they came from? You would have starved."

"But don't you see, Battistella?" Shock made Ziani speak gently. "Don't you see what you have done? You have turned me into a dupe. That woman will be laughing now, thinking of my face. I would rather have lived on *polenta*. I would rather have starved."

All strength now left him. His head fell back. "Please leave me," he managed to say. "Leave me to myself for a while."

They were the last words he spoke. He refused supper with a slight gesture of the head. When it began to get dark, Battistella brought in the candelabrum. He had lit all thirty candles as a special treat. But Ziani had slipped out of his chair onto the floor. The blaze was wasted on him.

RESTORATION THREE

◆

The Form Entire

I

Raikes worked steadily at the upper part of the Madonna's body, uncovering, centimeter by centimeter, the pale, untouched stone beneath the corroded surface. He had reached the clasp that held her cloak together at the neck; within a few days, if all went well, he would be repairing the ravages of her face. This, still blinded and blackened, seemed for the moment to repudiate the cleansed parts below.

The restored stone was clear, unblemished, without luster, revealed in this morning light as totally alien matter. However close the human likeness, it was impossible to forget the elemental substance of which the Madonna was made. Not like marble, Raikes thought: time brought a glow to marble, as the cuts softened and the salts accumulated, an appearance of warmth, something that might be taken for the transpirations of flesh. It was a marble body Pygmalion fell in love with. Perfect material for the Greeks, who wanted to bring men and gods closer. But stone of this dense impermeable sort was different; it belonged to the crust of the earth. Whatever shapes it assumed at the hands of man, it would always revert to kinship when the masquerade was over. The Madonna too. It was this that moved him, this temporary grace and beauty the savage stone had somehow been persuaded to bear.

From these thoughts he moved by a transition that seemed natural and inevitable to thoughts of Chiara Litsov, dwelling on her as patiently and lingeringly as the quartz cutter on the stone, remembering expressions on her face, things she had said, imagining the life of her body. There was, however, a difference: whereas the quartz cutter proceeded antlike, concentrating on one small patch at a time, Raikes's mind moved over Chiara in slow caressive sweeps, worshipful and sensual together.

Only discomfort brought him back from these thoughts to a sense of his present position, when some feeling of cramp or an aching muscle made him aware that he had been standing tensed for too long in the same place. Then he would straighten up, move away to the edge of the platform, and look out, sometimes over the little square below, sometimes across the roofs to the Lagoon.

He had to break off at eleven to keep his appointment with Dr. Vittorini; today he was to learn the results of his tests. These awaited him at the doctor's office, not the clinic, so he did not have so far to go. He arrived some minutes early but Vittorini saw him at once and after conventional greetings and some general remarks told him in his correct and careful English that he had an irregularity in the electrical impulses of his brain.

This had been said casually almost, following remarks about the frequency of fog in Venice just then and the high degree of moisture in the atmosphere, so that Raikes for some moments did not fully take it in. "What does that mean?" he said. He looked at Vittorini's composed face and felt the clutch of alarm. "Are you saying I've got brain damage of some kind?" he said.

"No, no," Vittorini said. "At least, not in the serious sense we usually attach to that phrase."

He glanced down briefly into the gleaming pool of his desktop. When he raised his head and spoke, it was as though to announce some curious fish glimpsed there.

"Nonetheless," he said, "we will have to suppose some lesion."

"Have to suppose?" Raikes stared at him. "Can't you see it?"

"It is not detectable on the x-rays, no."

"Then how on earth do you know it's there?"

"A kind of deduction." Vittorini smiled his charming smile. "We have also the charts from the EEG. They show a characteristic pattern of disturbance."

"Have you got them there? I'd like to see them."

Vittorini's smile diminished; it was clear that he would have preferred not to show them. Medical mystery again, Raikes thought. "It's my brain, after all," he said.

With the slight trace of a shrug, Vittorini looked among the papers on his desk, passed one to Raikes, who found himself looking at a series of wave bands, one below the other at intervals, the lower ones gently undulating, the upper three agitated and spiky.

"These waves register the electrical impulses of your brain," Vittorini said. "Their importance, of course, lies in the fact that such an abnormal record, obtained in the interval between attacks, establishes the diagnosis. Otherwise this might have been in doubt."

"The abnormal record being in this upper band, I suppose." Raikes traced with his finger the narrow, jagged crests. Behind his eyes and voice and senses this crazy agitation. It seemed incredible.

"You see the alternation of focal point and slow wave in the right temporal region," Vittorini said. "Highly characteristic."

"What is my condition then?"

"You have a neural discharge in the temporal lobe of your brain, Mr. Raikes, giving rise to very minor seizures. There is absolutely no need for alarm. The brain is not impaired; the seizures, as I say, are minor. The treatment is with drugs and presents no problems."

"Why now?" Raikes said. "I have never had anything of the sort before. Why now, at the age of thirty-three?"

"Who knows?" Vittorini sat back, spreading his beautiful hands. "Pathological change can take place in the temporal lobes at any time. Birth damage, a previous injury, some infinitesimal scar on the brain suddenly activated."

"But activated *how?*"

"Nobody can say, Mr. Raikes. The brain still presents many problems. As we grow older, things start to go a little wrong; only a little, but it is enough. I do not know, I am guessing, but some very slight loss of efficiency in the blood supply to the brain would have been sufficient to irritate this little scar of yours."

"This scar that no one can see."

Vittorini looked at him steadily for a moment. "Focal discharge," he said, "must always imply the presence of a localized lesion of the brain, even though the techniques available to us are not always adequate to demonstrate its nature."

"I see." Raikes compressed his lips with a sudden feeling of obstinacy. He had not liked this use of the word *must*. It sounded like a theological argument, reversed to prove the existence of matter. God's presence in the universe, the presence of this speck in his brain — the techniques available were inadequate to prove either. What had Vittorini to go on? A few marks on a sheet of paper. To argue from them to an invisible wound was like arguing from a flower to the Almighty.

As if sensing these reservations on his patient's part, Vittorini said, "I think I understand how you feel, Mr. Raikes. You are perhaps offended because I am insisting on a material cause for these experiences of yours when you see them as significant in some other way. Incidentally, have you had any more since?"

"No," Raikes said, "not since I last saw you."

"That too is surprising. The hallucinations are unusually complex and highly organized; also they have a kind of consistency about them, very interesting. But I have had a lot of patients through my hands. You would be surprised at the number of manifestations in cases of this type. They are legion, Mr. Raikes. Depending of course on the physiological functions subserved by the temporal lobes."

Their eyes met. Vittorini's were brown and shiny. "It is entirely a physiological matter," he said. "I would not like you to have ideas about it that might impede your treatment."

He paused as if inviting a denial, but Raikes remained silent. With something like a sigh, the doctor reached for the pad before him and began writing. "I generally prescribe phenobarbital as the basic anticonvulsant," he said, without looking up. "Thirty milligrams twice daily to begin with. It may tend to make you rather drowsy, though this varies with the constitution of the patient. In any case, I should like you to try it for one week. If it proves to be too much of a soporific, we can add an amphetamine to control it."

"And if the attacks recur? Do you increase the dosage of phenobarbital?"

"No, no. We do not want to have you sleeping all the time. No, we would supplement with another drug, Epanutin, for example, or Dilantin. That is a combination I have found successful. But I should like to see you again, a week from today, so that we can see how things are going."

"Very well," Raikes said.

A certain kind of obstinacy about his condition and a need to conduct himself with dignity had occupied his mind during the interview. When he was out again, however, in the bright street, and as he walked slowly back toward the Apostoli, an obscure distress grew within him. He had been dubbed ill; an anticonvulsant had been prescribed for him, as if he were subject to fits; his visions had been dismissed as the result of a malfunction. He felt lonely in the crowded street and somehow stricken.

Halfway down the Strada Nuova he found a pharmacy and obtained the phenobarbital. He had already made a resolution not to start taking the stuff until, as he put it to himself, he had thought things out. One great advantage of this policy, only half acknowledged, was that it might well require several days, making it therefore pointless to visit Vittorini again so soon.

He had turned off to his left toward the Grand Canal with the vague idea of sitting near the water, having a drink somewhere, recovering his morale. Almost at once he was brought up short. In the window of a small gallery, among an expensive-looking clutter of *objets trouvés* in wood and stone, ceramic birds, structures of wire and metal, he saw a Litsov bronze, a fragment of Chiara.

The gallery bore the name of the proprietor, Balbi, in gilt lettering above the door. Raikes remembered suddenly that Wiseman had mentioned Balbi's gallery as being one used by Lattimer. He entered and found a young woman at a desk. Of Balbi himself there was no sign. He asked the price of the Litsov. It amounted to more than five thousand pounds in English money. Wiseman had been right then. Still, the sum astonished him. He asked if there were others, and the young woman said no, this was the last. They had sold four Litsov bronzes in the last two months. They were in demand; this one would go soon. Signor Balbi was anxious to obtain more of the artist's work, but it was difficult to get hold of. In fact just now it was impossible; she did not know why exactly. Signor Balbi was complaining about it just the other day. It was not only in Italy that Litsov's work was highly regarded; he had great critical success everywhere; his prices were going up all the time. Now would be an excellent time to buy. It was an investment, one the *signore* would not regret.

Raikes explained that he was not rich enough to make investments. Exposed as a nonbuyer, he felt obliged to leave. Once again outside, he looked closely at the gleaming object in the window. It had a quality he remembered from the other pieces he had seen at Litsov's house, careful beauty of shape, an element of perversity in the mingling of forms.

It was while looking at this half-metamorphosed fragment of Chiara Litsov, feeling the distress induced by his visit to Vittorini subside at thoughts of her, that the notion came to Raikes that he had been guided to this place somehow; with this came the instant resolve to go and see her, at once, as soon as possible, without delay.

2

However, there was the work to be cleared up. Then it was time for lunch. It was early afternoon before he was able to set off for Chiara's house. By this time his mood had changed from excited anticipation to a sort of nervous fatalism; he felt he was embarking on a doubtful venture, bound to it in fact, though appointment there was none, dread of refusal having prevented him from phoning the Litsovs. Part of his nervousness was caused by the thought that he might not after all be welcome.

There was a corresponding change in the weather. Though brilliant in the earlier part of the day and during his visit to Vittorini, there had been a slow hazing of the sky in the interval. As he stood on the Fondamenta Nuova waiting for the Burano boat, mist was gathering already over the water, fluffing the sunshine.

He had no difficulty in finding a *sandolo* to take him from Burano.

The approach was as he remembered it, though the islands to the north and west were half obscured by the haze, their outlines glimpsed only occasionally. The tide was up, the flats were covered, the surface of the water like dull silver as the reflections were absorbed in the mist. Gulls flew high above; there was clear light in these upper reaches, and the birds' wings and breasts emitted flashes of brilliance as they turned in flight.

The Litsovs' boat was tied up alongside the landing stage.

The walk to the house was marked in stations of recognition. These sounds of slapping and creaking he had heard before while mounting the steps; this was where he had seen the lonely figure of Chiara in her red scarf; this was where Wiseman had greeted her; here he had stood when first he looked into her face.

His apprehension increased as he walked down the path toward the door. It was unconventional, extremely so, just to turn up like this, without any kind of warning. Supposing they are in bed together, he suddenly thought. He overcame the impulse to turn and walk away. Then she had opened the door and was looking at him. Her face was completely without expression for a very brief moment, then broke into a pleased smile.

"Simon, it's you," she said. "How very nice to see you."

He could detect no special consciousness on her face; but his awkwardness was increased by the knowledge that she must see his importunity, see the meaning of such a visit, uninvited, unannounced — the meaning of it was there in his awkward hesitation on the doorstep, his eyes that belied the merely social intentions of his smile. "I hope you don't mind," he said, close to her in the narrow passage. "I wanted to see you."

"I'm glad you came," she said. She was smiling, but her eyes regarded him steadily. With rising heart Raikes thought he saw a contradiction in them similar to his own, some attempt to hide feeling, avoid declaration. Whatever the truth of this, her next words showed no such intention. Pausing at the door that led off the passage, turning to him, she said, "I have often wanted to see you."

She was near enough for him to smell the scent she had used; near enough for him to see, as she looked at him, the tawny, warmer flecks in the otherwise cool eyes; near enough too for him to watch some slight irresolution appear on her face, some impulse checked, the impulse to look away, he suddenly realized, to turn aside before a moment arrived when it would be too late. Quite deliberately, standing there at the door, she survived this hesitation, continued to look steadily at him. The next moment Raikes had taken her by the shoulders and kissed her on the lips.

The kiss did not last long, but it lasted long enough for him to feel an unmistakable response. His heart was pounding as he stood back. Chiara looked at him a moment longer, then swiftly leaned forward and kissed him lightly on the cheek, immediately afterward opening the door to let him through.

She did not take him this time to the room where Litsov's bronzes were displayed, but to a much smaller one at the back of the house with windows that did not look over the Lagoon but gave a view of dark twisted pine trees shrouded in mist and the roof of a long low building beyond — Litsov's studio, he supposed.

He watched her move about, his whole being concentrated on her movements, the second kiss she had given him — swift, friendly, full of promise — present in his mind. He would have liked to tell her that he thought of her constantly, that he loved her, that he was ready to bless the universe for the fact of her existence. However, shifting in his armchair by the window, balancing his cup of coffee, he said none of these things; words of true feeling were difficult, impossible, at this stage, with interest declared but intimacy not yet arrived at.

They spent some time talking about not very important matters, things that Raikes kept little memory of — perhaps because of the events that followed. Then quite suddenly she said, "Oh, I have something for you. I was going to send it . . ." She stood up, smiling. "It is for you," she said, "and yet your presence here put it out of my mind. That is strange."

She was out of the room some moments, then returned with an envelope, which she handed him. "When I wrote to thank my aunt," she said, "I happened to mention the year you had told me your Madonna was carved, 1432. That is right, isn't it? It was by chance really; I was trying to explain why you were interested.

Well, it seems that the good soul found something dated in that year, a copy of a letter — the family correspondence was collated and printed privately in the mid-nineteenth century sometime, by my great-grandfather, I think. One of the few Fornarini to have had studious tastes. There is not much private correspondence surviving from those years, hardly any. Marcantonio Fornarini was at the court of Naples during the 1430s and he wrote regular diplomatic dispatches, but they went directly to the Signoria, and were kept in the state archives. This letter is by Federico Fornarini, who was a younger brother of Marcantonio, according to my aunt. It seems to be a reply to some previous letter, but there is no trace of any. I have put it into English; I thought you might have problems with the language of the fifteenth century."

"I have problems with the language of the twentieth," Raikes said. "I am very grateful to your aunt. And to you too, of course," he added, though as he sat there holding the long white envelope, he could not have said whether his gratitude was for her help or for the marvelous fact of her being in the world at all or — more basely perhaps — for the beauty of her legs, which he had been strongly aware of from the moment she sat opposite him in the low chair.

Something of all this must have appeared on his face, for after a moment she said, with some slight confusion it seemed, "You can look at it now if you like. You will be disappointed, I'm afraid. There is nothing much in it and no references to the Madonna."

At this moment, glancing toward the window, Raikes saw a tall, slightly round-shouldered figure emerge from the thick belt of mist surrounding the pines and start walking toward the house. "Your husband is on his way over," he said. He noticed that Litsov was dressed very formally, in a gray suit and black shoes.

"Litsov is in a bad mood today," she said. "He has been upset by something, I don't know what."

Raikes said, "I'm sorry to hear that." He was glad that this time she had not found it necessary to tell him how highly strung her husband was. After a moment's hesitation he slipped the envelope into an inside pocket. "Are you worried I will say something to provoke him," he said, "in my well-known clumsy way?"

"No," she said, "it is not that; besides, you are not clumsy. No, his work is not going well, I think, and when that happens, he always blames circumstances or other people. He is very — "

"Highly strung? Yes, I know."

Raikes was in an angle partly obscured by the door, and Litsov did not see him immediately on entering. He advanced some paces into the room and said abruptly, "I'm going to take the boat." Turning slightly, he saw Raikes. The look of indignant solemnity on his face seemed to deepen.

"Simon Raikes," Raikes said, getting to his feet. "I came to lunch some time ago."

"I remember you," Litsov said. "I never forget faces. We had a discussion about form. I think you saw my point of view."

"Oh, yes," Raikes said. "I *saw* it, all right." Quickly he enjoined caution on himself. He mustn't start arguing with Litsov again. Something pompous about the man provoked him now as it had done before.

"The boat?" Chiara said. She looked astonished. Raikes had the impression that her face had paled since Litsov had come into the room. "Why are you dressed up like this?" she said.

"That should be obvious." Litsov's face collapsed suddenly in the strange lipless smile that Raikes remembered. It was clear that though upset and even angry about something he was at the same time pleased that he had taken a decision — pleased too, it seemed, by the expression on Chiara's face, which was both surprised and alarmed. "I am going to the mainland, my dear," he said. "I am going to Mestre."

The suit was sharply creased, obviously not much worn. It looked incongruously smart on Litsov's angular, slightly stooping figure. He had dressed with care. A dark blue handkerchief protruded in neat folds from his breast pocket; his narrow pink tie was secured by a tie pin with a large pale stone in it, an opal perhaps; his black shoes were highly polished.

In all this, as in that triumphant and vindictive declaration of intent, there was something childishly defiant, or so it seemed to Raikes; something touching almost, because it was weak and accompanied by such solemn self-consciousness of manner. By announcing it, dressing up for it, he hoped to convince the adults that he was serious. The smart suit, the neat tie, the polished shoes, they were all designed to show Chiara that she needn't argue: he *must* go; nothing could prevent it — was he not dressed for it?

"I'll just have some coffee first," he said.

"But how do you think you're going to get there?" Chiara said. "Have you seen the fog that's coming up? In an hour or so it will start getting dark. You don't know the channels."

"I know them well enough."

"It's too dangerous, Paul. You can't go."

Up till now Litsov had been maintaining an air of nonchalance, smiling from time to time, helping himself to coffee, though it was obvious that he had been badly put out by something. Now the smile disappeared. "Of course you don't want me to go," he said. "I know that."

"I'm thinking of the dangers."

"Oh, yes," Litsov said, in a peculiar and disagreeable tone. "Why don't you take me then? You know the Lagoon better."

Forgetting his resolve to keep out of it, Raikes said quickly to Chiara, "If it's too dangerous for him, it's too dangerous for you."

"That's just an excuse," Litsov said. "It may interest you to know that I did a spot of phoning this afternoon while you were busy gardening. That surprises you, doesn't it? My well-known aversion for telephones . . . No, I don't want to discuss it," he said quickly, as Chiara seemed about to interrupt. "I've decided to go myself and find out what's happening."

"Why not get in touch with Richard?" Chiara said. "Or I'll do it, if you like. He could tell you what the situation is."

"No doubt he could." It was a sneer, almost. "I have no intention of getting in touch with Richard," he said.

An uneasy silence followed this remark. Chiara's face still wore the strained, slightly abstracted expression with which she had greeted her husband's announcement. Raikes felt embarrassed. "How is your work going?" he said.

"My work is going well," Litsov said. "It is other people who don't seem to be doing their job." His eyes were on Chiara. "And not only Adriano," he added, after a moment.

"You have the casting done on the mainland, I believe?" Raikes said, still valiantly persisting.

"I do everything here but the actual mold for the casting. And the firing, of course. I make the model and the rubber mold; I even assemble the wax sections."

"Who delivers the models for you?"

As Litsov was beginning to reply to this, Chiara broke in sharply. "Paul," she said, "I'll take you across, if you like — as you say, I know the channels better than you — but you'll have to wait until I come back from dropping Simon. You can't go off with the boat anyway until Simon has been taken back. It shouldn't take long."

Litsov paused for what seemed a long time. "Very well," he said at last. "I'll wait for you."

Taking this as his cue, Raikes got to his feet and said he thought he'd better be on his way. They left Litsov there, in his smart suit, helping himself to more coffee.

Immediately outside they kissed again, but briefly. The mist was thicker now. Pale water met the pale sky in a seam that was undetectable — only occasionally parting to show a darker line. Far out, softened and diffused by the mist, yellow lamps marked the deep-water channel. At the landing stage he noticed that the tide was lower: there was a glisten of mud here and there; dark fronds of seaweed broke the surface; the mooring stakes revealed blackened stumps.

Chiara had lit the lantern in the stern. In dark beret and long raincoat, she handled the boat with complete assurance. She was unfaltering in all things to do with physical action.

The muffled waste of water closed round them. The sound of their engine was all the sound in the world. Where sea and sky parted there were darker bars, mere darker levels in the haze, discernible as land because gulls walked and waded there. As they drew nearer to Burano, Raikes made out the stooping figures of men ankle deep in the shallows, looking for clams — they appeared to be cautiously walking on the water.

At Burano he had expected her to cast off immediately and return, but she stepped out with him onto the jetty and tied the boat up. "I feel I need a drink," she said, "before going back."

They found a café on the main square. After no more than a sip of cognac, she went to make a phone call. It seemed to Raikes that she was away rather a long time. When she returned she said abruptly, "I've told him I'm not coming back tonight. It's too foggy already and it will be dark soon. It's just too risky."

"I'm sure you're right," Raikes said. "I expect he was furious, wasn't he?"

"Who? Oh, Paul . . . Yes, he was, as a matter of fact. If I go back, you see, he will make a fuss and try to insist on taking the boat out. And that would be dangerous, you know." She seemed suddenly to have become tense and somehow defensive. "Too dangerous for me," she said," and I know the Lagoon much better than Paul." It was almost as if she expected him to argue.

"I think you're right." Raikes did not know whether he was experiencing excitement or fear. Not quite looking at her, he said, "Do you mean you're not intending to go back there tonight at all?"

"He would only argue and make a scene," she said. "No, I think I'd better come back with you to Venice."

3

On the way back they did not speak very much. Chiara seemed nervous and preoccupied. Raikes was conscious of a tension almost painful at her nearness, at what he sensed to be her availability, at the constraint that kept them apart still. He knew they would make love that night, sensed that she knew it too. The sounds and sights of the journey — the steady noise of the engine, the darkening air, the blurred yellow lamps of the markers slung across the Lagoon, the mournful cries of steamers lost in the mist — had for their only function the celebration of this knowledge.

On the quay they stood hesitating for some moments. Then Chiara said she would go to a hotel she knew of, not far away, five minutes' walk along the Mendicanti, near the Civil Hospital.

"I could put you up," Raikes said. "I thought, you know, it might be awkward for you at a hotel, not having any luggage and so on."

"Well," she said, "they know me there, you see. I've stayed there once or twice before when the same thing has happened, so they would understand about the luggage."

"The same thing?"

"I mean when I have been prevented from going back home."

"I see, all right, yes."

"It would be better. Your Signora Sapori might not like it, you know, if I stayed there. She would come to only one conclusion, and that would be the right one. I do not want to make your life difficult."

"I wouldn't care how difficult you made my life," Raikes said.

"In that case there is even more reason to be careful. The best thing is for me to go and register at the hotel, make sure of a room and so on — it is not the full season yet, but one should always make sure in Venice. Then we could have dinner together somewhere, if you like."

"Would you like me to come with you?"

"To the hotel? No; *non vale la pena,* it is near. I have nothing to carry. Why don't you wait for me? There is a bar, just here off the *fondamenta* — you can see the sign. Why don't you have a drink there and wait for me? I will not be long, perhaps half an hour."

Raikes agreed and they separated there on the quay. He stood and watched her fawn raincoat merge into the misty light and disappear. Suddenly he was reminded of the evening of the conference, when he had watched two figures, Lattimer's and another's, at the farthest limit of vision, where the lamplight dissolved in mist. He was sure now that Chiara had been the other one. Why had the two met there? He wondered about this, as he sat over his Punt-e-mes, waiting for her. Lattimer had looked worried somehow, not as if he were going to a lovers' meeting. Involuntarily his mind moved to the exhibits in Lattimer's "museum," among them those wiry, beribboned tufts. There was something not quite sane about Lattimer, something monstrous in his appetite for victory. In other times he would have collected scalps or heads, instead of works of art . . . They had known each other before her marriage to Litsov; hadn't he said that, or implied it? There had been familiarity in his words and smile, that evening when the whiskey made him boastful . . .

She had taken off the beret and put up her hair so that it lay on top of her head, revealing the strong neck, the delicate temples, her ears, which he could not remember seeing before. He thought she had put on eye make-up, too, in this brief interval. She came through the bar serious-faced, her head held up, looking for him among other people, and he felt his heart constrict at this luminous seriousness of hers, at the thought that it was for him — at least now, this evening.

She did not want to stay for a drink so they left immediately. They had dinner at a small restaurant near the Scuola di San Marco and shared a bottle of Sicilian wine. Raikes hardly noticed what he ate, nor much of what they talked about. She too seemed in a curious way preoccupied, not vague but rather excitable and disconnected in the things she said. Her eyes were very bright and she was flushed — circumstances he thought due to the wine.

Over the coffee that kind of pause descended which is not awkward exactly but results when everything has been said but the one essential thing.

"I'd better get the bill, I suppose," Raikes said. He began casting those wary glances of the Englishman who wants to catch the waiter's eye.

"The hotel is called the Perseus," she said. "It is between the hospital and the Mendicanti Church, a small hotel. My room number is twenty-six — on the second floor. If I go back there now, and allow about fifteen minutes . . ."

"Yes, all right," he said. He was struck, as he had been before on the quayside, at the clear, definite, and precise way in which she dealt with all these practical matters. It was as though she had worked everything out in advance. Women are great planners, he thought, rather uneasily. Why had they not gone together, booked a double room in the first place? No one would have been any the wiser. But of course they knew her at this hotel . . .

"Go straight through," she said. "No need to ask at the reception desk. Just go directly to my room."

"Yes," he said. "I'll wait here for a while. I'll have another drink."

She smiled at him as she got up. "Don't drink too much," she said.

The fifteen minutes passed slowly for Raikes. It was still fairly early when he left the restaurant, not much after ten. He found the hotel without any trouble; no one took particular notice of him as he crossed to the lift. The second floor corridor was deserted.

Chiara's room was lit only dimly by the small bedside lamp. She faced him without saying anything. He took her at once into his arms and began to kiss her. The skin of her face was hot; her mouth too was hot and her lips parted under his kisses. He felt the pressure against him of her abdomen and the front of her thighs. After these first kisses she pressed close against him for a while, face hidden. Then, as if with some access of urgency, she panted and raised her face again, in haste, seeking his lips. No words were exchanged between them. Raikes had time for some slight feeling of surprise at this wordless burning haste of hers, after the previous cool arrangements. But at these further kisses his own excitement began to mount; her haste was communicated to him. Suddenly it was as if all the desire he had ever felt was focused on this one woman in his arms. His clothes constricted him, the blood was beating in his temples, he could not distinguish her clamorous breath from his own.

Three or four staggering dance steps brought them to the bed. Here, moaning and fumbling, they undressed each other as far as impatience would allow, stripping off whatever would get in the way. He abandoned his attempts on the gray dress, removing only the flimsy garment beneath it — his own trousers still clung to his knees. As soon as he put his hand on her she cried out. She cried out again when he entered. Her body, the thighs that strongly held him, were burning with the same fever as her face. Raikes had never experienced such passion in a woman. She reached orgasm almost at once, within a few moments, in a series of sighing shudders, not painful or violent, but like a long release.

He stopped moving, surprised into patience, still rigid inside her, made forbearing somehow by the contractions of her pleasure, the sight of the flushed face that smiled at him. Very gently, in spite of murmured complaint, he withdrew, completed his own undressing and hers. Naked, she was very beautiful to him, her breasts softly mounded as she lay there on her back, the nipples large and prominent, the thighs rounded and strong, displayed carelessly now, half parted in the abandonment of her release. An emotion of great tenderness came to Raikes, contending with the urgency of his desire. He was erect still. He kissed her on the eyes and brow and mouth and slowly entered her again and heard her murmur and felt her body quicken and this time begin to move against him, heard and uttered the intimations of orgasm — his own came first with a sensation so strong that deep groans broke from him. His spasms brought her to it; she called out as if in surprise and her body convulsed violently so that he was almost thrown off, like a spent wrestler.

Afterward they lay side by side, looking up at the ceiling, in which there was a faint but extensive tracery of cracks. He found himself telling her a good many things in the next hour or so as they lay there, the lamp still on, her body calm beside him. He tried to tell her first of all about his feelings when making love to her, and before they had started — how much he had wanted it, how even then he felt that he adored her. "Not just afterward," he said; "*before,* you understand. It isn't so common to feel adoring *before,* you know, because basically by that time you usually feel so excited . . . I was excited too, that is the extraordinary thing."

He was absorbed by what had just happened, the preternatural wisdom he felt he had shown, waiting long enough for her to be able to come again. Some instinct of grace had saved him from his own importunate haste. Surely only love could produce such instincts. "You are the one woman in the world for me," he said. "It has never been like that before."

Certainly it had not been like that with Margaret, who worked in the prints department of the museum, who had shared an apartment with him for several months. They had got on well enough in a way, but their lovemaking had not been successful. "There was nothing in it, it was just an act, you know," he said. "She went along with it. We remained completely separate people." This had been symbolized perfectly by the manner of their parting. They had sorted through the books and records together, each calmly and amicably claiming his or her own. What a way to part. Raikes grew voluble at the soullessness of it. "It's amazing," he said, "how closely tied we are to *things,* to material objects. The division of property was the really important thing, not what we actually said to each other. That is how we convinced ourselves we were really serious about breaking up. You know, it is like 'With this ring I thee wed,' only in reverse."

She herself talked little, saying nothing of her previous life or loves. She replied to him in a slow voice, looking up at the ceiling. Twice she reached for her watch from the bedside table to look at the time. He tried to tell her about the impact on him of their first meeting, how stricken he had been, how remote and unattainable she had seemed. "I never thought you would look at me," he said.

In the joy of the contrast between this state of affairs and his present felicity, he turned to her again. He touched the skin of her shoulders, tracing the form of the bones beneath; he kissed her cheek, and the side of her neck, and her breasts, feeling the nipples harden between his lips. She pressed close against him and he felt himself stiffen against her stomach. He would have moved onto her but she stayed him, sitting up herself, pulling the sheet clear so that she could look down at him. He closed his eyes under this scrutiny and after a moment felt her hands caressing him. Then she had knelt astride him, lowered herself carefully onto him. She sighed as he entered, and uttered his name.

This time they took longer; their movements were more deliberate. He saw her face above him as he moved to her rhythm, rose and fell with her, thrusting to penetrate as deeply as he could; saw her face still straining upward as she rode him, vague, uncertain, strangely yearning; saw the green eyes closing and the face preparing for its pain. "I love you," he groaned. "I love you."

Still he could not sleep. When the lamp was switched off, he talked on for some time in the darkness — glad of the darkness in fact, as he plunged into telling her about his visions, what Vittorini called the hallucinatory content, though he did not mention his visits to the doctor, describing only the things he had seen or thought he had seen, the feeling, the vertigo, the resonance of laughter, wet bodies, straight shadows, the statue amid the foliage, the two faces of the same girl.

"That is strange," she said, in a tone he did not quite understand.

But he was sleepy now, as if lulled by these confessions, and sleep came to him before he could ask her what she meant, what she really thought.

Somewhere toward morning she woke him, reaching for her watch to see the time. "I can't sleep," she said, in a tone of complaint, like a child. A moment later he felt her kisses on his face and body. She was burning hot again and her skin felt dry, feverish. He was still half asleep, not properly ready, but she maneuvered him inside her and panted and turned her head restlessly while he stiffened slowly, growing till he filled her and they both made noises of delirium. Raikes felt ecstasy approach very slowly, even reluctantly, from some infinite distance, like a wary god. When it came, however, it was cataclysmic, threatening his whole being with extinction. He fell back from it exhausted, passing instantly from this foretaste of death to the oblivion that is its simulacrum.

Almost at once — or so it seemed to him — she was shaking him awake. He thought at first that she wanted to make love again. But her tone was sharp, businesslike. "It's nearly half-past six," she said. "If you go now, no one will see you."

"Won't there be someone on duty there?" he said.

"This is a small place. There is no one on duty at night. The day clerk will be here now, but he is not at the desk till after seven — not till they start serving breakfast. He goes to have his coffee with the waiters."

"You seem to know the place well." Raikes was prey to sudden, disagreeable suspicions. "Have you smuggled people out before?" he said. She was sitting up in bed and he was aware of the beauty of her breasts.

"I told you I have stayed here," she said. "I have tried to pay the bill at this time and there was no one there. You must hurry."

She seemed to grow agitated now, passing a hand rapidly through her hair. "Please hurry," she said. "Even if someone sees you, they will only think you are going out to get a paper."

Raikes thought this doubtful, but saw no point in saying so. "When can I see you?" he said, struggling into his clothes.

"I want you to go back with me," she said. "You know, to help me to explain what happened, why I couldn't go back last night.

He would have been waiting for the boat, you see, but of course it was too dangerous."

He looked at her in surprise. Her face was pale and bore the defenseless, unprepared look of early morning. While he watched, she passed her right hand slowly down her left arm from shoulder to wrist in the curiously narcissistic gesture he remembered, self-protecting and self-loving. It came to him that she was frightened of Litsov.

"But you phoned," he said; "you phoned from Burano. He knew you weren't coming back."

"Yes," she said, "that is so, of course, but it will help if you come with me. Please, Simon."

"I don't mind," he said, "if that is what you want."

"I can meet you in an hour — less."

"It won't take that long to pay the bill, will it?"

"I paid the bill last night. Since I had no luggage, it seemed better. No, I am going to have breakfast here."

For some reason Raikes was completely taken aback by this. He stared at her without speaking.

"That is the normal thing to do," she said, almost primly. "In this situation one must do what is normal."

Was this the burning creature of the night?

"I'll wait for you outside, then," he said.

"Well, not quite, perhaps. Wait at the entrance to the *ospedale*. It's just around the corner. No, just a moment. You'd better go back to your apartment first. Have your coffee there, as usual. I'll telephone you later. You must go now, please."

To his enormous relief, reception desk and lobby were deserted. He heard a clatter of dishes from the dining room, but as far he could tell no one saw him leave. Disheveled, strangely demoralized, he stepped out into the opal light of morning.

It was not until he was back in his apartment, sitting with his coffee, that he remembered the letter. It was still there in his inside pocket. The single sheet of notepaper had been folded twice. Slowly, almost absent-mindedly, he smoothed it out and began to read Chiara's large, angular writing. She had not bothered to translate the formal opening:

All'Illustrissimo Signor Conte Maffeo di Rovereto

Fear not any displeasure on my part from the Council in response to your intercessions. In my eyes and theirs it stands to your credit and to the credit of your noble name that you should express thus your sense of the obligations all of us owe to those who in any way depend on us. In this you show your right feeling and the dues imposed on all who are inscribed in the Rolls, and these moreover are dues which keep together the fabric of our state and preserve the Signoria. Moreover, I well understand the feelings of your lady wife and her sympathy with any from her native place. Know that the Bernardoni family stands high with us and we would do much to mark this respect.

However, in this matter I am powerless to help. The Council view the case with severity. What you say concerning the character of the girl is true and should act in some mitigation but the Council take the view that this is becoming too prevalent now, this disregard for life among the people, and so there is need for exemplary punishments. Therefore I can do nothing in this matter though wishful to please you in all ways in my power.

Believe me to be, Illustrissimo Signor Conte, now and always at your service.

Federico Fornarini

Raikes sat for some time puzzling over this, obscurely disappointed. In spite of Chiara's words he had been expecting something more obviously significant. The letter was dated October 19, 1432, and had clearly been written in reply to some request for favor, probably a plea for the girl, who seemed to be mixed up in some crime or other, perhaps murder.

He looked again at the names: di Rovereto, Bernardoni. They meant nothing at all to him. Suddenly he remembered Wiseman, that cherubic knowledge about the patrician families of Venice, the day they had lunched together in the sunshine on the Riva degli Schiavoni. It seemed half a lifetime ago now, his meeting with Chiara had distanced all else before. It was not nine o'clock yet; possibly Wiseman would not have left for his office.

He went quickly downstairs to the telephone, feeling a certain frailty along the insides of his thighs as he did so, reminder of the night past. He found the number in his diary, dialed hastily, and was relieved to hear Wiseman's gentle, equable voice at the other end.

"Di Rovereto, Bernardoni . . . No, I can't tell you offhand, dear boy. Not very important families, I fancy. The first sounds Venetian. I can find out, of course. No trouble at all. Leave it to Uncle Alex."

Chiara's call came at half-past nine. They met on the Fondamenta Nuova at the Burano boat stage. During the trip back they stood close together, not speaking much. Her face was very pale. He put his arm round her shoulders and felt the tension in her body. She would not be looking forward to facing Litsov; he was not looking forward to it himself.

The boat lay as they had left it, hull wet with the deposits of the mist. This was thinning now, yielding place to sunlight, as they nosed out of the little harbor and turned eastward, the great tower of Torcello on their left, rising clear into a softly livid sky.

It was a journey that was becoming familiar to Raikes. As they drew near to the island, he noted again, in spite of his nervousness, the silvering of light on the meshes of fish traps staked in the distant shallows, the gleams of broken water beyond, where sandbanks lay just below the surface. Over all the scene, to Raikes's view at least, there lay a sort of moving, shimmering presence, as if some being of immortal lightness and inscrutable purpose were moving over the water, displacing the mist here and there, admitting the sun in arbitrary patches, sudden transforming glitters of light.

Crouched on the little wooden jetty, helping to tie up the boat, he noticed fronds of dark green seaweed groping in the shallow water. Small crabs moved languidly against the black moss at the foot of the wall.

Silence lay over the house as they approached. The door was unlocked. As they walked down the passage, Chiara called her husband's name, twice, but there was no reply. "He'll be working, I expect," she said. "I'll go over to the studio. You wait here."

When she had gone, Raikes stood for a moment or two in the

passage. Then he opened the door to the main living room and passed inside. The curtains were still drawn in here. There was an oil lamp on the table, still burning, though the flame was flickering, almost spent. In this light, and the daylight filtering through the curtains, the bronze sculptures emitted shifting gleams, as if uncertainly signaling. A faint smell of paraffin hung on the air.

He had blown the flame out and was moving to draw the curtains when he heard her quick steps in the passage. He turned and saw her framed in the doorway. "He forgot to put the lamp out," he said.

"He's not there," Chiara said. "He's nowhere in the house at all."

She made no move to come farther into the room. Raikes hesitated for some moments. "He must be somewhere," he said. He had the feeling that she was waiting for him, that she did not want to be alone any longer. "Of course he might have got a boat somehow," he said. "Last night, I mean, later on. Must have been quite a bit later, well after dark, anyway. He could have phoned someone he knew."

"Litsov doesn't like telephones," she said. "Still, if he was really determined to go . . ."

"Funny he should have left the lamp on. We'd better have a look round the island, I think — he may still be here somewhere."

But there was no sign of Litsov anywhere. He was not among the pine trees, nor the tangle of shrubs and bushes, nor the old foundations and ruined walls of former houses that led down to the shore on the north side of the island.

They covered the ground together, Chiara several times calling Litsov's name. "Something is wrong," she said, and he noticed that she had begun trembling. "If he had gone to Mestre, he would have left a note."

"But if he was angry with you?"

"All the more reason. I know him. He would have wanted to show me that he didn't need me, that he had gone in spite of me."

"Well, he is not here," Raikes said, rather helplessly.

Nevertheless they began again, picking their way among low walls grown over with briony and ivy, scrambling through hollows where the old foundations had subsided, poking into thickets clogged with the bleached débris of old tides.

"Do you think he could be hiding somewhere, deliberately not answering?" Raikes said, as they once more emerged onto the rocks of the foreshore.

"As a game, you mean? No, he is not like that."

Patches of mist still hung above the surface of the water, shot through with sunlight. Some disturbance must have occurred out in the Lagoon, though they heard and saw nothing; perhaps the passage of a large boat. It had its faint aftermath here, small eddies and ripples among the stones of the shore, a whole series of kissing, lapping noises. Some few feet out from the edge a dark mass of kelp simmered very slowly, occasionally breaking the surface into shivers of light. Beyond this, in deeper water, were a few leaning, half-rotted stakes — markers for a navigation channel long unused. Moss glistened dark emerald on them where the falling tide exposed it.

There were a number of largish boulders on the shore and for no particular reason Raikes scrambled onto one. Had he not done so, he would probably have noticed nothing until the water was lower. Now, at first casually, then with increasing attention, he found himself looking from this eminence at a small glimmering shape out there among the dilapidated stakes, something that reflected the misty sunlight striking the surface of the water. With a distinct feeling of absurdity, Raikes sat down on the rock and began to take off his shoes and socks.

"What are you doing?" Chiara said.

"There is something . . ." Raikes said vaguely. He began to wade out, stepping gingerly through the thin ooze of mud and the squirming seaweed. As he approached the stakes, the water rose above his knees, soaking his rolled-up trouser bottoms. By this time he knew what he was going to find.

Litsov's body lay submerged in two feet of water. He was trapped among the stakes, looking up at the light that broke through onto his face — only a few inches separated his slightly open mouth from the air. He was puffy-looking, but he had a certain nobility, staring up, the long hair lifting round his head. The jacket of his suit was still buttoned, the tie still neatly knotted. Even the blue handkerchief in his breast pocket was still in place. Only his left sleeve, riding up his arm a little, detracted from the smartness of his turnout.

There was time, in this terrible exchange of glances, for Raikes to remember the other face gazed at through clear water, time for him to feel the strangeness of the coincidence. Then he had taken Litsov by his sodden shoulders, raised him clear, begun to drag him toward the shore. Unsure of his footing, he stumbled and floundered, ducking the drowned man yet again. As he heaved Litsov onto the shore, the splash and scrape of the heavy body, his own groaning breath, Chiara's sounds of distress, all merged and became indistinguishable.

He did not yet look at her. Doggedly, knowing it was hopeless, he worked to revive Litsov. He noticed a deep gash, washed livid, on the drowned man's forehead, above the staring right eye.

Behind him he could hear her crying. *"Non avrei dovuto lasciarlo,"* she said, over and over agin. *"Non avrei dovuto lasciarlo."*

"Non era colpa tua," he said. He got up from Litsov and went to her. "You couldn't have known," he said. "It wasn't your fault."

"You don't understand," she said. *"Il dottore mi aveva avvertito.* Vittorini told me to watch for signs of an attack."

"Attack?" he said. "Did you say Vittorini?"

She raised a face from which all trace of color had gone. "I told you Litsov was an invalid," she said. "He was an epileptic."

4

The shock of this was still in his mind while they waited for the police, remained during the days that followed, softening gradually to a sense of irreconcilable elements, some obscure failure of logic or natural correspondence. As he continued to work on the Madonna, he sought for something, some link that might explain this feeling of discrepancy. Possibly, of course, it was no more than an instinctive repudiation on his part of any too close parallel between himself and the dead man. Litsov, it seemed, had been an epileptic. This was what he, Raikes, was too, or so Chiara had stated, while they drank brandy in the kitchen and he dried his clothes and tried not to think of Litsov reclining in sodden state on the shingle. His own attacks were milder — Litsov had sometimes fallen down and lost consciousness — though attacks could get more severe, she had said, dry-eyed and firmer-voiced now, after the brandy, though her hands were shaking still. Especially if, like Litsov, one omitted to take the pills regularly. Raikes did not tell her that he had not yet taken any pills at all. Vittorini had prescribed phenobarbital for them both, he had been dismayed to discover.

"They don't use the term so much nowadays," Chiara had said, pausing and breathing deeply with a visible effort at control. "I thought it was that when you told me about those things, those visions of yours. But after what Vittorini said to you, I'm sure of it."

The same self-protective obstinacy he had displayed before the doctor made him doubtful of this, but he had admired her courage, the reserves of fortitude that enabled her to bear up in this way, after such hideous events — the floundering recovery of her husband's body from the sea, the useless attempts at revival.

He was working on the Madonna's face now, area of utmost delicacy and danger. In spite of his now considerable experience with the quartz cutter, he was still afraid of making some false move that would damage her irreparably: there might be room for error in the draperies; there was certainly none in the face. The mouth bothered him a good deal: there were encrustations of diseased stone between the lips and in the slight concavity above them; leprous deposits that had thickened and coarsened the whole mouth, totally obscuring its expression. He was working now, with the greatest care and concentration, on the lower lip.

As he worked, he went over, in the same painstaking detail, the finding of Litsov's body: the face first, merely a glimmering object to begin with, then the swollen gaze, the meekly open mouth — as if to receive a biscuit, Raikes had thought afterward. Otherwise neat and tidy . . . In his gray suit he had seemed to be still demonstrating an intention of some kind, as if showing the world that he was dressed for a purpose and meant business . . . An obscure horror stirred in Raikes at this thought of Litsov's immaculate appearance under the water, only that left sleeve riding up a little. He had been dressed up for drowning, not for any visit to the mainland. He had fallen forward, struck his head, drowned without struggle in a foot or two of water. Afterward the tide must have drawn him deeper in, rolled him over somehow, nudged him about until he got caught among the stakes.

This was the obvious explanation, and presumably it was what the police believed had happened. It was five days since he had seen or spoken to Chiara, so he had no idea what developments there had been, if indeed there had been any. Litsov had a medical history as an epileptic; the autopsy would have revealed how much phenobarbital there was in his system, hence whether he had been taking his regular dosage. It was all straightforward enough. But the sense of incongruity, of logical wrongness, remained.

He wondered whether his uneasiness was due simply to the fact that he had not himself told the whole truth to the authorities. In the interval before the police arrived, Chiara, though trembling still and deeply shocked, had found the firmness and clarity to warn him. They must keep to their story now, she had said — or, rather, they must make sure their story was consistent with the appearances they had already created. They had spent the night separately, she at her hotel, he at his apartment. They had met the following morning and returned to the house together.

"Everything else we can tell them just as it was," she said. "The drink at Burano, the phone call, the dinner, everything. After dinner I returned to the hotel and you stayed in the restaurant. You had another drink, settled the bill — then you went back to your apartment. I phoned you next morning and asked if you would return with me."

"But why?" he said. "Why not make a clean breast of it?"

She had seemed incredulous, almost, at this. He did not understand: they had already made the pretense; they would have to keep to it now. Otherwise it would look suspicious. "They will think it has something to do with my husband's death," she said. "It will look as if there was a conspiracy. Besides, and most important, they will think we have been lovers for a certain time before, and so, you see, they will suspect all kinds of things. You do not know the Italian police as I do. They think love a great motive . . ."

There had been a note of contempt in her voice. Contempt for the police or for the emotion of love, he wondered now. In spite of her vehemence he had gone on making objections. Supposing someone had seen him at the hotel? Wouldn't it be even more damaging if some witness came forward later?

She had gone to him then, taken his hands. She knew he hated lying; she felt the same; but he must think what there was at risk. Why should anyone have particularly noticed him in the hotel? Why should anyone make a connection between them? It was unreasonable to think that anyone should do so. Did he think he had been more conspicuous then because he was proposing to hide something now?

Her logic, the brief calm that had come to her aid for the purposes of argument, astonished him. He was confident, too, in his own mind, that no one had noticed him in the hotel. As he hesitated still, wondering what kind of risk she had meant, she turned abruptly from him and stood apart with lowered head. "Don't you think the shock of his death has been enough?" she said.

This appeal, her distress, moved him in a way that argument perhaps might not have done; what seemed her loneliness at this moment brought the beginnings of tears to his own eyes. He moved to her, took her in his arms. "Don't distress yourself," he said. "Don't worry about it. I love you. We'll do as you want."

Close in his arms, face hidden against his chest, she said, "There is one thing more, darling, but it doesn't involve telling any lies. I don't think we should say anything about Litsov wanting to leave the island last night, do you? There's no point. It wasn't really serious anyway. By mentioning it we would give the impression that it was important somehow."

In the event, on the first occasion at least, not much had been required of him — or of Chiara either. Considering that a man had died, the statement, taken from them jointly, seemed brief to Raikes, even cursory. They related the circumstances in which they had left Litsov the evening before, their return in the morning to find him drowned. Within a couple of hours, their statement had been taken, the doctor had made a preliminary investigation, Litsov was under a tarpaulin sheet in the police launch. It was in this same launch that Raikes himself returned to Venice, keeping his back to the body, heavy with the knowledge of his lies.

The heaviness was with him still, almost like a foreboding, as he blasted delicately at the Madonna's mouth. Her lips were revealed now, the line of them clearly marked, faintly, tenderly smiling. It seemed to Raikes suddenly that he knew those lips, that smile. Abruptly he switched off the quartz cutter and stepped back for a better view. The mouth was wider, the lower lip fuller, than in the severer classicized Madonnas common earlier in the century. Something pagan almost, in that long, faintly curving smile. Delicacy there, however, and supreme skill on the sculptor's part, in the fading line of the mouth and the sharply indented corners — almost as if drilled. But that was unlikely surely, at this period . . . What did the mouth express? Pleasure, welcome, some quality of shy excitement? Yet the body was turned away . . . Again it came to him that he knew the mouth, knew that faint but indubitable smile. Yet the memory eluded him, remaining at the border of consciousness, ungraspable, like his sense of unresolved contradiction in the circumstances of Litsov's death.

The same evening, at his apartment, he had had a further visit from the police, a single police inspector in plain clothes, smiling, courteous, speaking quite passable English. Sitting there, the policeman opposite in an armchair, he had been requested to go through his story again. He did so, repeating the version of events which was now official, which had become more real and solid than the wraith of truth he and Chiara were concealing. The night of love was canceled out almost, relegated to some dim margin of time. Both of them, jointly and severally, had denied it. Yet it was there to spring back again at any moment, though not now as love but guilt.

He longed for Chiara, for her physical presence, for the reassurance of her smile and her touch. But she had asked him not to visit, not to phone, not to make any attempt to establish contact. There was policy in this as well as feeling, he recognized that; and he had respected her wishes.

There were small variations, new questions, new details that had to be supplied. Why, the policeman asked, had they decided to go on to Venice? Why not stay at Burano for the night? In his case, of course, it was clear; he had an apartment to return to.

Raikes thought it probable that they had already questioned his landlady, Signora Sapori. But she had been in bed already when he got back. He was often late. And in the morning, when she brought his coffee, he had been at his table, as usual, writing up his diary. He always made his own bed . . . Yes, in his case it was clear, but why had Signora Litsov elected to go on to Venice with him? The policeman's eyes were glistening, long-lashed, good-humored. Raikes explained that there was a hotel the *signora* knew of in Venice, where she had stayed once or twice before when a similar thing had happened. She had thought it better to go there, since they knew her, and of course, having no luggage . . . the fog . . .

The policeman nodded, Yes, naturally. There was, however, a remaining look of what seemed speculation in his dark eyes. Signor Litsov did not leave the island very often, hardly ever in fact. He was something of a hermit, everyone said. Yet on this occasion he was dressed as if to go somewhere or meet somebody. Did he mention anything of the sort? No? And why, after all, had they decided to go back together to the house in the Lagoon, he and the *signora?* The next morning, that is.

This was basically a difficult question and one that for some reason had not been dealt with in the original statement he and Chiara had made to the police. What made it difficult, Raikes realized now, was that he did not really know why himself, but he knew it was important not to suggest there had been a quarrel or bad feeling of any kind. She had asked him to go, he said. She had phoned his apartment and asked him to go. But why? the policeman insisted, widening his handsome eyes. She wanted me to add my explanations to hers, Raikes said. She wanted him to understand why she had not been able to return the evening before. But she had phoned already, wasn't that so? Yes, that was so . . .

This policeman, like policemen everywhere, was capable of long and terrible pauses. Suddenly Raikes remembered his success with Biagi and the workmen on the subject of female caprice.

"She took it into her head," he said. "They get these ideas . . . *Si mettono in testa queste idee.*"

As if in a dream he saw the inspector smile and shrug, heard him say, "*Non si sa mai,* you never know . . ."

"You never know," Raikes repeated eagerly. "How can you know what they will get into their heads? *Che ci possiamo fare?*"

The inspector was smiling broadly as he took his leave. "*Non si sa mai, eh?*" he said. "You never know what they will get into their heads."

5

On the evening of the sixth day, while he was occupied with his diary, Chiara phoned. Would he collect Litsov's belongings from the Central Police Station? The police had completed their inquiries; it had been concluded that Litsov died by misadventure. She had taken his agreement for granted, it seemed: the police would be expecting him to call. He must take some means of identification with him.

Her voice was warm, immediate, instinct with a special kind of promise, and Raikes was deeply stirred by it, after the days of not seeing her, of thinking about her constantly. "When can I see you?" he said.

"You can come over tomorrow, if you like."

"Do you want me to bring the things?"

"Things? Oh . . . no. I don't want them. You will come tomorrow, won't you? I miss you so much."

"I miss you, too," he said, and his throat tightened at the urgency of the truth in these simple words. He could not come until late afternoon, he explained: there was his work, and an official meeting at the offices of the Soprintendenza, and then he had promised to have a drink with a friend, a fellow named Steadman, whom he didn't think she knew.

"No, I don't know him," she said. "Come whenever you like. There will be no need for you to rush off this time."

Excitement at the promise in these words, at the thought of seeing her, the enormous relief of knowing that the police inquiries were over, made it impossible for him to return immediately to his diary. He walked restlessly about the room for some time. So prompt was he to suggestion where Chiara was concerned that the mere sound of her voice worked immediate physiological effects on him, and these were slow to subside. It was half an hour before he was collected enough to sit down again at his desk, take up the threads of what he had been writing.

One of the mysteries surrounding the Madonna is why no account has remained to us of her stay at the Casa Fioret. This suggests some element of deliberate suppression. Piero Fornarini in his correspondence with his cousin makes what looks very like a play on words when he refers to the donor — who was presumably the owner of the Casa Fioret at that time. It seems this man had asked for his name to be kept out of things, as also the circumstances of the Madonna's installation. This is distinctly odd. He had a miraculous Madonna on his hands, he agreed to have her placed in a prominent position, then he spent a good deal of his time — and quite a bit of money — trying to keep the matter quiet. Fornarini says he should be called Cornadoro, Golden Horns. The immediate connotations of this are that he was rich and a cuckold. Or perhaps merely that his horns were productive of money for Fornarini. At any rate, he was rich enough to ensure Fornarini's silence; and if the horns part of it is right, he would have a reason for wanting to keep things hushed up. Names ending in oro *or* ore *were not uncommon in the period. One possible course might be to trace all such names recorded in Venice in the middle years of the eighteenth century. Far beyond my resources at present. By no means certain of success in any case — it might not be a pun at all. I have to admit that this whole line of inquiry comes to a dead end here, for the moment at least.*

I am hoping for some information from Steadman tomorrow as to the life and work of this Girolamo, who I am now sure actually carved the statue in 1432, on commission from the friars of the Supplicanti. What I should like to get are some more details of his career, particularly afterward. A man of that order of talent must have produced more work, not necessarily in Venice, but somewhere. *Also, of course, why did the friars reject it? Was Girolamo's Madonna too naturalistic, too much a sexual being for them? There must be more to it than that. Maddening to think that the whole story is there, if only I could put my finger on the clue that would unravel it. There must be bits and pieces lying around — in some attic or archive, on some obscure shelf. Not so much unraveling; more like putting a jigsaw puzzle together . . .*

My attacks, as Vittorini calls them, have not recurred lately, not for some weeks now. He was surprised to hear that himself. I have not taken any of the phenobarbital yet — nor at the moment do I intend to. I haven't been back to see him either. I am convinced that if only I could interpret them properly those things I saw would help me to understand the history of the Madonna. It seems to me just as likely or more likely that a disturbance in the impulses of the brain, this neural discharge, as he terms it, could be caused by psychic intimations as by some hypothetical lesion in the tissue somewhere. I am committing this to paper, though I would hesitate to say it to anyone, but I think it is possible that the statue is imbued with some kind of energy and that through constant proximity over a period of time, concentrating on her as I have done, something of this could have been communicated to me. I know this is an extraordinary thing to say.

Raikes sat back abruptly. That feverish incredulity had come over him again. Could an image of stone be affected by what human beings did to her and near her? Could this in its turn affect other human beings years, centuries, later? Fornarini's pun, if that was what it was, even the Madonna's sanctification, were mixed up with sexual treachery. It was the day we were together near her that I knew I was in love with Chiara. There were no more visions after that. All that randiness when I first started the work . . .

He had gone about Venice in a state of tumescence. All focused on her, on Chiara. Even now, he thought, just listening to her voice on the phone . . .

Only once her tone had changed, and that was when he had asked about Litsov's things. She had been very definite that she did not want them. Of course she would not wish to be reminded of such a terrible experience. Not even some small thing that he might have had about him . . . She was able to dissociate herself from the past; it was a great gift. Bereavement took different people different ways. Chiara was one of those who seek for consolation in the senses: she would try to warm herself, not sit out in the cold. Like a cat . . . that gesture of hers was catlike, too. That was why her voice promised him so much, barely a week after her husband's death. The night they had spent together, had she been in flight from some misery then? If so, she kept her head well, he thought, remembering the clear and definite instructions she had given him before and after. Two different Chiaras: the ardent creature of the night, the cool tactician of the morning. It came to Raikes suddenly that he did not really know her.

Litsov, of course, he had known even less. Litsov was summed up in other people's phrases, a recluse, a bit of a hermit, highly strung, his prices are going up, Litsov has genius, my husband is an invalid, Litsov dislikes telephones . . .

He had overcome his dislike that day at least, the last of his life. He had phoned to Mestre, spoken to the people who were casting his work. He had learned something that disturbed him, something that determined him to go and see them — there and then, without delay. Childlike, he had dressed up to demonstrate his intention. In this immaculate state, waiting for the return of the boat, he had had a fit, fallen, and choked to death in shallow water. He had not taken his phenobarbital that day. Perhaps he had forgotten, his feelings being disturbed. The same drug, Raikes thought, prescribed by the same doctor. Had Litsov too had abnormal wave patterns, an invisible, undetectable scar on the brain?

These and other questions presented themselves to Raikes in the course of the evening. Most pressing of all was the severely practical one that came to him as he was undressing for bed. What was Litsov doing down by the water? What could have led him, in the fog and gathering darkness, knowing there was no boat, to go stumbling about at the landing stage?

6

Next day he began work early — before eight. He had slept badly, waking frequently with feelings of oppression and foreboding, but felt no tiredness now. She was nearly complete; it was a matter of hours, a day or two more at most. There was only her face. The headdress he had done already and all the deeply indented parts where the headdress framed the face, leaving by conscious contrivance only the features themselves, so that the completion of the Madonna would resemble an unveiling: she would be restored to the world. It seemed fitting to Raikes, properly ceremonious, that he should end his work like this — and in particular with her eyes and brows. He was troubled still, as he worked, by something he sensed as familiar in the faintly smiling mouth.

The meeting with Manatti at the Soprintendenza — something between a social call and an informal report — took less time than he had feared. By noon he was back at work again. He was involved in the extremely delicate area around the nostrils and the folds at the sides of the nose. An error of judgment here, and the Madonna could be permanently disfigured. All thought, all speculation, left Raikes's mind as he worked. His whole being was concentrated on the exactly judicious use of the delicate, savage, faintly hissing instrument clutched in his hand between thumb and forefinger; even the knowledge that he was to see Chiara later that day was pushed into the background of his mind.

Progress was extremely slow. He was obliged to pause frequently to wipe the dust from his mask. Fear of abrading the healthy stone — something that could happen in a few seconds of lapsed concentration — made him more nervous and tentative, more reluctant to bring the quartz cutter close. In this absorbed solicitude for the Madonna's face his lunch hour came and went, unnoticed. When cramped muscles and strained eyes made him stop, it was midafternoon; the lower part of the Madonna's face, to the bridge of her nose, had been cleaned, and it was time for him to start getting ready to meet Steadman.

They met at Florian's, as arranged — Raikes's idea this, as he intended to go on afterward to pick up Litsov's belongings at the police station. They sat in the shade of the awning and watched the life of the *piazza* for a while and had some expensive beer. Raikes felt hungry now, belatedly, and ordered a toasted cheese sandwich.

"I suppose one has to come here once on every visit to Venice," Steadman said. He looked relaxed, as far as his saturnine cast of feature could allow, and slightly tanned — the weather had been sunny in London. "How have things been here?" he said.

Raikes thought briefly about telling Steadman what had happened but decided almost at once against it. He did not know the people, for one thing. But there was more to it than that: it was somehow his, Raikes's, own territory, one he had not found his way about in yet. It was too soon to admit anyone else. "Oh, much as usual," he said. "I haven't seen much of the Tintoretto people. I had a cup of coffee with Miss Greenaway the other day. You'll have seen her, I expect."

"Pauline? Oh, yes. Barfield has got the plaster off, I gather. You're not really looking too well yourself, you know."

"I'm all right," Raikes said.

Steadman waited for a moment or two, then looked away across the square. "Things are getting that summer look," he said, his eyes on a group of fifty or sixty Germans flocking round a vociferous guide with a bright red umbrella, which she held aloft and waved to draw the attention of strays. "You won't be here that much longer now, will you?" he said. "The old girl must be nearly finished. I'd like to have a look at her, by the way, when the restoration is complete. I want to take some pictures, as a matter of fact."

"Of course," Raikes said. "I've done everything but the face. Well, I've done the lower part of the face too. It won't be long now. It's an amazing bit of work. Even the perspectives . . . You can see it in the draperies, but it's particularly clear in the face. She was intended to be seen in half profile, from below — though not so far below as at present. So the artist kept the forms on the farther side more nearly on the same plane. You can see it in the cheeks, the farther one is distinctly less modulated."

Steadman nodded. "It is what I said before," he said. "These devices were not employed at all in native Venetian Gothic. Commonplace enough later, of course, all over Italy. No, your man came from somewhere else or was trained somewhere else."

He paused, looking rather closely at Raikes. "Piedmont is what you think, isn't it?" he said. "I did a little work on it in London. Quite frankly, there isn't a great deal. Artists came to Venice in the fifteenth century from all over Italy, even Florence, though it was usually the second-raters who came from there. So obviously there must have been some from Piedmont too. The trouble is that most of the work was done in combination with others or under the direction of others, and so it is not recorded anywhere. Most of these people were what today we would call migrant workers. A number of them would have been highly talented; a few might have had genius — there was a lot of it about. But we shall never know their names."

"I see, yes." It was clear that Steadman was settling into his stride. His voice was eager; he had forgotten to be hard-boiled and laconic. The pause had been for effect only. "Plenty of work, in any case," Raikes said, by way of encouragement.

"Oh, yes, no shortage of work, though they tried to operate a closed shop from time to time. Building going on all over the place, tremendous demand for statues. There are some references to a stone carver from Piedmont named Donato Baffo, who was employed in the workshop of Bartolomeo Bon. He is known to have done two of the water spouts on the façade of the Ducal Palace — very accomplished and delicate work. But that was in the 1450s. The best bet is the one you must have had in mind when you set me on to this business. No good trying to look innocent, Simon. You must have known there was a contract in existence between the Supplicanti in Venice and one Girolamo Piemontese for a Madonna Annunziata."

"Well, yes, I did," Raikes said. "I suppose I should have told you. It seemed a long shot, you know."

"Still does," Steadman said. "There's no record of whether the work was ever done, there's no description of it anywhere, there's no connection with the present location of your Madonna. Annunciate Virgins were being commissioned all over the place at that time."

"Do you know anything about this Girolamo?"

"All that is known about him comes as a footnote to the life of Jacopo della Quercia, the Sienese master. Girolamo Piemontese is known to have worked in Bologna, at San Petronio, as an assistant to della Quercia. How he came to Bologna, no one knows. He is mentioned by name in connection with the reliefs round the main doorway, but this would have been under direction, not independent work — probably. Nobody knows, of course. He left Bologna in a hurry; again, nobody knows why — possibly some trouble with the authorities. Then he turned up in Venice and seems to have lived obscurely until he obtained the commission from the friars."

"They rejected her, you know. At least, they didn't use her on their church. Could this have had something to do with the style or execution of the work? There's a very sensuous treatment of the drapery, for example. The friars might not have approved."

"Too sexy, you mean?" Steadman considered a moment. Then he said, "I don't think it is very likely. One doesn't know, of course. The Supplicanti were an ascetic order, it's true — though this Venetian lot doesn't seem to have been, or not for long. More of that in a moment. Asceticism was seen as a sort of bloodless martyrdom, you know. By emphasizing Mary's purity, the friars could see her as a model, and in that case the more abstract the method of composition, the more removed in time and space, the better. All the same, this was fifteenth-century Italy. The cult and depiction of the Madonna were well developed by then, and very delicate and varied grades of emotion were finding expression through her, among them the erotic. No, I think there would have been a fair degree of tolerance at the time. Mind you, asceticism has its other side too, and I think that is what may have gone wrong with the Supplicanti."

"How do you mean?"

Steadman drank some more of his beer. "I did some work on them too," he said. "Once I had discovered the connection. Of course, if you had not been so devious, Simon, I would have known the connection earlier."

"I should have told you," Raikes said again. But he could see that the other man bore no grudge; was even, in his rather morose way, enjoying the situation.

"I have a theory about them," Steadman said. "Nobody knows for sure why they were expelled from Venice. This stuff about indiscipline and debauchery doesn't get us very far. If it had been only individuals, they would have been dealt with as individuals.

It had to be something collective, something dangerous to the establishment. It wasn't political, or the secular authorities would have been involved. As far as I can see, that leaves heresy. Now the only heresy I could think of that might tie up with sexual malpractices, no pun intended, is gnosticism. Art history takes you into odd corners sometimes — I once did a paper on gnosticism in relation to early Christian sculpture. So I knew there was a standard work on the subject by a man called Abrahams."

Steadman paused and drank again, obviously savoring the moment. Then he said, "It's got a reference to the Supplicanti in the index, Simon. It seems that the founder of the order, a man named Matteo da Polenta, had been a follower of the Christian gnostic Pipo Fiorentino, who was burned for heresy in 1302."

"What did the heresy consist of?"

"They saw the physical world as irredeemably evil. There was nothing to be done about this; it began with the *descensus angelorum*, the mingling of spirit with substance in the creation of the world. The business of the soul was to repudiate the body and so reach awareness of its divine origin. Seems mild enough now, but these beliefs were passionately held, and they were regarded as a serious threat to a church which was set on affirming the sacramental nature of the world through the doctrine of the Incarnation. Serious enough to burn them when they caught them, in preceding centuries anyway. All the same, they lingered on here and there."

"In an established monastic order? At the tail end of the fifteenth century?"

"Why not? They were a flagellant order, weren't they? Contempt for the flesh can take various forms. You can leave it alone, you can flog it, or you can debase it through perverted practices. I think it was the third way that the Supplicanti took and that's why they were kicked out. None of which helps you much with your Madonna."

"I don't know," Raikes said. "Paradoxical, isn't it, if they despised the flesh so much that they should commission a Madonna Annunziata, one of the great Christian symbols of flesh sanctified?" He paused for a moment or two, then he said, "What happened to Girolamo afterward? Did you find anything out?"

"Absolutely nothing. No more commissions, no more references to his name at all. A complete blank."

"Surely it's unusual for someone to disappear like that, without trace?" Raikes found it difficult to keep the disappointment out of his voice.

"Not really. He disappears from our view, that's all. There are gaps of years in even the best-documented lives of the period. Our lad may have married well or come into money. He may have decided to give up the trade of carving for something a bit more regular."

"Give it up?" Raikes said. "He would never have done such a thing. I know he wouldn't. This is an *artist* we're talking about."

He paused. It was a dangerous moment for him to do so. "An artist," he said again. Suddenly, without warning, emotion had him by the throat; he felt his eyes threatened with tears. "What nonsense!" he said loudly. "You think that is what people do?"

"I'm sorry," Steadman said quickly. "I didn't mean to sound glib about it. There could be a thousand reasons. I didn't realize you were so sure this Girolamo was your man."

Raikes swallowed, feeling ashamed already, though whether of his emotion or his rudeness he did not know. "Please take no notice of me," he said. "I'm a bit on edge, I think. I've got no proof at all."

One of Steadman's rare smiles came to his face, lighting up its rather somber lines. "I wouldn't let that deter you," he said. "Nobody else does." He paused for a moment or two, then said in different tones, "Listen, Simon, I know it's none of my business, but you're looking distinctly under the weather. I suspect you've been spending yourself on that stone lady of yours. Why not take it easy for a day or so at least? We could go over to the Lido tomorrow if you like. Have a swim, have lunch."

"It's a nice idea," Raikes said. "I'm so near the end, you see. There's just her face."

"After five hundred years, another day wouldn't put her out too much. Still, of course I can see you want to get her finished. When it's all done, we'll have a big celebration dinner."

"That's a marvelous idea," Raikes said. "We'll have Barfield and Muriel in their best bandages."

"And Owen, with a coil of rope."

"Slingsby and the Japanese, carrying art object in box."

"Sir Hugo."

"That tiny editor, Beamish-Smith, for an improvisation on the theme of flesh tints. We could sit him next to Pauline."

"On second thoughts . . ." Steadman frowned and compressed his lips, as if debating the matter with himself. "Let's have a drink, just the two of us," he said after some moments. "I don't want the expense."

This made Raikes laugh a good deal. He was inclined to laughter now, after his earlier inexplicable outburst. He was smiling still as he watched Steadman make his way across the square, through a confusion of sunlight and parasols and pigeons, in the direction of San Moise. He himself went off in the opposite direction, toward the Molo. He paused outside the Sansovino Library, gazing at the alternating lion and human faces above the central arches. The lions looked unexpectedly benignant and mild, the men distinctly ferocious, and this too seemed very funny to Raikes in the slight hysteria of his present mood, though whether the joke was deliberate or merely an accident of time was difficult to determine. High above, along the topmost balustrade, too far away for their expressions to be read, white figures in attitudes of tension and turning looked down from every pinnacle, as if in some petrified apotheosis.

From here he made his way directly to the police station, explained to the policeman at the desk who he was, and produced his passport in proof of it. There were two men sitting on a bench who did not seem to be policemen at all and Raikes felt obscurely offended at the thought of having to collect the dead man's things in front of other people, not even officials. It seemed to make light of poor Litsov somehow.

In the event he was asked to go into an inner room, bare but for two upright chairs and a table with a mottled glaze on it. Litsov's things were brought to him here in a large brown bag. He would have taken them as they were, without examination, in his haste to get away, but one was not allowed to do this, it seemed; there was an official procedure. The contents of the bag had to be checked against a list, signed for.

The policeman, who was fat and rather expressionless of feature, explained all this to Raikes, afterward slowly laying out the articles one by one on the table: jacket and trousers, tie, socks, underclothes — pathetically Litsov had been wearing brief, jaunty red underpants. The clothes had been washed and ironed — by whom, Raikes wondered. Was there a subdivision of the force responsible for this? The shoes were dull, with white tide lines on them. Some loose change, bank notes, a wallet, a photograph, a little silver pillbox, quite empty. He had not carried much about with him. No wrist watch . . . The wallet was lined with plastic, so the photograph had not fared too badly. Under the stolid gaze of the policeman Raikes picked it up. It was a close-up of Chiara, blurred and streaked but still recognizable, smiling.

When the first intimation came to him of something wrong, he could not have said. He was looking down the list the policeman had handed him, not really checking the items, making a sort of pretense of doing so, preparatory to signing. After all, it didn't matter much, he thought; no one wanted these things if Chiara didn't. Though she might well have second thoughts when she came to a calmer acceptance of her loss . . . His eye moved over the list, considering items at random, passing on. He saw they had the tie pin down, *una fermacravatta,* and he glanced at the table to see if it was there. It was next to the pillbox. Beside it was a single cuff link, silver and black, in the shape of a small medallion. Raikes picked it up. It was quite heavy, a disc of some black stone, rimmed with silver, rather unusual.

"Only one?" he said to the policeman. *"Un gemello solo?"*

"Si, signore, soltanto uno."

"Where is the other one? *Dov'è l'altro?'*

The policeman raised his shoulders in a slight shrug — his first movement since putting the things on the table. *"Se guarda la lista . . ."* he said. "If you look at the list, you will find only one."

Raikes saw at once that this was true: it was down there as *un gemello,* a cuff link. "Yes, I see," he said, rather vacantly. *"Soltanto uno."*

The policeman's stolidity seemed to intensify, if that were possible. The matter clearly presented no difficulty to his mind. A man drowns, it is an agony, things might well have become detached.

The only way to look at it, Raikes thought vaguely, signing the receipt, restoring the contents to their bag, taking his leave. No one, after all, would *steal* a cuff link. But the policeman had not seen Litsov in the water . . . At the moment of stepping out onto the street, Raikes remembered that left sleeve riding up the arm a little. Of course, because the cuff link must have been missing then. But that had been the only sign of disarray. Everything else had been in place. Even his handkerchief . . . Litsov had not flailed about; he had not been roughed up by waves. He had been unconscious; he had choked quietly in shallow water; there had been no struggle at all.

7

Clutching the bag, Raikes walked for some time without much noticing which way he was going. His mind, always very tenacious, was occupied with a simple logical series repeated over and over again. Could Litsov simply have forgotten or omitted to wear the other cuff link? This was unlikely: he had been dressed with conspicuous care, prepared for the world — Chiara had exclaimed at sight of his debonair tie pin. Besides, it would have been noticeable; one of his shirt sleeves would have been loose, or had a tendency to flap, or been in some way obviously different from the other. Anyway, it was not the sort of thing you would forget to do. You might put on odd socks or forget to do up your fly, but you would know you hadn't a cuff link in; you would feel the difference. It had to be supposed that when he and Chiara left the house, both cuff links were still in place.

Very probably at any rate, he thought. He began to feel the need for a drink. Somewhere behind his dogged reasoning he sensed something terrible beginning to loom, but he couldn't stop. He saw Litsov's blank stare again, that meekly open mouth. What could be imagined as happening to him in the water that could have left his handkerchief and tie in place and at the same time pulled one of his cuff links through four separate apertures in four separate thicknesses of sodden cotton?

He was crossing the Campo San Marino now in the direction of the Church of the Miracoli. At the north side of the canal he hesitated for a while, then turned left. After a few steps it came to him that he should be going in the opposite direction, toward the Fondamenta Nuova, to catch the Burano boat for his visit to Chiara. But there was something he should do first. What was it? Of course, he must put Litsov's things somewhere . . . Could the cuff link have been lost during recovery of the body or by the police later? No, it was missing when I found him, sleeve of both jacket and shirt had ridden up, baring part of the left forearm. Of course at the time I did not associate this with . . .

At the Miracoli Bridge he paused irresolutely, his desire for a drink increasing. Could someone have *taken* the cuff link? At this moment he heard his name called and, turning, saw Slingsby bearing down on him in what looked like the same billowing fawn suit, as if he had been in limbo since their last meeting, waiting to materialize again.

"Well, hello there," Slingsby said. "Mr. Raikes, isn't it? How goes it? How is the stone lady?"

Raikes felt his hand enfolded in a larger, softer one. "She's fine," he said. "I'm not far off the end now. There's only her face."

"That's just great," Slingsby said. The pink expanse of his face eddied with suggestions of pleasure and approbation, though the small blue eyes were as anxious as ever. A compound odor of gin and peppermint creams came from him.

"What brings you this way?" Raikes said.

"I've been looking at the marble panels in the Miracoli Church. That is something I do from time to time. It is a wonderful thing, Mr. Raikes, and a deeply reassuring thing, to discover a beauty and harmony that depend on no depiction of the human form or other humanized motifs."

Slingsby paused, making delicate fidgety motions just below his chin. "I do not like the human image," he said. "Not really. Not deep down. If you ever want a trip on a downward slope, go from these beautiful marble panels to the sculptures at the Giovanni and Paolo Church; severe, yes, restrained, yes, but our ugly passion for self-replication is evident already. From there to the grotesqueries of the Ospedaletto; finish up with that hideous, degenerate face on the *campanile* of Santa Maria Formosa — the gratuitous ugliness of which inspired your John Ruskin's wrath and disgust."

"Not mine," Raikes said. "I don't like Ruskin much. Besides, he was wrong. That face on the *campanile* is now thought to be a realistic portrait of a person actually suffering from a painful and degenerative disease." Of course, he thought, if someone did take the cuff link, then that person must have witnessed Litsov's death or found him dead, and since he did not try to save him or get help or do anything at all . . . But why take a cuff link?

There was only one conceivable reason.

"I hope you don't think that disproves Ruskin's point or mine," Slingsby said. "Facts like that have got nothing to do with truth. Somebody *chose* to carve that face, for a joke I guess — Venice is full of jokes. Would you care for a drink?"

"I'd like one very much," Raikes said.

They found a table in the café bar of the Miracoli on the corner of the square. Slingsby asked if they had gin and relaxed visibly when told that they did. "I like gin," he said. "It's a clean drink." Raikes asked for cognac and swallowed half of it at once.

"There's another reason why I like those panels," Slingsby said. "They are reasonably secure from deterioration over the foreseeable future. You can't say that for the external stonework."

Raikes nodded, saying nothing. It could be seen from the greater fixity of his regard that Slingsby was returning to his obsessions, now that the flurry of the encounter had died down. It was necessary only to keep up an appearance of attention. She will be waiting for me, he thought. Moving about the house, alone in it, alone on the island, Lagoon water glimmering all round her, the water where her husband died. She had stayed on there in the house. He had thought this was courage . . . We might have a fire later, and the oil lamps on, something to drink, and we would talk, sit close together in the firelight. When I hear her voice and look into her face, everything will be all right again; these hideously breeding maggots of doubt will shrivel and die . . . But not in that room where his bronzes are, those polished ambivalent fragments. Five thousand pounds. *Litsov is my creation. My husband almost never leaves the island.* Never again anywhere now . . .

"This is granite we're talking about," Slingsby was saying. "A granite obelisk. At one stage of its career this obelisk lay prostrate on the delta silt of the Nile, at Heliopolis, for five hundred years. Five hundred years, Mr. Raikes, lost and forgotten, soaking up soluble salts by capillary migration and at a tremendous rate — this is flood-plain silt we're talking about. Yet did the salts in those pores hydrate? No, sir, they didn't. And why? You know and I know the answer to that." Slingsby advanced his face a little, pausing for effect. "Atmosphere too dry," he said, carefully stretching his moist little mouth round the words. "All the same if it was five *thousand* years. Now you put that obelisk up here, or in New York's Central Park, or on the London Embankment, and in two years the surface would be dripping off it. Two years."

"I know," Raikes said. "It's amazing."

"See it as a courtship ritual," Slingsby said. "That is the way I have taken to thinking of it. Borrow a leaf from the naturalist's book. Strictly heterosexual, of course. The water drops we should see as female, the hungry and highly motivated SO_2 as male. The randy sulphur dioxide swirls about, just longing to get into the pants of the H_2O, have its way, swarm down onto the stone in aqueous solution, a nuptial flight that ends in a bath of sulphuric acid."

Slingsby paused, staring solemnly at Raikes, his hands busy with their curious plucking motions in the air before his chest. "For sexual intercourse, read hydrolization," he said.

"Are you having another?" Raikes said. "I'm going to."

"Yes. Double gin, please. Think of it cosmically. Think of the dangers to stone in the atmosphere, even without the interference of man. Think of the dissolved gases and ions concentrated in the dust, impalpable, invisible to the naked eye, the influence of oceans and desert flats on the sulphate and chlorate content, the continuous mixing of the air masses by winds and vertical updrafts . . ."

It was clear by now that Slingsby was talking himself into a state of nervous agitation. Threads of saliva stretched at the corners of his mouth. His little blue eyes stared affrightedly. "I can hardly stand to think about it," he said.

Raikes stirred and spoke with an effort. "I thought it was only in literature that the Americans had an Apocalyptic school," he said, attempting a smile. "There is something I was wondering about, I'm afraid it is changing the subject . . . Do you by any chance know how many casts a sculptor is allowed to make of a particular work?"

Slingsby blinked and moved his bulky shoulders, as if emerging from some dream. "Casts?" he said. "We are talking about metal sculptures?"

"Yes."

"As many as he wants, I guess. So long as he doesn't call them originals. He wouldn't want to make copies; depreciates the currency. Normally speaking, he would scrap the molds after the first casting."

"Yes, quite. No, I meant originals."

"I'm not sure," Slingsby said. "I think I read somewhere that the U.S. Bureau of Customs currently recognizes the first four as originals, no, maybe it's six. I don't know about the British."

"Probably much the same with us." Raikes finished his drink and stood up. "I'll have to rush off, I'm afraid," he said. "Various things to see to — rather pressing."

He was in such haste to get away before Slingsby offered to accompany him that he almost forgot the bag.

8

He walked back toward the Miracoli Canal, moving quickly at first, slowing down when he was out of sight of Slingsby. It was almost six o'clock. He had eaten little that day, but he was not hungry. He was feeling the effects of the two brandies taken on an empty stomach, and he stopped on the way home to drink some coffee. Back at his apartment he washed and tried to rest for a while, but he could not rid his mind of questions, dared not try. He held consciously now to his perplexity, tried to creep farther in, as if it were a cave of refuge, as if he could hide in this twilight from the appalling certainties massing at the mouth.

He was on the point of leaving again when Signora Sapori came up to say that there was a phone call for him, *un Signor Lattimer*.

Standing in the narrow hall, Raikes held the receiver in silence for some moments while he controlled his breathing. "Hullo," he said at last. "Raikes here."

"Simon? I've been trying to get you all afternoon." Lattimer's voice was impatient, slightly hectoring, as always. "This is terrible news," he said. "I've only just heard about it. I've been away on business these last few days. You found him, didn't you? It must have been —"

"When did you go?" Raikes said.

"What?"

"When did you leave Venice?"

There was a short silence. The line crackled faintly. Raikes could sense the creature at the other end processing this question, computing the nature of the seeming irrelevance.

"The same evening poor Paul was drowned," Lattimer said at last. "Luigi drove me to the airport. Flights were delayed, though, because of the fog. Simon, I haven't got much time, there's a lot to do, as you can imagine. He left no will, you know. Chiara has asked me to see to things."

"Yes, of course."

"I believe she asked you to pick up Paul's things from the police."

"Yes."

"Quite unnecessary. I'm sorry you had to go through that."

"I didn't mind so much." Lattimer could not have known about this, not until his return. Chiara must have told him. An unpleasant surprise. What had *he* told *her?* Did she know, he wondered suddenly, about that long, windowless shed in Lattimer's garden?

"Everything in order, was it?" Lattimer's voice was normal, casually brisk.

"Everything the police had in their possession was handed over to me," Raikes said deliberately. In the pause that followed, he sensed once again that his words were being processed, felt over for what they would yield, by a mind that was isolated and tenacious and beyond responsibility somehow. He listened for perhaps six seconds to the low crackling on the line, pictured the staring composure of the other's face. The certainty that Lattimer had killed Litsov came over him like a wave. He felt a chill of fear, not of the man himself but of his own knowledge, his alacrity to grasp the evil. "She doesn't want them," he said, striving to keep his voice steady.

"Well, that's the point, that's partly why I'm ringing. The fact is that she does want them after all . . . She's in a state of shock still, you know."

"Yes, of course."

"She was rather expecting you this evening, I gather."

"Yes . . . I may not be able to make it now."

"In that case, I wonder if I could send Luigi round to pick up the things?"

"Of course," Raikes said. "I'll leave them with the landlady. I probably won't be at home myself."

The arrangement once made, Lattimer rang off fairly abruptly. Replacing the phone, Raikes became aware that he was sweating. What code or bond had kept him reticent, had kept them talking like that, within those conventional limits?

It was quite impossible to remain at home any longer. The brown bag he left in the care of Signora Sapori, its contents complete save only for the cuff link — this he took with him. He had no particular idea of a destination. Once in the street, he turned on impulse toward the northern part of the city, crossing the Misericordia and Sensa canals, coming out finally on the wide rectilinear expanse of the Sacca, that great square bite in the northern shore of Venice. Here, below the bridge, he found a quiet place to sit, facing out toward the Lagoon, with the long façade of the Palazzo Contarini opposite and the white walls of San Michele just across the water.

Behind him, out of sight, the sun was setting. The wide expanse of the Lagoon opened out beyond the mouth of the Sacca, pale and luminous, with a straight track of red across it. From moment to moment, as he watched, this faded and spread, as if bleeding into the water. I could still go, he thought. A few minutes' walk would take me onto the Fondamenta Nuova, right alongside the Burano boat stage. I could phone from Burano, she would come for me . . .

She had phoned from Burano herself, that night. She had phoned to say she was not coming back. So Litsov had no reason to hang about in his suit near the water. Litsov, whom I hardly knew, whom I did not want to know or think about, because I was falling in love with his wife; Litsov the pompous Platonist, with his shyness, his irritable vanity, blankly noble brows, not a likable man. With that talent for making shapes of metal. Turned into a mere drowned shape himself. Because you see, Raikes told himself carefully, that is what was done to Litsov. He had not been dressed up for drowning at all. *He had been drowned because he was dressed up,* because he was intending to go to the mainland, because he would no longer stay in the prison of the island, laying the golden eggs. That is why she did not go back that night, not because of the fog, not because it was difficult or dangerous, but because she did not want to return with the boat. She made sure he would not get off the island. And then, of course, from Burano she had phoned Lattimer . . .

Raikes stirred and sighed. It was the only possible explanation. Otherwise, how could Lattimer have known what Litsov intended to do? What coincidence could have brought him out through the fog and the darkness of that evening? They must have been cheating Litsov for a long time, perhaps since they first installed him on the island. Something to do with the casting, making extra casts from his molds probably, selling them as originals. Easy to do, on an international market. And at the prices Litsov was beginning to command . . . Lattimer would have all the necessary connections. It was a perfect set-up. *Litsov is something of a recluse, you know.* Then they had gone too far; he had become suspicious. But why had they held back his work like that, at the end? It had been only a matter of time, surely, before he found out. Had they taken this into account, *foreseen* it? And the phenobarbital — presumably there had been no traces in his system. The fact that Litsov had been prescribed the same drug, by the same doctor, had made a deep impression on Raikes. Had Litsov refused, like himself, to cloud his visions? But no, Vittorini would have made a statement to the police. Litsov must have been in the habit of taking the drug, otherwise they would not have been so ready to see his death as misadventure. So it must have been kept from him somehow, or reduced, not just on that day, but *before.* Was that why they were holding his work back? Prices would rise after his death, for a while at least. In that case, sooner or later, one night or another, dressed up or not . . .

His mind flinched away from this. Who would answer such questions now? Who would even ask them? Not himself, certainly — he had decided that already. It was still possible to believe that she had not wanted or intended the death. In a sense it didn't matter. It was enough for him that she had *known,* from the moment of making the phone call, all through the night they had spent together. She had been feverish, restless, unable to sleep. He had supposed, he had allowed himself to believe, this was because of him . . . I must go to her, he thought, talk to her; a few words would be enough. This is in *me;* I am fabricating evil. My mind the host to it. No words even; a smile, a look from her eyes.

But as he watched the flushed water fade slowly, saw the zones of the surface marked off by varying depths, Raikes knew he would not go. In moments not consciously registered but quite irrevocable, between the red and gray of this evening, some complex blend of logic, self-abnegation, an instinct of retreat, had corrupted his love forever. This corruption was the truth now, beyond question. She had used him for her pleasure as she had used him for her safety. It was the thought of this pleasure that he found least endurable. Had she wanted distraction, or had what she knew excited her further? She had been in heat, and her mind all the time cool, self-regarding, planning her safety. The sense of this mystery visited him like nausea, and for some moments he felt he might be physically sick. This, or something like it, must be the truth, his mind insisted. Everything he knew, everything he could remember, confirmed it. While they sat at dinner, while she gave him those precise instructions, Lattimer had been crossing the shrouded Lagoon toward the island, making his way across this very water, clear now and luminous to the horizon. Perhaps at the moment she cried out and shuddered in his arms, Litsov, who carried her picture in his wallet, had been choking his last.

Out in the Lagoon groups of black stakes marked the entrance to the deep-water channel. The surface was darker around them, as if they were somehow staining the water. Dark objects darken in this light, pale ones increase their pallor, Raikes told himself, attempting by just observation to lessen the horror of his thoughts. If we had known each other longer, long enough for me to understand or make an attempt at understanding, or to have acquired some intimate knowledge of wrongs done to her or harm suffered. But there had not been long enough for more than this pain of betrayal. Once more he remembered that gesture of hers, which he had thought so out of character, that stroking of the hand down the arm, at once self-protective and self-loving. It was money she had wanted. With money you can ensure your safety with your pleasure. What had she said that day? *I want to be eternal . . .*

He took the cuff link from his pocket and looked at it closely: a disc of black stone, basalt probably, about the size of a man's thumbnail, with a thin rim of silver; the part that went through the buttonhole was a thin oval, also of silver. Lattimer it was who had spoken about the importance of things, of material objects. Who would have thought that such a very small thing as this, an insignificant artifact of stone and silver, of no particular value or beauty, could have revealed so much? Because of course, Raikes told himself in that same careful way, this object, which is not proof of anything at all, carries certainty with it. It was as if everything, the whole story, had been there, just behind, waiting to form.

There were random elements, of course. Chiara had acted on impulse, seized the occasion of his visit, the pretext of the fog; she had risked something — perhaps not much — to have someone to sleep with that night; she had taken a chance on his being willing to lie about it, implicate himself. Lattimer too, though the impulse was of a different kind: he could have waited, he could have had the pick of Litsov's possessions; but he had needed to despoil the body freshly killed, needed a trophy to add to the others in that windowless shed in the garden. And he himself, was he not the worst, who had improvised the story, imprisoned himself in it, with no more to go on than this object in the palm of his hand, scattered memories, a process of deduction flawed by his own self-contempt? How could he have thought she might love him? *Non si sa mai.* Strange creatures . . . *Who knows what ideas they will get into their heads?*

This echo frightened Raikes, and he got up to go. Darkness was not far off now. To the west the first lights of Mestre had come on. The water was pale gold across the whole surface of the Lagoon, covered with very faint corrugations. Suddenly the harmony of this vast rippled platter was disturbed by the passage of a *motoscafo* out toward San Michele. By the time the wake had died away the gold had gone, sea and sky were a uniform pale violet. Raikes stood for some moments longer, looking northward across the water. Out there in the gathering darkness was the speck of land that contained her. A luminous point, he had thought it once. His throat tightened. Another kind of man was needed. Not me, he thought. Nor the police either. I have been here before; this is not the first time; I have taken this path before.

He turned his back on the water and began to walk away in the direction of San Alvise. But almost at once, by a sort of homing instinct, he turned off toward his church, the place of his labors. He did not want to see anyone, talk to anyone. By disposition he was solitary — under stress he would always turn inward. Now he was glad of the approaching darkness, the relative quiet of the streets in this northern area of the city.

The *campo* was almost deserted. There was light around the café, and a few people were sitting within the enclosure made by the trellis and the potted shrubs. To Raikes's intense dismay, as he was passing through this zone of light he heard his name called and next moment found himself confronted by Barfield, who was wearing a striped tie and a smart navy blue blazer with glinting brass buttons.

"We're sitting over there," Barfield said, with unwarranted familiarity, as if they had arranged to meet and it was sufficient now to indicate the place.

"I was intending —" Raikes felt suddenly bereft of all will and energy. Glancing in the direction indicated he saw sharp-featured Muriel in a red dress and clashing amber necklace, head tilted in the act of draining a glass. "I don't think —" he began again.

"We're celebrating, old man," Barfield said. "Join us for a quick one?"

Helplessly Raikes allowed himself to be escorted to the table. He greeted Muriel with a bow and sat down. "Fixed fate, free will, foreknowledge absolute," he said. "That's Milton."

"This is Barolo, very good stuff," Barfield said. "I'll get another glass."

"What are you celebrating?" From where he was sitting he could see across the square to the dim façade of the church, make out the boxlike structure halfway up, within which his Madonna awaited the last stage of metamorphosis. Tonight, he thought; I must finish her tonight. Then tomorrow . . . It would be easier to face things if he had finished.

"We've got the first of the paintings back on the wall." Muriel was wearing lipstick tonight and had granted her mouth too generous a shape with it. *"The Woman Taken in Adultery,"* she said.

"Consolidated, cleaned, restored, forgiven," Barfield said. "Sorry, I was thinking of the hymn. *Reframed.* Good as new. It's the first to be completed, you know, so we thought we might make it a social occasion. All work and no play makes Jack a dull sod." His manner was more relaxed than usual, a fact that Raikes attributed to the workings of the Barolo.

"We asked Owen," Muriel said, in her cross-patch fashion — no change in her, at least. "He hasn't turned up yet and we've been here nearly an hour. And Pauline, of course . . ."

"Perhaps they have other fish to fry," Raikes said. His voice sounded curiously pure and detached to him, as if his words were distilling on the air rather than straggling from his larynx. He was in some neutral zone where warring elements meet and sheer off: Muriel's celebratory perfume, Barfield's gleaming buttons and his stripes of some obscure club or association, the house in the Lagoon with water slopping at the landing stage, Litsov's meek mouth.

"Well," he said, "congratulations anyway."

"We could never have done it," Muriel said, "could we, Jerry, if we hadn't spent so many nights working late?"

"And you were handicapped," Raikes said vaguely. "Broken limbs, dislocations, and so on." It was to their groans in the darkness that his quest had begun. *Oh, Jerry, Jerry, Jerry.* All the saints and Virgins staring down. "You battled on," he said.

It was the right note. From the way Barfield was pouring out his Barolo, from the irritable but pleased stretching of Muriel's reddened mouth, he could see that these remaining Tintoretto people were once more fully in their heroic role. This was Homeric stuff, the sweet carousing after hardships suffered and dangers survived.

"Well, of course," Barfield said, "we've had our ups and downs, haven't we, Muriel? But that's what life is about, isn't it? And you've got to be humble. We can't know everything, can we? I mean, we don't even know one another. Wasn't it you who talked about people trying to learn about death by measuring corpses? That was early on, when we were just beginning here. I won't tell you a lie, I was put out at the time. But you were right. Facts don't get us all that far. And even when it comes to facts we never get the essential ones."

"How do you mean?"

"Well, take Tintoretto. We can analyze his paint surface until we know every color he used; not only that but how he made them, the constituent elements. For example, we know that he made his gesso by roasting gypsum, grinding it to powder, and binding it with animal glue. We know to the month when he gave up the gesso preparation and started painting on a dark ground. We know how he made the dark ground. We can look at a window frame and we can say this was done with white lead and a coarse brush. We can say that is arsenic sulphide; we can dissolve this in chloroform and prove it to be indigo. Every stage, from the first brushstroke . . . But we don't possess, and we never will possess, the one essential piece of information."

"What is that?"

"What did he use" — Barfield widened his eyes in the visionary way Raikes now remembered — "what did he use to give his colors that quality of vibrancy? How is it that they do not fade? He used something else, some additive, some drying agent, completely undetectable by modern science."

"If it's undetectable, how do you know that it's there at all?"

"It must be there. How else can you account for the special quality of radiance in late-fifteenth-century Venetian painting? Titian has it too. People have always recognized it. The Venetian Secret, they call it. They knew something we don't."

"You may be right," Raikes said, "but it seems odd to me to pin your faith on a material explanation, and one that is completely undemonstrable. It rather contradicts what you began by saying." He rose to his feet with a sense of effort. "I'll have to be getting along," he said. "Are you working late tonight?"

Muriel giggled, a rather startling sound. She said, "We're not dressed for it."

"We're going to have dinner when Owen comes," Barfield said.

In haste to forestall an invitation, Raikes began at once to move away. "Well, have a nice time," he said. He crossed the lighted area adjoining the café, gaining with a sense of release the shadows beyond. He crossed the square on the far side, made his way round the curved projection of the apse, and began immediately to climb up his ladder.

For reasons still not clear to him he had never succeeded in obtaining a light from official sources; the matter had been passed from one authority to another without any result. Finally accepting defeat, Raikes had provided himself with two strong, battery-operated lanterns which he could hang at different levels from the scaffolding. These he lit now and hung up, on either side of the Madonna's head.

His equipment was as he had left it, under the tarpaulin sheet. Half mechanically he donned overalls, cap, and mask. Within a minute or two he was at work on the last remaining area of pollution, delicately, despite his tiredness, clearing the blackened, clotted gypsum from the sockets of the eyes, stroking away with the hail of particles the badger stripe of bleach that ran from the forehead to the bridge of the nose. The cutter hissed in fading or intensifying volume, combining with the hum of the compressed nitrogen fueling the motor to make a varying pulse of power. Raikes shut his mind to all thought. The world was reduced to this small, dusty enclosure, the Madonna's face, the steady white light of the lamps.

When he stopped finally it was almost midnight and her face was without blemish, her sight restored. He knew now whose face it was — it was as if he had known all along, had unconsciously resisted the knowledge. That faintly smiling, dreaming face, the curve of the mouth, the eyes narrow and long, the wide, rather low forehead; he had seen them before: it was the face of the drowned girl, unwilling and yet complaisant, expressing a sort of secret complicity in her own death. It was the face that had looked at him through clear water, the same he had seen blurred and indistinct through some thicker, less transparent medium. Of course, he thought, she must have been the model; Girolamo used her for his model. Was she the naked, laughing girl in the room with the straight shadows? That band round her neck . . . She had died by violence; he knew it suddenly. And yet the face had been peaceful, slightly smiling, like the one before him now. The drowned do not smile. He thought of Litsov's solemn stare, the meekly open mouth accepting death like a sacramental biscuit.

He had stepped back to the rail, surprise at this recognition flooding his mind. Afterward, when he tried to think about the next few moments, it seemed to him that he had ceased quite to look at the Madonna, or had relaxed his attention in some way without turning it on anything else. It was in this unguarded moment that Raikes felt the hush and resonance, the sense of exposure and isolation, the half-sweet, half-fearful sensation of swooning, and he was looking again at the statue. The scale was the same; there was the same distance between them; but the air had darkened. There was a sense of space; the source of illumination was not now the lamps but the Madonna herself, as she glowed in the darkness with a radiance of her own, a soft enveloping flame of light, strangely local and contained, not reaching into the darkness all around. This time the sense of swooning was more intense, Raikes's balance was lost, and he sank to his knees on the platform.

How long this lasted he had no means of telling; he was still kneeling when he came to himself again, with that belated alarm, the Madonna above him, the bright lamps on either side with moths fluttering round them, her face turned slightly to greet the angel's news.

He walked back to his apartment in a state of suspended consciousness, noticing nothing of his surroundings. In the dim light of the hall he saw that the brown bag was no longer where Signora Sapori had placed it in readiness. Luigi must have been there, then.

On the hall table there was a letter for him. He took it upstairs with him and read it in his room. It was from Wiseman, apologizing for not answering his queries earlier, explaining that he had been away for several days attending a conference in Milan. Unfortunately, there was not much to tell. He had found both names in

Capellari's *Origin of Illustrious Gentlemen.* The Rovereto were an old but not particularly distinguished Venetian family ennobled only after the Serrata of 1296. Matteo was a second son. In 1415 he had married one Maria Bernardoni, who bore three sons and outlived him by ten years. The Bernardoni were Piedmontese, with large estates up near the French border, very powerful in local terms but too remote to have much influence farther south . . .

Piedmont, he thought at once. That must be the connection, but through the wife. In that case it was the artist, not the girl . . .

He was exhausted. Standing there in the chilly silence of his room, still shaken by that terrible radiance of the Madonna, wrestling with the implications of Wiseman's letter, worried by Luigi's sinister promptness, he felt a sudden overmastering need to deaden his nerves, achieve some peace. Without thought, without debate, he went to his drawer and took out the plastic cylinder that contained his phenobarbital. He filled a glass with water from the hand basin and took thirty milligrams, the dose Vittorini had prescribed.

9

Within half an hour oblivion descended on Raikes and he slept without stirring. He rose at his usual hour, aware of a slight heaviness in his limbs, but clearheaded, with all the details of what he intended to do that day firmly present to his mind.

As soon as he was dressed he got out his diary. This would be one of the last entries. With none of his usual hesitation he put in the date at the top of the page, *June 16,* and began.

The Madonna is now completely restored, her whole surface free of corrosion. The first and main consequence of this is that she will have to be sealed with the least possible delay. Naked as she is, she is extremely vulnerable to further pollution. The air of Venice is a killing agent, as Slingsby remarked to me once, and it works with terrifying speed on exposed stone. If she were left for long now, longer than a day or so, even in this drier weather, it would be like curing someone of a fever, then stripping off his clothes and turning him out of doors. I am planning to do the sealing later today, using wax acrylic and a propane burner. That done, my work in Venice will be over.

It is clear to me now, in the light of Wiseman's information, that this Matteo di Rovereto was Girolamo's patron, and that the letter from Federico Fornarini which Chiara got for me is — must be — a reply to some previous letter from di Rovereto asking for clemency on Girolamo's behalf, not on the girl's, as I first thought. The wording is ambiguous, but the real clue is in the Piedmontese connection. Di Rovereto's wife was a Bernardoni. Natural she should take an interest in him — perhaps it was through her influence that he obtained the commission in the first place. Odd to see a Fornarini cropping up in this earlier period, right at the beginning of the Madonna's career. But they were numerous enough, I suppose.

If I am right and it is Girolamo that is being pleaded for, the girl's character acts in mitigation of him, not of herself, so she must be a bad character, and a public bad character in those days must surely mean a prostitute. All this seems reasonable enough. He must have been accused of some crime in connection with the girl. Was she the victim? Disregard for human life, the letter said. Murder then, or serious assault. She was the victim, yes. Is she the drowned girl? In that case, the model for the Madonna, the drowned girl, this hypothetical whore, are all the same woman. Yes.

But in that case . . . She was smiling, though she had died violently. I'm convinced that everything I have seen in these famous attacks of mine has contained some truth, some relevance to the Madonna, even the things I do not understand and perhaps never will. So it must mean something, this smile. Did I make some mistake, get the message wrong? Perhaps I simply transferred the smile from the living face to the dead one — the kind of thing that happens sometimes in dreams. Or could there be a different order of truth in it, something emblematic? Was she smiling because she had been vindicated in some way? Or avenged? And the light that shone from her, from the Madonna. That was the miracle, of course; that is what they saw, or had a strong impression of seeing, three hundred years later, in the garden of what is now the Casa Fioret. The light came from her. There is some sort of sexual treachery here too. Hush money to the Bishop. This Cornadoro, whoever he was, the cuckold, he laid golden eggs — like poor Litsov.

I am at the end of things now. There is only one more thing I can think of doing.

Raikes paused, and the horror descended on him that had never been far away since his visit to the police station the day before, when Litsov's things had been handed over. It was this, he saw now, that had invaded and darkened his sense of the past. The same stain spread over both, the same elusive presence, everywhere answering, but never sufficiently, to the pressure of his mind, the touch of his curiosity. Like a sponge, he had said. Everywhere you touch it . . . But dirty liquid, in past and present alike, no pure distillation this, rather an ooze of treachery and crime. Everywhere his mind looked, there was the same flinch of horror, even in the small details of memory: the blackened stakes at the landing stage, the groping weeds, the languid crabs against the wall . . .

He was rescued by the appearance of Signora Sapori with his breakfast. He had no appetite, but he drank the coffee. With it he took another thirty milligrams of phenobarbital, and when, shortly afterward, he left the house, the plastic cylinder went with him in his jacket pocket.

It was still early and cool, though the sky was almost cloudless — a few last wraiths dissolving without stain in the luminous east, over the Adriatic. A thin mist still lay on the water, but all the promise was for a hot, clear day. Raikes took a *vaporetto* to the station, crossed the canal by the Scalzi Bridge, and began to walk in the direction of the Frari. In the maze of narrow streets south of San Simeone he went wrong twice and had to ask the way. He came out finally on the north side of the Campo dei Frari and found himself by a lucky accident exactly where he wanted to be, immediately in front of the large, square-fronted building which houses the Venice state archives.

In the little cubbyhole of an office he made a preliminary explanation, in his careful Italian, to a pale, sleepy attendant in uniform. He was asked to wait. After some minutes a youngish, courteous, bald man arrived. He listened carefully, brown eyes mildly intent on Raikes's face.

"Yes" he said, "it is possible to refer to the records. You must have someone with you, unfortunately, *devo accompagnarLa,* since you have no authorization, you understand . . ."

"Yes, of course," Raikes said. "Thank you. It shouldn't take long."

"Is it the proceedings of the *signori di notte* or of the *quarantia* you would like to see?'

"I'm not sure about the difference."

"It is a murder, you say?"

"I think so, yes."

"In that case it would be the *quarantia,* almost certainly. They were the higher court. So we must look at the records of the *avogadori di comun.* They presented the evidence in criminal cases. We have no detailed records of the evidence, but we have the notes that were made on completion of the trials."

They went up three floors in a lift and passed into a long room with tables down the center, shelves of volumes up the walls, a steady, evenly distributed light from high windows. There was another, much older man, working at a small desk, who rose when they entered. After some consultation with his colleague and some maneuvering of a stepladder at the far end of the room, he took down a thick quarto-sized volume from one of the upper shelves and brought it to them.

"Each volume covers ten years." The younger man smiled. "*Tanta criminalitá,*" he said. "A lot of crime." He laid the heavy book on the table. "Perhaps the *signore* would like to sit here?"

Obediently, Raikes sat down and drew the book toward him. With the two officials maintaining a discreet distance, he began to look through the pages. These were the original entries of the magistrates, page by page, a bare statement of dates, names, verdicts, punishments. In many cases a brief laudatory phrase had been appended, as if to compensate these unfortunates for the harshness of their fate.

He found what he was looking for quite soon. It was an entry for November 6, 1432 — scarcely a fortnight after the date on Fornarini's letter to di Rovereto. Girolamo shared the page with two others: a young man named Francesco Natal, apprentice sailmaker, sentenced to three years in the galleys for stealing sacred objects from the church of San Samuele (*"giovane dotto e intelligente"*), and a sixteen-year-old maidservant, burned for arson (*"galante e bela"*). Below these, at the foot of the page, Girolamo Satta, stonemason, age thirty-three, hanged for the murder of Bianca Pellegrino (*e morì valorosamente"*).

My age exactly, Raikes thought. He felt that oppressed sadness we feel when reluctant suspicions are confirmed. The brevity of the entry, this terse disposal of a human life, appalled him. It had ended here, then.

For some time longer he sat looking at the names, as if they might provide some clue to this remote act of violence. Girolamo Satta, Bianca Pellegrino. Laughter in a sunlit room, water on naked bodies, lines of shadow . . . This was why no more work had come from the hand of Girolamo Piemontese. No voluntary abdication this, no private failure like his own, but a death in public view. *"È morì valorosamente,"* he died bravely. Raikes became aware again of the slight but pervasive heaviness of his limbs, a thick feeling in his tongue, not unpleasant.

He closed the book, stood up; the attentive officials came forward. The mutual courtesies, the descent in the lift, were barely registered in his consciousness. He found himself out in the open again, in the sunshine. The air was full of pigeons, loud with their wings. Something must have alarmed them, he thought. He looked blankly for some moments at the façade of the Scuola San Rocco across the square, then began to walk slowly in the direction of the Grand Canal. At the San Tomà landing stage there was a boat just casting off and he scrambled aboard at the last moment.

The weather in this brief interval had become brilliant. As they passed beneath the Rialto Bridge and rounded the upper loop of the canal, he was forced to squint against the dazzle from the water, the shimmer of pale brick from the celebrated façades on the opposite bank. Venice had paled in this drier air; the reddish tones of damp had gone; colors were everywhere more delicate now, more quiveringly responsive to light.

He descended at San Marcuolo and made his way northward to where the cleansed Madonna awaited her final seal of wax. He was anticipating this eagerly, the comfort of the cool stone under his hands, the safe enclosure of the cubicle, the hours of physical work and the boon of weariness that would follow them.

However, as he began to cross the *campo* toward the church, his sense of gaining sanctuary vanished at a stroke: Chiara Litsov was standing alone at the side of the main doorway. He had an immediate, craven impulse to flee, but she was looking toward him, she had seen him. It was clear that she was waiting for him there. Drawing near, he saw that she was smiling. "I thought I'd find you here," she said. "What happened to you last night?"

She leaned her face forward to kiss him. He felt the brief warmth of her lips on his, felt his own unwilling response. Awkwardly he placed a hand on her shoulder. "I didn't expect to see you," he said, realizing that of course he should have expected it, should have known. Responsibility for severance did not rest with him at all; it was she who would not be able to tolerate silence, uncertainty, the thought that something had gone wrong.

Something now in his tone or touch seemed to alert her; she raised her head to look fully at him, seemed about to speak. Then she moved away a little, the smile disappearing. "What's the matter?" she said. "Aren't you glad to see me?"

"We can't talk here," he said. "Come up with me."

He led her across to the foot of the ladder. The repairs to the church floor had been completed two weeks previously; there were no workmen standing about today to take an interest in her ascent. She went up before him, sure-footed, negotiating the narrow rungs with entire confidence. Then they were standing together in the small enclosure, with its odors of dust and sun-warmed plastic — odors of refuge hitherto for Raikes.

He had time to marvel at the resplendent whiteness of the Madonna, work of his patient hands, her face and upper parts radiant in the sunshine; time to remind himself that she was vulnerable still, that there was the need to seal her beauty against the aggressive impurities of the air. Then he turned to Chiara and said, "I picked up your husband's things yesterday." His tongue felt thick and slow. He looked at her as if in hope that this bare statement would explain all, resolve all. But she was silent still. "Then Lattimer had them picked up from my house," he went on. "Did he bring them to you?"

"No, he phoned to say he had disposed of them."

"Did he say anything about them?"

"No, what should he say? He said only that he had disposed of them. To spare me pain, he said."

"To spare you pain?" An involuntary twist of a smile came to Raikes's lips. "Chivalrous fellow," he said.

She was looking at him narrowly now and it seemed inimically. "Why are you speaking to me like this?" she said.

Of course, he thought, Lattimer would say nothing, why should he? He was cool, even if he was mad. Slowly, haltingly, looking away from her in shame, sometimes at the dreaming face of the Madonna, sometimes across the rooftops to the glitter of the Lagoon, he told her the stages of his suspicion, of his knowledge.

"Only you could have phoned Lattimer," he said. "No one else knew that your husband was set on going to the mainland. That was unexpected, wasn't it? His decision to go, I mean. I could tell from the way you reacted. You and Lattimer were in it together; you were using his molds to make extra casts, then putting them into circulation as originals. I priced a sculpture at Balbi's gallery. Litsov was prolific as an artist, wasn't he? Five thousand pounds a cast would not have been a bad return on no outlay to speak of. Then he got suspicious."

He looked at her finally. She had turned white, but her eyes continued to meet his without wavering. There was a slight frown on her face, a look of what seemed genuine puzzlement.

"But what has made you think that someone phoned Richard?" she said. "Me or anyone? Why should you think that anyone went to the island at all? The police have said that Litsov was alone, that the death was accidental."

"There was only one cuff link," Raikes said. He was in the corridors of the nightmare again now, with the fat, shrugging policeman and the brown bag. "Only Lattimer would have been capable of doing that," he said. "He took one of Litsov's cuff links after drowning him. He . . . collects things, you know. I suppose you know;

you and Lattimer are obviously on intimate terms." He paused for some moments, then added heavily, "I have thought and thought about it. There is no other explanation. You must have known it."

"Known it?"

The sudden rage in her voice dumbfounded him. He had not envisaged her reactions very clearly, being too much subject to the hideous unease of saying such things to her; but whatever he might have imagined, it was not this voice, not this white face of anger and contempt.

"Known it?" she said again. "How would I know such a thing? Do you think he would boast of it to me? To you, more likely. It is you who are interested in fetishes, not us; you, all these dirty little boys who cannot grow up. Is it my fault the fool is still *in calzoncini corti,* what do you say, in shorts?"

"In short trousers," Raikes said.

She had paused for breath, looking at him with no abatement of rage. Indeed, his correction seemed to make her angrier. "Ah, thank you," she said. "So you are the detective who says who is guilty at the end of the book and everyone is astonished by his cleverness. Tell me, why do you come to me with this talk of a cuff link?"

"I did not come to you." He was nettled by this misrepresentation. "You came to me," he said.

"But of course," she went on, "there is no one else, is there? You will not go to the police because you are not a man for that, and besides it would be useless, you have already lied to the police in various ways. In any case you have no proof at all. What is a cuff link? You can't even prove he was wearing them both. You are as mad as Richard, with your cuff link."

"I lied to help you," Raikes said. "You asked me to do it."

"Shall I tell you why you have spoken like this to me?"

"I wanted to give you a chance to explain."

"To you?" She made a sudden passionate gesture with the flat of her hand, waist high, as if cutting outward at something. "Why should I? What claim do you think you have on me? I am not accountable to you."

"Who then?" Raikes said. "Who are you accountable to?"

"You don't see me as I am — how can I talk to you? Because we spent a night together and liked it, that gives you rights over me? You come with that air of reasonable, injured man. 'Oh, dear, I am disappointed in you. I did not think you were that kind of woman.' *What kind of woman?* Tell me, please."

Raikes was bewildered. She had struck him before as reticent, rather. The spate of words, the furious mimicry, were completely unexpected. "I didn't say —" he began.

"And all the time," she broke in impetuously, "the real reason has got nothing to do with Litsov. It is your self-esteem that is hurt, because you think I used you for my safety and had my pleasure from you at the same time and said nothing, all commonplace things, but you had decided I should be your Madonna."

"Commonplace? Do you know what you are saying? Those are not commonplace things in my world."

Even to his own ears this sounded self-righteous and rather ridiculous. "You are quite wrong anyway," he added. "I was not looking for a Madonna." How had he got into this position; how had it come about? She had somehow forced the thing onto the plane of argument, and he was losing. With all the trump cards in his hand, he was being obliged to defend himself. "Quite untrue," he said.

"It is true, Simon. You go at once into a dream about women. I knew it from the first time we met. I saw it on your face that day we met on the path and I had been planting the seedlings. Simply it was a person doing some work in the garden, but that could not be enough for you, could it? I saw you then beginning to make a shape for me. You do it and we are fools and we join in the business. Then again — though by that time I was beginning to like you a lot — I saw the same stupidity, that day in the *campo* of the Maddalena, the poetry of Marin — *Me vogio êsse eterna* — remember?"

"Of course I remember. It was on that day I first knew I was —"

"But you *are* eternal, you said. I saw myself in your eyes, and I was pleased because I am a fool too, but then I thought, *Cosa vuol dire, questo signore?* What does he mean? I meant only that I want to live, I want to be alive forever, but you meant the Eternal Feminine or some such rubbish. *Non fare il cretino,* Simon; there is no such thing. Now, because I have failed to be the Madonna, you want to turn me into Jezebel, you want to be the Hercule Poirot of Venice and prove everything with the aid of a cuff link."

She paused for a moment, then said, with an extraordinary, driven vehemence, "I am *myself,* not your distortions. I *enjoyed* deceiving Litsov. Money, other men sometimes. What other way was there? It was *action.* Stuck there on the island to assist his talent, cook and clean for him, strip to be his model, stand or sit or lie while he cut me up into fragments? Was that enough? It was enough for *him.* All his sex went into those bits of metal."

"Did you and Lattimer sleep together?" The question, so long in his mind, sprang from him now without premeditation, forced out by her admissions.

"It is not really your business," she said, "but no, we didn't. I need to be strongly attracted before I can do that."

Raikes struggled to suppress the pleasure these few, almost careless words of hers had given him. He said. "You could have left him, couldn't you? But of course you might have found yourself pushed for money. Well, you are rich now, you have it all."

"Simon," she said, with a sudden change of tone, "don't let us stand here arguing anymore. I never intended Litsov's death, but he is dead. We — you and I — we are still alive. If you are a man you will look at me and see me and take me as I am."

She had noted his pleasure, he realized, the shameful gratification he had somehow not managed to conceal. She was formidable — he knew it now — as delicate in perception as she was quick in mind; and intent, focused to register his weakness. He cast about in his mind for an answer.

"That night in the hotel," she said, "it has never been so good with anyone else. That is the truth, I promise you."

"If I am a man?" he said slowly. "You talk as if you had the only notion of what a man is. You are doing the same thing you accused me of."

"Why do you talk as if we were in a courtroom? Listen to me: you could sculpt again. It was the great disappointment of your life, you said so. Now you have the choice to make again. You could give up your work at the museum. I could help you."

"Help me?" He looked at her almost incredulously. "I should

have thought you'd had just about enough of helping sculptors," he said. The color was back in her face and her eyes were bright. She was serious; he was suddenly convinced of it. It was monstrous, but she was entirely serious: she wanted to take him on, make a sculptor of him. The offer was naïve, perverse, delinquent, all at the same time. He looked closely at her face, the delicate bones at cheek and temple, the green-tawny eyes, the wide, sensuous mouth, lips slightly parted in the eagerness of her feelings. He struggled to imagine what her motives might be, and failed. In this moment of uncertainty, he experienced a sudden strong impulse of sexual desire for her. He looked away quickly, in case his eyes betrayed him.

"I need to *believe*," he said. "I need completeness, somehow. I don't quite know how to explain it. People call me a perfectionist, but that's not it really. I think it's partly why I turned away from being a sculptor. Now I think I was wrong to turn away. That's why I wanted the past so much, you know, the complete past of the Madonna. But all I have got is fragments. With you too it's the same. I don't understand you. I have looked too hard and I have somehow convicted myself. I don't know if you can see what I mean. I have corrupted my own feelings about you and about her."

"Because of a cuff link?" she said.

He was silent for a moment or two. Then he said, "Because you left him there."

She had moved closer to the Madonna. For a few moments he saw the two faces together, the vivid flesh and the immaculate stone. Then, with that devastating ability to sense what he might be feeling, she said, "The man who made this was different from you, Simon Raikes. He had courage to finish something."

He remained silent. She waited a moment longer, then turned away and began to climb down the ladder. He made no move to stop her. When she had gone, he stood motionless for several minutes, feeling alone and bereft. In this stricken silence he became aware gradually of the presence and predicament of the Madonna, the mute demand of the vulnerable stone. He would work; he would concentrate; he would shut his mind to everything else.

He had everything he needed: the wax acrylic, the propane

burner — these had been in readiness from the beginning. He set to work with devotion, beginning as before with the hem of her gown, using a narrow, house-painter's brush to apply the preservative, determined to neglect no smallest part of her. Anything missed the air would swoop on, deposit its contaminants there, set up once again the process of decay.

He worked unremittingly, the turpentine smell of the preservative in his nostrils, using the brush sometimes, sometimes his hands, working the glutinous stuff into the pores of the stone, stroking it into the complex folds of her clothing. As he settled into the caressive rhythm of the work, he found himself, despite all resolutions, thinking intently about Chiara, going over the details of their interview. It seemed to him now that he had taken the wrong attitude toward her; he had assumed the air of a superior being. No wonder she had been angry . . . Her first anger had not been with him, however, but with Lattimer: anger and contempt — a proof she had not known of that despoiling of the dead? Yes. No reason to think she knew Lattimer would kill him, or even do him physical harm, though she must have had some idea of it, of the possibility of it, otherwise why go to such trouble to establish an alibi? Or was he attributing too much calculation to her? She had panicked, phoned Lattimer, kept away. It was all he could with any certainty accuse her of . . . But she had not had a look of panic. He strove to recall her demeanor during that evening. Tense, stimulated. His great mistake, he saw it now, had been to adopt that accusing attitude, give her no real chance to explain. She was cheating Litsov, she admitted that. Still, the way she put it . . . Energy like hers, pent up and frustrated, might well find an outlet in such a way. Could she really be blamed for it? *All his sex went into those bits of metal.* He remembered her, on the day of his first visit, standing somehow lost among those fragments of herself. And Lattimer, with his trophy tufts. Hers not among them. *She did not sleep with Lattimer.* For some reason he believed this implicitly. She slept with *me.* I have been too harsh with her, he thought.

All the rest of the morning and well into the afternoon, as he worked on the statue, these thoughts continued to revolve in his mind. He felt no hunger. There was still the slight heaviness in his limbs, but his hands obeyed him well. He had reached her face now. With brush and fingertip he coated cheeks and brow, smoothed the wax into her eye sockets, nostrils, the indentations of her hair, the faint curve of the mouth.

Last of all came the burning. When he was sure, as far as humanly possible, that no part of the Madonna had been left untreated, he played the flame of the burner over her, sealing the whole surface with brief but intense blasts of heat, welding the wax onto the stone to form an unbroken film.

In the late afternoon he stepped back from her, his eyes stinging. She was impregnable, impervious, proof against corruption — for how long, he wondered. Fifty years, a hundred? My lifetime at least, he thought. She stood there now as he had envisaged her on his arrival, as he had aspired to re-create her, resplendent in the warm pallor of her stone, her body in tension between reluctance and desire, her dreaming face turned away, that arm held out, guarding.

She was finished; his work was done. He would make his report, the work would be inspected, the scaffolding taken down. Then he would see her as men had been intended to see her, from ground level, thirty feet below. I have been looking from too close, he thought. I have distorted things. No more visions . . . From the moment of swallowing the first thirty milligrams he had accepted the doctor's view, he saw now, agreed that there was a lesion in his brain, undetectable but beyond question there, resulting in neural discharge in the form of hallucinations. Perhaps the sense of evil was merely a neural discharge too, that sickening sense of mystery which had come to him the evening before, as he watched the light fade on the water, fingered the trivial, inconclusive object of silver and stone. Yes, he had been looking from too close. I must try again, he thought; I must see her again.

He looked up at the slightly averted face of the Madonna. Something more was needed, some offering, placatory, sacrificial. *Of course.* He crouched down, groping and peering among the draperies of her robe, behind, where the molding was a little cruder. Finding an incision deep and narrow enough, he took the cuff link from his trouser pocket and inserted it edgeways, pressing down until it was wedged firm, with no part projecting. With his fingers he smeared wax into the crack until it was level. Then he whisked the flame of the burner over, sealing it in.

The Burano-Torcello boat came in as he was descending at the Fondamenta Nuova. Within a few minutes they were heading north, the white walls of the *cimitero* receding on the left, the shimmering, depthless expanse of the Lagoon opening before them.

He had planned, on arriving at Burano, to find someone with a *sandalo* who would be willing to take him at once to the house on the island. However, standing on the little quay, distracted by shifting reflections of houses and boats in the harbor water, he experienced a sudden loss of nerve. He needed a drink first. He walked away from the harbor past stalls hung with lace, found a small café on the corner of the square, and despite the heat asked for cognac. He was halfway through it when he realized he was in the same café he and Chiara had gone to, where they had had the drink together, when she had said she was returning with him to Venice. Because of the fog, because it was too dangerous . . . She had made the phone call from here.

The realization, combining with his nervousness, was suddenly too much for him. Again in that oddly automatic manner, his hand went to the small cylinder in his jacket pocket. He had intended to take the second half of his dose, if he took any more at all, late that evening before going to bed. Now, rapidly and surreptitiously, using the rest of the brandy to help him, he swallowed down a further thirty milligrams.

Making his way back to the quay, negotiating for a boat, he felt no immediate change. He found a man willing to take him, and within minutes they were on the way, heading out into the bright waste of the Lagoon. The sun was high; the day was cloudless, windless. Here and there small groups of gulls floated, looking less like birds than bright buoyant crystals precipitated on the surface by the action of the light.

The boatman stood at the prow, lunging forward with his single oar. He made no attempt at conversation, and Raikes was glad of this, glad to let the silence of the Lagoon settle round him. The sun was hot on his face. He narrowed his eyes in an attempt to make out the distant shapes of land; but it was too much of an effort and after a while he desisted, content to watch the water cleaving with their passage, listen to the creek and splash of the oar. A certain torpor was beginning to descend on him; the feeling of heaviness had intensified and he had again become aware of his thick, unagile tongue. It occurred to him that he had been unwise to mix brandy with the barbiturate. He had not eaten much either, he suddenly remembered; in fact he had eaten nothing at all since the day before, with Steadman, at Florian's. What had Steadman said? Their conversation was remote now, as if it had taken place in some other phase of life altogether. He had spoken of the Madonna cult, yes. The few known facts about Girolamo's life. The Supplicanti, still nursing their heresy after two hundred years, devising strange sins for the sake of heaven. Contempt for the flesh can take various forms. Among them, murder. Girolamo — could he really have choked the life from the woman who had given him his Madonna?

The Litsovs' boat was in its accustomed place. The tide was up; water brimmed against the supports of the jetty, covered the seaweed, concealed the algae line on the shore rocks. He paid the man, thought briefly of asking him to wait, decided against it. He began to climb the steps up from the landing stage.

As he reached the path at the top and began to walk along it, the same familiarity descended on him as before, the sense of passing through stages of intensely significant experience. This had become a landscape of his own shaping, charged with his love, silt and sand and stones of it; clay color of the path, caked now with heat; detritus of past tides in the nondescript shrub; constant glimmering presence of the water.

He passed the place where he and Wiseman had come upon her gardening, turned the bend of the path, approached the house in its cluster of pine and willow. The nervousness was there still, though blunted by his lassitude and a certain sense of slowness in the movements of his eyes.

No one came in answer to his knocking. He tried the door, found it unlocked, and stepped inside, calling her name as once, on a misty morning, she had called Litsov's. He began to walk down the passage, looking into rooms, calling several times again, experiencing as he did so the vague beginnings of panic.

She was nowhere to be seen. Silence resettled heavily in the intervals between his calls. He passed through the kitchen out to the path at the rear of the house. This led through a grove of listing, etiolated willows to Litsov's studio. Beyond, the gleaming Lagoon again became visible, absolutely motionless, unbroken to the horizon. His fear grew. There was the boat, the unlocked door — she must be on the island somewhere. She had offered herself and he had rejected her. A woman scorned. And Litsov's death still in her mind . . . He remembered the quiver in her voice when she spoke about courage. What had she said? *The courage to finish something.* He had not answered her, barely looked at her, made no attempt to stop her leaving. It was here, between the trees and the shore, that they had searched for Litsov that day, calling this way and that, rooting about in hollows, in the tangle of shrubs, the overgrown rubble of old houses. But it was in the water they had found him . . .

When he was through the trees, the full force of the sun struck him. He took off his jacket. He was sweating. The brightness of the light and the effects of the drug combined to make it difficult for him to focus his eyes. Reluctantly, yet with a sense of inevitability, he began to walk toward the water.

He found himself above the small beach of gray shingle on which, with the distraught tones of Chiara in his ears, he had heaved the drowned man that day. At the water's edge he saw a white garment, strangely isolated and distinct on the bare pebble, lying as it had been carelessly or hastily dropped. With an immediate leap of alarm, he began to walk forward, scanning the water. To his amazement, he made out the movements of a swimmer. Someone was swimming there, half lost in glitters of light, performing an elegantly leisurely backstroke not twenty yards from the dark cluster of stakes where poor Litsov had been entrapped.

He heard his name called, saw her wave. The water between must have been too shallow for swimming, because she stood up at once and began wading toward him. It seemed to him that she was naked, but his eyes were not focusing well and she was still half concealed in the intensity of the light. The resistance of the water lent her grace; she walked without shrinking or uncertainty, head up, sure of her footing, followi .g a known way among these flats of mud and weed.

Rooted there, immobilized, moisture filming his eyes and slightly blurring his vision, Raikes watched the pale gold, glistening form emerge, saw the bright swirl of water around it, the flashing ripples made by the thrust of the thighs, saw the lineaments of flesh emerge from the heart of light, the straight shoulders, dark nipples, plunging lines of the pelvis, black pubic bush. As she stepped out onto the shingle she was smiling.

Last Words

The arm, the left arm I decided to change. Bianca had to return the next day — she agreed to come in the morning. She had taken to wearing a thick veil and would not remove it until she was inside my room, giving as a reason that someone was following her, but she was always fanciful she liked dressing up and making mysteries, her hold on reality was not so strong as yours or mine my lord so I did not take the veil seriously or her later talk of a protector, which I now regret. She refused to name him and this made me the less inclined to believe her.

I had the arm down against the thigh but this was wrong because it closed off the lines making the body too passive and so the tension was lost. It is true of course that she should be passive she must accept the news, the angel does not come to give her a choice but to inform her of a destiny, she has been chosen as the vehicle for Christ Incarnate. Moreover it is in the nature of women to be passive, Aquinas has said it, man is the vital source of life, *la virtute attiva,* and it was Eve's sin that she corrupted this. We know that the soul is infused by God forty days after conception in the case of a boy and eighty in the case of a girl. Why does God give man the primary soul if not to give him also the forming and controlling of things? (Of course in the case of Our Lord the soul was infused instantly, perfect and sanctified.)

So she must by her female nature be passive but on the other hand the Holy Virgin was afraid at this moment, the visit of the shining angel took her by surprise. In the commentaries of the Fathers we are told that Mary was alarmed by the magnificence of Gabriel, and she said to him, O thou fire-being how shall I believe thee? Also it has been said though I forget by whom *non quemvis angelum mittit ad virginem,* it was no ordinary angel that God sent but His *fortem archangelum.* So the position of the Virgin's arms should show not only her humility but also the instinct to guard herself. I have seen a Madonna Annunziata by della Robbia which has the left arm extended also one by Matteo Raverti which he made for the Duomo of Milan but the arm is held higher and merely a gesture to express surprise. I wanted more than this. Then I thought again of how Adam and Eve after eating the forbidden fruit covered their genitals, not their hands or mouths, which had done the deed. This is a sign that they themselves knew their sin was the impulse of desire. They had carnal desire for each other after eating the apple and this was all Eve's doing. Then I saw my Madonna's arm could serve as a *figura* for Eve's arm to show the sin of the Fall redeemed. The wine Eve pressed for mankind poisoned them but the vine that grew in Mary nourishes and saves the world. And also the name Eva if reversed gives us Ave of the angel's greeting and that is the reason it is written *Funda nos in pace, mutans nomen Evae.* All this I saw only gradually. And there were changes in the angle of the face and the arrangement of the draperies.

During this time we talked together as I have said. She gave me the gossip of the town and I spoke about my life — how I ran from herding goats to apprentice myself to the Carthusians at Pavia where I learned some Latin along with the stone carving and afterward ran away again to join the forces of Andreolo Belcapuzo and fought in the Lombardy wars. All this before I was twenty years of age. Then I stayed behind at Bologna where I worked as an assistant to the Sienese master della Quercia and it was then I began to understand my talent. She asked me about the quarrel that night in the tavern concerning which Rodrigo Nofri has testified that I uttered treasonable speeches — all lies, my lord. Nofri has been bribed to perjure himself. I explained to Bianca that the Florentines began it by staring and then the Muranese who was with us said something about the hat of one of them because they were dressed in the trumpery French fashion with rainbow-colored hose and feathers in their hats, which no Venetian would dream of. But it was their talk of Carmagnola that made me angry. I was not drunk at all, whatever the tavernkeeper says. My lord, Carmagnola was a poor village boy from Piedmont as I was, from the same region as your illustrious lady wife and so I was defending your family also, and he went on to become the greatest *condottiere* in Italy, victor of Como and Adda. Lodi he surprised and put its lord in an iron cage, in his twenty-fifth year he was created Count of Castelnuovo di Scrivia, with lands and titles. He humbled Pandolfo Malatesta. He restored the domains of the dukes of Milan, then turned against them to fight for Venice at a salary of one thousand ducats a month, this was the man these fops were abusing and it is well known that though Florence is allied to Venice the Medici are treacherously seeking a separate peace and everyone in the room knew it and was against them, but I said nothing even when they imitated my accent, only asked them not to speak of Carmagnola. Then one of them said he thinks this Carmagnola shits gold and pisses *acqua nanfa* and I said I do not say he pisses *acqua nanfa* he pisses *acqua morta* like everyone else, who says he pisses *acqua nanfa?* You are a pisspot I said and whatever he pisses his piss is better than your spit (because he was spitting as he grew excited). Who are you calling a pisspot? he said and I saw his hand go across his body and I stood up. I was telling this to Bianca and growing angry as I remembered it but when I looked up from the lower draperies where I was cutting the folds I saw that she was laughing at all this talk of pissing and I laughed too, seeing it was not worth being knocked senseless for. He punched me with his sword hilt, a French sword with a basket guard, having no room for a thrust, though I drew blood from him also, catching him in the armpit with my *stortella,* which I carry only for my defense. Not a deep stab, but he did not go unscathed. And so we laughed together at this. Other times too we laughed together. She laughed often. Never again now.

My lord that poxed-out hag of a Fiammetta (my landlady Maria

Nevi) has testified that she saw me through my window drowning Bianca in effigy by submerging an image of her in liquid and that is why witchcraft has been added to the charges against me. But this is based on ignorance as well as malevolence, and the ignorance is not hers only but belongs also to my judges for accepting such an accusation. It is true that when I had finished the clay model I made a copy, rather rougher, and afterward immersed it, but this was for the purpose of transferring the proportions to the block of stone. Anyone who knows anything of the matter knows that you must always study the block to be carved, you must see the form that is imprisoned there which is also the form that is imprisoned in your mind. Therefore it is important to decide, or to see, before attempting the first cut, where the form is, the depth from the surface at which the key points of the figure exist. Now one very good way of doing this — it is a method I learned from the Florentine Sebastiano Macchi when we worked together in Bologna — is to suspend your model in a glass-sided vessel similar in shape to the block with a hole at the bottom which you can plug, then you fill it up with liquid to cover the model — the liquid should be pale and opaque, a mixture of water and pulped mastica is what I find best — and so by removing the plug you can reduce the level and the model is revealed and you see the exact section of the part to be carved. The levels correspond with predetermined measurements on the stone, and a calibrated pointer for measuring distances toward the center is also necessary.

This then is how I drowned Bianca in effigy, this is my witchcraft. She herself saw the figure standing in the liquid and she laughed at it, such things amused her, like a child. I remember that she brought her face up close to the glass to look at the face of the model and she laughed. It is true Bianca was drowned, half choked with a cord first, then drowned, but it was a coincidence. Or perhaps it was done on purpose to incriminate me. I did not kill her. Why should I want to kill her? I used her for —

I hear his step outside. More than one. Somebody is with him. It is too early.

I knew him as soon as I saw him enter with my ox of a jailer, taller even than him but slimmer, his pageboy behind and a secretary of the Consiglio in a blue cloth gown; saw that stiff face all the men of the family have and the long furrow between nostril and mouth and the faint twist of contempt on the lips. I knew him as I know his brothers, having seen them in ceremonial procession walking in rank among the notables dressed in the red damask of the Senate and in favored position, close behind the Doge himself. This one had risen higher since then, he wore the black now, not the red, the long-sleeved gown and brimless cap of office. My death entered with him. No man could have a worse enemy than Federico Fornarini. And he was more than a senator now, more than a knight of Venice, he was one of the Ten.

He sent the others to wait outside in the passage, though within call if needed, and he closed the door carefully. He wanted no hearers for what he was going to say except only me and he had come so I could hear it from him. He was careful, always careful of himself, like all his cursed family, even with them outside there he kept the distance between us, standing with a hand on the dagger inside his robe. The other hand he clapped to his breast as he made me an exaggerated patrician bow. So, he said, you are Girolamo these are your quarters, better than the goat pen in Piedmont you come from. Indeed yes I said but there have been better times between. Why do you honor me with a visit? I came to tell you in your stinkhole here he said, speaking quietly. I want you to know.

Even across the room I could smell the fragrance of his person, he had bathed himself in civet to come here, risked the breath of infection for it. Then I knew my death had entered with him. It was you then? I said. You were the one she spoke of. I came to tell you, he said again. When they take you and hang you in the *piazzetta* you will know whose hand made the noose. Yes, I will know I said. I am not a dog I looked him in the eye. I would ask you to sit I said but there is just the one stool and that is mine and the floor is dirty and there is rat shit about and rats too. Scum of a stone cutter he said the rat shit is yours. You had her killed I said. Your people bribed the witnesses.

His smile grew more pronounced at this. I also conduct the hearing, he said. I take the evidence and with my learned colleagues assess it. I have the advantage of them, of course. It has been interesting, my friend, very entertaining, to read these daily effusions of yours. Alfredo is a faithful animal, he brought them straight to me. Your patron, I regret to say, saw nothing of them. He paused for a moment and his face changed, the smile left it and he looked at me with hatred. It was interesting, he said, to read of your frequent screwing of my whore.

Give me a weapon, I said. Weak as I am. Then we would see the color of your blood, which no one has had a chance to do since your *bravi* do all your fighting. Thus I sought to provoke him but it was useless he was too cold, besides he wanted a felon's death for me. The smile was back on his face now as he looked at me. So this is the justice of Venice I said. God will punish you. That may be he said but you will not see it, I on the other hand will see your hanging, I will see your feet kicking and your eyes bulging out. I will see that the executioner gets a *bene andata* to prolong the business as these fellows know well how. Did you forget my name?

I never knew you were the one, I said. But why kill her, why have Bianca killed?

She was my whore, he said. I had my times to visit her and she knew them. I went there on the day and at the time and she was not there. *Figurati,* I Federico Fornarini, I arrive and the creature who keeps the door tells me Bianca is not here. Not here? Then where? She cannot say. Imagine it, I am compelled to ask where my whore is. Moreover the doorkeeper knows, I see the knowledge on her face, even I see something of a smile there. I leave instantly of course but I set a man to watch the house. He reports to me. She arrives fifteen minutes late, hot with haste, carrying a bag. I do not question her, I have her followed. So I learn the truth.

You continue to visit her, I said, and you — Yes, he said, I fuck her just the same. That is what she was for. I do not show displeasure but she is marked for death. I fuck her and have her watched and when the time comes I have her whore's life snuffed out.

He took two steps back toward the door, hand still inside his gown. She brought it on herself, he said, speaking more quietly. I was generous with her. I did not ask too closely how she spent her time. Then I call and she is not there. The fool was dressing up for you. I did what was necessary. There are people who look to me.

God help them I said.

You too he said. A convicted felon. And also, to sweeten your thoughts, your botch of a Madonna which is now in the possession of the Supplicanti, it will never be used on their church. I have spoken to their Prior. When I explained matters to him he began at once to see the statue's imperfections. Whatever pious reasons they give out for rejecting it, the Supplicanti are too recently settled in Venice to disregard my wishes or risk the displeasure of my family. So you will die, Girolamo, you sodomizer of your mother, and the Madonna will die with you.

He looked at me again for a few moments without speaking more, the twist of a smile still there, though his face was white and sick, and I knew in that moment that he hated me also for my talent. Then he went out, looking like a bat from behind with his long sleeves trailing.

My lord there is little left to say. I know my words are not reaching you. I think I have known it from the beginning. All the time the jailer was betraying me. He said yes, you can trust me, you have my promise. He nodded his big head. Then he gathered up my papers and carried them to Fornarini, to laugh over and destroy. However, it has become habit with me. Death will come soon enough, I will not anticipate it by falling silent now. So I write to you a few words more, though knowing it is hopeless. The light is failing but I have a lamp now, they have given me a candle lamp. Alfredo came back with it. Yes, he said, I have orders to give you a lamp. I know whose orders. He wants me to plead for life but I will not, I do not address these words to him, shame of his race, with not courage enough even to do his own killing.

All the time I was carving the stone Bianca came to see me. She came when there was no need. She dressed in the *vesti della Madonna.* She stayed when there was nothing to do. She cooked meals or she cleaned the room. The weather was hot. I worked on the statue and sometimes in the midst of my work sometimes afterward we made love together. (She did things with me, Fornarini, that she never did with you. What they were I will not say. But believe it. Moreover she took no money.) I got water from the pump and we washed each other from the bucket. And she laughed and cried out at the cold water. Her body was beautiful.

And all the time she must have been frightened. I did not take it seriously. She was fanciful in any case and she liked to make mysteries. She had little sense, *una cervellina,* but she would have known what kind of man she had to deal with. She knew what could happen to girls of her trade, the broken bones, slashed face, the beating and gang rape of the *trentuno,* the dumping ground of the Lagoon.

She knew the danger and still she came. I think it was because she had no existence of her own. That morning, when I went to announce I had chosen her out of all the women in Venice she was installed there with her doorkeeper and her goldfinch and the damask hangings and her book that she couldn't read. Being the Madonna was a part for her to play, she lost herself in it. Yes that must be the reason. We never spoke about love. Now I am to die but what is my fault? Who can say I harmed her? I would not have hurt

Bianca. She always did as I asked. Once only we quarreled. That was when she said she could not see my light and I was offended and told her to go away, but then she said she could see it. She cried and said she could see it.

I do not believe you. Would they hack her to pieces? Me they will kill but not the Madonna. And so not me. The star does not lose virtue by putting forth its ray or the mother by bearing a son. Nor can the creator of forms be diminished or eclipsed. There is natural light, there is the light of God with which objects can at any time be imbued, and there is the light that lives in creation. All things are in threes. The pagans believed that evil comes with the descent of spirit into material bodies but we believe that spirit comes as radiance from the face of God that first enlightens the angels then illumines the human soul and finally the world of corporeal matter. And this is again three and the reason is that God governs things by threes and these themselves are also governed by threes and so there is the saying that *numero deus comparare gaudet.* For the Supreme Maker first creates things, then seizes them and thirdly perfects them *primo singula creat, secundo rapit, tertio perfecit.* Fornarini, murderer, you do not understand this, but all who are makers know it.